KT-177-461

C334311195

THE EDGE

By Jessie Keane

THE ANNIE CARTER NOVELS

Dirty Game

Black Widow

Scarlet Women

Playing Dead

Ruthless

Stay Dead

THE RUBY DARKE NOVELS

Nameless

Lawless

The Edge

OTHER NOVELS

Jail Bird

The Make

Dangerous

Fearless

JESSIE KEANE

THE EDGE

MACMILLAN

First published in 2019 by Macmillan
an imprint of Pan Macmillan
20 New Wharf Road, London N1 9RR
Associated companies throughout the world
www.panmacmillan.com

ISBN 978-1-5098-5494-3

A CIP catalogue record for this book is available from the British Library.

3 5 7 9 8 6 4

Printed and bound by CPI Group (UK) Ltd, Croydon, CR0 4YY

To Cliff

ACKNOWLEDGEMENTS

To the team who get me there – you know who you are. And the pals (Steve and Lynne, I'm looking at you!) who make life worthwhile. Special thanks to Louise Marley, who patiently explains technology to me while I blunder along in cheerful ignorance. And grateful thanks to Tobias Backer Dirks, SERC Shooting Officer, for the fine details. Any mistakes are mine, not his. And to all my Facebook and Twitter friends and fans who catapult me every time into the top ten *Sunday Times* bestseller list, thank you, thank you, thank you! Your support means such a lot, guys. Big hugs from me.

1

1980

It was seven in the morning, and it was freezing, a yellow-grey cast to the clouds that spoke of snow. The north wind bit like a rabid dog. The shivering staff were readying themselves to go back into the huge supermarket warehouse on the outskirts of London after their tea break. Perishing out here. But at least it was fresh air, a break from the monotony of inside.

'Right, better get to it,' sighed Jane, casting one last look around the bleak landscape of the industrial estate before crushing the stub of her fag out beneath her heel.

It wasn't exactly pretty by the wire fence, where they stood hunched against the searing wind, and the job was boring as fuck, stacking this, moving that, but it paid the bills. She was up to her eyeballs in debt after the usual Christmas blow-out. Buying the kids presents she could ill afford. Well, could *not* afford, not since their dad, the rotten bastard, had taken to the hills last June. So the job had to be done. Love it or hate it.

She took one last wistful look at her *Sun* newspaper. Mrs Gandhi had won the election in India, the steel strike was ongoing, and the Ruskies were swarming all over Afghanistan, trying to wipe out Afghan army units or the mujahideen, no one seemed quite sure which. Jane folded the paper, shoved it under her arm. Same old shit. Happy New Year!

'Yep, we'd better,' said her mate Susan, and chucked the remains of her tea onto the scrubby patch of grass, moving along with everyone else toward the high warehouse wall.

Nobody took any notice of the armoured van coming down the road beside the perimeter fence behind another, larger lorry. The payroll van came at this time every week, no big deal. But then the huge eighteen-wheeler juggernaut in front of the van carrying all their wages suddenly braked, jack-knifing to a halt in front of it.

The payroll van screeched to a standstill.

Everyone stopped and watched, open-mouthed, at what was happening twenty yards away from them.

What the . . .?

Now *another* van, dark green, roared up and slid, scorching rubber, close to the back of the payroll van.

'Jesus, what . . .?' The workers stood transfixed, disbelieving.

Men were pouring out of the juggernaut and the green van.

'Christ almighty,' gasped Jane, clutching at Susan.

The men wore body armour, balaclavas, rock-climbing helmets, heavy boots and overalls. Some were carrying shotguns and others had pistols. Two of them got out chainsaws from the rear of the green van. They shimmied under the payroll truck and the chainsaws roared into life as they cut into the truck's hydraulic cables.

'Christ, they're gonna take the money!' said Susan. Like iron filings to a magnet, all the workers shrank back against the wall of the building.

'Look . . .' Jane said. One of the guards inside the van was picking up his radio.

'DON'T!' said a hooded man standing in front of the van. He was holding something up in each hand; both items were green and circular.

'What's he doing?' whispered Jane, trying to blend into the wall, make herself invisible. All her co-workers were doing the same.

'Look!' said Susan, her voice shaking.

'Those are limpet mines,' said one of the men further along the line – Tezzer, who was in the Territorials of a weekend, strictly for the piss-ups with his mates. He was white as a sheet. 'Someone ought to *do* something,' he muttered.

'Yeah?' asked one of his co-workers. 'Well, you'd be a fucking good choice for that.'

It was a standing joke in the warehouse – everyone sneered at Tezzer and his tough-guy act. They were all sick of hearing Tezzer brag about what a fearsome 'soldier' he was.

'I mean . . .' started Tezzer.

'Yeah, go on, Tez,' said a couple of the others, and soon there was a chorus of encouragement.

Jane and Sue watched, appalled, as Tezzer took a few steps forward.

'No! Don't . . .' said Sue faintly.

One of the men who'd arrived in the juggernaut had spotted Tezzer. Now he was coming at a run. 'Get back you bastard!' he yelled.

Tezzer froze to the spot, too scared to move back or forward. The man from the juggernaut took this as a sign of rebellion and ploughed in, clouting Tezzer in the midriff with the butt of his shotgun.

Shrieks went up from the line of workers. Tezzer doubled over, clawing at the man with the gun, grabbing at his helmet as he went down. Tezzer's fingers caught in the man's balaclava, dragging it askew and then off.

They all saw it: thin blond hair, runty, wrinkled features, a mouth twisted in a snarl, gold chains at the man's neck.

'You *fucker*!' the man shouted, and clubbed Tezzer with the shotgun's barrel.

'Oi!' Other men were starting forward, shocked at what had happened to Tezzer. He might be a boastful little prick, but *this* wasn't on.

'I told you! Get the fuck *back*!' roared Runty, and he let a deafening shot off into the sky. Ignoring the writhing Tezzer lying on the ground, he yanked his balaclava on and slapped the helmet on his head again.

'Christ! Look!' muttered Jane to Sue.

The man holding the mines had pressed a button on one, arming it. Red lights started flashing. Then the other one. Now he was fixing both onto the bonnet of the payroll truck. He was staring into the cab of the vehicle with clear intent.

Touch that radio again and you're dead.

The guard inside the van put the radio mike down and raised his hands in surrender.

Traffic was building behind the scene of the robbery. Commuters were trying to get to work. One of them got out of his car and came up to see what was happening, and the watching workers let out horrified gasps as one of the raiders fired over his head. The man scuttled back to his car.

'The police will come,' said Jane, trembling. 'Won't they?'

Susan wondered what the police could do about this little lot, even when they got here. And where were the building's security guards? The warehouse had eight of them. What were they doing? Sitting by the fire in the control room, the fat bastards? They should be out here, doing some-bloody-thing. Although Christ knew what.

'We ought to get back indoors,' said Susan, but she

couldn't move after that gunshot, and nobody else was moving, either.

The chainsaws fell silent. The two men came out from under the payroll van. One went to attack the hinges at the rear.

Those are black hands, noted Jane. The man wasn't wearing gloves. And there were black dreadlocks trailing down his back.

He went over to another big lorry, parked opposite and pulled away a length of tarpaulin to reveal a massive metal spike. Then he jumped up into the cab, and reversed at full throttle. There was an almighty *boom* and the spike punched a hole in the armour plating of the van.

'Oh *shit*,' said someone in the queue.

The man threw the truck into reverse and rammed the spike home again with another ear-splitting crash. When he did so, a grin showed up in the mouth hole of his balaclava. Jane saw gold.

'RIGHT!' shouted one of the men – and they were in, unloading the bags of cash in double-quick time and shoving it into the green van.

Police sirens were sounding in the distance. Jane and Susan stood there, quivering, as one of the gang paused at the back of the van, looking around, looking at *them*.

His shotgun swung in their direction. Was he smiling? Mocking them?

'Fuck,' whispered Jane, feeling her bowels loosen.

'Tell your boss: this is a present from Thomas Knox,' he shouted over the freezing roar of the wind. Then he turned away, jumped up into the green van.

It was done, over.

Three million quid had just been lifted from a warehouse that paid protection money to Kit Miller.

2

Usually, for most people, Friday was a good day. Herald of the weekend. But not for Detective Inspector Romilly Kane. She was on the phone to her husband Hugh. 'I'm going to be late again,' she was telling him. 'Sorry.'

'S'OK,' said Hugh.

She could picture him standing there in the shabby little kitchen of their – well, *her* – place near Ladbroke Grove. He'd be leaning against the counter. Dark-haired, bearded, and a passionate advocate of every left-wing cause going. He was Hugh the caring person. Everyone's huggable friend, the social worker. They'd met through work when they'd both been on a nasty child-abuse case five years ago; a year later, they were married. She'd kept her own name. Maybe that had hurt him, who knew? And he'd moved in with her. Well – sort of.

Ah, sore point.

What Romilly had learned about Hugh since they'd married was that he was an expert at sitting on fences. Hedging his bets. At first he'd talked about selling his place and both of them pooling their resources, buying a new place that was wholly *theirs*. But that plan had been abandoned. He'd kept his tatty little bachelor flat, going back there weekly 'to see everything was OK', sometimes staying overnight. Once, Romilly had snapped and raised the issue and it had sparked a fierce argument. It was then that she realized he was *never* going to sell it. And he was never going to properly buy into their marriage. The flat was his way of keeping his options open.

She'd given up arguing with him about it. Hugh was everyone's friend, but it was all show. The reality was that he was too unfocused and lazy ever to commit to a meaningful relationship. It had reached the point where she was actually glad of his regular absences – and she knew that wasn't a good sign.

So, hands up: their marriage wasn't going terrifically well. They'd both plodded on with it, living day to day, ignoring the awkward moody silences, the unasked questions.

Do you still love me?

That was one Romilly thought she already knew the answer to. And there was another one, equally important: *Do I still love you?*

Truthfully? She knew the answer to that one, too.

'Sorry,' she said again. 'Ten at the earliest, I reckon.'

'OK, don't worry. No problem.'

DCI James Barrow was coming toward Romilly's desk and his eyes told her there was something important on his mind. A skinny six-feet-six-inches tall, he wore rimless glasses, had a long, weathered face and a shock of faded-ginger hair. He was a nice man and Romilly both liked and respected him.

James was well-balanced, dedicated, pushing fifty, long-married and not often given to excitability.

'Got to go,' she said to her husband, and put the phone down.

'Wages van robbery,' DCI Barrow told Romilly as she started shuffling bits of paper around her desk. Much as she tried, her desk always looked like an explosion in a paper factory. He handed her *another* sheet of paper, with the details of the robbery on it. She scanned it briefly. 'How much?' she asked.

'Three mill,' he said.

Romilly straightened. 'You *what*?'

'Better get out there,' he said. 'SOCOs are on it.'

'Yes, sir,' she said, standing up, hitching on her jacket, snatching up her bag. She went through to the outer office where the rest of the major crimes team were beavering away. 'Harman!' she bellowed to her bulky, bright-eyed and prematurely balding DS, way down the other end of the room.

Harman looked up.

Romilly waved the sheet of paper. 'We're on,' she said, and Harman grabbed his coat.

3

DI Kane and DS Harman arrived at the warehouse and found a scene of chaos. SOCOs milling about in white coveralls, police tape strung up around a procession of vans, cordoning off the whole area, police cars parked up five-deep. Romilly grabbed one of the officers and asked to be filled in.

'Bomb disposal are on their way,' he said, indicating the wages truck with two mines stuck to its front. 'Limpet mines. Not a huge blast, but enough to kill anyone at the wheel. Scary people, these. Ex-military maybe. Armed to the teeth, by all accounts.'

'Anyone hurt?'

'One hero who thought he'd have a go,' said the officer. 'Carted him off in an ambulance, but it don't look too bad.'

'Christ alive,' said Harman, looking over at the shattered wages van. The two mines on its front were still flashing red.

'Three million,' said a SOCO, shaking his head. 'Not a bad payoff, eh?'

Romilly and Harman headed inside the warehouse. It was huge, stacked with shelves up to its vast ceiling. She snagged a passing blue-overalled worker. 'Where's the manager's office?' she asked.

He pointed out a row of glass-fronted offices at the top

of a set of stairs on the far side of the building. 'It's the first one,' he said.

The two detectives went up the stairs and were confronted with a closed door marked 'Kevin Batley, Manager'. Harman knocked at it. It was flung open instantly.

'Yes? What the fuck is it now?' a short, balding man asked them angrily.

'You're the manager?' asked Romilly. Over his shoulder, she could see a white-faced young woman sitting by a desk inside the office.

'I am.'

Romilly showed him her warrant card. 'I'm DI Kane, this is DS Harman. We'd like to ask you some questions about the robbery.'

The phone was ringing. The woman picked it up and spoke.

'Is this necessary right now? I'm up to my arse in it here,' Batley said.

'Head office,' said the woman at the desk. 'Shall I . . .?'

'Tell them Mr Batley's busy. For the moment. And that he'll ring them back as soon as possible,' Romilly told her. Then she turned her attention to Kevin Batley as the woman relayed what she'd just said to head office. 'Let's talk.'

'What, right now? You do realize there's a fucking *bomb* outside my building?'

'Bomb disposal are coming,' said Romilly. 'We need to talk *now*, Mr Batley.'

'Christ, all right. If we bloody must. Julie!' he bellowed at the woman as she put the phone down. 'Give us a minute, will you?'

Julie stood up and slid past them all, out of the office, and went off along the landing.

'Right! Come in,' he said, ushering them inside and

closing the door. He went around the desk and sat down. 'So, what do you want to know?'

'Anything you can tell us. Anything you saw. Any detail will help.'

'I didn't see a damned thing. There'll be CCTV, of course. Security will have seen the whole thing happening from the monitors – it was them who phoned your lot while I sat up here all unaware that I was about to be blowed to kingdom come.'

'Limpet mines only cause damage in the immediate area of the blast,' said Harman. 'You're safe up here.'

'Was there anyone out there when it happened?' asked Romilly.

'Yes. About thirty of the workers. They're all inside now. And fucking traumatized.'

'We'll need to speak to all of them.'

'Bastards! You know what they're saying? That it was an organized crime gang that did it. One of those gangs you people never seem to tackle.'

'What?' Romilly was frowning at him. 'How d'you know that?'

'They fucking-well announced it, didn't they,' said Kevin. 'One of them said this was a present from Thomas Knox. *Everyone's* heard of that bent bastard.'

'Who would be stupid enough to announce their involvement in a robbery?' Harman asked Romilly half an hour later, when they were trudging down the stairs with Kevin Batley leading the way.

'One gang trying to make trouble for another?' she suggested.

'Maybe it's a double bluff.'

'Or maybe a challenge.'

Batley was calling the workers together, clapping his

hands and standing on a pallet to give himself a little height. They gathered nervously, some of them still looking shaken from their experience.

'We want to know everything you saw. However insignificant,' said Romilly. 'If any of you think you have something that could help in our investigation, please hold up your hand now.'

Several did. One woman stepped forward and said: 'I think one of them was black. He had black hands. No gloves, not like the others. And I saw dreadlocks down his back. And he had gold fillings in his teeth.'

'And you are . . .?'

'Jane Mowbray,' she said. Harman was taking notes.

Another woman piped up: 'We all saw another one. Tezzer knocked his hat and balaclava off. He was scrawny. Tatty blond hair. Wrinkles. He wore gold chains. And his teeth were bad.'

'Anything else?' asked Romilly.

Silence.

'Look, if that's all, can we get on?' asked Kevin Batley.

4

There was happiness, and then there was what Daisy Darke felt when she danced in Rob Hinton's arms at their engagement party that same evening. The lights were low in the big living room at the back of Ruby Darke's house, and it was hot in here despite the cold outside, with nearly a hundred people crammed in, all of them high on booze, sugary cake, too many sandwiches, sausage rolls and cheese straws. Everyone was pleased, after the excitement of Christmas, to have this celebration to ease them through the end of the January doldrums. The DJ they'd hired for the night had Peaches and Herb on the turntable, singing 'Reunited'. It was a smoochy number and one that made Daisy smile, because she and Rob *were* reunited, after quite a long time apart.

Five years ago, they'd split up. Mostly that was down to Rob, not her. Rob had a chip on his shoulder about Daisy having grown up in the palatial Brayfield House with her bastard of a father Lord Cornelius Bray and her supposed 'mother', Lady Vanessa – who had turned out not to be her mother at all. Ruby Darke was her true mother, but Daisy had been to finishing school and spoke with a plum in her mouth, and she knew that Rob had tried to get over it, he really had, but for Christ's sake he was an East End boy and she knew it grated.

So, he'd finished it.

Daisy was aware that his mother Eunice had called him a fool.

Daisy's twin brother Kit, who was also Rob's boss, had come to her defence and kicked his arse royally over it.

But Rob had been unmoving. It was *over.*

For a long time after that, she knew he'd deliberately steered clear of her. And then one day – this had been about a year ago – they'd bumped into each other unexpectedly at Kit's house, and that was it. They were back on again. So here they were – yes, reunited. And engaged.

The smoochy number drew to a close and the DJ put on a fast track by the Bee Gees. Daisy and Rob left the dance floor, and so did a few other couples.

Ruby and Kit came over. Daisy thought again how very alike her mother and brother were, both of them dark-skinned, black-haired, and stunningly attractive. Ruby was wearing a simple lime-green shift, Kit was in a black bespoke suit. Daisy was so proud of him. She thought that Kit had grown in stature over the years. Once, her twin had worked as an enforcer for big noise Michael Ward. Michael had owned clubs, restaurants, snooker halls, and was paid protection by half the businesses in town. When Michael died, all that he'd owned had passed to Kit, his right-hand man.

'You happy, darlin'?' asked Ruby, hugging Daisy as Kit went on to where the bar was set up, then vanished into the next room.

'Happiest I've ever been,' said Daisy truthfully.

'Call for you,' said Leon, coming up to Ruby. 'Unless you seen Kit, he could take it . . .' Kit wasn't in sight right now, so she went off into the kitchen and picked up the phone.

'Hello?' she said.

Kevin Batley's furious voice bellowed out of the receiver at her: 'Would you mind explaining to me, you cowing *bitch*, just what the fuck we pay you people for?'

'Show everyone the ring,' said Rob's mother Eunice, who was sitting with her partner Patrick Dowling – Rob's father having died four years ago – and Rob's older sisters, Trudy and Sarah, and their husbands. So the happy couple did the rounds, and everyone oohed and ahhed over the sapphire with tiny diamonds clustered around it, all set in a platinum band.

'Beautiful,' the women gushed. 'Oh, that's lovely.'

'Must have cost you a fucking fortune,' said the men to Rob, pulling his leg.

'You've got great taste in women,' said Ashok, who also worked for Kit. He gave Daisy a kiss on the cheek.

'Yeah, but she's got fucking awful taste in men,' said Fats, another of Kit's employees. He gave Daisy a hug. 'What's she see in 'im, eh?' Fats asked Ashok and Daniel, Rob's younger brother. Daniel was the quiet middle child, not in-your-face assertive like his older brother Rob and not mouthy like his younger one, Leon. 'Ugly as sin and big as a house,' said Fats.

Daisy was giggling, her eyes dancing with mirth as she looked at Rob. Rob *was* big – six foot three – but he was all solid muscle, with fine, handsome features, straight treacle-blond hair and sexy khaki-green eyes. Every time she looked at him she thought, *God, I am so lucky.*

'Oi! You pair,' said Rob, pulling a laughing Daisy away from Fats and Ashok. 'She's spoken for.'

Ruby came over. She looked troubled.

'Everything OK?' asked Daisy.

'Yeah, fine.' Ruby gave her daughter a bright smile

before turning to Fats and snagging Daniel as he passed by. 'You two. With me.'

'What's that all about?' Daisy asked Rob, watching her mother's departing back with concern.

Daisy was getting used to the fact that Ruby, once a model citizen, had over the past couple of years become a key part of both the legit and criminal businesses that Kit ran. Ruby had her own interests, too – she'd acquired a Soho nightclub, for example – but her flair for business had made her an invaluable part of Kit's team.

'Whatever it is, Ruby'll sort it,' said Rob.

Finally they were able to escape outside, alone, just the two of them. Daisy shivered and Rob took off his jacket and draped it round her shoulders. He'd always looked after her, cared for her, stood by her, even when she'd been a total pain in the arse, and she loved him for that. She could feel his warmth trapped in the purple silk of the lining, enveloping her. Rob pulled her into his arms and kissed her. Now the noise was *really* cranking up in there, the DJ was playing 'YMCA' by the Village People, and everyone was singing along. There was a lot of stamping of feet and clapping and shouting. Rob and Daisy had to stop kissing, they were laughing so hard.

'It's been a great night,' said Daisy.

'Fucking fantastic,' said Rob. He stared down into her eyes. She was a beautiful, statuesque, corn-gold blonde, blue-eyed like Kit her brother, but with a complexion like fresh summer rose petals. 'You gorgeous thing,' he murmured.

'*You're* the gorgeous one.' Daisy snuggled up. 'We're going to be so happy, aren't we?'

'Yep,' said Rob.

They were interrupted by Daisy's six-year-old twins barrelling out of the door. There was a blast of hot air, a crash of singing voices, a hard disco beat and a glimpse of many hands forming the letters Y M C A.

Matthew yelled, 'Uncle Rob,' and flung himself at Rob, who laughed and hoisted him up for a hug.

Luke, always the quieter one, fastened himself to Daisy's legs like a large limpet.

'How ya doin', soldier?' Rob asked Matthew. 'Having a good time?'

Matthew nodded and cuddled in. Rob smiled into Daisy's eyes over her son's head.

'We're going to be fine,' he said. He ruffled Luke's hair, who gave him a shy grin. 'That right, Luke?'

'Yeah!'

5

An hour after he'd made the call, Kevin Batley sat tied to one of his own kitchen chairs, bloodstained and battered, and reviewed the situation. He hadn't thought today could get any worse, but he'd been wrong. Usually he was cock of the walk; king of all he surveyed. He strutted around at work, in a place as big as an aircraft hangar, watched the staff straighten their spines and work that bit harder whenever he passed by. He enjoyed his job. The power of it. His to hire and fire. His to goose behind the filing cabinets if he so chose. Which his little dolly-bird secretary wouldn't ever complain about, because she wanted to hold on to her job. It paid well, even if it meant working with him.

So tough shit, Julie.

But today wasn't like any other day he had ever experienced. Three mill in wages, gone. Bloody *bombs* outside his patch. Today was the sort of day where you were happy when the bastard finally came to an end. And you hoped you would live to see tomorrow – but right now? That was doubtful.

First, *it* had happened. The robbery. So sudden it made your eyes water. So violently efficient it had shocked him and everyone else in the warehouse to the core. *His* responsibility, of course. The buck stopped with him.

When panicky members of staff came hammering at his

door he'd told them to piss off and shut up. Too bad he couldn't do the same when the police came knocking. And after enduring their stupid questions he'd had to put up with more of the same from his superiors upcountry, who were already in touch with the insurance people. And then he'd got the roasting of his life from the chairman of the supermarket chain.

Jesus, what a day.

'I'm still waiting,' said the woman.

Despite the dire straits he was in, Kevin Batley noticed what a looker she was. He'd never actually seen her before, not close up. He'd heard about her, of course. He'd dealt with her son, Kit Miller, just once – and that had been a pretty damned scary experience, not one he cared to repeat. The man had left him in no doubt he was fucking *dangerous*. Since then, all he'd seen of the firm that *his* firm paid protection to was Fats, who came and collected the money every fortnight. Fats, who was now clouting him in the head like he was a punchbag.

The call from the chairman was where it had all gone wrong. He'd received the bollocking. Taken it on the chin and up the arse. Afterwards, smarting, *stinging* with resentment, red in the face with humiliation, sweating with stress, he'd put the phone back down and wondered if he would still have a job come Monday. He had security guards about the place, why hadn't they done something? Too slow. It had all been too *sudden*. He'd sacked four of them, straight off. The ones he didn't like, anyway. The other four he'd spared. For now. He was a beneficent ruler, all-powerful. Couldn't *believe* the Chair had spoken to him over the phone like he was some fucking lowlife office junior getting a carpeting. He had his own designated parking space at the front of the building, and his Aston Martin was parked in it. He *ran* this place. And yet they talked to him like that, like he was nothing.

It was all too much.

Not thinking – furious, wounded – he had snatched up the phone and called the number. When it was answered, it sounded like a party going on at the other end. Oh, they were having *fun*, were they? When he had been living through the worst day of his entire life? He'd demanded to speak to Kit Miller himself, or to the mother, Ruby Darke. She was the one who came on the line, and by Christ he was ready for her, *incandescent* with rage. That was when he'd said the words he now wished he could snatch back.

'Would you mind explaining to me, you cowing *bitch*,' he'd said, 'just what the fuck we pay you people for?'

Huge mistake.

Now here he was, sitting in his own home, tied up and punched to fuck. She'd showed up with two heavies, Fats and some other guy. On his fortnightly visits to collect their fee, Fats was all smiles and courtesy. No courtesy now, though. None of that. Fats and the other one had battered him about the head until his ears rang. He was bleeding from cuts all around his eyes and chin.

'Don't mark him up too much,' said the woman.

So they'd started on his middle. The woman stepped daintily back as he shook his head and a crimson droplet fell near her black suede court shoes. He yelped as a punch landed right in his belly, which was soft from too many expense-account lunches.

'Still waiting,' she said near his ear.

'I'm s-sorry,' he gasped out.

'Louder,' she said.

'I'm sorry!' he shouted, and started to sob.

Ruby Darke stared down at the man. You couldn't let disrespect go unpunished, but right now, seeing him broken and pathetic, she felt some sympathy for him. Kevin Batley was an arrogant little man used to chucking his weight about. He'd just miscalculated, that was all.

She nodded to Daniel. Rob's younger brother had joined the family firm a couple of years ago. He was a lean young bruiser with a patient, solid presence who was getting very handy on the firm. Ruby liked him. He was much easier to deal with than the youngest Hinton boy, Leon, who was fiery and unpredictable. Then she nodded to Fats, who was an old hand in such matters.

The two of them loosened the wire binding Kevin's wrists.

'They say anything, these people? When they were taking the cash?' asked Ruby. She was not an unreasonable person, and Kevin Batley did have a point; the warehouse paid protection to the family firm, and it was down to them to rectify this situation if they could. So he was *right* to be upset. But not abusive. She couldn't tolerate that.

Kevin shook his head. His eyes widened in wild hope as his wrists were freed. They weren't going to hurt him any more.

Without a word, Ruby and the two men made their way to the back door, now hanging from its frame where they'd kicked it in and come storming into the house.

'Wait . . .' Kevin licked his dry lips, wincing as his tongue touched a sizeable, oozing split there.

Ruby Darke turned back. She looked so bloody *civilized*, that's what struck Kevin. She was tall, slender and neatly groomed in a lime-green shift dress and black jacket. Half-caste, obviously, with her black hair gleaming in its tidy chignon. Long gold earrings catching the light as she moved. Her eyes were dark, speckled with gold. A beauty. But cold as ice. Back in the days when she was running Darkes, the chain of department stores that bore her name, she was known as the Ice Queen of Retail. But now she'd grown into something else. Something *deadly.*

He tried to think, but his brain felt like mush. Hadn't one of the girls – was it Jane? – hadn't she said . . .? Yes. Now he had it.

'An employee who's in the Territorials tackled one of the raiders, pulled off his balaclava. Everyone got a good look at him. Thin bloke. Gold chains around his neck. Blond hair. Raddled skin. Bad teeth. And one of the girls saw a guy with black hands, black dreads. And gold fillings, she said.'

'Anything else?' asked Ruby.

'Yeah. There is. As they were leaving, one of them yelled that this was a present from Thomas Knox,' he gasped out. 'He's one of your lot, isn't he?'

Ruby took a step towards him and her eyes were like flint.

'You fucking *what*?' she asked, very cold.

Shit, thought Kevin as the two heavies began to walk towards him. 'I mean, in the same sort of trade as you and Mr Miller,' he said in a rush.

The two men were coming closer, closer.

Ruby Darke was staring into his eyes, a cobra mesmerizing its prey.

Kevin knew then that the day wasn't over.

Not yet.

6

Thomas Knox was pissed off. First it had been the police, hauling him in for questioning about some robbery or other. And now he opened the door to his plush Hampstead pad and there was Ruby Darke, with whom he had once had a hot thing going, a *major* thing, and she was grabbing him by the throat and shoving him back into his own damned hallway.

Her eyes were crazy-mad, glaring into his. He was a big man, blue-eyed, blond-haired, and he'd *liked* the thing they'd had going together, he'd thought it was something special. But it had fizzled out and he was surprised to see her, and even *more* surprised at her obvious fury.

'Hello, Ruby,' he managed to croak. 'What the fuck are you doing? Chloe could have been here.'

'Oh, your wife? Not that I give a toss, but I just saw her leave. This isn't a social call. And I'll tell you what I'm doing,' she said, her voice flat and without emotion. 'I'm asking you a question, and I want a straight answer. I mean, *straight.*'

'Go on then,' he said, wondering if he was going to die right here in his own hallway. If she had a knife or a gun in her pocket – and she might – this could turn nasty in a heartbeat.

'Did you have anything to do with that warehouse robbery?'

'Christ! Not you too. I've spent most of the day down the police station, answering their stupid questions.'

'Did you do it? Was it you?'

'*No*,' said Thomas. 'Fuck's sake, of course not. Someone's playing silly buggers. It was nothing to do with me. I know Kit's over that side, why would I do a stupid thing like that, step on his toes, start a war between him and me?'

'You *swear*? Or by Christ, I'll slit your throat myself, I promise you.'

'On my life,' he said.

Ruby stared into his eyes for long, long seconds. Finally she pulled back.

'Kit was ready to come over here himself and rip you a spare arsehole,' said Ruby. 'But I said you would never do a thing like that. Not on his manor. Lucky for you, he's letting me handle it.'

'Well, you've handled it,' said Thomas.

'The men who did it said it was down to you. "From Thomas Knox," they said. What were we supposed to think?'

'That I'd be fucking mad to announce it?' he suggested.

Ruby narrowed her eyes and stared at his face. After their affair had ended, she'd heard on the grapevine that he'd married Chloe, a glamorous and much younger woman. She'd seen them around town a few times. Chloe Knox was big-breasted and blonde – a real-life Barbie doll. Ruby sometimes thought that *she* should have been Mrs Knox; but somehow the moment had never seemed right, and it had passed them by.

'I'll see you later,' she said, and opened the front door and was gone.

'Right,' said Thomas to empty air, staring after her as he

sagged against the wall. Mad bitch! He was wondering if she really would have slit his throat. Probably yes, if push came to shove.

She was hot as hell though.

Crazy as fuck, true – but still red hot.

That afternoon, Ruby was in the sitting room at the front of her Marlow house with Kit, watching copies of the CCTV tapes from the warehouse.

'I've spoken to Thomas,' said Ruby, as they saw the robbery unfold on the screen.

'And?' said Kit.

'And he says, on his life, this had nothing to do with him. Someone's mixing it.'

'Assuming he's telling the truth.'

'I think he is.' On the screen, Tezzer was being hit with the shotgun.

'Yeah, you think.' Kit looked at his mum. He knew her and Thomas Knox had been close. And now, this. Was Knox playing them? Or getting some sort of twisted revenge on Ruby? He couldn't be sure. 'Did you dump him? Or did he dump you? You never said.'

'Does it matter?'

'It might.'

Ruby paused, then said: 'I dumped him, OK? After I realized that he had a whole stableful of whores besides me. His new young wife, Chloe? She was one of them, and I guess she played the game smarter than the rest, because he upped and married her.'

'OK. Look – there's the bloke.' Kit froze the image. Blond hair. Scrawny. Bad teeth. Gold chains. 'Don't recognize him.'

Kit started the thing running again. There was the black

man, dreads down his back. A flash of gold when he grinned as he rammed the wages van.

'I'll show this to Thomas, maybe he knows them,' said Ruby.

'Yeah,' said Kit, standing up. 'And maybe, even if he does, he'll say he don't. Listen, I want a sit-down with Knox, soonest.'

Ruby eyed her son. In this mood, he was capable of a wrong move. 'No,' she said. 'I'll handle it.'

'The fuck you will.'

'I *will*.' Ruby stood up and looked him in the eye. 'Kit. If there's a moment, a single frigging moment when I doubt what he's saying, then he's yours. I promise you.'

Kit met her gaze, unblinking. Finally he nodded.

'Do it,' he said.

7

Barry Jones came into his DI's office in high excitement. Romilly and Harman were in there, talking over the case. Romilly was wondering if they'd missed anything.

'I just got off the phone with bomb disposal,' said Barry, hefting one heavy arse cheek on to the edge of Romilly's desk.

'Go on,' she said. This sounded promising. Barry was a big man, running to flab, his hair starting to go grey; he looked like a cosy house husband with his beige cardigans and ill-fitting trousers, but appearances were deceptive: Barry had an extremely agile brain.

'Clever really.' Barry was shaking his head in admiration. 'You know what those limpet mines were?'

'No. Tell me.'

Barry paused for dramatic effect, then said: 'Meat pies.'

Romilly squinted up at him. *What?*

'Yep.' He nodded. 'Tinned meat pies. Fitted with magnets and flashing lights. Painted green so they looked military. Only dangerous if you eat 'em. You ever had one of those bloody things? No meat. Pastry like lino.'

'You're kidding.'

He made the sign of the cross on his chest. 'God's truth.'

Romilly let that sink in. Fucking meat pie tins. Barry

hauled his bulk off her desk and made his farewells with a grin.

'Cheeky bastards,' said Harman.

'Clever too.' Romilly looked at the clock on the wall. Six. Christ! She wasn't looking forward to this. But she stood, gathered up her things.

'There's something I have to do at home,' she told Harman. 'I'll come straight back when I've finished.'

Romilly left her office, pausing at the door of the big main office where her team were still hard at work. It was all hands on deck over the warehouse job, the nick was a madhouse of action, ringing telephones and shouted conversations as the large team of detectives worked on it. Surveillance operations had been set up on six known criminals – including Knox – who could have been involved.

So far – nothing.

That bugged her. Seriously.

She was hoping the van used to ferry the money away from the scene would be found somewhere, dumped; but no. So there were rafts of coppers out now checking through all the car sales places, breakers' yards, anywhere a hot motor could be easily disposed of.

And they were hauling suspects in. People who were in this line of work, and were always on the police radar. For months her team had been covertly watching a scrap-metal merchant called Finlay who'd long been suspected of large-scale auto theft and armed robberies. It had turned up nothing; County had been bellyaching about the cost. Now the warehouse thing had kicked off, the police were all over Finlay like a rash, combing every yard he operated and all around his home, too, fully expecting to discover the get-away van.

So far – nothing.

They'd turned over all Thomas Knox's businesses, and drawn a big fat blank there, also.

Romilly was almost glad to get out of the building for a while. As she headed for the door, Bev Appleton, a DS and a friend of Romilly's for years, caught her arm. Bev was big, blonde and pretty, a married mother of two lively kids.

'You OK?' she asked.

'What?' Romilly jerked to a halt. 'Oh! Yeah. Fine.'

'Only you look like shit.'

'Thank you very much.'

'Just saying. Bad deal over the warehouse business,' said Bev. 'You *sure* you're OK?'

'Oh, the usual. That's all. Men. You know.'

'Maybe we can catch up later?' Bev's sharp eyes were still resting on Romilly's face.

'Sure, yeah,' said Romilly, and surged onwards.

She felt faintly sick. She'd set this up, no one had forced her hand. This was the decision she'd made, and now . . . now it was time.

She let herself in the front door quietly. Not creeping in, exactly, but she wasn't announcing her entry with trumpets and fanfares. And she heard them almost straight away. Noises upstairs. She put down her bag and went up there, pausing when she reached the top stair. *Am I sure I want to do this?*

Right now, she felt she was out of choices.

She moved along the landing, pushed open the master bedroom door.

And there they were.

Romilly stood in the doorway and watched her husband's bare arse pumping up and down between the legs of Sally, the barmaid from the Nag's Head. That sick feeling washed over her again. Her stomach churned and clenched. Well, she'd known, hadn't she? Really, she had. In her gut. She folded her arms and watched them for several seconds, until Sally's eyes flickered open and looked over Hugh's shoulder – and straight at her.

'*Jesus! Hugh!*' Sally yelped.

It should almost have been funny. But to Romilly it felt sad. Yes, she'd known at some subliminal level what was going on. But here it was, confirmed. Hugh sprang up like a startled deer, clutching the sheets around him. Sally lay there, spreadeagled, before she too grabbed for cover. Romilly stared at her. Then she said: 'Well don't just fucking lie there, Sal. Pour me a pint or something.'

'I . . . I . . .' Sally stammered, red-faced.

Romilly turned her attention to her husband. 'I'll be downstairs,' she said. 'When you're ready.'

Romilly waited in the kitchen, scanning the day's paper without taking much in. The strike was worsening, British Steel was talking about axing over eleven thousand jobs in Wales by the end of March. In Belgrade Tito's left leg had been amputated to stop the spread of gangrene. She shuddered and dumped the paper in the kitchen bin.

Finally, Hugh came down dressed in his bathrobe. She could hear Sally up there, scrabbling into her clothes. All a bit undignified.

Hugh's face was like thunder. 'You said you were going to be late again,' he said. 'Ten, you said.'

Romilly gave him a look. 'You *what*? Listen, Hugh. News alert. I'm a detective inspector. I catch criminals for a living. I set a simple trap, and you fell right into it.'

'Clever bitch, aren't you,' he sneered.

'Blimey, Hugh,' said Romilly, shaking her head. 'Whatever happened to the caring, compassionate social worker guy I married, eh? I never thought you'd turn out to be such a walking ruddy cliché, bonking the local bike because your wife doesn't understand you.'

'But that's the trouble,' said Hugh angrily. 'You *don't*.'

'Oh, I think I do. You're dancing the horizontal tango with Sally in my bed, in *our* bed. Why didn't you take her back to that cosy little hovel of yours?'

'I . . .' he started.

'I'll tell you why. It was to give me the finger, wasn't it? To say, "Fuck you, Romilly, what would you make of *this*?"'

'Is it any wonder that I've got to look somewhere else for affection?' he demanded. 'Fuck's sake! You're married to your sodding job, not to me. It's fucking *boring*. *You* are boring.'

'I see.' Romilly nodded, taking it in. She was a workaholic bore. Nice. 'Oh look, here comes your little playmate.'

Sally came thundering down the stairs. She cast a look in their direction as she passed the open kitchen doorway, then she scuttled out the front door and was gone. 'Bye, Sal!' shouted Romilly after her.

'So what now?' asked Hugh.

He looked, thought Romilly, like a sulky kid caught scrumping apples. Pathetic.

'Get any stuff you need together,' she said, going through to the hallway and picking up her bag. 'I want you out of here by the time I get back tonight.'

There! It was done. She walked out of the house and over to her car. The sick feeling had abated, a little. She tried to pinpoint how she felt right now. Down the road, she could hear Sally's heels clacking on the pavement as she made her escape. *Maybe I've just escaped too*, she thought. As she climbed into the driver's seat she turned this over in her mind, analysing it. She was good at analysing things. How *did* she feel? And it popped into her head, straight away.

She felt *relieved*.

8

The killer was a perfectionist, with a tidy mind; he was the sort of man who would feel compelled to straighten the tins in a food cupboard – supposing he ever had one, which he didn't. But if he *did*, he'd have them all facing neatly to the front, and arranged in date order. He was even neat in his personal appearance, always beautifully turned out; clothes clean and pressed, hair trimmed, shoes polished. Mess, disorder of any kind, upset him. Which was why he was looking in disgust around the room he was currently sitting in.

He was in a big, red-brick house in central London. It had huge bay windows and high-ceilinged rooms, so the actual proportions of the place were delightful; but inside, in this vast living room, years of dust and dirt had accumulated. The furniture looked tired, threadbare. Three yappy little dogs were hurling themselves around the room, snapping at each other in a game of chase, snarling and barking.

The killer hated dogs. Dirty, snivelling things.

Sometimes, when he was practising for a job, he used stray dogs as targets. Tidied them away afterwards, of course; he couldn't leave a mess.

He could smell the dogs in here. A pungent, eggy smell; raw and canine. He was trying to hold his breath, and failing. He could see a small brown deposit over in the far corner of the room. *Jesus*. How could anyone live like this?

'That's hardly mates' rates,' the man seated opposite him was saying. 'What, no discount for rellies?' he complained.

'Twenty grand now, twenty when the job's done. I think that's fair. You haven't told me the target yet. I've never liked the idea of flying blind.'

'These are the details.' The man handed over a folded scrap of paper and a small stack of photographs. The killer unfolded the paper and looked at it. Scanned the photos. Then he tucked them all in his pocket.

The dogs were still rushing around, panting, tongues lolling. One brushed against the killer's ankles, and he moved his legs quickly to one side. Filthy things.

'All right?' said the man.

'The date's fine. Gives me plenty of time to get things straight.'

'Good. I'll need to go to the bank,' said the killer's uncle.

He was thinking that his nephew – his brother Bill's boy – was weird as ninepence, wandering the country on his own, rootless. Jobless, too, except for these 'removals' he did now and again. You couldn't reach him when you wanted to. No address. No phone. Nothing. So he'd had to contact his brother, tell him he wanted a word with the peculiar bastard. His brother hadn't had a clue where his own son was. So he'd phoned his mother, the killer's grandma. The killer had stayed with her as a nipper after his mother – Bill's wife – had scarpered, and he still dropped in on special occasions – birthdays and so on – to see the old girl. Finally, weeks later, contact was made.

'I'll come back tonight,' said the killer, standing up. 'Say, seven o'clock?'

'Fine,' said the man, and his nephew left the room. The man breathed a sigh of relief. The bloke might be useful, and he might be his own flesh and blood, but still – he gave him the fucking creeps.

Catching the Tube, the killer went straight to a lock-up he kept under a false name over in Peckham. He opened up, collected his bag, relocked the door, and went to the hotel he'd checked into the day before. He changed his trousers because the dog had brushed up against the ones he'd been wearing, and put the dirty pair in another bag. When that was done he had a cup of tea, washed up the dirty cup, saucer and spoon, wiped down the tea tray. Taking a third bag with him, he headed back over to his uncle's place to collect his first payment. No dogs in evidence this time, and thank God for it.

Having done all that, he was suddenly in the mood to celebrate. Why not? He'd get dinner at one of the local restaurants, and then he'd start researching his target. No time like the present. He felt quite excited now. He always enjoyed the prospect of a kill. Dinner first – and after that he'd go to Soho to have a look at Ruby Darke's club, see if he could spot her there.

9

Crystal Rose was sitting in a giant champagne glass in Ruby's Soho burlesque club. The glass was overflowing with bubbles that glittered with rainbows as they drifted down onto the stage. Crystal, a tiny and beautiful brunette, appeared to be naked in the bubbles except for one ornate diamond necklace. She was lifting one leg provocatively, then the other, stroking her hands down over her own shapely limbs and smiling coyly at the audience.

To the background track of 'Diamonds Are a Girl's Best Friend' sung by Marilyn Monroe, Crystal twisted and writhed, then finished her routine with a flourish, standing up in the glass, bubbles lightly – suggestively – coating her nudity.

The lights winked out.

When they came back on again, two sequin-covered acolytes – Crystal's 'Rosettes' – had appeared and a set of steps had been placed in front of the huge glass. As Crystal Rose descended to stage level to rapturous applause, waving left and right, her two assistants covered her with giant white-feather fans tinted pink by the lights. She was ushered off the stage, blowing kisses to her audience.

Ruby Darke watched it all with interest. Crystal was *good* but God she was a pain in the arse. Ruby ran this single club as she had once run a countrywide retail business – with an iron fist in a velvet glove. She surrounded herself with a good team but sadly also had to contend with very young and gorgeous girls like Crystal, who were hell to handle. Capricious. Demanding. But necessary, drawing in the punters like bees to honey.

One of these days, Ruby thought, burlesque was going to go mainstream like it had back in the day when she had been onstage at the Windmill. After selling her business, she'd visited strip clubs and lap-dancing clubs, wondering if she might take one of those over and expand it, but she hadn't really wanted involvement in them; it wasn't her thing. And then she'd seen current-day burlesque being performed, and instantly she was sold. It was teasing, artistic, sexy but not lewd. It was very like what she'd done when she'd been young and foolish and in love with that rat Cornelius Bray. Of course, Cornelius had turned out to be a son-of-a-bitch bastard, and it had all ended badly, but still – the burlesque had triggered a nostalgia in her. She loved it, and it seemed the punters did too.

'She's good,' said Laura, the club manageress, a six-foot redhead with huge, shrewd blue eyes, who was sitting beside Ruby at her table near the stage. 'And Christ, don't she know it.'

'She's better than good, she's terrific,' said Ruby. 'Draws the punters like no one else.'

Crystal was a hit, there was no doubt about that. Ruby looked around with satisfaction. The club was packed tonight. Every night Crystal appeared, there were people queuing fifty-deep at the door. Ruby was pleased. She'd started this club mostly to give herself an interest after she'd sold the Darkes chain of stores, and to help launder some of Kit's cash through the tills, but it was making a pretty healthy profit in its own right.

'Trouble is, she only wants three nights a week,' Laura

sneered. '*Family commitments*, my arse. She's making enough out of us on those three nights not to bother herself with working too hard the rest of the week. Lying at home painting her toenails is my best guess, while watching TV. Which leaves us short of acts,' said Laura.

'Yeah, but we've advertised. No bites?' They'd put ads in all the papers.

'Some. But we want quality, like Crystal – and that's rare.'

'The agency not sent any new ones over?'

'No one I'd care to put on stage.'

The general theme of the club was discreet erotic retro – so when Crystal wasn't dazzling her adoring public, the acts comprised of Forties-style performers with their hair in victory rolls, singing old hits like 'Boogie Woogie Bugle Boy'. Those acts went down well. But Crystal was a bigger draw.

'What about her two acolytes? The Rosettes. One of them like to step up? Take centre stage?' asked Ruby. The Rosettes were Crystal's younger sisters, and they seemed terrified of her.

Laura shook her head and smiled grimly. 'Have you *met* Crystal?'

Ruby had to smile. Crystal was queenly, bossy, a right regal pain in the backside.

'You want to start world war three? Crystal would go *apeshit* if she wasn't head honcho over the other two. Older sister syndrome. You know what that's like. Oh look,' said Laura, gazing over toward the club entrance.

Ruby looked and felt her innards shrivel. *Shit.*

'Ain't that Thomas Knox?' Laura glanced from him and back to Ruby. 'He's one of the big boys around here. A local face. Didn't you and he . . .?'

'Yeah, we did. Once. Ancient history,' said Ruby.

Last time she'd seen Thomas, it was in his hallway and she'd been spitting mad. They *still* had stuff to square away, him and her. *This* time – for the first time ever, so far as she knew – he was bringing his young trophy wife into her club. What the *fuck* was he playing at?

Ruby couldn't resist the urge to examine Chloe in minute detail. Mrs Knox number two – the faded and faithful number one having been kicked to the kerb years ago – was a heavily made-up blonde who was wearing a red silk shift dress that very nearly covered her huge, balloon-like breasts.

'Hot, isn't he?' smiled Laura.

'I wouldn't know,' said Ruby, giving her a scathing look, turning her attention firmly away from Thomas and his wife. Was he taking the piss?

'Well, *I* wouldn't say no,' said Laura.

Ruby watched from the corner of her eye as he and Big Tits were led to a table by one of the hostesses. He passed by Crystal, who was just taking her seat, her eyes darting everywhere, her smile neon-bright – *Look at me, I'm the star of the show* – beside a neatly dressed man with dark hair.

'Wouldn't kick *that* out of bed,' said Laura on a sigh, watching Thomas with narrowed, predatory eyes.

Ruby shrank into her chair as he flicked a glance in her direction. She reached for her voddy and orange and drained the glass.

'What I think is—' said Laura.

'Laura,' Ruby cut her off.

'What?'

'Shut the fuck up.'

Ruby was in the bogs an hour later, washing her hands and repairing her make-up, when Tits showed up. Ruby wasn't exactly surprised, because Chloe had been shooting her cold looks ever since she came in the club.

Ruby cast a sideways glance at her in the mirror, but said nothing. Another woman, a big brunette, paused at one of the sinks, combed out her hair, departed. Soon as she was gone, Big Tits launched into The Speech.

'What you need to do,' she said flatly, 'is stay the fuck away from my husband.'

Ruby paused mid-lippy. 'Sorry?' she said.

'You heard. I got friends, you know. I got people around town who tell me things.'

'Good for you,' said Ruby, popping the lipstick back into her bag.

'You been to my home. People *saw* you.' Chloe sent a scathing look over Ruby, from head to toe. 'I know he had a thing with you once. But look at you. You're not even *young*.'

'Youth is overrated,' said Ruby, heading for the door.

'I *told* you . . .' Chloe started, stepping in front of Ruby.

'Get out of my fucking face,' said Ruby.

'You don't scare me,' said Chloe, but Ruby could see uncertainty in her eyes.

Ruby leaned in closer and Chloe recoiled. 'Don't I? Well I bloody should. Now *shift*.'

Chloe shifted, and Ruby swept out of the room.

10

'She's stunning, isn't she?' said Crystal, seeing that her companion's attention had been pulled away from her as Ruby Darke came out of the powder room and returned to her table. Crystal frowned. *She* was always the centre of attention. It was hardly a good start, him ogling other women. And Ruby was *old.* Well past it.

'Hm?' His eyes came back to hers.

'Her. Ruby Darke. She owns this place.'

'Does she?'

'Yes, she does,' said Crystal, still miffed. 'And now she's in business with her son and they say the deals are *distinctly* dodgy. Lots of under-the-counter stuff going on. Do you fancy her?'

He'd come backstage, given her all the chat, saying how much he loved her act, he was a huge fan, would she join him for a drink? Her sisters had squawked that she was too busy, she was exhausted after her performance, but she had overruled them, saying, Of course, why not? He was very fuckable, with dark hair and dark eyes, his face fine-boned, angular. Pity about that thin judgemental mouth.

But he was beautifully turned out. Expensive cologne. Yeah, why not?

Now here he was, looking at other women. This did not sit well with Crystal. *She* was the star, no one else. She turned her attention from him as he ordered champagne from Joanie, one of the club hostesses. She watched the act onstage; three tubby girls in GI uniform singing something about Uncle Sam.

'You're exquisite,' he suddenly whispered in her ear. His mouth brushed her skin and she shuddered. Yes, she was. And he'd better remember that. Her. No one else.

'Am I?' she was half-smiling now, preening as Joanie came with the champagne in the ice bucket.

The hostess unpopped the cork, poured out two flutes, and left the rest on ice.

'Bloody fantastic,' he said, his breath like a feather against her flesh. 'Here's to you. You are *such* a star.'

He was holding his champagne flute out. Her bad mood dissolving, Crystal lifted her own glass, clinked it against his, smiled, and drank.

The killer was annoyed with himself. He was going to have to be more careful. Maybe too many brandies after dinner; he was relaxing too much. Crystal didn't know it, but he'd stared at Ruby Darke not with sexual interest but in a dispassionate and predatory way – the way a cat would look at a helpless mouse before it gobbled it down.

They'd chatted, laughed, and after that he'd been careful not to let his attention waver again because he wanted sex tonight. He quickly discovered that voluptuous and dazzlingly attractive though she might be, Crystal was also a fucking nightmare: arrogant, mouthy, telling him more than he wanted to know about her act, how useless her sisters were, and that *she* had always been the star of the family and one day soon she was going to make it big, go to Hollywood, the works.

Yeah, yeah, he thought.

'You could do it,' he told her. 'I'm sure you could. You have star quality.' She lapped that up.

'You worked at the burlesque club long?' he asked her.

'Nearly a year.'

'What's she like to work for – Ruby Darke?'

'All right.'

'Her family show up much? I think there's a daughter. And a son?'

'Don't know. I saw them once. Odd thing, that. Daisy, the girl, is white and Kit, the son, looks half-caste like Ruby. But they're twins. Born on the same day. Weird, yeah?'

'I suppose it can happen. Never thought about it. You ever spoken to them?'

'No.' She stared at him, eyes narrowing. 'What is this – twenty questions?'

He dropped it. Didn't want to have to work to get her out of another sulk. Even bed with this tedious woman was a look-at-me performance. Both mildly drunk, they got a taxi back to the hotel where he'd booked a suite – cash on the nail – as Mr Ted Smith from Preston, Lancashire. He started kissing her the instant they were inside the door, mostly to shut her up; he wanted sex, not another monologue on how marvellous she was. In the bedroom, she started doing an elaborate striptease while he watched from the bed, pretending to be turned on but actually getting pretty annoyed. He'd *seen* all this shit earlier in the evening, now all he wanted was the sweet release of a quick uncomplicated fuck, then eight hours' sleep.

When she danced closer, sliding her undone bra left and right, he grabbed it, pulled it off, tossed it aside. She smiled and covered her nipples with her hands, coyly. She was tiny in stature, but large-breasted, nipples big as beer mats. It was a combination he liked very much.

'Oooh, does he like it rough?' she teased, smiling.

He grabbed her and dumped her on the bed. Leaned over her, a flare of anger in his eyes. 'Oooh,' he mimicked her. 'Does *she* like it rough? Cos that's how she's going to get it.' She stared up at him, suddenly uncertain. Then he smiled brilliantly.

'Joking,' he said, and kissed her again to stop her yammering on.

After that, it was easy; he had a tried-and-tested ritual he always observed when in bed with a woman. Get it all out of the way, then on to the main event. Suck her tits. *Bite* her tits. Not too hard.

'Ow!'

'Sorry, I just want you so much . . .'

Then on to the magic button. They all had one, and some were more responsive than others. Crystal Rose went roaring through the ceiling after the merest touch, gasping and screaming. Theatrical bitch, she would. Might even be faking it, but who knew? Who cared? He slapped a hand over her mouth so that the people in the room next door didn't know his business, then shoved his penis into her and rode her like a showground pony until his own orgasm crashed over him. He drew out of her, limp, spent. Then he rolled over, away from her, and fell asleep.

He woke up with sunlight beaming into his eyes through a crack in the curtains. A room he didn't know. Well, no change there then. He was used to that, waking up in an alien environment. He liked it that way. No ties. He was happy drifting around the country, footloose. He'd check out tomorrow, go on somewhere else. Find somewhere near the target area for the job. Didn't know where yet. Didn't care.

Aware of movement, he opened his eyes fully. Someone was humming a tune. A woman. Yesterday came back and slapped him into full wakefulness. The job he'd taken on. The payment. Celebrating last night with fine wine, a good steak dinner and a so-so fuck with Crystal Rose, who never seemed to stop talking. She was still at it now.

'Honey? You awake? Where d'you keep your robe, I'm buck naked here and it's freezing . . .' A stab of alarm hit him as he heard the wardrobe door slide open.

He sat up in the bed, pushed his hair out of his eyes. She was peering in the wardrobe.

'You got some lovely clothes. Designer stuff,' she was saying. She pulled his Calvin Klein jacket off a padded hanger and slipped it on. 'Beautiful. The fabric's so soft. I'll wear this to make the tea, OK?'

Not OK. He hated anyone touching his things. And now . . . shit . . .

He sprang out of the bed but he was too late. She was looking in the bottom of the wardrobe, her curvy little bare arse up in the air. When she turned to face him, she held a handful of cash and her eyes were wide open with surprise.

'Holy moly, there's a *fortune* down here.' She glanced back into the wardrobe.

He'd left the bag undone. *Stupid shit, you left the bag undone and then invited the world's nosiest, mouthiest woman back for sex. You* moron.

'Hey!' Now something else had caught her eyes. 'Is that a gun? It looks like a gun. Do you shoot? My dad has a farm in Gloucestershire; he's a keen shooter,' said Crystal.

'Come out of there.' He was shoving the door closed, wrestling some of the notes out of her hand, all at the same time.

'All right, no need to be so rough,' she said, laughing.

He reached past her to his tie. Grabbed it. Looped it around her neck. And pulled tight.

Suddenly Crystal Rose wasn't laughing. The remaining

banknotes fell to the floor in a cascade as her hands flew to her neck to claw at the tie. Choking noises were coming out of her mouth and her face was turning brick-red as the blood was cut off. Her terrified eyes stared into his.

'I'm sorry about this,' he said through gritted teeth as he applied more pressure. 'I really am. But you shouldn't have done that. You shouldn't have looked in there.'

'Don't,' she managed to wheeze out.

'Sorry. Got to,' he said, and pulled the tie tighter.

Suddenly she went limp. Her eyes glazed over. He kept pulling, tighter and tighter, his hands aching with the effort. Then he heard liquid running and the *stench.*

'Oh fuck,' he grimaced. He'd never actually strangled anyone before; he much preferred the neatness, the cool distance, of a gun. Now he was shocked. He'd heard they did that when they were hanged. Voided themselves. And that's what she'd done. All over the fucking carpet. Shooting was so much nicer than this. But what choice had she given him?

None.

She slumped to the floor. He let the tie go and stepped back, his face crumpled with disgust as he stared down at the corpse still wearing his jacket. Well, he was never going to wear *that* again. He'd have to buy new.

'Silly cow,' he said, breathing hard, and started gathering up his money.

He didn't want any of that stuff getting on *this.*

11

DI Romilly Kane was down the nick, still talking to her team about the warehouse robbery and right now getting no-fucking-where. They'd hauled Finlay in, and had to let him go. Questioned Thomas Knox again, ditto. Turned up all the other faces they could, questioned them hard, searched premises, caused a general stir. Spread the search wider and wider for the getaway van. So far? Just a fat zero.

Getting into February now, and what did they have to show for it? Fuck all.

'Me and DS Harman took another look over at the warehouse, like you said,' said DC Phillips, a keen young woman with brunette plaits. 'Bately, the MD, looks like he's had an argument with a pit bull.'

Romilly frowned at her.

'Apparently he went home the night of the robbery and fell arse over tit down the stairs, smashed his face up good and proper, poor sod. He's still all colours of the rainbow,' Harman explained with a grin. 'This is definitely not his year.'

'Don't you think that was strange? The man with the gun saying "a present from Thomas Knox"?' said Romilly.

'I do,' agreed Harman.

'Announcing his involvement? Who'd be crazy enough to do that?'

'He's crazy like a fox, Thomas Knox. Maybe he *is* involved. Maybe he's expanding. Branching out.'

'And what? Telling everyone about it? Not clever.'

'Maybe he was issuing a deliberate V-sign to whatever lowlifes think they "own" that area,' suggested Harman. 'Damn sure someone does.'

'Yeah? *Who* does, exactly?'

'Miller mob, isn't it? Used to be Michael Ward's patch, big local tough, but Kit Miller took it over after Ward got done.'

'Bring me in Miller's file, will you?'

'Sure thing. So . . .' Harman let out a breath. 'We find those two blokes – the blond and the black – and maybe some pieces will start to fit.'

Romilly looked at the blown-up still of the CCTV from the warehouse, pinned up on the board. There was runty blond guy, and there was black guy with dreads.

'Get people out on the streets again, do door-to-door, take the pics of those two and see what's to be found,' said Romilly. They'd already done this, many times, but they had to keep slogging away.

She went back to her office, passing DCI Barrow's room as she did so. He called her in. She stepped inside and closed the door.

'Progress?' he said, peering over his specs.

'We're working on it, sir.'

'And you? How are you?'

Romilly gawped at him in surprise. Their conversations rarely got personal. 'I'm fine,' she said.

'Only there's been a rumour circulating.'

'Oh?'

'Rumour that your marriage has hit the buffers.'

'That didn't take long.'

'Has it?'

Romilly screwed up her face. She didn't want to talk about this. 'Sort of.'

'That's vague.'

'Well, it has.'

'You need time off? I could pass all this over to Turner. By rights, it should have been his shout, but he was away. Now he's back.'

'No. I'm fine, sir. Honest.'

'Help's always here, if you need it,' he said.

'Thanks.'

'OK.'

Romilly went. As she walked along the passageway to the door, she looked down at her left hand. There sat a plain little diamond engagement ring, and an even plainer wedding band. Both Hugh's choices, not hers. Had she ever really liked them? No.

Stickability was her middle name, and she'd stuck with a dead marriage when instead she should have dug a hole and buried the fucker. She took both rings off and dropped them into her bag.

Suddenly, she felt more free, more *herself*, than she had in a long, long time.

12

Fats went down the Mile End Road to collect from a couple of restaurants and a dry cleaner's there. He hadn't anticipated any trouble, and he didn't get any. All the owners paid up, offered him free meals, free cleaning on his suits. Which was only what he had come to expect; he was working for Kit Miller, who was a very big noise on these streets, and respect was due.

The Bill hadn't nicked anyone for the warehouse job in January, not yet. And Kit was still spitting mad over it. There was taking the piss, and then there was *that*. Three million quid lifted from a place that paid to his people. Not good. Not good at all.

And Thomas Knox, who'd always been an ally of Kit's, had been implicated. It was a dirty business. They were still trying to trace the two arseholes who'd been spotted on the day of the robbery – so far without success.

'You want to watch yourself, Fats,' said one of the restaurateurs as he handed over the wedge.

'What?' That sounded like a threat. Fats' eyes narrowed. What the fuck . . . ?

The owner quickly held his hands up. 'Don't misunderstand me. Just I had some blokes in here the other day, saying they could do the same job for less. I explained that we were very happy with Mr Miller. Which we are. Of course.'

'You told them no,' said Fats.

'Damn sure!'

'If they come in again, call the office. What did they look like?'

The owner described them. But neither one of them sounded like runty blond, or the black guy.

'You take care now,' said the owner.

'People see the warehouse getting done on our patch, they'll chance their arm, see if they can move in,' said Kit when Fats told him what had happened. They were sitting in the office behind Sheila's restaurant an hour later.

Sheila, who was long dead, had been gang lord Michael Ward's wife. Michael used to run this manor; now it was Kit's. Kit was sitting behind a tooled-leather desk where once Michael had sat.

'Cheeky bastards been on our turf, suggesting they could cut the owners a better deal,' said Fats.

Kit nodded, glanced at Rob, his head man, who was, along with Fats and Ashok, sitting in the small nicotine-stained office with him. Michael had puffed on expensive Havana cigars and Dunhill cigarettes while doling out orders to his boys in here – the ceiling was still coffee-brown, but Kit hadn't redecorated. The stains, the old furniture, everything in here reminded him of Michael, who had been like a father to him.

Kit wasn't a smoker. He wasn't even a drinker, not any more. He'd been there, done that; now he liked to keep himself fit, do some boxing down the gym, a bit of weight training. Keep his levels up so that he stayed fast, stayed sharp. Once, he'd been Michael Ward's chief breaker – just as Rob was now his – and he prided himself that he was no less fit now than he had been back then.

'No mention of Knox, I suppose?' asked Kit.

'No.'

'Owners turned them down?' asked Kit. From out in the main body of the restaurant, there came the noises of the waiting staff, chatting, laughing, and of glassware and cutlery being laid out ready for lunch.

'Too right,' Fats leered. He wasn't pretty, Fats. Lean as a whippet and wrinkled as a prune, he was fortyish and had never been a looker. But he was efficient and he was ferocious, which was all that Kit required. 'Happy with our service, see?'

Kit thought that they damned well ought to be. What his mob did was basically keep the peace on streets where the police were wary of treading. Around here, *they* were the law. Any hassle the owners got was instantly sorted out for them. Yes, they paid for the privilege – his boys collected from around forty restaurants and as many nightclubs and shops, plus ten snooker halls and a load of amusement arcades. But the deal cut both ways. What the owners of those places got in return was complete peace of mind, with robust help never more than a phone call away.

The London underworld streets were run nowadays pretty much as they had been ever since the sixties when the Richardsons and the Frasers held the south, the Regans the west. The Foremans had held Battersea, the Nashes covered The Angel, the Carters held Bow and part of Limehouse, and the Krays had held Bethnal Green. Old orders had changed, people had come and gone, but the rules still applied. You didn't piss around on someone else's manor. It just wasn't done.

Recently, Kit had set up a limited company with himself and Ruby as co-directors, offering security services to VIPs. It had taken off nicely, having established a reputation for providing solid, hard men, reliable and fearless. Work was pouring in.

So all was pretty much OK. Or it *had* been, up until the robbery. That had made him and his people look bad, and he was still fuming about it and wondering what the fucking hell was going on. And so far he wasn't convinced, as Ruby seemed to be, of Knox's innocence.

'You found those two arseholes yet? The two that got spotted?' he asked Fats. If they could track them down, maybe they could get answers instead of sitting here in the dark.

'Still trying. Everyone's on the lookout.'

'Well try faster. Try harder,' said Kit.

There came a rap at the door and it opened. The bulky besuited boy outside on the door – Daniel, the eldest of Rob's two younger brothers – let Ruby Darke and her daughter Daisy enter the office, then closed the door behind them. Both women were carrying a cluster of shopping bags and looked happy but exhausted.

'It's *crazy* out there,' said Ruby, flopping into a chair.

'We're hoping for some lunch,' said Daisy, dropping her bags and greeting Rob with a kiss.

'Hiya, beautiful,' he said. 'Bought me something nice?'

'It's all wedding stuff,' said Daisy. 'I tried on twenty veils this morning. Or it felt like it, anyway.' Kit rose to his feet, hugged his sister and kissed his mother's cheek.

'You OK?' he asked Ruby.

'Yeah, fine,' she smiled. 'Remind me why I bought that damned club though, will you?'

'Because you missed the business,' he said. 'I told you that you would, remember?'

'Yeah, well I must have been off my head to get into the clubland stuff. I've had nothing but trouble with that place. Mad chefs, demented brewers, and now a star turn that's failed to show without a moment's notice.'

'I've never been inside a burlesque club,' said Rob thoughtfully.

'Whoa, tiger, don't get too excited,' said Daisy with a grin. 'Burlesque is *art.* It's dance.'

'The fuck? It's stripping,' said Rob.

'Well yes, granted, but it's very subtle, very artistic.'

'That's right,' chipped in Ashok. 'I know about this. Each performer has her own particular set of moves. And if anyone else copies them, it's handbags at dawn.'

'So, not stripping?' Rob looked disappointed.

'Technically, yes, but . . .' said Daisy.

'Sounds bloody boring. Don't think I'll bother,' said Rob.

'Anything we can help with?' Kit asked Ruby.

'Yeah, find me another star like Crystal Rose by nine o'clock tonight.'

'This the one who's gone AWOL?' asked Rob.

'Without a word to me *or* her sisters, who help in her act. They showed up last night, thinking she'd follow on because she hooked up with some new bloke a couple of nights back. But she didn't, so I had to get up onstage and cancel. People were disappointed and it's a damned nuisance. Crystal's a pain in the rear.'

'An employee you can't count on is a liability,' said Rob, who was rock-solid dependable at all times and couldn't understand anyone who wasn't.

Ruby smiled at him. Soon he was going to be her son-in-law and she couldn't wait. He felt like family already, like a second son. He'd been her driver, and Daisy's, when they needed his protection.

You always felt safe with Rob. And best of all, he guarded Kit, stood by him, watched his back. Ruby felt that Rob would lay down his life for Kit; their friendship was that close.

'It'll all work out,' said Daisy.

'That's it, though. The agency's sending over a raft of performers this afternoon so I'm going to be knee-deep in interviews until six o'clock. It means a lot more work,' complained Ruby. 'Timing couldn't be worse, what with the wedding on Saturday and so much still to do.'

'You love it,' laughed Kit.

13

It was a beautifully crafted precision instrument, the gun. The killer'd had it specially made for him quite a while ago. It all slotted together for ease of transport: the butt, the barrel, the trigger, the screw-on sights and even the silencer. The silencer was important, because he needed to practise, and he couldn't do that down the club since the morons had chucked him out, so he had to do it in the woods, out of sight, and the silencer made it easy to do that quietly.

He picked up some shopping, including a marrow. He'd already calculated the distance he needed to get the hit absolutely right, but he wanted to get his eye in. He paced it out now, through the nettles and the ferns and the brambles that tugged at his camouflage pants. Then he tied the marrow up – chest height – to the low-hanging bough of an oak tree.

He went back to his shooting position, loaded the rifle, lined up and let off the first shot. It made a *phut* sound, with the silencer. Nice and quiet. But it missed the target, pulled to the right. He got a screwdriver from the toolkit in his pocket, adjusted the sights. Fired again. Missed. Again with the screwdriver. Took aim, exhaled slowly . . . and fired.

PHUT!!

The marrow flew apart like a grenade had gone off

inside it. Splatters of pale vegetable and clumps of its striped green skin flew in all directions.

Nice.

The killer smiled to himself. Satisfied, he dismantled the rifle and packed it away, whistling under his breath. He carefully picked up the spent shell casings on the ground – a good habit learned at the club; they called it 'policing one's brass'. He now felt he knew everything there was to know about guns, and more. The primer ignited the powder and then the firing pin struck, so all the spent casings were, of course, dented. Those idiots down the club didn't appreciate just how good he was. He was a Mozart, a Van Gogh – a genius in his field.

Well, fuck them.

Mission accomplished, he walked back to his car, surrounded by birdsong. Spring was coming, and primroses were coming up on the woodland banks, carpeting them in soft butter yellow.

He reached the car, popped open the boot. Then his smile died as he went to put the gun bag in there. Another thing occupied the boot, black polythene swathing it, tied with ropes and fastened with gaffer tape. Fortunately, Crystal Rose was so petite, she didn't take up much room. He squeezed the gun bag in beside her. Fucking inconvenient, she was. It had been the devil's own job yesterday. He'd had to buy a big sports bag, the biggest he could find, and cram her into it, zip it closed, get it out of the hotel and into the hire car he'd acquired, again giving a false name and paying in cash. On top of that, he'd had the job of cleaning up all the dreadful mess she'd made. He'd had to dump his best jacket in a large waste container, ramming it down among a ton of disgusting restaurant leavings, five miles up the road. He shuddered to think of it. All that muck in there. All the *mess*. He *hated* mess.

Now he had to dispose of the stupid nosy cow. Sighing, he wrestled the shovel he'd bought at a far distant DIY outlet from underneath her. Took out the pliers and the roll of tape. Then he stepped back, and slammed the boot closed once more.

14

Sometimes, Ruby Darke wondered how the hell she'd gotten into all this. *The apple don't fall far from the tree.* That was what her dad, Ted, had always said, when he wasn't running his corner shop, or belting her upside the head. Her mother had always been bad when you got right down to it, he said, and so was Ruby.

Ruby's two brothers, Charlie and Joe, had been crooks. They'd terrorized the workers down Smithfield meat market and dominated the post-war East End streets. While she – the one who was always sneered at and abused – had concentrated on the corner shop, turning it into a national chain. She'd been the straight one, the one who *should* have got the pat on the back.

But she never did.

Somehow, she had always felt the *lure* of crime. As a child, she'd been curious about the things her brothers got up to, and in adulthood there had been the men she'd taken up with. Michael Ward for one. And later, Thomas Knox.

There was a sexiness to it, she thought, a palpable *heat*, when you lived close to the edge. Now she was a part of Kit's organization, and money from the protection rackets was washed through this club and through many others that the company owned. She'd slipped into the life almost seamlessly, and now it was all she knew: sitting in on iffy deals, laundering dirty money, while all the time presenting a 'clean' image to the world, as she ran her Soho burlesque club, Ruby's.

Lately, however, she'd found herself wondering about the wisdom of being so involved in the day-to-day running of the club. This part – auditioning new acts – could easily be left to Laura the manageress, but no: Ruby had wanted to be the one choosing them, so here she was, running the auditions and bored out of her skull.

Her afternoon passed slowly. She sat through a tattoo-covered woman gyrating suggestively, followed by a jokey one, covered in balloons which she proceeded to pop one by one with a hat pin. Next up were two handsome young men in skimpy red bondage gear with tassels hanging off their peachy arses, calling themselves Boylesque. Then a terrifyingly huge, masked fire-breathing woman; a woman in black, sporting devil horns and Dracula teeth; and a Georgian shepherdess. Last came a trio of saucy can-can dancers, who were the only ones who even came close, but not close enough.

She was just packing up in her back office at the club, ready to go home, thinking with excitement that Daisy's wedding was this Saturday. Months of preparation had gone into it. There'd been so much to do, to organize. But now everything was in place, and it was *this Saturday.* Her thoughts were interrupted by a knock at her office door. She sighed. It had been a long, wearying day. She'd had fun this morning with Daisy, but this afternoon had really dragged.

'Yeah, come in. What is it? I'm finished for the day,' she warned, snatching up her bag, hoping it wasn't another act, turning up late on the off-chance. Or Laura with a problem. She wanted a hot bath and bed. Not much else.

It was the Rosettes.

'Can we have a word?' asked one of Crystal Rose's sisters.

'Sure you can.' Ruby suppressed a sigh, dumped her bag on the desk, and waited. 'Jenny, isn't it?' Jenny was the slightly more talkative one; Aggie was the one who rarely said a word. They were pretty, the pair of them. Watered-down versions of their glamorous older sister.

'That's right. Crystal hasn't called you, has she?' said Jenny.

Ruby shook her head. 'No.' She looked at the pair of them. 'She hasn't been in touch yet? Not with either of you?'

'No, and it's been three days,' said Jenny.

'Does she often do that? Go off with new men?' asked Ruby.

'A night, maybe. But not *days*,' said Jenny, while Aggie stood there chewing on a hangnail. 'And the thing is, you see, we phone each other all the time. Take turns. She'll say, "It's your turn tomorrow," so we phone her. Every day. We're always in touch.'

Ruby searched her memory. 'You don't live with her, do you? She's got her own place?'

Jenny nodded. 'We – Aggie and me – share a place in Earl's Court, but Crystal's got her own flat.'

'Well, have you checked it out? She might be there. Maybe she's too ill to phone.'

'That's why we wanted to talk to you,' said Jenny. 'To ask you. Would you come with us? I've got a key.'

Shit, thought Ruby.

Aggie, silent at the wheel, drove them to Crystal's flat in Barnes after Ruby had phoned home and said she'd be late back. Crystal's flat was the upper floor of a big Victorian house, reached by an exterior metal staircase. Ruby trudged up there after the Rosettes, cursing Crystal Rose for being a pain in the arse. She was probably up here in bed with her latest squeeze and would wonder what all the fuss was about. But no doubt she'd enjoy the attention; Crystal thrived on that.

But . . . she hadn't phoned her sisters, and she usually talked to them every day. Hadn't turned in for work, and Ruby thought she'd been quite happy at the club. Always pushing for more wages, but that was par for the course. So it was a little odd, all this. Slightly out of character.

First, Jenny rang the doorbell. No answer. She rang it again. They stood there. It was starting to rain.

'Got the key?' prompted Ruby.

Jenny nodded, produced it, put it in the lock. She opened the door.

'Crystal?' she called out.

The flat was silent. Jenny, Aggie and Ruby stepped inside.

'Crystal!' called Ruby loudly. 'You in here?'

The thing that struck Ruby as they walked further into the flat was all the *mirrors*. Every wall bristled with them, in every conceivable shape and size. The three women walked along the hall, into the bathroom – Ruby touched the flannel, the towels, all bone dry – then the bedroom – the bed neatly made, unoccupied – finally the living room – empty of life. At every turn, they were constantly confronted with their own reflections. Ruby could easily picture Crystal in here, chatting on the phone to her sisters while admiring her own profile, her superb little body, and purring with satisfaction over her own attractiveness.

'Doesn't look like she's been here for a while,' she said to the Rosettes as they stood, at a loss, in the hallway once again. 'Let's ask downstairs, maybe they've seen her.'

They relocked the flat and went back down the staircase

and knocked at the flat below. The girl who lived there hadn't seen Crystal Rose either, she was a long-haul air hostess and rarely at home.

'She's probably wrapped up in this new man and she's lost track of time,' said Ruby as they stood outside on the pavement.

'You think we ought to tell the police?' asked Jenny.

'If she's not back by the weekend, we will,' said Aggie unexpectedly.

They took Ruby back to the club in gloomy silence.

'I'm sure she'll turn up,' said Ruby as she got out. She thought of the washout auditions this afternoon, then of Crystal wowing the crowds with her champagne-glass act. 'Listen, why don't you two step up, take over the act, just until she's back?'

'Crystal wouldn't like it,' said Aggie with a set jaw, and that was the end of that.

15

On Saturday morning, Ruby was awoken by hammering and voices. Then a deafening screech of feedback from a microphone. For a moment she stared at the ceiling of her bedroom in her Victorian villa, unseeing, until it dawned on her what day it was. With a surge of real pleasure, she swung her legs to the floor, grabbed her robe and slipped it on, then went over to the window and pulled back the drapes.

Where two days ago the view had consisted of lawns, the blue oblong of the swimming pool and the flower borders, now there was also a big white marquee, with a red carpet leading to it from the house. People were scurrying about, carrying trays of glasses, lugging huge speakers, hefting boxes of plateware and cutlery. A dark-suited woman was threading cream roses, maidenhair fern and satin bows around the metal arch at the marquee's entrance. Another was hurrying around with a clipboard, giving orders – the skinny, nervy little wedding planner.

Ruby looked up. The weather gods were smiling on them today. Blue sky and sunshine! She threw open the window and breathed in deeply. It did feel like spring, now. Then she turned back into the room and looked over at the hyacinth-coloured silk dress and coat hanging in its protective cellophane sheath on the wardrobe door. The Philip

Somerville box containing the matching hat was on the mirrored dressing table. She couldn't suppress a grin. Days like this didn't come along that often, and they had to be treasured.

She glanced at the clock. Nine thirty, and the girl who was doing hair and make-up for her and Daisy was coming at ten thirty. Somewhere in the house she could hear Matthew and Luke, Daisy's twins from her disastrous first marriage, starting another fight, and Jody the nanny loudly telling them to shut up.

Ruby couldn't believe how blessed she was these days. Once, she had literally lived for nothing but her work. Having little else in her life, she had lost herself in statistics, turnover, profit and loss. But once she had been reunited with Kit and Daisy, her long-lost twins, everything had changed. Now she was a doting mother, an indulgent grandmother.

She hadn't regretted letting the Darkes stores go. And now she supposed she was as happy as anyone had a right to be. Reviewing her life, she thought that she was a lucky woman. She was pretty minted. She had her kids and her gorgeous grandkids. She had good health.

And there *had* been men. That aristocratic bastard Cornelius Bray. What a mistake *that* had been – but she'd got Daisy and Kit from him, so out of bad, good could come. Then she'd fallen for golden-hearted crook Michael Ward. She would have married him, but it was not to be. And after Michael's murder, Thomas Knox.

Ruby frowned. The question was, did she truly, completely *believe* his pleas of innocence over the warehouse job? Kit didn't, and she wasn't one hundred per cent sure herself. Knox was a real hardnosed gangster. Yes, they'd once had a hot affair. As a lover, he was second to none. But . . . did she trust him? Had she *ever* trusted him?

Suddenly the door to her bedroom was flung open. Daisy stood there wearing a white robe. Her corn-gold hair was loose to her waist and in wild disarray. Her skin was flushed and her blue eyes were glittering with happiness and a faint sliver of panic.

This was the best thing about her life, Ruby thought. Her kids. Big, beautiful, blonde Daisy and cool, dark Kit. Her twins. An accident of birth had seen them set off in very different directions in life – Daisy to live the high life with her father Cornelius and stepmother Vanessa, Kit to trawl the streets and somehow stay alive until Ruby managed to find him again. They looked nothing alike, Kit and Daisy. Coming from Ruby, who was half-caste, and Cornelius who was white, in a rare genetic fluke Daisy had been born pale-skinned like her father, and Kit had been born dark, exotic-looking, like his mother.

'Christ!' hollered Daisy in her cut-glass Home Counties accent. 'Why didn't you wake me? It's nearly ten!'

Ruby opened her arms. Daisy, laughing, crossed the bedroom at a run and joined her mother at the window. Ruby hugged her as they looked out at all the hustle and bustle in the garden below.

'Oh God,' said Daisy.

'What?' Ruby looked at her beloved daughter with concern. 'Nervous?'

Daisy bit her lip. Nodded. 'A bit.'

'Bad night?'

'Missed Rob,' she said.

Ruby smiled at that. Daisy and Rob had been living together in one of the two plushly furnished and spacious apartments over the garage block for over a year now. The twins loved it there, with the pair of them. One night apart? That wasn't so hard to endure, surely. She couldn't be more pleased about this match. Tough, East End boy Rob and posh, big-hearted Daisy. They were made for each other.

'After today you won't have to miss him, ever again,' said Ruby. She wasn't upper-crust, like Daisy. Daisy had been raised so differently to her. Ruby was an East Ender, like Kit, like Rob. He was going to be *so* good for Daisy, Ruby just knew it.

'Good.' Daisy hugged her mother hard, and shivered in anticipation. 'It's really happening, isn't it?'

'It sure is,' said Ruby, kissing her daughter's flushed cheek, feeling so happy for her that she could burst. 'Welcome to your wedding day, darlin'.'

16

When Romilly crawled home, exhausted after another hectic day, she found Hugh there, clomping down the stairs with two black bin bags clutched in one hand.

'Oh!' she said, startled. And pissed off. After a long day, if there was one thing she *didn't* need it was Hugh in her face.

This warehouse heist was driving her insane. They had pulled everyone in, putting everything they had behind it, both her and the team, but they had drawn a blank. The six major crims they'd watched – including that slippery bastard Finlay and Tom Knox – had pretty much been cleared of any involvement. She was starting to feel that all avenues had been covered. She hated that. *Something* had to give on it. And soon. It was now a case of digging deeper and starting again, from the ground up. Every second lost on this was evidence lost, so they had to break the back of it soon.

'Just picking up a few more things,' he said.

He looked sheepish. Well, he ought to.

'Not much to show for it, is it?' Romilly indicated the two bags he carried. 'Then again, I suppose most of your stuff is still back at that tip you call home. Smart move. Saved yourself some legwork there, Hugh, hanging on to that shithole.'

'Don't be bitter,' said Hugh. He was doing his wounded-pup look.

'Bitter? I'm not. Merely stating facts. Truth is, you always expected this marriage to crash and burn, didn't you? So it's no big surprise that it finally has.'

And damn, hadn't she half-expected it, too? Everyone knew that cops were impossible to live with. Mum had moaned on about Dad often enough, and he'd never got beyond detective sergeant. She was a detective inspector, and the pressure was *so* much more intense. Lots of coppers married other coppers, because at least they understood the pressures of the job: the hideous shifts you had to work, the horrors you saw and couldn't help but bring home with you.

She saw Hugh's eyes go down to her left hand. 'You're not wearing your rings,' he noted.

'That's right,' said Romilly. 'And you never wore a ring at all, did you? Bit of a clue there. Lack of commitment again. What, d'you want the engagement ring back? You going to give it to Sally? String *her* along for a few years?'

Angry colour flooded into his face. 'That was a cheap trick, what you did. You didn't have to humiliate her like that.'

Humiliate *her*?

Romilly opened the front door and stood there, stony-faced.

'Get out, Hugh. And before you go – give me your bloody key.'

17

'What the fuck did you let me drink last night?' Rob asked.

He was sitting at the kitchen table at Kit's house, where he'd spent the night. He was nursing a glass of Alka Seltzer and had thrown back a pint of water and a couple of painkillers. It was unlucky for the groom to see the bride the night before the wedding, so instead of being together in their cosy apartment over the garage at Ruby's place, Daisy had gone off to Ruby's and Rob had gone to Kit's, which was a tall and fiendishly expensive Georgian house a stone's throw from Belgravia. And Kit – his boss and today his best man – had got him and the rest of the small stag party, which included Rob's two younger brothers Daniel and Leon, completely rat-arsed.

'You were drinking Chivas Regal. And some vodka. Maybe a bit of port too,' said Kit, pouring out coffee for them both and sitting down opposite his best mate. 'Oh, and—'

'No! Don't tell me. I'll feel worse than ever.'

Rob was slumped at the table. He had just staggered down from Kit's spare room, having awoken to find that he hadn't even undressed last night. He had fallen spark out across the bed in all his clothes. Now his head was pounding and Kit was finding all this very funny. Rob watched his boss moving around the kitchen. Kit Miller, feared gang boss, getting all domestic.

'You'd make someone a bloody fantastic wife,' he said.

'Fuck off,' said Kit with a grin. 'What you need,' he said, going over to the fridge and pulling out eggs and bacon, 'is a fry-up. Line your stomach.'

'Ain't that supposed to happen *before* you start drinking?'

'Ah yeah. Spotted the deliberate mistake there.' Kit was hauling out the frying pan, slapping it on the stove, switching on the gas. 'Some people swear by prairie oysters.'

'I'm *not* eating – or drinking – raw eggs.'

'In that case, it's bacon and fried eggs,' said Kit.

'All right.'

Kit eyed his old pal with amusement as he put the bacon in the pan and heard it sizzle. Rob was the best, Kit depended on him absolutely. He'd provided solid back-up for Kit for so long that they almost moved together as one unit, neither having to explain a thing. But when it came to drinking, Rob was a lightweight. Kit, on the other hand, could put it away for England and barely feel the effects. Not a good thing, that. And there had been times – tough times – in his life when drink had threatened to rule him. But it didn't. And it wouldn't.

Kit Miller was *tough* and he was proud of that. He'd had a hard early life but it had made him resilient. Hard enough to take the knocks and stay standing. Knocks like life in the orphanages. And losing his old boss and mentor, Michael Ward, and Gilda, the woman he'd loved, both of them murdered. And then, five years back, Bianca Danieri had walked out of his life, saying she had to go search for her long-lost family, she needed time alone, and she hoped he understood.

He'd understood all right. It was a brush-off. He'd *loved* that mare, but she'd had a different agenda. He busied himself with the breakfast and thought *Well, fuck her.* Cocky as hell in his youth, full of swagger, Kit had grown up big style and he now had a cool, watchful presence. He had an athlete's inborn energy, good height, broad shoulders, curly black hair and café-au-lait skin. His face was arresting – his eyes, in particular, were startling, given his skin colour. They were a sharp, clear blue – the same blue as Daisy's – and radiated quick intelligence. His nose was straight, the nostrils widely flaring. His mouth was sensual. Such looks guaranteed that there were always women hanging around him, but mostly he took little interest in them.

Once, he'd had beautiful, golden Gilda.

Then, Bianca, white as the snow of her Nordic homeland.

For now, he was off women. As the bacon crisped up he broke the eggs into the hot fat and thought that women either let you down, screwed you over, or broke your heart. So who needed it?

He got the bread out, put it on the table with butter and orange juice from the fridge. Got out the cutlery and glasses. By that time the eggs were done. He went back to the stove, dished up, put breakfast on the table. Rob eyed it dubiously before picking up his fork and starting to eat.

Kit watched him. Rob was built like a ten-ton truck and had been his right-hand man for just about forever. He was handsome, burly, dependable as daylight. All the breakers and enforcers on Kit's payroll answered to Rob. Sure, Rob was – technically – Kit's employee. But he was also his best pal in all the world. He was like a brother.

'Better?' Kit asked.

'Hmph,' said Rob. He put down his knife and fork, sank his head into his shovel-like hands, scrubbed them across his face. Upstairs, it sounded like Daniel and Leon were starting to get up. Rob glanced up at the ceiling, frowning. Then he looked at Kit. 'Christ, am I really doing this?'

There was something in Rob's face that made Kit's attention sharpen. 'What, you got cold feet?'

'Nah.' Rob heaved a sigh and picked up his cutlery again. 'It's not that. Just this fucking hangover. And business stuff. Listen – we got to have a talk soon. A *serious* talk.'

Kit looked at Rob in surprise. 'OK. You sure it'll keep?'

There was heavy footfall on the stairs. Daniel and Leon burst into the kitchen.

'Yeah,' said Rob. 'It'll have to.'

'What, no brekkie for us?' said Leon, nicking a slice of bacon from Rob's plate. Rob slapped the youngster's hand away, his face like thunder.

'Show some fucking respect,' he growled.

18

The killer got into position bright and early to check that all was OK. He settled down. Got comfy. Took the pieces out of the carrying bag, looked it over. All fine. Slowly, carefully, he assembled the rifle. It was a nice day; no wind, that was good. A bright spring day in England, what could be better? Well, some things could, he thought. A beach paradise break, for instance. Couple of weeks in Barbados at a five-star hotel. But *this* would pay for *that*.

He had the first twenty grand tucked away safely. After today, there would be another twenty. Soon as he'd collected the cash, he'd select one of the fake passports he kept to hand – you could buy the things for a song on the black market, they were ten a penny – and take off somewhere.

He'd scouted out this area, gone in the local pub, kept his head down and his ear to the ground. People chatted, and he listened. He'd discovered that the owners of the apartment he now sat in were already living the Caribbean dream. They were in Antigua, and would be out there for another month. It was perfect. The place wasn't alarmed. He had a set of skeleton keys, and easily found one that fitted the lock on the front door. Once he was in, he stayed there, quiet and watchful; no one was any the wiser.

Inside, the apartment was a mediocre little place with dodgy plumbing, set in an outwardly grand and picturesque

Georgian block cloaked in thick green creeper that would turn scarlet in autumn. The place was near the shops, but he hadn't been into any of them and now that he'd gained entry to the apartment he didn't go to the pub any more, either. He got his groceries at a distance, and didn't bother with booze or newspapers. Oh, he glanced at the headlines sometimes, but the outside world didn't bother him much. He saw silly pictures of Henry Cooper and Kevin Keegan arsing around in a fake boxing ring, promoting Brut after-shave, and shots of the Humber Bridge under construction. Nothing of any interest to him.

No one knew he was here, he was sure of that. He'd been wearing disposable surgeon's gloves the whole time he was in here, and already this morning he'd given the entire place a thorough clean. Granted, his dabs weren't on any police file, but why take a chance? Why give the filth anything to work with?

You could see the river from here. It was pretty. Swans glided, ducks squabbled. Light danced off the surface as canal boats chugged past. A nice place to live, this picturesque village near Marlow on the Thames. And the most important thing he could see from this vantage point?

The church.

Quaint old place, it was. Norman, he reckoned, judging by the squared-off tower. He knew a bit about things like that. Aisles and naves and flying buttresses and stuff. He liked churches. Felt a deep sense of calm wash over him whenever he stepped inside one. Which wasn't very often, granted, but he liked them anyway. Not all the God stuff, but the architecture, the detail. Brilliant.

He picked up the gun again, rubbed it down almost lovingly with the cloth, hauled up the sash window and leaned the barrel out a little so that the tip rested on the stone sill. He hooked his finger into the trigger, fastened his eye to the sight. Adjusted the crosshairs until everything looked perfect. The big arched oak door of the church was so sharp and clear he could see the knots in the ancient wood, could pick out the black metal studs embedded in its gnarled surface.

His finger tightened on the trigger.

Boom, he whispered.

He sat back, replaced the rifle on the floor, pleased. All fine. He glanced at his watch. Ten o'clock. He'd grab some breakfast and then all he had to do was wait until it started. Or *ended*. He liked endings. They were neat.

19

'Right. Let's have a look at you,' said Ruby, grasping Daisy's shoulders and directing her gaze toward the full-length cheval mirror.

'Wow,' said the wedding planner, standing off to one side, still clutching her clipboard.

'You look *wonderful.* Both of you,' said the girl who'd styled their hair and done their make-up. She was packing her kit away now in a square silver case, but even she paused at this moment and stared.

Ruby, in her hyacinth-blue silk coat and dress with a matching hat, looked the picture of elegance, but all eyes were drawn to Daisy, who had wanted something simple for today, something *rustic.* So her corn-gold hair was loose, the waves cascading, gleaming and lustrous, on her bare shoulders. Her gown was in the milkmaid style, scooped low at the neck, fastened with pearl buttons at the back, the bodice tightly fitted, the skirts flowing out loosely to the floor, covering her white sandals.

Daisy carried a messy, casual bouquet of lush, cream roses and fronds of baby's breath. On her head was a circlet of the same flowers, holding the plain, simple veil she had dithered over and finally selected as *the one.* Her face glowed with happiness.

'You've never looked so beautiful,' said Ruby, feeling tears sting her eyes.

The planner, a manic smile fixed to her face, heard movement outside and rushed to the window. 'Oh, the car's here. How about a picture? We've still got time. You both looking in the mirror? The photographer's still downstairs.'

'No pictures. Not now,' said Ruby firmly, her eyes meeting Daisy's. The rest of the day would be hectic and noisy, they would be on show. This moment was theirs alone, private and peaceful, mother and daughter.

Already they could hear Matthew and Luke downstairs, all dressed up and ready to go in their pageboy outfits, shrieking and running around, giving poor Nanny Jody hell. Matthew would be throwing off his purple velvet bow tie and waistcoat. Mattie was an extrovert and loved to shed his clothes at every opportunity. Luke liked to undress behind the furniture.

Ruby looked at her gorgeous daughter and said: 'No doubts? You're sure about this? One hundred per cent sure?'

Daisy smiled. 'Dead sure,' she said.

'Right then. We're on.' Ruby reached up and pulled the veil down over Daisy's face. 'Come on, let's go,' she said, and caught Daisy's hand in hers. Ruby blinked hard, gulping back an emotional tear. 'Your public awaits.'

The Rolls Royce Silver Ghost purred through the streets, the uniformed chauffeur smoothly guiding the car. It was only a short drive to the church, and they could hear the bells pealing before they'd even come close. When they arrived and the chauffeur opened the door for Daisy while Ruby exited from the other side, the joyous sound of the bells being rung was almost deafening.

The photographer – a nervy little chap with crinkly

brown hair, assisted by a dumpy woman who looked like his wife – took a photo of Daisy emerging from the car, then of Ruby and Daisy beside the car. Finally he posed them in front of one of the vast yews to the side of the path leading up to the church and took more shots – one full-length, the other three-quarters.

As the vicar came out from the church door they saw Jody in her best dress holding on to Matthew and Luke, who were shouting and twisting like a pair of dervishes. Mattie's bow tie was missing. No surprises there. As they saw Daisy coming closer, the twins started bawling for her. Daisy blew them a kiss and made a firm 'keep the noise down' gesture, which they ignored.

The vicar shook Ruby's hand, greeted Daisy. Jody ushered the twins inside, and the vicar ushered Daisy and Ruby into the church.

'I'll signal,' he said, and hurried off to the high altar.

Daisy looked at the crowd gathered inside the church. Cream roses and matching satin ribbons decorated the end of every pew. She could see Lady Vanessa Bray, who'd raised her until she'd been reunited with Ruby, staring across the aisle at Rob's mother Eunice.

Daisy frowned at that. Vanessa was a terrible snob, and the Hintons were common folk. Eunice was saying something to her youngest son, Leon, who was today sharing ushering duties with the middle son, Daniel. She saw Leon listening, stony-faced, then he quickly moved away.

Eunice's face was a picture of hurt, and Daisy felt for her. Rob always said that Leon was a gobshite and unrelentingly nasty to their mother.

God, families!

All right, Eunice was tarty and she tended to dress that way. Her skirt today was a bit too short, the matching shell-pink top she wore a little too plunging at the neckline. But

Daisy hoped that Vanessa was going to be polite. She didn't want anything to spoil this day.

Her eyes moved on, and she could see Kit up at the front, and *there was Rob.* He was looking back. He saw her standing there, and smiled. Then the organ started to play, the vicar raised a hand. Everyone inside the church rose to their feet. Ruby and Daisy walked up the aisle to 'Here Comes the Bride'.

20

The killer had watched the guests arriving and filing inside the church opposite, all of them dressed up to the nines, smiling, chatting. Big, happy day for them. Payoff day for him, the culmination of two long, boring weeks. Now it was *showtime*.

At twelve noon the bride arrived with her mother. He saw the vicar greeting them, watched them go inside. He settled back, lined up the gun so that the sights were *smack* on the door area. Still no wind; that was good. Nothing to compensate for. Forty minutes, he reckoned. He'd watched a couple of weddings here last week to be sure, and forty minutes was the usual time. He relaxed. He waited.

It was such a beautiful wedding. Everyone said so, afterwards. The bride had been heartbreakingly lovely. The groom *so* handsome. It was obvious how deeply in love they were.

It's just so tragic, they all kept saying. *So awful.*

Hymns were sung, prayers offered up. The register was signed, and Daisy and Rob emerged from the vestry and walked back down the aisle as husband and wife, while the photographer set up his tripod outside the church door. The happy couple were smiling at people they knew as they passed by, Ruby and Kit following close behind them,

Jody tugging Daisy's twins along in their wake as Daniel and Leon, and all the guests followed on. Chatting, kissing, Daisy and Rob stepped into bright, spring sunlight, dazzled and blinking after the cool dark of the church.

A perfect day.

But then the killer fired.

And down in the churchyard, hell opened up.

21

The bells were ringing, clanging in Ruby's head. Everyone was talking, laughing. Confetti was flying, floating down in the still air, masking the happy couple in fluttering pinks and blues and yellows. Daisy was laughing; bits of the stuff were falling down the front of her dress. Rob's treacle-blond hair was peppered with it.

No one heard the shots. All that happened was that suddenly the photographer pitched forward, knocking over his tripod, smashing the Rolleiflex camera perched on it to smithereens.

The photographer's wife let out a cry and flung herself down beside her fallen husband.

Smiles dropped from faces. Had he suffered a heart attack? Ruby looked at Daisy, but Daisy, who was clinging on to Rob's arm, was pitching forward too, falling to her knees. Ruby's mouth fell open. Her eyes moved to Kit. Time seemed to stand still as she stared at his face, which was frozen in disbelief. There was blood on the back of the photographer's camel-coloured jacket, high up on the right shoulder. His wife stared at it – and then she started to shriek.

Kit was looking around. Left. Right. Ruby saw his eyes fasten on the building opposite. A glint of something, there? She wasn't sure. Kit was reaching for her, shoving her roughly to the ground.

'Down!' he shouted as she stumbled and fell. 'Everybody down! Gun! GUN!'

Now there was more screaming and the bells were still ringing. Everyone scattering, diving for cover. Ruby, scrabbling on the ground, all the wind knocked out of her by the force of Kit's push, her knees grazed, her heart beating madly, thought, *Oh shit! The twins!*

She looked around frantically, couldn't see them. Then she glimpsed Jody's yellow and blue floral dress inside the church door. Jody had them. They were safe.

'Stay down!' Kit shouted, and in the midst of chaos, screaming, mass hysteria, he was off. Leaving them. Running away.

'Kit!' Ruby yelled after him.

But he didn't stop.

22

Kit was sprinting full pelt. He charged through the doorway of the Georgian building opposite. People passed him, stopping to stare, but he paid them no attention. He shot up the stairs, thinking, *My sister's wedding. Whoever did this is* dead.

He thought it was the first floor. One of the windows on the right.

There had been a glint there, a flash. He was *sure*.

The bells were still ringing and he was running up, up, up, and now he was on the landing and it forked; there was a line of doors. *Which one?*

Christ knew.

He was sweating and the blood was thrumming crazily in his ears. He tried the first one. Locked. He raised a fist, hammered at it. Couldn't wait. Took a step back, kicked it open.

A little grey-haired woman was crossing her carpeted living-room, staring at him in terror. 'What are you—?'

He didn't wait. He went to the next door, tried it. Locked again. No time for niceties. He stepped back, kicked out. It juddered open. He peered in, expecting the pile-driver force of a bullet to stop him in his tracks at any moment. But the place looked empty. He carried on into the flat. The fucking bells were still ringing. He moved into the living room. There was a mangy old Chesterfield sofa, a threadbare rug. A fireplace. He went over to it and hefted the poker lying there into his hand. Looked around him, feeling his flesh creeping but too mad, too *enraged*, to feel fear.

Moving more stealthily now, he looked at the sash window, open; the church clearly visible. He pushed the entrance door to the flat closed and moved along the interior hallway. Trod carefully into a bedroom, then a bathroom. Nothing. He moved back to the living room. Went over to the window and looked at the floor. Three spent shells there. He picked one up, put it in his pocket. He sniffed the air and smelled cordite.

Across the road he could see the chaos in front of the church. He could hear the bells and the screaming. People panicking, running.

He turned and left the flat, went back to where he'd ruined the old lady's door. Pushed it open. She was there, mouth open, face white. She was trembling and her eyes were fastened on the poker in his hand. Kit dropped that hand behind him, held up his free hand in a calming gesture.

'It's OK. You're OK,' he said quickly. His mouth was dry as ashes. He had to swallow to get the next sentence out as adrenaline pumped furiously through his veins. 'Fire escape?'

She said nothing. With a quivering hand, she pointed to the left.

Kit pulled the door shut again and moved off along the hall. At the end of it was a solid fire door. He depressed the bar handle and shoved it open. Stepped out onto a metal stairway, his feet clattering on the thing. A gusting breeze lifted as he stared down the flimsy-looking zigzagging metal structure to the cobbles below at the back of the building. Bins down there. A few cars, parked up. No movement.

Nothing. If there had been a shooter here, he was gone.

'Fuck it,' said Kit loudly.

He went back to the shooter's flat, wiping the poker as he went. He replaced it. Then he went back down the stairs and out of the building.

23

It was still madness outside the church. The vicar had come out, seen what was happening, gone back inside. Suddenly, the bells fell silent.

The photographer's wife had stopped screaming. Now she was kneeling, crying hysterically, staring down at her fallen husband. There were people staggering about among the gravestones, people crawling back to their feet, their faces blank with shock. Ruby was still on her knees. When she saw Kit coming back, she stood up. As he came hurrying up the church path he saw that her tights were torn and there was blood snaking down from her knee to her calf.

'You all right?' he asked her.

She nodded. She was looking at the photographer, lying face down on the gravel. 'Christ . . .' she moved forward to help him. Daisy blocked her path.

'Are you all right?' Ruby asked her, clasping her shoulders, pulling her in for a hug. Then she stopped. Froze. Saw the blood on the front of Daisy's dress. Daisy's bouquet was on the ground, mangled by the panicked footfall of her guests. Her eyes were dazed.

'Oh God!' Ruby burst out. 'Where are you hit? Where?'

Daisy lurched sideways and sagged against the church

wall. She seemed unable to speak. Kit hurried to her; he could see she was about to collapse.

'Daisy! Where are you hurt?' he said urgently, slipping an arm around her, holding her upright.

She was shaking her head. Pointing with a trembling hand.

'Rob,' she whispered.

Kit and Ruby looked for Rob. He was on the ground.

'What the f—' Kit looked around for Fats. 'Fats! Here!'

Fats came over, white-faced. 'Boss?'

'Hold on to Daisy. Stay with her.'

Kit moved away from his sister and flung himself down beside his best mate. There was blood on the front left of Rob's jacket, just above the cream rose buttonhole he wore. The rose was delicately spattered with red. His face was very pale, his eyes closed. Kit stared at him in horrified disbelief.

'No, no no . . .' he muttered, thinking *the blood was Rob's, it wasn't Daisy's at all.*

'Ambulance!' he shouted at anyone who would listen. 'Phone for an ambulance, someone! Hurry!'

'Done,' said a voice from the crowd. 'It's on its way.'

With a shaking hand, Kit placed his fingertips against Rob's neck. For one terrifying instant there was nothing. Then he felt a fluttering, stumbling pulse. He took out a handkerchief and applied firm pressure to the wound. Didn't dare do CPR, he was afraid that would only cause more damage. He looked up desperately at Ruby, standing there with Fats and a stricken Daisy.

'Hold this,' he said, and Ruby knelt down and held the handkerchief to Rob's chest while Kit stripped off his jacket. Taking back the handkerchief, which was now soaked red, he reapplied pressure to the wound and laid his jacket over Rob to keep him warm.

'Don't you fucking dare leave me, you silly cunt,' he told Rob. His voice shook. 'Not today of all days. You hear me?'

'Rob! Rob?' It was Eunice, Rob's blonde, blowsy mother, shaking off the heavy restraining hands of her partner, Patrick Dowling, and surging forward with a panic-stricken face. She fell to the gravel beside her eldest son. 'What's happened? What is it?' she said, clawing at Rob's arm as if that could wake him and stop all this madness.

'Leave him, Eunice,' said Ruby. 'He's going to be all right. Just give him some air.'

'What the *fuck*?' Daniel came up and stood there, ashen, staring down at his fallen brother. Leon was at his shoulder. He said nothing, but his eyes were fixed on Rob and he looked like he was about to throw up.

'My boy! Oh Christ! My poor boy,' wept Eunice.

Kit looked up at Daisy, standing there sheet-white in her blood-splashed wedding gown. Ruby hugged her.

'He's going to be OK, Daise,' said Kit, not believing it.

'Of course he is,' said Ruby. Over Daisy's shoulder she saw Jody peer around the open church door. Quickly, she shook her head. *Keep the kids in there. Don't let them see this.* Jody drew back into the church's dark recesses. 'Rob's tough as old boots.'

Some of the other guests were huddling around the photographer. One of them was now staring down at the man and shaking his head. He was patting the shoulder of the woman kneeling, weeping, at the photographer's side.

'This can't be happening,' said Daisy. Kit could see stark terror in her eyes.

'It's going to be OK,' said Kit. He checked for Rob's pulse again. Oh Christ. Weaker. 'Hang on, Rob,' he muttered. '*Hang on*, you old bugger.' He felt tears start in his eyes. He clung on to Rob harder. 'Christ's sake, mate. Don't . . .' And his words choked on a sob.

*

It felt like an age until the ambulance arrived, but it was only ten minutes. When the paramedics stepped in to take over, Kit stood back, let them do their stuff. He looked down and in faint surprise saw that his hands were stained bright red with blood. *Rob's* blood. His head was empty of everything but what he'd felt over these last desperate, hideous minutes.

This must be shock, he thought. *This must be what it feels like.*

'What happened?' the paramedics asked, looking at the two casualties.

'They were shot,' said Kit, and then everything changed. The police rolled up, blue lights flashing, getting warily out of their cars, keeping their distance. A couple of minutes later a plain car drew up; more officers. And these had guns.

Kit looked at Daisy, who had slumped down and sat hunched on the church steps. What could he say to her? This was worse than bad. This was a living nightmare.

Daisy was staring at him. He saw the hope there in her eyes, the pleading. But he couldn't tell her what she wanted to hear. Tears started to cascade down her cheeks. Ruby crouched beside her daughter, trying to help but unable to. What should have been the happiest day of Daisy's life had turned into a disaster.

24

Romilly slept late on Saturday. She awoke to find herself alone in the very bed where Hugh had cavorted with Sally. She hadn't even had time – or the inclination, or the strength – to change the sheets yet. And she knew that her reaction was skewed. Any other wife, surely, would have been tearing them from the bed the instant that tart vacated the premises. Putting on fresh. Wiping out the memory of what had happened here.

But not Romilly Kane.

Because she was *relieved* to find herself alone in the bed, and actually? She didn't much *care* that she'd finally caught Hugh out with his cheating. She thought again of Hugh's indignation, his anger, at being discovered. She'd known for a long while that *something* was going on. Barbed comments from him, a general lack of any real interest between them. So she'd laid her trap and *snap!* He'd wandered into it.

She rolled over in the bed. It smelled stale and once again she thought of Sally and Hugh in here, playing hide the sausage. *Yuck.* But lots of space to stretch out now. Hugh was a big man and she was six feet two inches tall. Truthfully, she'd felt a low-level annoyance for quite a long time when Hugh thrashed about in his sleep in the night and woke her – which he did, often.

Christ, I have to sleep she'd always thought on waking. *The job! I have to sleep, or I can't function.*

Massive responsibilities rested on her shoulders. So she couldn't be little wifey. She was a detective inspector and her brain was ticking away like a metronome most of the time. She couldn't bring herself to give Hugh the strokes and pats he seemed to want.

Yeah, I'm just a boring bloody copper. And Hugh's right. I am *married to the job.*

And this is where you end up, she heard her mother's whiny little voice saying. *Alone. No husband, no children. Just you, Romilly, on your tod. Is that what you want?*

She sat up. It was daylight and she didn't have a clue what time it was. Reached for the alarm clock, which she hadn't set. Looked at it in disbelief.

Gone midday. Time to get going.

'Christ,' she muttered, and swung her legs to the edge of the bed and sat there. She could hear traffic passing on the road outside.

My marriage is over.

She kept thinking that. But she couldn't seem to summon any sense of sadness over it. It was done, finished. It had been dead in the water for a long time. So, forget it. Move on.

Romilly rose from the bed as her phone rang. She picked it up.

'Hello?'

'We got a shout, ma'am,' said Harman's voice.

'What is it?'

'St Michael's Church, Mitchell Underdyke. Shooting at a wedding. Armed officers are there.'

Jesus, thought Romilly.

25

As Rob and the photographer were loaded into two separate ambulances, everyone watched in silence. Even the wedding planner was quiet for once, pale-faced and shaken. The place was thick with filth, cop cars pulling up one after another, lights flashing, black-clad men getting out of a plain car. Armed officers everywhere.

'I'll go with Daisy,' Ruby told Kit.

He nodded. 'I'll follow in the car,' he said.

The photographer's wife was going with him to the hospital. Poor woman, Ruby couldn't imagine what she was going through. Clive Lewis had come here to do his job in all innocence, and this had happened. She caught Jody's eye as the nanny was battling with two howling twins in the church doorway. 'Look after them, yeah?' Jody nodded numbly.

Taking Daisy's arm, Ruby walked her down to the gate and into the ambulance after Rob. The armed officers moved past them, talking into radios.

'If anyone wants to come into the church and sit . . .?' the vicar offered, appearing at Jody's side, looking shaken.

No one did. They all stood there, staring at the bloodstained gravel, as the ambulances roared away.

'Everyone else,' said one of the beat police, raising his

voice, 'stay where you are. Police officers will move among you and ask questions.'

'I'm going to the hospital,' Kit told him. Not waiting for a reply, he turned and walked away.

When Kit caught up with Ruby and Daisy, they were sitting in a small, grey-painted waiting room in the bowels of the hospital building.

'What's happening?' he asked them.

Ruby, her arm around Daisy's shoulder, looked up at her son with bleak eyes.

'The photographer's dead,' she said, her voice unsteady. 'There was nothing they could do. They said it was instantaneous, he didn't suffer. They've taken his wife off somewhere, I don't know where. I think they've sedated her. She was shattered.'

Kit sat down opposite the two women. He was almost afraid to ask. 'And Rob?'

'They took him straight into surgery.'

Kit looked at Daisy. Her face was like a waxwork dummy, devoid of expression. Her white wedding dress was stained red. She still wore a circlet of flowers on her head, and her veil and her corn-gold hair were peppered with bits of confetti. Ruby had taken off her hyacinth-blue silk coat and draped it over her daughter's shoulders. Daisy sat and stared dully at the floor.

'Daise?' he said. 'You OK there?'

Her eyes raised, very slowly, until they rested on his bloodstained hands. 'What?' she said.

'Are you all right?'

'You're asking me *that*?' Fury flared in Daisy's eyes and her voice was sharp as a knife. 'Someone is right at this minute cutting open my fiancé's . . .' she paused and then corrected herself . . . 'My *husband's* chest to try and dig a bullet out of him, a bullet that was meant for *you*, so no, I'm not bloody all right.'

'She's very upset,' said Ruby to Kit.

'Upset?' A horrible rictus of a smile twisted Daisy's mouth. *'Upset?'* She glared at Kit. 'You're like a fucking cancer, aren't you? You corrupt everything around you. You've even changed Mum. It's down to you, what's happened to Rob.'

'Daisy—' started Ruby.

'It's true. This is all down to *him*.'

'Oh, come on,' said Ruby.

'What, you don't think so?' Daisy twitched away from Ruby's enfolding arm; she was staring at Kit with venom. 'I think Rob saw something. And he was trying to shield *him* from it.'

'What?' Kit thought of the flash of metal in the window across the road from the church. Had Rob seen it too?

'You heard. He unbalanced me so I fell. He was moving toward you. He saw something and he was doing his damned job. Even on the day of his wedding he was protecting *you*.'

Ruby was staring at Kit now. 'You ran off, into the building over the road. Did you see something there?'

'I thought I did,' said Kit.

'But you didn't find anyone?' Ruby asked.

He shook his head.

'Did you speak to the police?' asked Ruby.

'No, I came straight here.'

Daisy glared at her brother. 'Rob's in there being sliced up like ... *oh Christ* ... a Sunday joint, all because of you. That poor little man who was taking the photographs is *dead*, because of you. *You* were the target. Not him. Not Rob. The photographer's already in the morgue, and I don't know, I just don't know what's going to happen to Rob. Christ, he could *die . . .'*

Daisy dissolved into shuddering tears and Kit stared at her in anguished silence. In the past he had been a target for other gangs, and had got this far in life by fending them off – yes, with Rob's help. He probably was the target. Nothing else made sense. Daisy was right to shout and scream at him, to say *it's all your fault.* Because it was.

Someone came and stood in the doorway. It was a tall, cadaverous man, middle-aged and with a neat, grey goatee beard. He was wearing a green cap and a stained green gown.

'Mrs Hinton?' His calm brown eyes went to Ruby, then to Daisy sitting there in her wedding dress, and his face softened.

Ruby got to her feet. 'What's happening? How is he?' she asked.

The surgeon shook his head. 'I'm sorry. We did all we could.'

'No,' said Daisy, her face blank, standing up, seeming for a moment to sway on her feet. 'NO! This can't be happening . . .' She was almost screaming now.

'I'm so sorry,' said the man again.

'No, no! It can't . . .' Daisy was shaking her head, over and over. Ruby grabbed her, held on tight.

'No, it's not true. I want to see him. I want to see Rob.'

'Yes, you can see him. In a few minutes. Of course you can,' said the man gently, and then he withdrew.

'Daisy . . .' Kit was on his feet too now, reaching for her.

'Don't touch me, don't you fucking dare!' she shrieked. 'This is you. This is all *you*, you *bastard*! Rob is dead. And it's *your fault*!'

26

Feeling as if she was floating through hell, Ruby went in with Daisy to see Rob.

'I don't want *him* in there with us,' said Daisy, looking with hate-filled eyes at her twin.

'All right,' said Ruby soothingly. She looked at Kit. 'Wait for us, yeah?' They went into the room.

'He looks like he's sleeping,' said Daisy as she stood at Rob's bedside.

Ruby couldn't bear it. Her daughter should be the happiest woman in the world today, and it had all been snatched away from her. She stared down at Rob's still face and thought that Daisy was right; it was as if he was sleeping.

They had covered him with a sheet right up to his chin, and wheeled him into this impersonal pink-and-white painted room somewhere off one of the main wards.

Yeah, he's asleep. He's asleep and this is all a dream, and in a minute I'll wake up and laugh about this, thought Ruby.

Only she didn't feel like laughing. She didn't think she'd laugh, ever again. As she watched her daughter bend over Rob's lifeless body and lay her head in the hollow of his shoulder, she felt tears overflow and run down her face. Rob had been Daisy's love, but he had also been Ruby's friend; no, more than that. He had been like another son. Rob had saved her, guarded her, taken care of her. Of

Daisy too. Of *both* of them. And of Kit. And yes, Daisy was so angry with Kit, that was natural, but she would eventually see that turning on Kit was not the answer. They had to be strong for each other now and stay together, a family unit – not bicker among themselves.

Daisy was weeping, sobbing against Rob's unresponsive body. Ruby could only watch in anguish. His treacle-blond hair was combed, his strong face composed, his eyes closed. It seemed that at any moment he would open them and smile up at them standing here and say: '*What's up with you two? Who died?*'

Her daughter was in pain.

Her dear friend was lost to her.

Someone's going to pay for this, Ruby promised herself.

27

Kit sat down, feeling that the bottom had just dropped out of his world.

Rob was dead.

He couldn't take it in; didn't *want* to. His best mate. How was he going to cope, how was he going to go on, without Rob at his back?

But then – minding his back had got Rob into this. Daisy was right. He felt bone-deep grief. And anger.

A moment later, Rob's brothers and sisters arrived, and his mum Eunice with her partner, and Kit had to tell them the worst news they'd ever had in their entire lives.

'Mr Miller?' someone asked.

Kit didn't know how long he'd been sitting alone in the waiting room, staring at the floor. Down the hall, Rob's mother Eunice was sobbing her heart out. Rob's sisters, Trudy and Sarah, were with her. And his brothers, Daniel and Leon. Kit could hear Leon asking over and over who the *fuck* could do a thing like this.

But worst of all was the sound of Daisy crying. She was shut away in a room with Ruby and with Rob's dead body, but her cries carried along the hospital corridor and wrenched at his innards. *My fault,* he thought.

The female voice repeated his name. 'Kit Miller?'

He looked up. A tall, soberly dressed woman of about thirty was standing in front of him. She had a shock of wild dark-brown curls tied back with black cord. She was looking down at him with serious dark eyes, set in a pale, oval face. A stocky, thin-haired man of around the same age stood behind her.

He had the eyes of a cop, or a criminal. And so did she.

'I'm DI Kane, this is DS Harman,' said the woman, and they both flashed their warrant cards.

Kit stood up. He was six feet two inches tall and she was looking him straight in the eye. Not many women did that. His eyes slipped down to her feet. No heels. This girl was *tall.*

'Yeah, I'm Kit Miller,' he said.

She was gazing at him in that special way cops reserve for those who they know operate on the far edges of the law.

'Mr Miller, we have a situation here,' said DI Kane. 'A double shooting at a wedding. I believe your sister's . . .?'

'Daisy Darke,' said Kit. 'Her fiancé, her *husband*, I mean. He was shot. And the photographer.' *And I think that poor sod got in the way. Just like Rob did.*

'The vicar said you ran away when the shooting started.' Her eyes were staring into his. Curious. Mocking. Behind her, Kit thought he saw DS Harman suppress a smirk. Kit looked at him, and the smirk dropped away.

'That's right,' said Kit. 'I ran away.'

'Really? Only a couple of the guests think different. That maybe you saw something, and went for it. Maybe you saw the gunman?'

Kit wrestled with himself and then thought: *Maybe they can actually help. Who knows, perhaps they can find this fucker faster than I can. And if that's the case, I have to tell them.*

'I saw metal catching the sun at a first-floor window over the road,' he said.

DS Harman got out a notebook and started writing things down.

'So you ran *toward* what you thought was someone with a gun.'

'There was nobody there. He'd already gone.'

The DI looked at him steadily. 'Mr Miller,' she said, 'I need you to show me. Right now.'

'Wait up,' said Kit in exasperation. 'I've got my mother in there in bits over this. And my sister. And there's Rob's mother, his brothers and sisters. They're all bloody devastated. I can't just fuck off. Not now.'

'I'll give you an hour to see everyone safely home,' she said. 'And then you'll show me. And once that's done, I'll have to speak to your sister – I'm sorry, but it's necessary. This is a murder investigation, Mr Miller. We don't want to lose any time on this. I'm sure you understand.'

28

It was a miserable drive home, with Ruby hugging Daisy, who was slumped across the back seat beside her, and Kit at the wheel. Ruby knew she should have sought out the wife of the photographer before she left the hospital, but she couldn't. All her concern was for Daisy, who seemed simply *broken*. She had to focus on her daughter and push everything else to the side. Over the coming days, Daisy was going to need her badly. And so was Kit.

Kit parked up the Bentley beside a couple of other cars and a purple catering van with *Soul Food* writ large on the side of it on the gravel drive in front of Ruby's place. They went indoors to be met with silence, inactivity. All the happy preparations of the morning were done, and now should have been the time for celebration. The house should have been rocking with happy laughter and music.

Champagne should have been flowing. But it was eerily quiet. It didn't look like any of the guests had come back here, and they wouldn't, Ruby was sure of that.

As they walked into the hall, the wedding planner, still clutching her clipboard to her chest like it was a lifeline, came out from the kitchen and stared at them.

'I didn't know what you wanted me to do,' the woman said, shrugging helplessly. 'The caterers, all the food . . .'

'Tell them to take it away,' said Ruby. The thought of

food gave her the dry heaves. And, oh Christ, the wedding cake. Daisy mustn't see that. '*All* of it.'

The woman hurried off into the kitchen, closing the door behind her.

'Daisy, go into the sitting room. I'll make some tea,' said Ruby.

Throwing Kit a vicious look, Daisy shrugged off Ruby's blue silk coat so that it drifted to the floor and went into the sitting room. Kit made to follow, but Ruby caught his arm.

'Don't. Leave her for a while,' said Ruby. Upstairs, she could hear Matty and Luke arguing. They fought night and day, those twins, but they were in good hands. Jody was wonderful with them. And thank God for it, because right now Ruby couldn't spare a thought for anything but Daisy.

Fats, still wearing his cream rose buttonhole, came into the hall from the kitchen. It was only then that Kit remembered he was still wearing his buttonhole. He unfastened it, threw it aside.

Ruby picked up her coat, hung it up, and followed Daisy into the sitting room. 'Tea, Daisy? Or coff—' Her voice died on her.

Daisy was standing in the middle of the room, motionless.

Fuck, fuck, fuck! thought Ruby as she walked in. There, piled up on a long trestle table in front of the bay window, were the wedding presents. Pink balloons on ribbons decorated each end of the table, and floral swags that matched Daisy's bouquet and headdress were draped along the front of it.

'Oh Christ – Daisy, I didn't think . . .' she said.

Daisy walked forward and stood in front of the table, running her trembling hands over the gifts spread out there. When she turned to Ruby, her face was wet with tears.

'I wish I'd died too,' she said.

'No!' Ruby rushed forward and hugged her. Daisy stood there, rigid, unresponsive. 'Rob wouldn't have wanted you to say that. He was a fighter and he'd want you to be the same. And you have the twins. You're a mother, Daisy. You have to go on.'

'But I'm not like Rob, am I?' Daisy sobbed. 'I'm not that tough. I want him here, with me. And instead he's in a *morgue*.'

'I know.' Ruby cradled Daisy's head against her own. 'I know, sweetheart. It's awful.' She wanted to say something wise, something comforting.

But there were no words.

All she could do was hug Daisy tight, and let her cry.

Kit sighed as he watched them both from the doorway. Daisy turning on him like that at the hospital had hurt. Then there'd been the hysteria from Rob's mum and his sisters, loud fury from Leon and silent hostility from Daniel. Everyone was blaming him, and shit, they were right to do that. He knew it.

This *must* have been meant for him.

He went into the downstairs cloakroom and stood looking at himself in the mirror over the basin, wondering what the fuck to do now. His gaze drifted to his bloodstained hands. He literally *did* have Rob's blood on his hands. He turned on the tap and washed them clean, splashed his face with water. The blood swirling in the sink smelled metallic and for a moment he felt his gorge rise and wondered if he was about to hurl. But he didn't.

He heard someone knocking at the front door and he went back out into the hall and opened it. DI Kane and her sidekick Harman stood there.

'Time's up, Mr Miller,' she said.

Kit nodded and turned in the doorway. 'Fats? Keep an eye on everything here, OK?'

'Will do,' said Fats.

Kit stepped outside and pulled the front door closed behind him.

'OK, let's go,' he said.

29

It was hard, going back to the church. The police were still there in force, people in white suits taking photos, POLICE DO NOT CROSS tapes being slung up in a criss-cross pattern in front of the church door. As they got out of the car, Kit could see the stain of Rob's blood still there on the gravel. Confetti drifted along the pathway up to the church door, driven by the lifting breeze. He looked away. No fucking use, dwelling on things.

'So, Mr Miller.' DI Kane stood with him and DS Harman under the shade of the lychgate. Harman took out his notebook again. 'Tell me what happened here – in your own words.'

The sun was shining.

It was a beautiful day.

Rob is dead, he thought.

Kit said: 'We came out of the church. Rob and Daisy first. The photographer was out here with his tripod and camera, his wife – I think – with him. Everyone was shouting and the bells were ringing. Couldn't hear yourself think. The guests were throwing confetti. Tons of the stuff. We were all half blinded, what with that and the sun in our eyes.'

'But you thought you saw . . .?'

'The photographer went down first and I saw the blood

on the back of his jacket, so I glanced up and that was when I saw something. Metal. In the window up there.' Kit pointed to the Georgian building opposite.

'And you ran off, over there.' DI Kane was staring up at the window now, her back to the church. She turned her dark eyes on Kit again. 'One of the residents complained to our officers. Someone kicked her door in.'

'I wasn't sure about which flat when I got up there,' said Kit. 'I just knew I had to get whoever it was before they fired again. That's all. There was an old woman and I scared her. I apologize for that. I'll pay for the damage to her door. But I wasn't thinking straight.'

'And at that point you didn't know Mr Hinton had been a victim of the shooting?' she asked.

'No, I didn't. I only realized that Rob was hit after I came back down.'

'Let's go up,' said DI Kane.

The three of them crossed the road and went over to the building. They entered beneath the decorative Georgian portico and went up the stairs.

'The old lady,' said DI Kane as they climbed, 'Mrs Portman, she's gone to stay with her daughter. She was very distressed. She said a dark-skinned man with black hair and wild, staring blue eyes kicked in her door and stood there with a poker in his hand. Where did you get the poker?'

They paused outside Mrs Portman's shattered door.

'I got the poker from the other flat,' said Kit. 'But the flat was empty; whoever fired the gun was gone. There were spent shells on the floor by the window.' He looked at the floor. The two shell casings he'd left there were gone. 'I went back to the old lady and asked her where the fire escape was. She told me.'

'We've reason to believe that three shots were fired. We

picked up two spent casings from here. Did you pick up any, Mr Miller?'

'No,' said Kit.

'She said she was too frightened to speak when you came back a second time. She thought you were going to murder her.'

'She *gestured*, OK? And I tried to reassure her, but how the fuck could I, standing there with a poker in my hand? I went out on the fire escape but I was too late. He'd gone. Arsehole must have moved like greased lightning.'

There was a uniformed police constable now standing outside the door to the flat where the gunman had fired the shots. Police tape was draped across the broken lock. DI Kane nodded to the man, and he moved the tape, let the three of them inside.

They stood in the centre of the living room. An old sofa. A TV. A coffee table. The window was still open, and the view of the churchyard couldn't have been bettered.

DI Kane tipped her head toward the fireplace. 'The fire-side implements – particularly the poker – were dusted for prints. But none were found.'

'It's been warm for the time of year,' shrugged Kit. 'If he was staying here, I don't suppose he used the fire at all.'

'We didn't even find your prints on it,' said DI Kane, eyeing him beadily.

'Maybe I wiped it down before I put it back.'

'Why would you do that?' *Force of habit.*

'Listen. Picture the scene, can you? I was at my sister's wedding and then someone started shooting. I thought the gunman was up here so I ran up to try and stop the bas-tard. I don't know *what* I was thinking. I was acting on instinct. Maybe I did wipe the poker – so what? It wasn't *me* up here taking potshots at people. I'm not the man you're after.'

'Right,' said DI Kane. 'You know of anybody who'd want to target you, Mr Miller?'

'No. Not a soul,' he lied. And he could see in her eyes that she *knew* he was lying. Of course she did. She'd know the ins and outs of every villain on her patch; and he was one of them. 'If there's nothing else, can you drop me back at the house? My family need me there.'

'Sure,' she said, and DS Harman snapped shut his notebook and tucked it away. 'If you think of anything else, you'll let us know, yeah?'

'Yeah. Sure,' said Kit.

They went back downstairs and walked over to the car. As they did so, Romilly Kane watched Kit Miller. She knew of him, of course. Everyone on the force did. But she'd never brushed up close against him before. Bastard fancied himself, that was for sure. Thought he was irresistible with those come-to-bed eyes and his fit, toned body. He was a villain and she hated villains. But . . . It was a *big* but.

She was trying to think of anyone of her acquaintance who would run, unarmed, *toward* a man who was picking people off with a gun.

And she couldn't think of anybody.

Not a single one.

30

After they'd taken Kit back to Ruby's place, the police stayed on, questioning Daisy and Ruby. Then Jody got a grilling, while Ruby looked after the twins in the now empty kitchen. DI Kane left first, leaving DS Harman to follow later. All evidence of wedding preparations inside the house was gone as if it had never been. Kit poured himself a whisky and wandered out into the garden to get some air, try to take it all in.

Rob was dead.

He stared at the marquee, vast and white in the sunlight. The DJ was moving his speakers out of there, trudging round the side of the property with them to put them back in his van. He saw Kit watching him and ducked his head. Kit walked down to the marquee's flower-clad entrance and looked inside. A woman was putting cutlery back into a cardboard box. Another was taking the floral displays from the centre of the long tables and packing them away, too. The caterers had already taken the three-tier wedding cake away, and thank God for that. No way did he want Daisy seeing *that* today.

He drank some of the whisky and wondered what to do. Rob was in the morgue. And whoever had *put* him there – and the photographer – was still wandering about free.

And that person could give killing Kit Miller another try at any time.

Where to start?

What to do?

His mind was spinning. Once, he'd taken to the bottle hard, and he felt like doing that again right now. Drown his sorrows, because for sure he had plenty of them. For ten years, Rob had been at his side, covering his back and pulling him away from excess, always the voice of reason whenever Kit strayed too close to the edge.

Now, Rob was gone and Kit felt that a part of himself was gone, too. It was as if he was standing beside a huge cliff, and it was crumbling steadily beneath his feet. Soon, he would fall. He couldn't help but think of this morning, when he and Rob had talked over breakfast, neither of them knowing that it would be for the last time.

Christ, it was heartbreaking. And poor bloody Daisy. She'd be lost without Rob, too. Someone who had been such a big part of both their lives – and their mother's – was gone from them forever, and it hurt. It hurt like hell.

Someone cleared their throat behind him. Kit turned. It was DS Harman.

'Let's talk indoors,' said Kit.

Kit led the way into Ruby's study. It was a tiny, tidy room with one buttoned, tan leather chair set behind a plain desk, and a wheel-back chair for visitors. He closed the door behind them, flopped down in the leather chair. Drained the last of the whisky, placed the glass carefully on the desk.

'So,' he said. 'You lot got any ideas?'

'It's knowing where to start, isn't it?'

'Meaning?' Kit eyed the detective sergeant steadily. The firm had a lot of coppers on the payroll, and this DS was one of them. Kit didn't like bent bobbies much. He *particularly* didn't like this one with his bolshie manner and jokey expression. And he wondered what Harman's sexy, tumble-haired DI would say if she knew the truth about him.

'Come on,' said Harman. 'You got a ton of enemies and my guess is those two poor saps just got in the way. My lot won't usually take too much bother over it. Mind you, Kane could be the exception. She's like a dog with a bone, that girl. Persistent. Can't give up even when she knows she shouldn't bother. But the shooting element? Nobody likes that.'

'Right.' Kit mulled that over. *Shouldn't bother?*

Harman shrugged. 'Live by the sword, die by the sword, right? The photographer's the innocent party here. And your mate caught an unlucky one. I reckon they were aiming for you. And they missed.'

'Yeah. Got you.' Kit stood up. He walked around the desk and in one swift movement grabbed Harman by the front of his shirt, swinging him round. Harman lost his footing and hit the study wall with a crash.

'Hey! What . . .' he burst out, winded.

Kit still had hold of Harman's shirt front. He slammed Harman's head back against the wall, hard.

'Jesus!' the man yelped.

Kit came in so close that he could see the enlarged pores all over Harman's beaky little nose.

Harman wasn't smirking any more. 'Listen,' growled Kit.

'Wait! Don't . . .'

'Shut the fuck *up*, you tosser.' Kit gave his head another whack on the wall.

Harman shut up.

'Just listen,' said Kit through gritted teeth. 'My best mate died today, you smart-arsed little tick. You want to follow his example? Keep going.'

Harman's eyes were wide with fright. 'I'm sorry, all right? I didn't mean no disrespect.'

Kit gave the man a shove, sending him staggering sideways. He watched Harman in disgust.

'You keep me informed of anything and everything. I want the bastard in that window found. I want to know everything your DI knows. *Everything.* No exceptions. You got me?'

'Sure,' said Harman, straightening his clothes, visibly shaken. 'Sure.'

'And what about those fuckers who did the warehouse? You got anything yet on the two who were spotted?'

'Nothing,' gulped Harman. 'Not yet.'

'Well step it up a gear, all right? Now fuck off.'

When Harman was gone, Kit sat down at Ruby's desk. He was thinking about what Rob had said that morning, about needing a serious talk, but it would keep. Now he would never know what had been bothering Rob. *Business stuff.* Meaning what?

He took the spent shell casing out and looked at it, long and hard. Then he put it back in his pocket, took out the spare key he kept and unlocked Ruby's desk drawer. He took an item out, and went in search of his mother.

31

Kit found Ruby crossing the hall. 'How is she?' he asked her.

'Devastated,' said Ruby as DS Harman went over to the front door and let himself out. Her eyes followed him, then she turned back to her son. 'I don't like that bloke. He give you anything?'

'Not a thing,' said Kit, still fuming at Harman's words. Rob had 'caught an unlucky one'.

Unfortunate, but you get close to mud and some of it might one day stick to you. That *bastard.*

'He'll keep us posted, though?'

'He will.' Kit nodded toward the stairs. 'I ought to speak to Daise,' said Kit.

'Jesus, don't do that. Leave her be for now. I'll stay with her. She'll calm down. Don't worry.'

Kit looked around, his movements agitated. He felt the loss of control in this situation, everything sliding into chaos. He handed Ruby the cloth-wrapped item he'd just taken out of her study drawer. Ruby's eyes widened. 'Christ,' she murmured.

'Keep it with you in your bag,' he said. 'And keep it loaded. It's only a .22 but that's enough to stop anyone at close range. Don't look at me like that. We got to be prepared.'

'God,' said Ruby, putting a shaking hand to her face. 'All right. I will.' Her eyes filled with tears. 'What the hell's happening? Rob! I can't believe it.'

He squeezed her arm. 'I've got to go.'

Fats came into the hall from the kitchen, followed by the wedding planner.

'I'm going to see Rob's folks,' said Kit.

'I'll come too,' said Fats.

'No,' said Kit. 'I want you here. Watch Ruby and Daisy and the boys.'

He went out to the Bentley, took a package out of the boot and got in behind the steering wheel. Shrugging off his jacket, he slipped on the shoulder holster and got his gun out of the glove compartment, loaded it and slid it home. Put his jacket back on. Then he started the engine.

32

Rob's mother was in hysterics. Her daughters Trudy and Sarah were trying to console her, but she was beyond that. As soon as Leon saw Kit coming in, he put himself in Kit's face.

'What the fuck's going on?' he demanded aggressively.

'That's what I'm going to find out,' said Kit.

'Cop said they were aiming for you, and got Rob instead,' said Leon, his blue eyes cold with fury.

Kit took a breath. Harman! Useless loose-mouthed *bastard.*

'Ease off, bruv,' said Daniel, catching hold of Leon's shoulder.

Kit looked at the two Hinton boys. Rob had been the oldest and the best of them, Kit's firm right hand. Now he had to make do with these two. Daniel was OK. He was young, sure, but solid and dependable, whereas Leon was forever flying off the handle and kicking over tables, too full of youthful exuberance. No doubt about it, Rob's younger brothers were keen as mustard, but were they Rob? Could they *ever* be?

For a moment, Kit thought he was going to get a sharp right-hander from Leon. Maybe he even deserved it. But the moment seemed to pass. 'What the fuck can we *do*?' Leon demanded.

Kit paused for a beat. 'What Rob would have done in the same situation, I guess.'

Kit looked around the living room. Rob's mother was hunched on the sofa, still dolled up in her wedding finery and in floods of tears. Trudy and Sarah were on either side of her, their husbands hovering nearby. Eunice's partner, Patrick Dowling, got up from the sofa and came over.

Kit eyed the man up. Patrick was a big bloke – bigger than Kit – in his fifties, packed with muscle and a fair bit of fat. He ran a dodgy car dealership, Rob had told him, and he had a prosperous fuck-you air about him. His face was the brick-red of the heavy whisky drinker, broken thread veins radiating out from his nose like rays from the sun. His hair was thick and grey, his eyebrows bushy enough to almost have a life of their own as they drew down angrily over his fierce and bulbous brown eyes.

'What the fuck's going on, Miller?' he asked loudly.

Kit was silent for a long moment. 'When I find that out, I'll let you know,' he said.

'Take it easy, Patrick,' said Daniel, looking uncomfortable. 'Rob knew the risks. He accepted them. It ain't Kit's fault.'

'Take it *easy*? This ain't bloody good enough. Things like this happening,' bawled Patrick.

'You're right,' said Kit, and walked over to where Eunice sat huddled on the sofa. She looked up at him, her face drowned in tears, her mouth pulled down, making her ugly.

'My condolences, Eunice,' said Kit.

Eunice nodded, her eyes red with crying and full of fear when they met his. Kit Miller's name was mentioned in the same breath as the legendary London gangs – the Krays, Nashes, Richardsons, Carters, Foremans – and Patrick might be bold enough to call him on this, but she wasn't.

Patrick Dowling was there beside him again. 'You want

to fuck off out of it, Miller,' he said. 'We don't want you here.'

Kit turned and stared at Patrick, long and hard. Finally, bug-eyed with suppressed fury, Patrick looked away.

Kit turned his gaze to Eunice, said: 'We'll find who did this. That's a promise.' Then he left.

33

Days had gone by and the weather had turned. On Daisy and Rob's wedding day, the sun had shone and everything had seemed bright and hopeful. Now a humid fall of steady rain misted the garden, shrouding it in gloom as Ruby looked out.

Press photographers had started to gather at the gates, so every trip in or out of the house was a nightmare of flashing lights, shoved microphones and shouted questions.

'Some fucker in the police must have tipped them off,' Kit told her, and he put another two boys on the gates in case they tried to intrude further.

The marquee was gone. What should have been such a happy day for them all was gone, too. Daisy did nothing but sit in one of the main house's spare bedrooms – she couldn't face going back to her apartment over the garage block, the one she'd shared with Rob – day after day, gazing out at the lashing rain, seeing nothing. She barely ate. Not even the twins induced a flicker of interest in her.

'I'm going into town this afternoon,' said Ruby, going upstairs to find Daisy still sitting in a chair by the window, staring out. Ruby went to stand behind her daughter's chair. She touched Daisy's shoulder. No response.

'Oh?' Daisy was wearing a dressing gown. Since taking off the bloodstained wedding dress and giving it to the police as evidence, she hadn't bothered getting dressed again.

The doctor had come, prescribed tranquillizers. Daisy had taken them. Now she just sat there, saying little. Ruby understood her daughter's pain – *of course* she did, Daisy's pain was like her own – but she was beginning to get the urge to shake her, all the same. Daisy had children. She had to think of them. And she was young; somehow, however impossible it seemed at this moment, she would have a future. It wouldn't involve Rob, but there was still hope, there *had* to be.

'Going to the club. Want to come?' asked Ruby.

Daisy raised her head and her eyes met her mother's. Ruby thought that her daughter's eyes were like pits that led straight into hell; their expression was utterly bleak. 'No,' she said.

'OK.' Ruby patted her shoulder awkwardly. There were no words she could use that would ease Daisy's agony. It was best to say nothing.

Ruby made her way along to the nursery. The twins were playing, Jody was with them. They seemed fine. Kids were resilient. More so, she thought, than adults. She told Jody where she was going, then went downstairs to the hall. Fats was sitting in the chair by the door. He stood up when she appeared.

'I'm going to the club,' she said.

'I'll drive,' he offered.

'Thanks.' Ruby hesitated. 'So long as there's someone here to stay with Daisy . . .?'

'Daniel!' hollered Fats.

Daniel appeared in the kitchen doorway, slurping down coffee. 'Yeah?'

'We're going out. You stick close to Daisy. Don't let anyone bother her,' said Fats.

'Sure thing.'

Ruby took up her coat, umbrella and bag, aware of the comforting weight of the handgun inside it, and Fats opened the door. She was halfway out when the phone rang.

'I'd better get that, hadn't I? I don't want Daisy disturbed.' Ruby went back to the hall table and picked up. 'Hello?'

'Mrs Darke?' asked a quavery female voice.

'Yep,' said Ruby.

It would be some idiot selling something. She waited impatiently while silence fell at the other end of the line.

'Who is this?' she demanded finally.

'It's Mrs Lewis,' said the voice.

'I'm sorry, do I know you?'

'The photographer. Clive Lewis. I'm his wife.'

Christ! She should have gone and visited the poor woman, she knew that. But losing Rob had been so awful, so devastating, that somehow the days since the wedding had slid past and all her good intentions had been lost in the general chaos.

'Mrs Lewis,' said Ruby more gently. 'I meant to call on you. I'm so sorry for your loss.'

It was as if the woman hadn't heard her. 'There's something I have to show you,' she said.

'Oh. What is it?'

Ruby couldn't think of a single thing this poor mouse-like creature could show her that would be of any interest at all. She remembered her, shadowing her husband on the day of the wedding; nearly invisible in a muted blue tea-dress and clumpy, comfortable shoes, watching anxiously as each shot was taken, being jostled by crowds of guests and constantly being asked to stand aside so that they could take shots too, over the photographer's shoulder. Mrs Lewis had been carrying a small camera of her own. Why, Ruby didn't know.

'Come to the studio,' she said. 'Can you come now?'

'Well . . .'

'I think it might be important.'

34

Fats drove Ruby through the press scrum and out. Their first stop was the photographer's studio. It was a neat little shop, the facade painted burgundy and with *CL Photos* picked out in large, gold Gothic script over the top of a big plate-glass window. The studio was shoehorned into an unremarkable line of shops that included a launderette and a dry cleaner's, and there were vast prints of brides, misty close-ups and sharp full-length shots that showed big swirling wedding dresses and voluminous net trains off to their best advantage, all set out in the window to entice punters inside.

Ruby remembered coming here with Daisy when she booked the photographer, months ago. It seemed longer now. Much longer. In another world, where Rob was alive and everything was as it should be. The firm took protection money off this row of shops. The thought caused Ruby to frown. She supposed a photographer didn't make that much money; but still, Kit – and, indirectly, she – took a cut from their profits.

Fats parked up the car, and Ruby got out, ran across the rain-battered pavement to the door. It opened to the tinkle of a bell, and Ruby stepped inside, letting down her umbrella.

The studio seemed empty. A bit cold. No lights on, and

there were a lot of lights, gold uplighters that should have been switched on to accentuate the many enlarged prints that lined the tobacco-brown walls.

'Mrs Lewis?' called Ruby. 'Hello?'

'Mrs Darke?' Mrs Lewis appeared in a doorway at the back of the shop, holding a cellophane and paper package. *A grey woman*, Ruby thought. She was featureless, expressionless. Clearly, she had never been eye-catching, but grief had bleached her out even more, increasing her pallor.

'Yes, that's me,' said Ruby, not bothering to correct her. She'd never married; never been a 'Mrs'. She moved forward, extending a hand. Mrs Lewis took it, shook it. 'This is all so awful,' said Ruby, thinking that the woman's grip was cold and damp, like holding a fish.

'Yes,' she said vaguely. 'It's terrible.'

Ruby stood there, not knowing what else to say. Kit's business was a dangerous one. Her family mixed with bad people. Somehow, this poor little woman and her husband had trod too close to them and paid the price. She felt bad about it. There was no doubt in her mind that the bullets had been meant for Kit.

'You said you wanted to talk to me . . .' said Ruby at last, as Mrs Lewis seemed in no hurry to break the silence.

Mrs Lewis nodded, and finally she started to speak.

'People think a photographer's life is glamorous and artistic. But this is a business that has its own problems,' she said. 'We used to issue picture proofs without payment upfront, and then people started finding fault with the pictures – perfectly good pictures – to knock down the price. So we had to start taking full payment upfront—'

'Mrs Lewis,' interrupted Ruby, wondering where the hell all this was leading, thinking of Fats parked out there on a double yellow – not that the local plod would bother him, but still – and also thinking that this was a total waste of time.

'Hm? Oh yes – anyway – sorry . . .' Mrs Lewis held up the package and walked over to a small ornate desk. She paused to collect her thoughts and started in again: 'Another problem we've had is brides blinking. They don't have the sun in their eyes, because of course Clive always shoots . . .' Her smile faltered . . . 'He shot into the sun. Only very good photographers can do that. I've heard people muttering right behind my back at weddings, saying, "Oh, these photos aren't going to be any ruddy good, the fool's shooting into the sun!" Of course, they don't know what they're talking about. He was a brilliant photographer, my Clive. So in demand. He travelled all over the country taking photos, covering weddings, conferences and events. He always made brides look like angels. Even if they were plain, Clive could make them appear wonderful.'

'So . . .' Ruby prompted when the woman paused.

'Yes. The brides. They blink. They get nervous. We did a wedding once where the bride closed her eyes in *every* shot. As soon as she heard the shutter click, she closed her eyes. Nervous reaction. Ruined all the photos.'

'Yes, so . . .' said Ruby.

'So after that, we decided that what we'd do is this: while Clive used the Hasselblad or the Mamiya or the Rolleiflex – big-format cameras with fabulous lenses – we would double up the shots. I always carried Clive's old 35mm Leica around my neck, and replicated every shot he took, for back-up.'

'Right,' said Ruby, watching as Mrs Lewis tipped out a batch of five-by-four colour photos onto the desk. In one of them she saw Daisy, smiling, getting out of the wedding car. And then there she was, herself and Daisy, both of them standing beside the bonnet of the Silver Ghost.

'Oh God,' said Ruby, feeling tears prick her eyes. Daisy looked so beautiful. So happy. 'It's so tragic,' she said to the woman standing beside her.

'It is,' said Mrs Lewis, patting Ruby's arm. 'The Rolleiflex was smashed when the tripod fell over and the police have taken that, along with the film it contained. But I still have what I took on the Leica – they didn't ask for it and, by the time I thought of it, it was too late, the police had left, I was at the hospital, it was all chaos.'

'I know,' said Ruby.

'Anyway, I got them printed off, with our usual firm, and they came back today. I don't know what I was thinking. I was . . . numb, I suppose. Just going through the motions. Working, because I couldn't think what else to do. Oh Lord . . . poor Clive.'

It was Ruby's turn to pat Mrs Lewis's arm. They stood there for a moment, united in grief. Then Mrs Lewis straightened with a sharp sigh.

She's a tough old bird, thought Ruby. *She might look frail, but she's not.*

'*This* is the one I wanted to show you.'

She held the print out to Ruby, who took it and looked. It was a full-length shot of her and Daisy. Ruby remembered Clive Lewis taking it, setting up the tripod, arranging Daisy's dress, getting the shot just right. He'd been a perfectionist. And it showed, right here. It was a magnificent shot, backlit by the sun, the car's metalwork gleaming; truly fabulous. She remembered Mrs Lewis there too, shooting close by her husband's shoulder. Taking a back-up shot. *This* one.

'There,' said Mrs Lewis. 'In the background, you see?'

Ruby looked. She hadn't noticed before, but there at the upper left edge of the shot was the beautiful Georgian building over the road from the church, heavily clothed with a vivid green Virginia creeper.

And there . . .

'Shit,' said Ruby, her breath catching.

'See it?' said Mrs Lewis.

There at an open first-floor window on the far side of the building was a glinting tube of metal; the sun had caught it. Behind it, she could see the outline of an angular, dark-haired figure. Kit was right – there was a shooter in that window. That *was* where the shots had come from.

Ruby felt sick as she thought of that arsehole up there, about to ruin her daughter's happiness forever. She looked at Mrs Lewis and saw tears standing in her eyes.

'My Clive never hurt anyone,' she said. 'Not a soul. He didn't deserve this.'

'I'm so sorry,' said Ruby, guilt scorching through her like wildfire. Kit's way of life – shit, *her* way of life now too – all this had been brought down upon an innocent man, an unlucky bystander who'd got in the way, and upon Rob who had dived in front of Kit, protecting him – or trying to, anyway. 'I am so very sorry.'

'The police will have got something very similar from the Rollei,' said Mrs Lewis, her chin trembling but her mouth clamped in determination. 'But I thought that your family ought to have this. I know you have . . . influence. See what you can make of it. You take this.'

Ruby took the print from her. Their eyes locked. 'Do you have family, Mrs Lewis, someone to look after you?'

'I only had Clive,' she said.

Clutching the print and feeling like shit, Ruby went back out to the car where Fats was waiting.

'Right,' she said. 'Let's get on over to the club.'

35

Peachy Percival had once been an ace safebreaker, able to crack open any damned thing at a moment's notice. Before that he'd been in the army. He still had a keen interest in small arms, and could be relied upon to discreetly supply certain items if they were needed, for a price.

Peachy's missus greeted Kit at the front door, and led him through the house and out into the back garden and down to a six-by-three wooden shed. Inside it, with the door standing open, was Peachy, a stooped wire-haired veteran of many a mob adventure, humming along to Frank Sinatra and a swelling brass section on the portable radio, his half-moon specs slipping down his big curving nose as he sharpened a chisel on his lathe.

'Peachy!' she yelled, sending Kit an apologetic look. 'He's deaf as a post. PEACHY!' The old man turned, saw Kit and the missus standing there, and switched Frank off.

'Mr Miller,' he said, stopping the lathe.

The missus withdrew, leaving the men alone, shaking hands.

'Sad business at the wedding,' said Peachy. 'Sorry to hear it.'

'Thanks.' Kit took the spent shell casing out of his pocket. 'Can you tell me anything about this?'

Peachy turned it over in his hand. He looked up at Kit,

then pushed his specs up onto the bridge of his nose and said: 'This the one . . .?'

Kit nodded.

Peachy examined the thing again. 'It's a 7.62 millimetre. Fired from a high-velocity rifle. Can't see any obvious distinguishing marks. I'll have to get it up closer, under the magnifier, check for striations. Can you leave it with me?'

'Yeah. I can. But look after it, Peach.'

'With my life,' said Peachy.

36

Today Ruby's club was quiet, empty of patrons, empty of life except for two cleaners, who were hoovering and hollering at each other over the din of the machines, out in the main body of the club. Ruby went into her office, Fats following and stationing himself on a chair outside the door.

Ruby took off her coat. Relieved to be alone for a moment, she turned on the TV and was instantly sorry. The news was on: a shooting at a wedding in the previously quiet village of Mitchell Underdyke, two people dead and the police had no leads yet. She switched it off, sat down at the desk and put her head in her hands, heaving a long, heartfelt sigh. Mrs Lewis's small, pale face sprang into her mind and she let out a groan, guilt crippling her all over again.

That poor woman! All she had in the world was a modest business, and the firm had been dipping into the Lewises' earnings for years, providing protection. Worse, doing a simple job for the same firm had now killed the photographer. Without him, what would happen to the business? It would fold. It had to. Leaving Mrs Lewis without an income.

Christ!

It would be up to the firm to support her. That was only fair. Then Ruby thought of Daisy back at the house, nearly catatonic with grief, staring out of the window at nothing. And of the photograph now sitting in her handbag, the glint of a gun and someone behind it. Aiming at . . . at Kit, of course.

The boss of the business. The one to take out.

Her son was in mortal danger.

And he was even more vulnerable now, without Rob minding him. Ruby hated the idea of that.

She sat up, trying to focus, pushing away the panic that threatened to swamp her. She still had a business to run. Whatever else was going down, work had sustained her over the years. Her eyes drifted to the telephone. The answering machine light was blinking.

She didn't want to talk to anyone, not now. But she reached out, pressed *play message* all the same. You had to force yourself to keep going forward, because really, what was the alternative? Collapse? Give up?

Ruby Darke had *never* done that, not in her entire life.

It was Jenny, one of Crystal Rose's 'Rosettes'.

'I wanted to check if you'd heard anything from Crystal,' said the girl in her high, nasal voice. 'Can you phone me back? I'm on . . .' She reeled off a number.

Ruby wrote it down, stopped *play* and dialled out to Laura's home number. The manageress picked up straight away. 'Hello?'

'Laura, it's Ruby. Crystal's sisters are climbing the walls. Has that cow Crystal contacted you?'

'Nope. Not a peep from her.' Laura's voice took on a note of concern. Ruby had told her about the shooting at the wedding. 'Ruby, is there anything I can do?'

'There's nothing anyone can do,' said Ruby tiredly.

'How is Daisy?' Laura tutted. 'Christ! Stupid question. Look – anything you need, just shout, OK?'

'I will.' Ruby disconnected. Then she phoned Jenny's number. 'Laura hasn't heard from Crystal. Not a word.'

'I'm calling the police,' said Jenny.

Ruby stared at the phone. Ordinarily, she would dissuade Jenny from police involvement, but now, after the shooting, there were police crawling all over the sodding place anyway, so what the hell difference would it make?

'You have to do as you think fit,' she said.

'I will.'

As she put the phone down, it rang again. 'Hello?' said Ruby.

There was silence, followed by faint breathing.

'Hello?' Ruby repeated.

'You want to leave him alone,' said a female voice. 'I'm warning you.' It was Big Tits.

'Leave who alone?' asked Ruby.

'You *know*.'

Ruby had met up with Thomas again, briefly – but only to give him the CCTV tapes from the warehouse to look at. She was due to meet him again soon, right here at the club. It was all arranged.

'I think you must have the wrong number,' said Ruby, and slapped the phone back onto the cradle.

37

Days later, Daniel was sitting inside the front door at the Marlow house, flicking through the daily paper and not even seeing it, feeling gutted, disorientated, locked inside a nightmare he couldn't wake from. Jody the nanny had gone out with the kids, Ruby had gone out to the club, and the house was silent.

His big bro was dead. It was all too hard to take in. He'd always loved Rob and looked up to him. Rob had taught him all his fancy ninja moves. Sparred with him – and with Leon too, though not so much because Leon was a moody sod. It was Rob who had taught them how to be *tough*. How to kick arse and chew bubblegum. Now they would have to – somehow – go on without him.

Daniel wanted to find out who'd ripped his family apart this way, but here he was, doing what Kit told him to do as always, standing guard. Daniel hated sitting around, 'guarding' people. There was no one here to guard, not really. Daisy never came out of her room, anyway, so what the hell . . .?

His thoughts were suddenly cut off.

Daisy was coming down the stairs.

She was wearing a cream, belted mac, tan suede knee-high boots. No make-up. Her hair was a mess.

She looked pale, blank-eyed.

He straightened in surprise and put the paper aside.

'I'm going out,' said Daisy.

'What?' Daniel stood up. 'Where?'

'Out,' said Daisy, crossing the hall with a determined stride.

Daniel shook his head. 'No. Hold on. Where are you going?' He was thinking the hospital, the morgue. He didn't want to go back there but maybe she did. And if she *did*, he would have to go too.

'Not your business,' she said, opening the front door. The rain lashed in.

Daniel snatched his jacket from the back of the chair and put it on. He grabbed Daisy's arm.

'It is my business,' he said. 'Kit said to keep an eye on you. You can't go out alone. Tell me where you're going, and I'll come with you.'

'Get off me!' Daisy shook her arm free. Her eyes flared with temper. 'Leave me alone. I am going out, that's all you need to know.'

Christ! thought Daniel. Kit would have his guts if he let her wander off unattended, the state she was in. He thought of the jackals of the press, down by the gates. They'd mob her. And drive? The way she looked, she'd speed herself straight into the nearest brick wall. He went to the hall table, snatched up the pen there. Flicked a glance back at Daisy, but all he saw – to his alarm – was an empty doorway. The wind was gusting through, a few of last year's fallen leaves swirling inside the hall.

Daisy was out of sight. *Gone*.

'Shit!' he said loudly.

He quickly scrawled *Gone with Daisy* on the notepad and sprinted after her.

38

DI Romilly Kane was down the nick in the major crimes unit. After the case conference, she'd pulled the file on Kit Miller, and found it pretty bulky. Then she'd padded through to her desk with a muddy cup of the vending machine slop that passed for coffee and settled herself down to read through it. It didn't make very edifying reading, either. Dragged up in a variety of children's homes then let loose on the streets, 'security' was always the cover for Miller in adulthood.

He ran 'security' on club doors, provided 'security' for celebs or visiting diplomats. No mention of the protection rackets, of course. No one who paid protection to these people ever spoke about it. Of course not. Accidents could happen if they did. Maybe their shop would burn down. Or their kneecaps could suddenly get busted. Who knew? It was a dangerous world.

Further back in the file, she read about a murder enquiry where Miller had been questioned but released without charge. A man had got a thin dagger plunged into his heart. *Tito Danieri* was the man's name.

Now *there* was a guy with a thick file too. Tito's family had been immigrants from Naples, who'd made their home in Clerkenwell – known as 'Little Italy' because there were so many Italians settled there. Tito was a nastier type of thug altogether than Miller, but there was a connection. A falling-out over a woman, and the death of one of the major faces who ran the streets – Michael Ward, who Kit Miller used to work for.

Tito and his dad, Astorre, had been notorious for strong-arming the owners of clubs around Soho until they caved in and passed the businesses over to the Danieri clan. No concrete proof of that, of course. Tito had also been charged with running a raft of underage prostitutes smuggled in from the continent, girls he got hooked on heavy drugs so that they never strayed for fear of missing their next fix. Again – not proven. Charged but later released due to lack of evidence. No girls willing to testify.

Charged and released.

Maybe Kit Miller *had* plunged that dagger into Tito Danieri's heart. After all, there'd been a big upset among the London gangs before that – Michael Ward, who'd been romantically linked to Miller's mother Ruby Darke, had been shot, and Tito had been in the frame for it. Kit Miller had been Ward's right-hand man. And there had definitely been a fight over a woman. So . . . maybe.

And maybe – if he'd done it – Miller had done them all one huge fucking favour, got that scum Tito off the streets once and for all.

DI Kane picked up a black-and-white photo of Miller.

Romilly had thought it when she'd met up with him and she thought it again now: *handsome bastard.* It was the first time she'd ever actually been *startled* by how good-looking a man was. She'd heard of a poll where people voted for the appearance they thought most attractive, and the top result was those who were a mix of black and white. Kit Miller fitted the bill perfectly. He was stunning, with a brutal, brooding physicality about him. And oh how he knew it. Loved his fucking self, didn't he.

DS Harman came and slumped into a chair. He placed a folder on Kane's desk. She closed the Miller file and gave him a questioning look.

'Misper unit had this come through,' he said.

Romilly eyed her DS without expression. She didn't like him, but so what? There were plenty of her colleagues that she didn't like. Particularly the big-mouthed, preening arseholes – a description that applied to quite a few of the male detectives at the nick. But you didn't have to be best buds with someone to work effectively with them. One of the other DIs on the major crimes team, Karen Sharp – and she *did* like her – had warned her, 'Watch your back with that one.' She reckoned DS Harman was two-faced and possibly on the take. Romilly herself had long since come to the same conclusion. So far, she hadn't done anything about it. Maybe soon, she would.

Romilly picked up the file and flicked it open. 'Can't Sharp take it?'

'Thought you'd want to.'

Crystal Rose, burlesque performer, Romilly read.

Then she saw it and let out a *humph* of surprise. 'She works at Kit Miller's mother's club.'

'That's why I thought you'd want it. She works at Ruby's. Or she *did*. Hasn't been seen in just under a fortnight.'

'What, and they've only reported it now?'

'Nervous about getting us involved maybe, ma'am. Just passing it along, like they asked.'

Romilly closed the file and glanced up at the board at the side of the office with its scribbled notes and gruesome pictures of a big man with treacle-blond hair lying dead from a gunshot wound to the chest. A small frizzy-haired guy – the photographer – face-down on the gravel, blood on his back, also dead. She and the team had a double-murder investigation on here, a major warehouse robbery too. A missing girl would take them off track. But . . . it *was* interesting that the girl worked at Ruby Darke's club. The wedding. The robbery. A missing dancer. And all three events tying in to Miller and his family.

'Did we get the prints off the films – the one that was still in the broken camera and the other ones in the photographer's jacket pockets?'

'Just come in.'

'Bring them through. Who reported the girl missing? Was it Ruby Darke?'

'Nope. One of Crystal Rose's sisters. Jennifer.'

'Maybe Crystal's done a moonlight flit before. Perhaps she'll turn up.'

'The sister says she went off with a man that evening.'

'Right.'

'Girls these days, eh?'

Romilly eyed him steadily. 'CCTV in the club?'

'Sure there is.'

'Get on that, will you?' Romilly paused. 'How about all the witness statements at the church? The guests?'

Harman gave a snort. 'No one saw anything. No one heard anything either. They're all deaf, dumb and blind.'

'Be interesting to have another word with Ruby Darke. Why's she got a different name to her son?'

'It's in the file. She had illegitimate twins, Kit and a sister. The sister was white. Kit drew the short straw, he was dark-skinned and nobody wanted him. Different times back then, see? So he was pushed into orphanages, and he was named there too. Kit Miller. And he's kept the name.'

He'd had a rough upbringing. So did millions of other people; they didn't turn to a life of crime.

'What about Miller's father? He didn't want to know him either?' she asked.

Harman blew out his cheeks. 'Dear old dad was aristocracy. Cornelius Bray. *Lord* Bray. Ruby Darke's a looker, and he fancied a bit. Didn't like the idea of having a half-caste child like Kit though, so he just raised the daughter, Daisy.'

'Cornelius Bray? Didn't he die, some accident?'

'That's right.' Harman stood up. 'I'll bring in the prints.'

39

'Give me those, *right now*,' shouted Daisy.

Daniel had come haring out of the house at a run, seen her about to get into her Mini out on the gravel drive at the front of the house, rushed over and – in the nick of time – snatched the keys off her.

'No,' he said. 'No way.'

'I said *give* them to me,' roared Daisy.

'Don't be a bloody lunatic. You can't drive, you're tranked up to the eyeballs. *I'll* drive, just tell me where you want to go.'

'Give me those *fucking* keys.'

He shook his head.

Daisy punched him in the face. Daniel turned away at the last minute and her fist hit his left cheekbone instead of his nose and teeth. All the same, it sodding well *hurt*.

'You mad cow,' he said, grabbing her arm and hauling her round the front of the car, rain-soaked and struggling. He opened the passenger side and literally *threw* his boss's sister into the passenger seat, locking it after her. Then he went round to the driver's side and got in.

They both sat there, breathing hard.

'You finished?' he asked, sticking the key in the ignition.

Daisy threw another punch. It clunked against the side of his head and made his ears ring.

'Oh for fuck's—' said Daniel, holding up one arm to fend her off.

Daisy hit him again, ducking under his defensive arm to land a punch on his abdomen.

'How the *fuck* did Rob ever put up with you?' he burst out. 'You crazy bitch, will you *stop doing that*?'

Daisy stopped. More because she was winded, Daniel guessed, than because he'd asked her to. He lowered his arm cautiously.

'Right,' he said, feeling his heart still thudding fast in his chest, wishing Leon had caught this gig and not him. 'So. Tell me where you want to go.'

'I don't know where I want to go. Out. Away. Anywhere.'

'Daisy . . .' Daniel started.

'I want to score.'

'What?'

'Some crack. Something. Anything.'

Christ, he so wished this was Leon's job. Or Fats's. Or *anyone's*. He stared at her. She meant it. She was off her head with grief over Rob, and she wanted drugs to blank it out.

'Daisy, fuck's sake . . .'

'Yes, Daniel,' she said.

'No.'

Her blue eyes glared into his. 'I'll tell Kit you came on to me,' she said flatly. 'Days after your brother's death, you came on to me, *forced* me to have sex with you.'

'You *what*? What the hell are you saying?'

'Who d'you think he'd believe? You – or me, his sister?'

They sat, eyes locked, for long moments. Finally Daniel looked away and started the engine, clipped on his seat belt, his face grim. No matter how he looked at it, his arse was in a sling. If Kit found out he was enabling Daisy in taking drugs, he would be fried; and if Daisy told Kit those lies about him, and if Kit *believed* them – and he might; after all, Kit didn't know Daniel that well, not yet – then he'd be finished too.

'So you want to get high? Really?' he asked her.

Daisy didn't speak. She just nodded, staring out through the windscreen at the pummelling rain. 'You done this before?'

She nodded again.

'All right. I know a place where we can score. But you're going to do this under *my* terms. OK? Not yours.'

He started the engine, and drove.

40

'I heard what happened to Rob,' said Thomas Knox, coming into Ruby's office at the club that evening.

He closed the door, took a seat. Looked at Ruby, who was watching him in silence. *Could* she trust him? Thomas was dodgy as fuck but, until now, he had always been on her family's side. Was that still the case, though? He *could* be looking to turn them over. He could even have got together with one of the other mobs and decided to double the strength, maximize the clout. Who knew? There could be more trouble on the way, while he sat there all smiles and sympathy.

'Rob Hinton was the soundest man I knew,' he said.

'He was.'

'Kit must be sick to his stomach over this.'

'Yes. He is.'

'I'm sorry.' Thomas sat and stared at her when she said nothing.

'Your wife,' said Ruby.

'What about her?'

'She's been in touch. That night you came in the club with her, she warned me off in the bogs. And she's been on the phone to me, too.' Ruby stared at him.

'Saying what?' he asked.

'To leave you alone.'

'Chloe's off her nut. Thinks she sees affairs where there are none.'

'What did she think of the club? Did she like it?'

'She liked it. That girl in the champagne glass? Very clever.'

'Yeah, that girl who, incidentally, has gone missing,' sighed Ruby.

Thomas gave her a questioning look.

'Crystal Rose,' she explained. 'The girl in the glass.'

'What, got fed up with the job?' He eyed her with those cool blue eyes, very steadily.

'Don't know. Her sisters usually keep in touch with her every day, and they haven't been able to speak to her. She's not answering her phone. She hasn't been back to her flat. It seems odd.'

'Taken off somewhere with a fella?' he suggested.

'Out of character. One night, usually. No more. Anyway.' She threw him a thoughtful look. 'I'm giving you the benefit of the doubt on the warehouse job. I'm holding Kit back on this, you realize. He's not in a good mood. Right now, he'd like your balls on a spit.'

'He's too smart to start a full-out war over something like this,' said Thomas.

'I don't think he'd much care. But I do. I don't want him winding up dead.'

'So . . .?'

'Tell me again. Swear to me that you are in *no way* involved.'

'I told you. I'm not. And I can prove it.'

'How?'

'I can help you find those two men who everyone got a look at on the day. Skinny little runt with blond hair, gold jewellery and bad teeth. Big black guy with gold fillings and dreads. Saw 'em clear as day on the CCTV.'

'All right,' said Ruby, thinking that, although all this was making her feel stressed out like an overstrung bow, he was still gorgeous, and she could easily get back into something with him if she wasn't very careful.

Nah, I'm over all that, she told herself.

But she wondered if she truly was.

41

Peachy phoned the office at the back of Sheila's restaurant a couple of days after Kit had paid his shed a visit.

'Mr Miller,' he greeted Kit.

'You got anything, Peach?'

'Yeah. Don't know if it helps too much though. As I told you, it's definitely a 7.62mm. I've looked at it all ways, but there's no distinguishing marks. None. I don't know if it helps, but it's a bore that's used in most gun clubs for target shooting. Might be a place to start.'

'Right.' Kit looked at Fats, who was sitting by the desk counting twenty-pound notes from the morning's milk run. 'I'll send Fats over to pick the casing up. Thanks, Peach. It's appreciated.'

'No problem.'

Kit put the phone down.

'What?' asked Fats, pausing in his counting.

'Pick up that spent shell from Peachy for me, and bung him a ton, OK? Then sort out a list of all the gun clubs in the London area,' said Kit.

'I'm on it,' said Fats, passing the wad of twenties over to Kit before making for the door.

42

DI Romilly Kane was sitting in Jenny and Aggie Rose's chaotic little flat in Bermondsey, a weak cup of grey tea in front of her on the coffee table. Beside her was DS Bev Appleton. The two Rosettes were on the sofa opposite, staring at Romilly as if she had all the answers. She wished she did.

'Most missing people come back after a day or two,' said Romilly.

They nodded; said nothing.

'As this isn't the case with your sister, what we are proposing is that we will search her home address first,' said Romilly, thinking of the weird places they'd found 'missing' persons in the past – in cupboards under the stairs, skulking in loft spaces, hiding from angry creditors, pestering ex-lovers or dodging bailiffs. Some of them were just sick of the world and sunk deep in depression.

'We'll take some photographs of her flat's interior,' she went on. They'd be looking for signs of a struggle, of blood, anything that might indicate that Crystal had been harmed or was being held against her will. 'Then we'll want to talk to any other relatives of Crystal's . . .' Romilly paused. 'Is that her real name? Crystal?'

'Beatrice,' said Aggie. 'Beatrice Fuller. Fuller's our family name.'

Romilly and Bev both made a note of that. 'Middle names?' The sisters shook their heads.

'The other relatives,' Romilly continued. 'Mother, father . . .'

'Mum's dead. Dad lives abroad. Spain. Almeria.'

'Fine. Grandparents?'

'All dead. Sorry.'

'OK. Uncles, brothers, cousins, boyfriends, anybody you can think of. Please put together a list with all their contact details, and we'll take it from there.'

They nodded.

'The man she was last seen with in the club, was that a steady boyfriend?'

'No. Someone new,' said Jenny.

'We've been in touch with the club owner and we're going to see her now. There'll be CCTV from inside the club, we might be able to get a better idea of this man's identity.'

Then they would do door-to-door down the streets outside the club, and the same at Crystal Rose's home address. If all *that* yielded nothing, they would work out a media strategy, asking the public for information on the whereabouts of the missing girl.

'Her bank details, we'll need them. Can you get them?'

'I know where she keeps them,' said Jenny. 'Why . . .?'

'To see if she's touched any of her accounts in the period she's been missing.'

'Right,' said Jenny, her face pale.

This was starting to look *serious.*

43

Daniel drove Daisy up to a dingy, rubbish-strewn back street in Stockwell, parked up the car and took the keys out of the ignition. Then he turned to her.

'Stay here,' he said. 'Don't get out of the car. Keep the doors locked. If anyone bangs on the window, even if it's a little kid, ignore it. Talk to no one. They'd eat you whole and spit out the bits, so listen to what I'm saying. I'll be quick.'

Daisy sat there in silence while Daniel was gone. Before five minutes had passed, someone *did* bang on the window, a smiling tattooed man who mouthed: 'How *you*, pretty?'

When she didn't so much as glance at him, he gave her the finger and moved on. Two women who were probably prostitutes passed by, giving her evils, thinking she might intend to cash in on their patch. One of them kicked her door, hard, in passing. She didn't react. Three hooded youths took up station on the other side of the road, watching the car, watching *her*. A flicker of fear began to creep along the edge of Daisy's grief-numbed senses.

What the fuck was she doing here? Once, she'd done this sort of thing, lived the wild life, gone to raves and crazy parties, pushed her luck, thought it was the smart, the trendy thing to do. But she hadn't lived like that in a long, long time. And Daniel was right; this place felt dangerous.

She could hear police sirens. And now the three young guys were pushing and shoving each other, shouting, grinning, bustling each other out into the road – and closer to the car.

When the key suddenly turned in the driver's door, she nearly shrieked.

It was Daniel.

'It's all kicking off up there,' he said, getting behind the wheel and indicating with a nod of the head the tower block up ahead of them, the one he'd gone into. 'One of the usual boys who deals round here has been selling ganja and coke to some other dealers, only it *ain't* ganja or coke, it was tea leaves and stuff. His missus told me that six men smashed their way into the flat three nights ago for a chat with her husband, then they flung him out the window. From the tenth floor. He still had the TV remote in his hand when they scraped him off the pavement.'

Daisy's heart was hammering. The boys had seen Daniel get in and now they'd gone off, down the road. 'Did you get it? The stuff? Or is *that* fake too, just talcum powder or something?'

Daniel was staring at her and shaking his head. 'Yeah, I got it. And it's the genuine article. Now let's go somewhere private and get this done, if it's what you really want. But I'm telling you, Daisy – this is the first and last time. I mean it. Rob would have my *guts* if he could see all this going on.'

'Yeah, but he can't, can he?' said Daisy, her voice harsh with emotion. 'Because Rob is *dead*.'

'I know. I know,' said Daniel, starting the engine. 'Let's get the fuck out of here.'

44

When Leon dropped Ruby home, passing the press thronging at the gate, she saw that Daisy's Mini was not on the drive in its usual spot. Feeling a pang of alarm at this, she hurried indoors, and found the note on the hall table in Daniel's handwriting.

Gone with Daisy

Ruby called up the stairs to Jody, asking if she had any idea where Daisy had gone, but Jody didn't. Ruby was worried, but at least Daniel was with her. She had barely time to get her coat off when the doorbell rang. Fats answered it. The tall female police detective with the mound of long curly dark hair stood there, with DS Harman right behind her.

'Can we have a word with Ruby Darke please?' asked DI Kane.

Fats stood aside, letting the pair of them in.

'Come through to the sitting room,' said Ruby, and led the way in there.

When they were all seated, Ruby asked: 'Can I get you some tea? Coffee?'

'No thanks,' said DI Kane. 'Firstly – we've had a missing persons report on a Crystal Rose who works at your club. We need to see all the CCTV footage for the past month. Specifically, we need to look at the night she disappeared.'

Ruby frowned. 'She's not back yet?'

'You knew she was missing?'

'The sisters told me they hadn't seen her or heard from her since she left the club with a strange man. I went over to Crystal's flat with them, but the place looked as if it had been empty for a while. I thought she'd show up. God, that's worrying.'

'We're on it, Miss Darke. About the shooting at your daughter's wedding . . . can we have a word with her now? Is it convenient?'

'She's out,' said Ruby. 'I think she probably got tired of being cooped up inside and wanted some air.'

'It must be terrible for her.'

'It is.'

'Can you think of any reason someone would want to shoot Robert Hinton?'

Ruby blinked, stumped for an answer. Rob? No. But Kit? Quite a few.

'I can't think of a reason,' said Ruby. 'No.'

'Miss Darke, if you know anything that might help us in our investigation into the deaths of Mr Hinton and Mr Lewis, please tell us. I'm sure you want to track down the killer as much – even more – than we do.'

'I do.'

Romilly held Ruby's gaze. Ruby didn't blink or glance away.

'But I really can't help you,' said Ruby. 'Not about the shooting.'

'We think that it was carried out from a first-floor flat in the Georgian building opposite the church,' said Romilly. Prising info out of Ruby Darke was like getting blood out of a stone. Personally, Romilly felt torn over this case. Yes, it was her sworn duty to investigate – but on the other hand, it reeked of gangland grudges. Shootings in public places were a no-no. There were law-abiding people to protect. Gangland flare-ups couldn't be allowed to impact on ordinary, innocent citizens.

'Oh?' said Ruby. She already knew that, from the print the photographer's wife had given her.

'Yes. Rest assured we are actively pursuing this matter, Miss Darke. Now, the CCTV . . .'

'I'll phone Laura, the manageress,' said Ruby, rising to her feet to indicate that she wanted to wrap this up. 'She can bring the tapes into the police station, marked for your attention.' *But not until me and Kit have had a look at them, and made copies*, she thought. 'Now, if there's nothing else . . . ?'

45

The thing with cocaine is, it makes you feel wonderful. Invincible. Euphoric. For a little while, anyway. Maybe thirty, forty minutes. It doesn't last.

'Is that all of it?' Daisy asked, and Daniel thought she looked so different.

They were in Daniel's flat over the garage at Ruby's place. There were two flats up here, and currently he was occupying the one at the back with the garden view – this one had been Rob's and Daisy's, and how he hated *that* fact. Leon had been given the one at the front that looked down the driveway to the gates beside the road. There had been a major reshuffling of security following Rob's shooting – and Daniel had drawn the short straw.

Daisy had wasted no time in snatching the little packet of powder off Daniel, tipping it out onto the coffee table, cutting the lines with a credit card, rolling a fiver and snorting the stuff up. She did it like a pro, like she'd done it a hundred times before, and that worried him.

Then she'd fallen back onto the sofa, and a look of bliss had slowly come over her face. Ever since the wedding, Daniel had got used to seeing her – when he *did* see her, which was damned rare – grey in the face, red-eyed, literally washed-out with grief.

Now, Daisy was smiling dreamily. And she was asking for more.

'No,' said Daniel, sitting opposite her. 'No more, Daisy. That's it.'

Daisy's eyes popped open and stared into his. 'I could make you get me more,' she said.

'No. You couldn't.'

'If I told Kit—'

'You can tell Kit any damned thing. That I fucked you with a banana, if you like. I don't give a shit. You're not getting any more.'

Daisy pouted, then giggled. *Giggled.* And his brother Rob – her husband – was lying dead in the morgue. Suddenly he felt disgusted with her. Worse, he felt disgusted with himself, too.

'We lived here,' said Daisy. 'Me and Rob. Rob and I. Both of us. Together.' She was looking around the room.

'I know that.'

'They're doing the post-mortem tomorrow,' said Daisy. The smile dropped from her face. She sat up, and her eyes met his. He could see the images marching through her mind, pictures of Rob, mighty Rob, *invincible* Rob, having his innards sliced open, his strong body invaded.

Jesus. Daniel stared at her in horror. Was *that* what had brought this on?

Yes. Of course it was. And who could wonder at it? The poor cow.

'Just rest there, Daisy,' he said.

'You're a nice boy, Daniel,' she said, closing her eyes.

Nice? Only his mother ever called him that. He was the middle son, the forgotten one. Leon had always been Eunice's favourite, no doubt about it. Trudy and Sarah were next in the pecking order, both as close to Mum as ticks on a cat's arse. Then Rob. Then came Daniel, bringing up the rear. He'd always felt like an afterthought. Largely missed, overlooked. Rob, as the firstborn, had been idolized. And Leon had been the spoiled baby of the family. He still was, Daniel thought, even though the idiot treated Eunice with contempt in return for her adoration.

Daniel stood up, went and poured himself a beer. As soon as she was more herself, he would take Daisy back over to the main house. It would all be OK.

But Daisy got up too, and came over to where he stood. There was something in her eyes that he didn't like. She reached out a hand, laid it on his chest.

'You know, I've never really noticed you before. Leon's stunningly good-looking, but you? You're . . . ordinary. A bit shorter than Rob, but stockier. Thick-set. And muscular,' she said almost consideringly. 'You're the dependable one, aren't you? The dull one. The one who stands by whoever needs him. What if I need you, Daniel?'

If you need me, I'll be there, he thought, but didn't say it, although it was true.

'You're off your head on coke,' he reminded her, setting his glass aside, avoiding her eyes which seemed to drag him toward her. And he couldn't let that happen.

'Daniel,' she said, her voice husky. Her hand moved on his chest, caressing.

'What the hell are you doing?' he asked, his head snapping up, his eyes blazing into hers.

'What do you *want* me to do?' she asked, smiling, and her hand trailed down over his stomach.

'You know, I've never noticed it before, but your eyes are like Rob's, aren't they. That strange green . . .'

He caught her wrist, stopped her hand moving.

'Ow,' said Daisy.

'I'm not Rob,' he said flatly. 'Remember that, will you? *I'm not Rob*.'

46

Kit showed up an hour after the police had departed. Straight away he asked after Daisy.

'She's out,' said Ruby.

'Out? Out where, for fuck's sake?' Daisy had spent the last fortnight staring into space. Now she was out? Doing what?

'No idea. Daniel's with her, that's all I know.'

Daisy and Daniel went back to the main house nearly three hours later, when everyone else had eaten and Ruby had helped Jody bathe the twins and put them to bed. Ruby and Kit were in the sitting room. Leon was in the kitchen, watching TV. Fats was on the door, reading the paper.

'I'm going up to bed,' said Daisy. She had a bad headache. Thinking back, she could remember drug hangovers from her distant past; they were a bitch. It had been a long time since she'd had one, but by Christ she had one now. All she wanted was to take some paracetamol, lie down, and hope to God she could sleep. And never wake up.

'No,' said Daniel, blocking her path to the stairway.

'What?'

Daniel grabbed Daisy's arm and walked her into the room where Kit and Ruby were sitting in front of the *Ten O'Clock News*. They both looked up in surprise.

'Daisy!' Ruby jumped to her feet. 'I was worried. Are you all right?'

'She's fine,' said Daniel.

'Yes, I am.' Daisy wrenched her arm free of Daniel's grip. 'I'm *fine*.'

Daniel pushed the door closed and then turned, bracing himself but shit-scared. He faced his boss.

'Daisy went out to score. I caught her as she was going out the door.' Daisy's jaw dropped. 'You *bastard*!' she burst out.

Ruby was staring at Daisy, transfixed. 'Is that true?'

'It's true.' Daisy's face was a picture of hostile misery. 'I felt so low. I just had to . . .' She trailed off.

'God alive, Daisy, what were you thinking?' snapped Ruby. 'What the hell got into you?'

'I couldn't stop her,' said Daniel. 'So I went with her. Made sure she was doing it safely. There was nothing else I could do.'

'Christ, Daisy!' said Ruby.

'You treacherous sod,' Daisy shot at Daniel.

'No,' said Ruby. 'Don't you dare have a go at him, he did the sensible thing. You didn't.'

Kit stood up. He looked mad enough to *spit*. His blue eyes radiated cold fury.

'With your two kids upstairs, you thought you'd go and do that?' he said quietly to his sister.

'I've lost Rob. I don't care about *anything*, not any more,' said Daisy, tears filling her eyes.

Kit reached out, took her arms and shook her, hard.

'Kit . . .' started Ruby, stepping forward.

'Are you kidding me?' he asked Daisy, his voice harsh with anger. 'Things get rough so you run off and start injecting?'

'I didn't inject. I *wouldn't*. I did a couple of lines of coke, that's all. I needed it. And don't fucking lecture me! This is all *your* fault. It's you they were shooting at. Not Clive Lewis. Not Rob. It was *you*.'

Kit was glaring. 'Where's your fucking backbone, Daisy? You can't be this weak. What the hell are you thinking of?' he demanded.

'I don't know!' Daisy shouted, the tears spilling over. 'I just . . . I couldn't . . . I didn't know what to do . . .' Her voice trailed away and she started to sob. Kit pulled her in close and held her, stroking her hair. 'Shh,' he said. 'I know, Daise. I know.'

Over Daisy's head, Kit's eyes met Daniel's.

'I had to tell you, boss. She was going to do something crazy, I couldn't stop her so I had to stick with her,' he said.

'You did right,' said Kit. 'And you did right telling me, too.'

Suddenly Daisy jerked away from Kit's grip. 'No! Don't touch me. Don't come near me. I fucking *hate* you.'

With that, she left the room. Kit looked at Daniel.

'Never keep anything like this from me, Daniel. I'd have your guts if you did. Go get something to eat now. Grab a beer. And don't worry. You done good.'

Daniel went off into the kitchen and found Leon in there. Leon was tedious – bouncy and quicksilver and acid-tongued – very different to himself. Leon had his jacket off and his tie loosened.

He was drinking a Coke and heating up a pizza in the microwave.

'Where you been, bruv?' he asked.

Daniel pulled up a bar stool and heaved a sigh of deep relief. He'd been sure Kit was going to burn his arse over a low light, but somehow he'd played it right. Fortunately.

'Gimme some of that pizza, will you. And don't ask

where I've been or what I've been doing, because, frankly? You wouldn't believe me if I told you.'

'That why I saw Daisy's Mini parked out the back of the garage?' asked Leon, watching his brother's face with shrewd blue eyes. 'Don't worry. No one else saw it there, only me. You always did fancy her on the quiet. What you been doing? Somethin' bad?' He made an obscene gesture.

'Shut your fucking face, Leon,' said Daniel.

'Trying your luck with her, now Rob's not here to stop you?'

Daniel catapulted himself off the kitchen stool, grabbed Leon and slapped his head down hard onto the kitchen counter.

'I said *shut up*,' he yelled.

Leon was laughing when Daniel let him up. 'Whew! Touched a nerve there, yeah?'

Daniel pointed a rigid finger in his brother's face. 'Never say anything like that to me again. *Never.*'

'Look at me, I'm shiverin' with fear,' said Leon.

'You ought to be,' said Daniel. Fuck the pizza. He went out the kitchen door and trudged over the lawn back to his own flat.

Touched a nerve.

Leon's laughter was still ringing in his ears.

Truth was, he *had*.

47

The police had searched Crystal Rose's home address, examining the immaculately tidy mirror-clad apartment thoroughly. They'd photographed everything. They'd looked in the loft, without success. Pulled everything out of the largish cupboard under the stairs, since the sisters had told them that Crystal was a woman of dainty proportions and therefore might fit inside it, and they'd found nothing but feathered fans and a spare bubble machine. They'd looked in cupboards. Nothing.

They had questioned her sisters again, and extended that familial search to include uncles, aunts, her dad in Almeria and a couple of cousins. Nothing. Gone door-to-door down the street from the club, and at Crystal's apartment. *Still* nothing.

Crystal hadn't used any of her cards since she'd vanished, which didn't look good. She didn't own a car – she'd travelled to work by Tube or taxi – so there was little chance of tracking her movements on any of the major roads. She hadn't contacted any of her relations, or her few friends.

They were hitting dead ends.

But there was still the CCTV from the club's interior. If that turned up nothing, they'd have to appeal to the public for information.

'How's it going?' DCI James Barrow asked Romilly as

she passed by his open office door at a fast walk, hitching her arms into her navy jacket as she went. Romilly paused and stepped into his office. 'We've got three bullets from the two vics and the church door, plus two spent shells from the room opposite the church with ballistics,' she said, pushing the door closed behind her. *And I think Kit Miller's got the third shell.* 'Awaiting reports, sir.'

'This misper too much on top of all that? I could re-allocate. By rights, it should have been Turner's shout anyway, but he came back two days and now he's off again, with the flu. Or Sharp's lot could take it?'

'No. It's fine.'

Romilly bridled a bit. The suggestion that she couldn't cope niggled her. She'd been coping all her life; she thrived on stress, and just as well. Policing was in her blood, like it had been in her dad's, and granddad's. Starting out as a greenhorn beat bobby, she'd worked her way up the ranks, breezing through her exams, getting into plain clothes with energy and an enormous amount of application. For the past two and a half years she'd been an effective SIO – Senior Investigating Officer – in charge of major crime cases. And she'd loved it. *Lived* for it. Maybe a little too much. Career first, life second. So maybe it *was* her fault her husband had chosen to fuck around. And now she was coming up to thirty years old. Her carefree twenties were behind her, and she'd barely even noticed them go.

'There could be links here,' said Romilly. 'Word is Kit Miller owns the part of town where the warehouse robbery went down. His mother Ruby owns the club the misper vanished from, and his sister's groom and the photographer got done on her wedding day. It's all a bit too close for comfort.'

'Your honest opinion?' he asked. 'On the church shooting?'

Romilly shrugged. 'Got to be gangland, hasn't it? Most likely. But we'll follow it through. To the bitter bloody end – as per usual. PM on the photographer's being done right now, then the groom this afternoon. I'm heading off over there.'

'OK. Don't let me keep you.'

48

The killer was back in the room again, with the dogs. He *hated* the fucking dogs. But he was pleased that he was about to collect at least a portion of the last twenty due from his uncle for a job well done.

Well, *ish*.

It bothered him that he hadn't picked up the three spent shell casings in the flat after the shooting. But there'd been that random, *bastard* puff of wind, ruining his shot, and then he'd seen Kit Miller, his third target, coming at a run and knew he'd been spotted. He didn't do hand-to-hand, he wasn't strong enough for that, and he knew that Miller would squash him like a gnat.

He had to clear out, fast.

And he had.

But it gnawed at him, leaving those shells behind. It was untidy, and he didn't like that. He didn't like the fact that he'd wasted Miller's shot, either.

'So, the money . . .?' the killer prompted. He'd waited more than a week for this. He'd been patient for long enough.

'What about it?' The killer's uncle grabbed one of the dogs and hauled it, slobbering, onto his lap. The killer stifled a wince. His uncle stared him in the eye. 'You got Hinton. You got Lewis. But you *didn't* get the one we wanted most.

You missed your chance with Miller, and I'm not paying you a single solitary bean until he's six feet under.'

'That's not fair. I fulfilled two-thirds of the contract.'

'I don't deal in thirds, sonny. I want the whole job done, *then* you'll be paid.'

'It's more difficult now. They'll be on guard.'

'Your problem, not mine.'

The killer felt rage in his heart as he stared at his uncle. There were other complications, too. But of course he wasn't about to tell his uncle about Crystal Rose and her unfortunate death. What with the shootings at the church and the girl going missing from Ruby Darke's club, he was worried that someone was going to make a connection. He told himself it wouldn't do them any good if they did, but still – he didn't like it.

He really didn't.

But what could he do? He had to pick his moment carefully, finish the job. And *then* he'd get his money.

49

It was the part of the job Romilly hated most, attending post-mortems. The pathologist, Derek Potts, was middle-aged, scholarly, gently smiling, and he always wore a natty bow tie. At Christmas he wore one with a snow scene and reindeer. He was like a favourite teacher, someone you'd be happy to have a chat and a pint of beer with down the pub. He treated each dead body respectfully, patiently; uncovering, slicing, weighing – everything was done with a steady, reverential air.

Romilly liked that.

She'd been at PMs in the past, conducted by other people, where the atmosphere was humorous and blasé, and that didn't feel right. She'd seen that sort of attitude sometimes down the cop shop too – it was the way some coppers dealt with the bad and the bloody-nigh unbearable. Like a biker's helmet on a dusty road with a treacherous turn, with a teenage biker's head still inside it and his body twenty feet away. Nasty stuff. Hard to take. So they made a joke of it, hoping that would somehow take the sting out.

Romilly stood back, clad in the same protective clothing as everyone else in this big, cool, Lysol-scented room, while Potts and his assistants worked on the body of Clive Lewis, the photographer. Under the glare of the lights, Mr Lewis was carefully dissected on the big metal table with the drainage channels.

The Y-section on the chest and abdomen was first. The high-pitched whirring of the saw put her teeth on edge as it sliced through the mortal remains of Clive Lewis. She looked away. Not that she was squeamish – she'd attended enough post-mortems now to be way past the throwing-up stage.

The sawing went on. She looked at the sink, where kidney-shaped and circular metal bowls were stacked, ready for containing the bits and pieces of what had once been a human being. One of the assistants brought several dishes over to the table. Time passed. The heart was being examined and weighed.

'Maximum damage here,' said Derek to Romilly. 'He couldn't have survived this shot.'

Next came the lungs. Then the kidneys.

'Oh! Well, that's a surprise,' said Derek suddenly as he sliced open the stomach bag and emptied its contents into a tray. He half-turned toward the detective inspector. 'Romilly? Come and have a look at this.'

Romilly approached the table, and looked.

'Fuck,' she said.

Derek smiled. 'Well yes. Quite.'

50

Tanya Bellifer taught yoga and she loved dogs. She was a fizzy little laugh-a-minute blonde with a ponytail and a cute, blue-eyed face permanently crinkled up with smiles. She lived with her boyfriend Andy, who was working as a forklift driver in a DIY warehouse at the moment, but he wanted to take his interest in bodybuilding into personal training. They were going places, they had their own house and a fucking great mortgage, a car each, and the only *slight* wrinkle in the happy-ever-after was her dogs.

They were big bastards, these dogs. A mother and daughter Newfoundland, each of them black as ink and huge. The mother weighed in at eleven stone, and the daughter was catching up fast. These two monsters ate more than both the humans in the household put together.

'They're costing us a fucking fortune, Tans. I'm telling you, they got to go,' Andy was always saying.

But they were her *babies*. She couldn't have kids, so the Newfies stood in. Maybe those damned steroids Andy took to bulk up were the trouble, who knew? She'd read that they increased muscle but shrank a man's gonads to the size of peanuts. Tanya adored her dogs, and if Andy wanted them gone, fuck him. *He* could go. She wasn't going to be parted from her doggies, no way.

She walked them in the woods behind the house every

morning and afternoon, fitting them around her classes; they were no trouble at all. Yes, they ate a lot, but what price could you put on love?

It was a bright morning, and she was glad of the dappled shade cast by the big oaks. Once she'd found a deer lying in here, sunbathing in a warm patch of sunlight. It had scarpered when she appeared, but she'd gone to the spot and felt the ground; it was warm. She'd sat there awhile, feeling at one with nature; peaceful.

Now she strode along, no time for sitting. She had a dental appointment to get to in a while so they were going to have to cut short their walkies this morning.

'Casey! Pucci!' she called as they hared ahead of her.

Time to get their leads on, get back to the house, smarten up.

'Come on, girlies, let's be having you!' she carolled.

They were quiet, somewhere up ahead, out of sight.

'Oh, flip,' she said, hurrying after them.

'Casey! Come on, come to mama, girls,' she called. They'd led her further into the woods than they normally did, and she had to get back to the house sharpish.

Then she spotted them ahead in a small clearing among the trees.

'Oh, you naughty girls,' she said, and hurried up.

Pucci, the baby girl, was pawing at the ground, exposing a bit of black plastic bag, while Casey, the mum, was yanking at something with her teeth.

'What you got, girlies?' smiled Tanya, coming up, clipping on Pucci's lead.

Casey didn't even look up. She was pulling at some grey-blue thing, a doll's hand maybe. Some kid had dropped their doll or someone had dumped household rubbish here, hence the bin bag. The smile dropped from Tanya's face as

Casey tugged harder. One of the doll's fingers came away and . . . *Oh Christ, that's not a doll's finger.*

Tanya staggered back a step. She felt bile rush up into her throat like acid as Casey snapped her jaws together and swallowed the digit. A half-choked scream tore its way out of Tanya's mouth. She grabbed Casey's collar and clipped on the lead and almost had to *drag* the dog off its find. There was a grey arm poking up stiff as a branch from the soil the dogs had disturbed.

Oh Jesus!

That's not a doll. It's a dead body.

Then the smell hit her and Tanya backed away, whimpering, gagging, pulling the dogs.

She started to run with them, stumbling, crying, back to the house.

51

'I think the twins should go and stay with Vanessa,' said Ruby.

Days had passed. Daisy had come out of her bedroom and was now downstairs in the sitting room.

This was progress. But Ruby couldn't forget what had happened the other night, Daisy going out with Daniel looking for a hit when she had two small children upstairs, depending on her. *Needing* her.

'What?' Daisy looked at her vaguely.

Ruby let out an exasperated sigh. She knew Daisy was suffering. But for God's sake! She was going to have to snap out of this. Vanessa was the twins' adopted 'grandmother', Lady Bray. She lived down at Brayfield in Hampshire, and would welcome the chance to see Daisy's children. Vanessa had raised Daisy for the first part of her young life and she adored Matthew and Luke.

Ruby had been thinking about this a lot, and it seemed like an ideal solution. An extended stay with Vanessa deep in the country would be a treat, a holiday for the kids. And it would give Daisy time to pull herself back together again. Hopefully. If she ever would. Right now, Ruby doubted it.

'Matthew and Luke should be with Vanessa for a while. Jody will drive them down there, stay on for a couple of weeks. That'll give you a break, and Vanessa will love it. So will the twins.' She expected an argument. An objection. But Daisy merely nodded.

'OK. If you think that's best.'

Christ, Daisy! Ruby eyed her daughter, thought of saying something cutting and then thought again.

All Daisy's dreams had been destroyed. She was *right* to feel this way.

'I'll go phone Vanessa, and tell Jody. There's no reason they can't go today.'

'Yeah. Fine,' said Daisy.

Ruby left the room and Leon sauntered in, closing the door after him. Daisy looked up at him in surprise. Leon rarely addressed a word to her. 'Something you wanted?' she asked.

Leon nodded. 'Yeah, there is. I wanted to know what the *fuck* you were playing at the other night. You could have got Daniel in big trouble. *Terrible* trouble.'

Something in Leon's tone penetrated the fog in Daisy's brain. She stood up.

'How *dare* you speak to me like that,' she said in her crispest, coolest Home Counties voice.

'I'll speak to you how I bloody well like. Fact is, girl, you got to get a grip. Dan didn't want to tell me what you were up to, but I got it out of him. I have to say, I am fucking *appalled.* Your mum won't tell you this because she's too soft with you, but I will. Shape up, will you? Way I see it is, Kit ought to have kicked your arse when you dragged Dan into your games. *I* would have, for sure.'

Daisy stared at him, seeing the gleam in his eyes. *He's enjoying this*, she thought. Tearing me off a strip gives him a hard-on. The *tosser.* 'I'm not listening to this.' Daisy was heading for the door.

'Yeah, you are.' Leon grabbed her arm and dragged her to a halt. 'You need someone to tell you this, Daise.'

'Don't you *dare* call me that.' Only Kit had ever called her Daise. And Rob, of course. The pain of it all lanced through her yet again, fresh and raw and hungry, biting into her head, her guts. Rob would never call her that again. 'Let go of me,' she said icily.

'Uppity little tart.' Leon let go of her arm. 'You know I'm right,' he said.

Without uttering another word, she swept from the room.

52

They got the call from local uniform. SOCOs were summoned and by ten thirty Romilly and Harman were at the scene of Tanya Bellifer's discovery in the woods. They showed their warrant cards and ducked under the POLICE – DO NOT CROSS tapes that had been strung up around the edge of the wood beside the road.

There were arc lamps set up at the body site in its small clearing, and a white forensic tent. Romilly spotted Derek Potts there, dressed in white coveralls. Four of the forensics team were carrying a stretchered something into the tent. Derek raised a hand to Romilly and stepped inside, following the SOCOs and their grim burden. Moments later, he emerged and came over.

'Romilly,' he greeted her.

'What have you got?' she asked.

'Small female, twenty to twenty-five years old. Strangulation. Very sad.'

'Is it our girl, you think? The burlesque dancer?'

'Almost certainly. Dog walker found her. Always the way, isn't it. Dogs and their keen noses. There's one odd thing.'

'What?'

'All her teeth have been removed. Post-mortem.'

Romilly stared at him.

'Fingerprints can vanish with time,' Derek shrugged. 'Teeth don't.'

Their misper had turned into a murder enquiry. 'OK to . . .?' asked Romilly. She indicated the clearing.

'Yes of course.' Derek moved into the clearing and Romilly and Harman followed. He pointed out the grave Crystal Rose had been buried in. 'She was in there, wrapped in black plastic bin bags. Couple of weeks, I think, which ties in with our vanishing burlesque girl.'

'OK to look around now?' Romilly stared at the shallow grave and tried not to shudder. The thought of that poor girl in there, rotting.

'Fine. All marked, all photographed,' said Derek, and turned and left her and Harman to it.

'Christ, what a way to end up,' said Harman.

'Tragic,' said Romilly. Giving the grave a wide berth, she moved around it, brambles catching at her jeans. She paused, taking in the scene. The wind whispering through the bare boughs of the trees. Sunlight shimmering through on to the forest floor. Far enough from the road and the surrounding bustle of housing estates to hear nothing but the sweet sound of birdsong.

It was idyllic.

And tainted by murder.

'What's that?' she said. The slanting sun was highlighting something vivid, something blue.

'Hm? What?' Harman's gaze followed hers.

Romilly moved off, crushing ferns underfoot and releasing their dusky scent into the air. The brambles thickened, catching at her jacket, scratching her hands. She surged on. Stopped by a tree. There was a small length of rope hanging there. Electric-blue nylon rope, tied to a low branch. In the shape of a noose.

'Kids messing about? Playing hangman?' suggested Harman.

'The loop's too big for a noose. Particularly a kid's one.'

Harman was looking at the ground beneath it. 'Bits of old fruit down here, by the look of it.'

Romilly took plastic gloves out of her pocket and snapped them on. Taking out an evidence bag and a scoop, she picked up some of the mouldy remains of the fruit and bagged it up.

'What the fuck's *that*?' asked Harman, peering closely at a scrape mark along the tree branch, near where the rope was tied on.

Romilly gave it a close inspection. Then she looked at the noose, the fruit. 'You got a penknife on you?' she asked.

'Sure.'

'What d'you think it is?' asked Harman, handing over the penknife.

'You ever see that film with Edward Fox? *Day of the Jackal*?'

'Can't say I did.'

Romilly was digging at the tree bark now, working her way around the scrape mark.

'Well, you missed a treat.'

She dug deeper, eased the knife right in, and yanked it back. A brass-coloured cylinder popped out and fell into her waiting hand.

'Shit,' said Harman, taking back his knife, staring in surprise at the bullet.

Romilly indicated the rope. 'Someone was target-shooting here. This wasn't kids playing hangman, this was someone perfecting their shot. And penny to a pinch of shit?' She waved the bagged rotten fruit in Harman's face. 'This was a melon. Check this whole area for spent shell casings.'

53

Ruby was at the club watching a rehearsal when Romilly called in. The DI was accompanied today by a large blonde wearing a navy-blue skirt suit and plain white blouse.

'Speak to you?' Romilly asked. Up on the stage, Jenny, the bolder of the Rosettes, was climbing into the champagne glass, having agreed – reluctantly – that she would try to take Crystal's place in the act. Marilyn Monroe was cooing 'Diamonds' over the sound system.

'We're too upset over Crystal to even think about this,' Jenny had said when Ruby asked her for the tenth time to at least give it a go.

'Come on, give it a try,' Ruby had coaxed her. And to her surprise, Jenny had said she would.

Now, watching the Rosettes up there on the stage, Ruby was thinking that it was a disaster. One of the many disasters happening in her life right now. Jenny was taller than Crystal, and she was having trouble folding herself into the bowl of the glass. Sister Aggie was on the stage, hands on hips, directing operations full-volume to make herself heard over the soundtrack.

Ruby led Romilly and the big blonde woman over to her office. 'Laura handed in the CCTVs at the station, didn't she?' she asked.

'She did. Thanks for that.' Romilly and the blonde

followed Ruby into the office and closed the door, shutting out Marilyn's breathy singing voice and Aggie's shouted instructions to an unsteady Jenny.

'Take a seat,' said Ruby, going round her desk and sitting down. Romilly and the woman sat. They all looked at each other. 'How can I help?' asked Ruby.

'This is DS Appleton.'

Ruby nodded, waited for them to get to the point.

'The night Crystal Rose vanished, she met a man inside this club,' said Romilly.

'That's right,' said Ruby. 'You should get a good look at him on the CCTV.'

'Yes. I'm afraid we're bringing bad news, Miss Darke,' she said.

'What is it?' asked Ruby, feeling nervous.

'Crystal Rose's sisters . . . can you call them in?'

'Of course.' Ruby stood, went to the office door. Aggie turned, and Ruby hooked a finger at her. *Both of you*, she mouthed. *Over here*.

Leaving the door ajar, Ruby stepped back into the office and in an uneasy silence walked around the desk and sat down. 'They're coming,' she said.

Marilyn's soundtrack was abruptly silenced. Moments passed. At last the door swung open and the Rosettes stood there, Jenny in front, Aggie behind, as usual. They came in, closed the door behind them. Suddenly, the little office was overcrowded, packed with bodies. Both Romilly and Bev stood up, offered the girls their seats. 'What is it?' asked Jenny. 'What's happened?'

'I'm so sorry. But we've discovered a body,' said Romilly. 'We believe it's your sister.'

Ruby stared at her in horror. Both the Rosettes were wide-eyed with shock. Aggie had a hand over her mouth. 'Oh God. No,' said Jenny.

Bev reached out and squeezed Jenny's hand comfortingly. Jenny snatched her hand out of the woman's grasp.

'How did it . . .? I mean, how did she . . .?' asked Jenny.

'We believe the cause of death was strangulation,' said Romilly. 'And now we want to find whoever is responsible, and bring them to justice. For that to happen, we're going to need your help.'

54

After an hour, Romilly left Bev Appleton in the club, still talking through events with the Rosettes and Ruby. Gladly, she stepped back out into the sunshine. PMs were the worst, but another painful part of the job was breaking bad news to the bereaved. She hated it, and was glad that it was done. As she made her way out, she bumped into Kit Miller, coming in.

'Oof,' she said in surprise at the impact, and fell back.

Kit steadied her with both hands on her upper arms. 'Hello, detective,' he said. 'In a rush?'

Romilly stepped away, shrugging off his grip. 'Not particularly. Actually, I'm glad I ran into you, I'd like a word.'

'About . . .?' prompted Kit.

'Let's walk,' said Romilly, and set off along the pavement, dodging other pedestrians. Walking, she didn't have to look at him, or think to herself how annoyingly cocksure and good-looking he was. Still, she was irritably aware of him swaggering along beside her, like he owned the world.

And maybe he did. For sure, he owned *this* one. These streets. As they walked on, people glanced at him, nodded. He seemed to exude a fearsome and yet somehow fatherly vibe, both benevolent and pitiless, and there was something deeply respectful in the way they looked at him.

'So? You got anything?' he asked.

Romilly shot him a sour sideways glance, cop to a man she *knew* was into crime. So what if he was hot? He was hot in other ways, too. *Bad* ways. But too clever, thus far, to be caught. 'I've got a lot,' said Romilly. 'And at the moment it's bewildering. A dead girl who worked in your mother's club. A hit at your sister's wedding that seemed to be aimed at you. A robbery that appears to tie in with you and your family . . .'

'Why would anyone want to shoot me?' he asked, all innocence. But she saw his jaw tighten.

'Because you are who you are.'

'And that is . . .?'

Romilly ground to a stop. Looked him dead in the eye. 'You know what I'm talking about.'

'Don't think I do,' said Kit.

'Extorting money from businesses.'

'What, me?'

Romilly sighed.

'Do you know anything about that supermarket warehouse heist?'

'I saw that on the news. No. Why would I?'

Romilly turned and started walking again. Kit fell into step beside her once more.

'Protection rackets are a dangerous game, I imagine. People – other gangs maybe – get envious. Start thinking they'll turn your lot over and step in,' she said.

Kit said nothing.

'He was your best friend, yeah? Rob Hinton?'

'He worked for me,' said Kit. 'Security.'

But Romilly saw the tension in him. Rob Hinton had been more than an employee to Kit Miller. *Much* more.

'What we want to avoid,' she said, 'is the idea that anyone could take the law into their own hands over this. I understand that you might be upset . . .'

Kit stopped walking and turned to her. 'I'm not upset,' he said.

Yeah, you are, thought Romilly. *You're ready to tear someone's head off over Rob Hinton's death.* But she'd prodded the wound, seen what was there. It was still open, still angry. Festering. And she'd issued her warning, so job done.

'The missing girl,' she said.

She saw the stress lift in him. 'Crystal Rose. The burlesque dancer.'

'She's turned up dead. Strangled.'

'Shit.' Kit paused mid-stride.

Romilly stopped walking too and turned to face him. 'About the wedding photographer,' she said.

'What about him?'

Romilly hesitated before informing him: 'During the autopsy, we found twenty bags of cocaine in his stomach.'

Kit stared at her, astonished. 'You serious?'

'Deadly. Our surmise is that he's been shipping the stuff round the country while doing photography jobs.'

'You've got to be kidding me. That little bloke was a drugs mule?'

'Photographers don't earn much. Drug dealers do.'

Kit thought about that. If Clive Lewis was shipping product, she was right; he was probably a good earner.

'You checked his bank statements?'

'We have. No good.'

He thought again of Rob on the wedding day morning, worried, needing to talk – about what? Business stuff, he'd said. Was it *this?* No, surely not. Rob knew that Kit never touched drugs operations. Not his field, and he despised druggies. But Rob always did the milk run on that arcade. Had Rob somehow got wind of what Clive Lewis was up to? Or was it something else that was bugging him? Something *worse*?

'Could be he's hiding the cash somewhere else. Or maybe washing it through another business.'

Romilly stared at his face. 'Is that what you'd do?'

'It's what anyone would do, if they regularly had a gutful of coke and a lot of payments coming in from it. What about the wife?'

'What about her?'

'You've spoken to her?'

'I have. And she seemed shocked by the news that her husband was carting drugs around the country. She *acted* shocked, anyway. As for payments? She claims to know nothing about any of it.'

Kit rocked back on his heels, his face thoughtful. 'Maybe she's lying.'

'Maybe she is. My feeling is, she isn't.'

'If Clive Lewis was fiddling someone on the drugs, it could get nasty. Christ, it could be, couldn't it?' His eyes met hers and to her surprise she saw a flash of pain in them: real, genuine pain, quickly replaced by anger. 'Those three shots could all have been for Clive Lewis. Maybe Rob got hit by mistake.' *Or maybe Rob was involved.* No. Why was he even *thinking* that? 'You got someone watching the widow woman? She could try to get access to the cash. The people who shot Lewis and Rob could contact her. Maybe Lewis was getting antsy, refusing to cooperate any more. And now they'll switch their attention to her.'

'I think that's unlikely. She's not a photographer. She's a stay-at-home type, if I'm any judge. And we can't spare the bodies,' said Romilly. 'Have someone sitting outside that studio for – what? Weeks, months? No. Not possible.'

'I can spare someone for that,' said Kit.

'No.'

'They'll get straight on to you, first hint of a sniff.'

'Absolutely not.'

Kit thought of Rob, lying dead on a slab, taking his mystery with him to the grave. He wanted to get to the bottom of this, and soon. 'I'm going to do it anyway.'

Romilly held her breath. 'Fuck!' she burst out. 'All right. Do it.'

'Anything else I can help you with, detective?'

'Don't bloody push it,' said Romilly, and walked off.

55

When Ruby got home to Marlow, it was chaos outside the gate. There were more journalists than ever, and the instant they saw her car coming they were firing flashguns, shouting questions.

'Miss Darke, you got anything to say about the shooting at your daughter's wedding? Or on the death of the girl who worked at your club?'

'Was this a gangland hit, Miss Darke?'

'Was your son the target, Miss Darke?'

'Are *you* a target?'

'How do you feel about the girl getting killed, Miss Darke?'

'Are you concerned that innocent people got hurt?'

'What the fuck?' said Ruby out loud, and the car swept in, the gates closing behind them, shutting the press out.

Christ, they were getting more rabid, not less. She hoped to God none of them tried to get into the grounds to come up to the house itself. Daisy was in a fragile state, Rob gone, the kids gone, she didn't need any of that shit. It was all so bloody awful. The Rosettes had lost a sister, Mrs Lewis a husband, and Daisy the love of her life. And now, after what Kit had told her following his conversation with DI Kane, there was even a question mark in Ruby's mind around quiet, grey little Mrs Lewis. Either Mrs Lewis was a bloody convincing liar, or she really was in the dark about what her husband had got up to on his travels.

Ruby was relieved to get indoors, shut out the world.

Leon emerged from the kitchen when he heard her come in.

'Where's Daisy?' asked Ruby.

'Upstairs. Asleep, last I checked.'

'And Kit?'

'Out and about.'

Ruby nodded and went on up. It was deathly quiet in the house without the rumpus and giggles of the twins; she missed her grandkids already. She went to Daisy's room, knocked lightly on the door and went in. The curtains were closed against the sunlight. When her eyes grew accustomed to the half-dark, Ruby saw that Daisy was in the bed, but her eyes were open; she was staring up at the ceiling, seeing nothing.

'Daisy?' Ruby felt a pang of alarm. If Daisy had been seeking drugs, had she taken something else, was she . . .?

Then Daisy's head moved; she blinked and her eyes fell on Ruby. 'What?' she said vaguely.

Christ, I thought you were dead for a moment there.

Ruby went over to the bed and sat down on the side of it. Her heart was beating uncomfortably hard and fast with the aftermath of fright. She felt like her world was falling apart, but she had to be strong for Daisy, not show a moment's weakness.

'How you doing?' she asked, taking her daughter's hand. Her heart was breaking for Daisy. She wanted to take her pain away, make it her own. But she couldn't.

'OK,' said Daisy. 'Leon said there's even more journos at the gate now they've found this missing girl who worked at your club.'

'Yes. There are.'

'Vultures.' Daisy shuddered. 'I saw the one o'clock news; they said they'd found her body in woods somewhere.'

'That's right.' Ruby sighed. 'The DI in charge of the case came over this morning and broke the news to Crystal's sisters. I was there.'

'They haven't got anybody for it?'

'No. Not yet. You going to get up? I could cook us something.'

'Not hungry.'

'Well . . .' Ruby stood up. 'I'm famished. I'll go and rustle up a snack. Sure I can't interest you?' Daisy didn't answer.

'Daisy . . .' Ruby stared down at her daughter in anxious frustration.

'There is one thing, though,' said Daisy.

'Oh? What?'

'I want Kit to sack that bastard Leon.'

'You what?'

'He was very rude to me. He's *always* rude to me, come to think of it.'

Ruby wondered about that. Maybe Leon had kicked off about the drugs, and Daisy hadn't wanted to hear it.

'I'll pass it on,' said Ruby, thinking that she wouldn't bother. Leon had just lost his brother; he had enough problems.

56

Down in the kitchen, Ruby made omelettes for herself and Leon. She turned on the radio, tried to cheer herself up. Darts were singing 'Duke of Earl'.

'What you been saying to Daisy?' she asked him as they sat at the breakfast bar eating. 'She wants Kit to fire you.'

'Someone had to tell her to get a hold,' he said, unabashed.

Ruby looked at Leon. The *mouth* on this chippy little fucker. He was nothing like Rob, nothing like blockish Daniel either. Leon didn't even *look* like his brothers. Or his sisters, come to that. Leon was almost classically beautiful. He had white-blond hair, aquiline features, stunning blue eyes. And he was fiery; he could lose his temper and ten minutes later have no clue what he'd got so enraged about.

'Take it easy with her,' advised Ruby. 'She's having a tough time.'

'We could all sit in the corner and cry. But it's no good falling to bits, is it?'

'Leon.'

'Yeah?'

'Button it for a change, OK?'

Leon wiped the bread around his empty plate and scoffed it down.

'Noted,' he said, and took the plates over to the dishwasher, doing a little one-two shuffle as the beat changed and Michael Jackson started in on 'Don't Stop 'Til You Get Enough'.

Ruby watched him. He had a lot of charm, Leon, when he wasn't being a pain in the arse. And at least *he* seemed to be coping with Rob's death OK, even if no one else was.

'How's your mum doing?' she asked.

'Oh, *Eunice*?' Leon never called Eunice 'Mum'. And he always looked sour at the very mention of her. 'She's OK,' he shrugged. 'Shocked, of course. Well, we all are.'

'You seem to be handling it well. Better than Daniel, I think.'

'Daniel's a fucking idiot. Thinks the sun's pulled up on a rope.'

'Bit harsh,' said Ruby.

Leon heaved a sharp sigh. 'I'm tired. So I'm turning in,' he said, and headed for the back door. He met Daniel, just entering. They passed each other without a word. Daniel closed the back door, locked it.

'I'm going to take my coffee into the sitting room,' said Ruby, switching off the radio and standing up. 'Join me, Daniel, if you like.'

Ruby went into the sitting room and sat down. This morning, she had left the print the photographer's wife had given her, the one of her and Daisy standing beside the Rolls with the Georgian building opposite the church in the background, on the coffee table. Now she looked at it and sighed for the ruination of what should have been a blissfully happy day.

Then she took her copies of the club's CCTV out of her bag and fed them into the machine beneath the TV. She watched as the night of Crystal's disappearance was replayed in black and white on the silent screen. She watched Crystal walk to one of the tables, a tall, thin, dark-haired man following behind her. They sat down; a while later, Joanie the hostess came over and left champagne in an ice bucket. They drank, talked. At one point Crystal's body language seemed to signal annoyance. Her companion was looking away from her, across the other side of the room, then his head swung back.

Ruby tensed.

Christ! Was he looking at me?

She could see herself there, in his eyeline.

Was he?

Daniel came in, pushing the door closed behind him, a mug of coffee in his hand.

'This from the club?' he asked, his eyes fastened to the screen as he sat down.

'Yeah.'

Daniel's attention wandered to the photograph on the table. 'The day of the wedding,' he said, picking it up to look more closely at it. He was quiet for a long moment.

'Daisy looks great in that shot,' he said at last.

Ruby said nothing. She'd always been aware that Daniel'd had a bit of a crush on Daisy when he was younger.

'And that . . .' He was peering closer. 'That's someone up on the first floor there, the shooter. The one who killed Rob.'

Ruby gazed at Daniel with sympathy. 'This is awful for you, for your family. We miss him, but you must miss him far worse.'

Daniel looked up, shrugged. 'We all miss him, don't we,' he said, swallowing hard.

Then he looked at the image on the TV screen. Back at the photo. He frowned.

'Ruby?'

'Yeah?'

'This . . . look at this, will you? Look at the shape of the head. The one who's in the photo, and the one who's on the screen? This couldn't be the same person, could it?'

57

Fats had provided a list, and Kit had started in on the gun clubs. He was going to each one in turn, showing them the shell casing, which they all – without exception, so far – recognized. But further questions drew a blank.

'You got any rogue shooters here?' he asked, time after time.

But the answer was invariably, What are you, police? Where's your ID? At which point he always felt a burning need to rip their heads off and beat them with the wet end. He wanted, he *needed*, answers.

When he returned, feeling dispirited, to the office behind Sheila's restaurant, he got a bell from Petey, one of his regular boys, calling him over to the Lewis studio. Petey was there, slouched behind the wheel in his old mineral-blue Ford Escort, thirty yards along the road. He wound down his window when he saw Kit approaching.

'Boss,' he said.

'Something?' said Kit.

'Just an update. Studio's open. A couple of people come in and out. Bloke from a photo lab, van marked *Pollack Photographic*, went in at twelve and came straight out again. Strikes me as odd though.'

'What's odd?'

'That the studio's open at all. Husband's dead. Wouldn't

you think wifey would shut the place up – mark of respect, at least? I mean, isn't she *upset* her husband's dead?'

'Might be glad to see the back of the fucker.'

'She's been down the shops a time or two,' said Petey. 'And she went to a lock-up Thursday. Came out with a laundry bag. Moving the old man's belongings around, I reckon. This is a boring bloody job. Think the police would cover it?'

'Can't spare the people,' said Kit, thinking of DI Romilly Kane telling him that. She was kind of cute, but she looked at him like he was the Antichrist, like she ought to have a crucifix or some damned thing in her hand for protection whenever she was with him. He didn't *like* assisting the Bill, but this was to catch Rob's killer, and he would work with *anyone* to achieve that.

Lock-ups and laundry bags, he thought.

'If she goes back to that lock-up again, let me know,' he said.

Romilly was surprised to come into the station next day and find Ruby Darke waiting for her. She had with her a well-muscled young man, solid as a bull and with treacle-blond hair and greenish eyes.

A minder. Well, she is Kit Miller's mother, once a model citizen but apparently now as crooked as a dog's hind leg, and that smooth bastard Miller seems to have minders to spare.

Romilly was simmering with anger at Miller. She had warned him not to get involved in police business, and instead, what did she find? That two gun club stewards had phoned in to the nick, saying there was a man going round asking questions, showing a shell casing, and it seemed odd, was he one of theirs? When they were asked to describe the man, it was obvious it was Kit Miller they were talking about.

Romilly ushered Ruby into the depths of the cop shop, sat her down, offered coffee, which she and her silent escort declined.

'We were looking at this yesterday,' said Ruby, pulling out the photo of her and Daisy by the Roller at the church. 'Daniel – this is Daniel. He's Rob Hinton's brother, the man who was shot at the church. The groom. Not the photographer.' Daniel inclined his head an inch.

'He spotted it first,' Ruby went on. 'The man behind the gun and the one on the CCTV with Crystal Rose. Look at the shape of his head. The long face. The skinny neck. And the thin wrists. We think it could be the same person.'

'No luck on the gun clubs?' Fats asked Kit later the same day.

'None.'

'Well, we've had a bit of good news.'

Jesus, could I use some good news. 'Go on then. Spit it out.'

'The scruffy blond bloke from the warehouse hit.'

'What about him?'

'One of the boys picked him up in a pub down the Mile End Road, chucking his money about, buying people drinks.'

'Where is he?'

'We got him stashed away.' Fats stood up, pulled on his jacket. 'Thought you'd want to talk to him yourself.'

'You got *that* right,' said Kit.

58

It was early Wednesday evening, and Daisy was on her own with Daniel on guard. Ruby was at the club, and Kit was out. After turfing a press photographer out of the back garden at about four, Daniel went to sit in the kitchen. He was careful to leave the door into the hall open so he could see what was going on; he didn't want a repeat of that drugs business. He passed the time watching rubbish telly and the news until six thirty. After that, he made beans on toast and, hearing Daisy coming downstairs, offered her some.

'No,' she said, sweeping through the hall and blanking him. She went into the sitting room and closed the door, shutting him firmly out.

Well fuck you too, he thought.

Since the drugs episode last weekend, she'd been ignoring him, cutting him dead at every opportunity. Well, fair enough. Let her stew. He heard the kitchen extension tinkle, meaning Daisy was on the phone in the sitting room. Maybe she was getting hold of herself at last. She'd started phoning the kids a couple of evenings ago and it seemed to be a regular thing now, and that was good. Poor little fuckers must be bewildered, suddenly sent off, after all that happened at the church. He reckoned they could be scarred for life.

When he'd finished eating, he loaded the dirty crocks

into the dishwasher, and sat through a soap opera in which it seemed all the women wanted to get married and all the men wanted to beat the crap out of each other. He looked at his watch. Later, when Kit got back, he was planning to visit his mum, see how she was doing. He was worried about her, and he knew she wouldn't get much sympathy off her supposed 'partner'. In his opinion, Patrick Dowling was a shit. Trudy and Sarah would see Eunice was all right, but he wanted to check in with her, all the same. Rob's death had hit her very hard.

The phone extension 'pinged', signalling that Daisy's call to the kids was finished. Then the phone rang. He didn't pick it up. Daisy was right there, she'd do that. He wasn't her social fucking secretary, after all. After four rings, it stopped and the call light stayed on. Daisy had answered.

Daniel got back to the soap. One woman was shrieking at another and yanking her hair. He tweaked the volume down, with half an ear listening out for Daisy in the sitting room, wondering who the call was from.

Eventually the light went out on the kitchen phone. End of call. Silence from the sitting room. He put the kettle on for a cup of tea and stood against the worktop waiting for it to boil. Then he heard the sitting room door open. Daisy crossed the hall and came into the kitchen and stood there looking at him with stunned, heartbroken eyes.

'What?' he asked, straightening in alarm.

'That was the police,' said Daisy. 'They're releasing Rob's body tomorrow. So we can make the funeral arrangements.'

'Oh shit,' said Daniel.

Daisy burst into hopeless tears. She flew across the kitchen straight into his arms. With no other option, Daniel grabbed her and held on tight. His sister-in-law, his brother's wife. The poor bitch, what a fucking disaster.

'I'm sorry, Daniel!' she sobbed out. 'I'm sorry I dragged you into that with the drugs. You didn't deserve it. I think I was out of my mind, I was crazy, I didn't know what to do.'

'It's OK,' he said, smoothing her hair. 'It's fine. You were upset. It's forgotten.'

'Christ, I'm sorry. Leon's right, I'm a complete *cow*.'

'Leon's talking out of his arse. Forget it. It was nothing.'

He patted her back, beginning to feel uncomfortable. Daisy was gorgeous, and as stable as Semtex. One false move and he could find himself in a whole heap of shit with this situation. Firmly, he pushed her back, away from him. He didn't *want* to – and that was the danger, right there. What he wanted was to go on holding Daisy, his dead brother's wife. And that wasn't on.

'Let's go get a brandy, you've had a shock,' he said, reaching for the remote and switching off the telly. 'I'll phone Ruby, tell her we've had the call.'

And then Ruby would come back here, and he wouldn't be alone with Daisy any more.

Safety in numbers, he thought.

He led the way into the sitting room, went to the drinks cabinet, and poured them both a Martell. He felt like he needed it too. Daisy sat down, wiped her eyes. The lamplight fell on her hair, highlighting it to spun gold. She tucked her long legs up underneath her; she had great legs. He thought of the suede boots she'd been wearing on their drugs expedition and quickly yanked his mind off that. He handed her the glass of brandy, picked up the phone and made his calls. Tried not to look at her.

Failed.

He wondered where Kit was. And he wished his boss would come back, right now.

59

Kit was walking around a man who was suspended by a heavy chain, upside-down, from the rafters of a big disused barn way out on the Essex salt marshes. There were covered-up cars, engine parts and wheels stacked up around the interior of the barn, but a space had been cleared for the moment. Kit owned this place, and next week it was going to be bulldozed, turned over, shoved back into the ground.

The lads had been out on the London streets, passing the word, looking for this man, the one witnesses described as part of the gang that robbed the supermarket warehouse. Word spread fast, on the streets. And now they had the small, runty, blond man with wrinkles, bad teeth and a fistful of gold medallions around his neck. They didn't have the black one. Not yet.

They'd tracked Runty down to an East End pub and the black had been there too, *also* flashing his money about – but the black had been stronger and quicker and had managed to leg it before they grabbed him. No matter. Him, they'd sort later.

Kit circled the man. There was blood all over the runt's face and blood on the concrete floor, and his bad teeth wouldn't be a problem any more because Kit had been laying into him with the baseball bat he held in his red-stained hands.

Kit's face and his shirt front and his suit had caught spatters of the runt's blood but he didn't give a shit. His boys, six of them, stood around, watching. They'd divested the runt of his gold neck ornaments, hauled him up on the massive chain meant for removing car engines. Then Kit had moved in.

'Who was really behind that warehouse job?' asked Kit.

The runt gasped down a breath, spat blood. 'Don't know what you're talking about,' he rasped out. 'Please . . . I dunno nothing.'

Kit thought of Rob, dead in a hospital morgue. He'd wanted to pulverize someone ever since the shooting, and now he had his chance. He took aim and smashed the baseball bat into the runt's skull again.

The runt screamed, rocking on his chain.

'Where's your mate staying, the black one? You tell me that and you might get out of here.' The runt was gasping, squirming. Kit drew the bat back again.

'No!' yelled the runt. 'I'll tell. All right? I'll tell.' He did.

'There. Easy, wasn't it?' Kit moved in and patted the man's sunken cheek. The runt flinched away from his touch. 'Now the rest. Who set up the warehouse job?'

The blond shook his head again. Kit walked off to the far side of the shed where all the boys waited, watching in silence.

He was simmering with suppressed rage. He wanted to smash something. Bring Rob back to him. But he couldn't. And knowing that made him furious. He turned to go back and start over, get the answers he needed, but Leon stepped forward first, pulled an army grenade from his jacket pocket. Before Kit could draw breath to stop him, he yanked the pin and lobbed the grenade. It hit the floor, bounced, and landed right underneath the runt.

'No!' he screamed.

Everyone scattered out the door.

The grenade exploded.

The runt stopped screaming. His head was gone.

Kit climbed back to his feet, his ears ringing from the blast. He stood there, breathing hard. Then he went back inside. The boys followed. In the shocked silence, blood dripped like a tap. He looked at Leon.

'You. Fucking. Stupid. *Maniac*,' said Kit, each word falling like a hammer blow.

He grabbed Leon and pulled out his gun and in fury shoved it up under Leon's jaw. Leon was balanced on tiptoe all of a sudden, his eyes wildly staring into Kit's, which were blazing. 'You fucking *cunt*. You jumped-up little son of a bitch! You listen to me.' Kit shook him, hard. 'You don't move until I tell you to.' He shook him again. 'You don't even *breathe* without my permission.' And again, harder. 'Now. Have you got that?'

Leon swallowed, feeling the cold metal crushing his throat.

'I got it,' he managed to whisper.

'You what?' Kit growled. 'I didn't hear you.'

'I got it!' Leon choked out.

'Fucking *fool*.'

Kit shoved Leon away from him, his face twisted with disgust. He slid the gun back into the shoulder holster. Leon backed away, clutching his throat. Kit turned to the others.

'Clear this mess away,' he snapped, and walked out.

60

It was gone two in the morning when Kit got back to Ruby's place. No press there now, no nothing. All dead quiet. He let himself in and was surprised to find a light on in the sitting room. He went in there, stood in the open doorway.

Ruby was sitting in her dressing gown, nursing a brandy. She looked up and straightened in her chair with a jerk of alarm when she saw his hands, his shirt, his face, all spattered with blood.

'It's not mine,' he said, reading her expression.

Ruby settled back. 'What happened?' she asked.

'Caught up with one of the blokes from the warehouse job.'

'Did you get anything out of him about it?'

Kit shook his head. 'Not much. Leon blew it. Finished it off too quick. Stupid little bastard.'

Ruby paused for a beat. 'Kit. He's cut up over Rob. Whatever he's done, you got to make allowances. He's young and impulsive. Christ, *you* were like that once. I suppose all he's trying to do is make a name for himself.'

'Well he has, and it's *cunt*.' Kit drew a steadying breath. He was still fuming mad at Leon. They'd been *that close* to getting some answers, and he'd blown it. 'Anything happening here?'

'The police phoned earlier. They're releasing Rob's body for the funeral.'

'Fuck.' Carefully, Kit slipped off his stained jacket and put it aside. He'd burn it later, and the shirt, and the trousers. He glanced down. And the shoes. He sat down opposite Ruby.

'Here, drink this.' Ruby passed over her own half-full glass. 'I couldn't sleep. Kept thinking about everything. The wedding day. And now the funeral.' She clutched her head as if it ached. 'And there was something else I wanted to talk to you about. You know the missing girl, the *murdered* girl, Crystal Rose? Well, the man in the club buying her drinks and the man in the window firing the gun, it could be the same person.'

Kit sat silently, absorbing this. He gulped down the brandy. Then he said: 'The police know?'

Ruby nodded. 'We went down the cop shop, me and Daniel. The Bill are going to put the club CCTV out on the TV news and appeal for information.'

61

'You fucking idiot,' said the man.

The killer was sitting in the house in central London again, the same one where he'd first accepted the job. The man sitting opposite him was literally quivering with fury as they both looked at the TV screen. On the BBC news, they were showing the CCTV from the burlesque club and asking for the public's help in identifying the man who was now shown walking through the club behind the murdered Crystal Rose.

'It's nothing,' said the killer. 'Forget it. They're never going to trace me from that.'

The dogs were at it again, small yappy things running around the room. The killer tucked his feet in so that they couldn't touch him. Fucking dogs, he hated them. But his uncle seemed to dote on the bloody things.

Although he wouldn't admit this, the killer didn't feel quite so sure of himself now. He stared at the screen, at *himself*, and wished he'd never gone in there, never fucked the little twat, never had to wring her stupid bloody neck.

Women were always trouble.

Why hadn't he remembered that?

His father had told him so, over and over, after Mother left when he was nine years old, taking her lapdog Kiki with her.

'She didn't care about you,' his father had told him. 'Or me, come to that. Thought more of that bloody dog of hers.

But we're all right on our own. Just you and me now, son. Just us.'

That dog had loved his mother but despised his father and even snapped at the son, whenever he came near. The killer had grown up an isolated only child, unable to make friends, but as he grew older women were his weakness and he found they were attracted to him. So he had no trouble getting female company. Keeping it? Quite another matter. After a few dates, they'd get tired of his lack of charm – that was something he reserved for first dates only, manufactured to get a woman into bed – and they'd scarper.

'What the hell are we going to do about this?' asked the man angrily.

'Nothing,' said the killer. 'What we do is *nothing*. We sit tight, that's all.'

'If any of this ever leads back to me . . .'

'It can't. It won't.' The killer was annoyed with himself for once again giving in to his sexual impulses. Usually, he kept himself to himself. He was happy that way. People, particularly women – thank you, Dad – were always troublesome in the end. He hated that he was so tempted by them. But he could control it. He *could.*

'Don't worry,' he told his uncle.

It irked him that he hadn't fully completed his task. On the day of the wedding, with Kit Miller running at him, he hadn't had time to retake the third shot and to pick up his spent shell casings, police his brass as he should have, as any good marksman would.

'It will be fine,' he said. 'You'll see.'

'It better fucking be,' said the man. 'Or I'll want a refund on that first down payment, I'm warning you.'

'A refund? Fuck *off.*'

'Then get on with it. Miller – I want *his* arse. All right? Once that's done, you'll get your cash.'

62

Jenny and Aggie Rose were down the police station at the invitation of DI Romilly Kane. DS Bev Appleton was sitting in on the interview. So was DS Harman, taking notes. Both the Rosettes were subdued.

Joanie Fletcher, the hostess who'd served Crystal and her date that evening, was in the other interview room, waiting, but no one expected to get anything of any use out of her.

'Is there anything you can tell us about this man on the CCTV. Take your time,' said Romilly. 'Think about it. Any small detail will help.'

'Nothing really. Except, when he came backstage, he said his name was John,' said Jenny.

Which was probably not his real name anyway. 'No surname?' asked Harman.

Both girls shook their heads.

'He was tall,' said Romilly. 'How tall?'

'Six-two maybe?' said Jenny.

'Taller,' said Aggie.

'Six-three then.'

'Thin, fat? Medium build?' asked Bev.

'Thin,' said Aggie. 'Real skinny. Thin in the face, you know. Sort of long.'

'Clothes?' asked Romilly. She pressed play on the

machine and the CCTV sprang into life again, the image of the tall man following Crystal Rose through the nightclub. 'Looks like a pale jacket,' she said.

'Caramel-coloured,' said Jenny. 'Camel, don't they call it? It looked expensive. You could see the hand stitching on the collar. Bespoke, I reckon.'

'Any marks, moles, tattoos?' said Romilly.

'Nice hair. Dark. Thick and straight.'

'Anything else?'

'No. Good skin. Smelled nice.'

'What smell would you say? What aftershave?' asked Romilly.

The Rosettes looked at each other.

'Musky,' said Jenny.

'Musky and sweet,' agreed Aggie.

There were a thousand musky and sweet aftershaves on the market.

They questioned the Rosettes for another half an hour before letting them go. Next they tackled Joanie Fletcher. Nothing. The man was tall, thin, good-looking. Nothing else. He'd paid cash. That was all.

After the Rosettes interview, Bev hurried off to her next case. When Romilly and Harman had finished with Joanie, Harman busied himself with paperwork. Romilly sat in her office, brooding. The man who was probably the last person to see Crystal Rose alive was tall, thin, dark-haired and neat in appearance and he smelled good. Him and a million others.

Then the phone rang, and it was Kit Miller.

63

'You're sure about this?' asked Romilly as she stood on the corner near the lock-ups with Kit.

'My boy said she's been back there once already since the wedding, on a Thursday morning. Now she's back and it's Thursday again. Visit number two. Might be nothing, who knows. But she's not taking stuff in there. She's bringing stuff out. You'd expect her to be clearing hubby's stuff out of the flat, right? Not taking more stuff back there.'

'You've been going round the gun clubs,' said Romilly.

Kit turned his head, looked into her eyes. Said nothing. He'd been doing a *lot* of things. Having a sit-down with Thomas Knox. Giving Leon a thorough bollocking for being so bloody hasty and depriving them of the answers they needed. None of which he was going to tell *her* about.

'We've had complaints,' she said.

'Complaints? About what?'

Romilly counted to ten. 'You did pick up that third shell casing.'

Kit shrugged and looked away.

Romilly sighed and returned her attention to the car parked in front of one of the lock-ups. 'Could be anything in there,' she said. 'Maybe things of sentimental value? Something to remind her of Clive Lewis?'

'Oh please. She's come out of there once already with a

laundry bag stuffed full of something, and I don't think it was some old git's pipe collection. You checked the bank statements, didn't you? There was no paper trail, nothing untoward going into the accounts from drug sales, but for sure it has to be going somewhere. Look out. Here she comes.'

Mrs Lewis was coming out of the lock-up, a big and clearly heavy blue tartan laundry bag in her hand. She put the bulging bag on the pavement and secured the lock-up door. Then she went over to her car, stuffed the hefty bag in the boot, and got in.

Romilly detached herself from their corner and legged it over to the car. She tapped hard on the driver's window and flashed her warrant card as Mrs Lewis started the engine.

'Police! Switch off the engine, please.'

Mrs Lewis's eyes widened in fear. Instead of switching off the engine, she threw the car into reverse. It leapfrogged back and smashed into the Volvo parked behind her.

'Police! Stop!' shouted Romilly, trying the door's handle.

Mrs Lewis was fiddling with the gears. She found first and the car jumped forward. Her door swung wide open and knocked Romilly to her knees. Kit stepped quickly in, leaned over and grabbed the keys, switching off the engine before Mrs Lewis could take another swing at reverse and flatten Romilly like roadkill. He hauled her back to her feet.

'You OK?' he asked.

'I'm fine,' she snapped, scrabbling free of his grip. She turned to the woman in the car. 'You're under arrest,' she said.

Before taking Mrs Lewis down to the station, Romilly first took the woman around the back of her car and popped open the boot. The laundry bag was full of money. A *lot* of money. Then she locked the car and took Mrs Lewis with Kit back to the lock-up. White-faced, hands shaking, Mrs Lewis opened up.

There was a big square slab of tarp-covered something in there.

Romilly stepped in and loosened the side ties on the tarp. She threw it back.

'Holy fuck,' said Kit.

Under the tarp was a massive pile of money. Romilly turned and stared hard at Mrs Lewis.

'It's nothing to do with me,' she said.

Romilly took the smaller woman's arm. 'Come on, let's get this secure and then we'll take you down the station. This will be impounded.'

Kit was watching all this with mild amusement.

'Does anyone else have a key?' asked Romilly after Mrs Lewis had locked it up and they stood outside once more.

'No. Well. Mr Hinton did,' she said.

Kit's amusement faded to nothing. He stepped toward the woman and she shrank back as she saw the expression in his eyes.

'What did you say?' he asked.

'Mr Hinton had a key. That . . . that's what Clive's note said.' Her face crumpled. 'What's going to happen to me?' she wailed.

Romilly and Kit stared at each other over the woman's head.

Rob had a key?

How the hell did *that* work?

'We're going down the station and you can explain to me what's been going on here,' said Romilly. 'All right?'

64

'I told you – he left me a note,' said Mrs Lewis, sitting in an interview room down the cop shop. 'I had to get the will out, didn't I. And the note was there too, in an envelope with the key and directions to the lock-up, and he said if I ever lost it, Mr Hinton had a spare. I never even knew he had a lock-up. So I went there, and there was all this . . . money.'

'And you had no idea the cash was there, before that?' asked Romilly as DS Harman sat slouched in a chair in the far corner, listening but saying nothing.

Mrs Lewis shook her head.

'But when I apprehended you, that was at least your second visit.'

'Well . . .' Mrs Lewis looked flustered. 'It was Clive's money, wasn't it. So it was also mine. And I must say, I was shocked to find it there. All that cash. I couldn't believe it. We'd lived hand-to-mouth for years. Clive was . . . well, I hate to speak ill of the dead, but Clive was very careful. Went into a panic every time a bill dropped through the door. Every time we took a big wedding order he'd say, oh that would pay so-and-so's bill. We never had a holiday. Never had a damned thing.'

'Go on,' prompted Romilly when Mrs Lewis hesitated.

The woman's mouth crumpled like she'd tasted something bitter. 'You know what? He was a mean bastard. Sitting on all that, hoarding it, and never telling me a thing about it – while I scoured the supermarket aisles for the shelf with all the bargains, and collected money-off coupons, and switched off all the lights in the flat, and bought clothes from charity shops. I scrimped and saved the whole damned time.'

'So you went there and found it, and took some of it,' said Harman. 'Twice.'

'It was mine, wasn't it. Clive's dead, I'm his widow. So yes, I took it.'

'And where is the money you took on your last visit?' asked Romilly. 'I have to remind you, Mrs Lewis, that the money was the proceeds of crime. And as such, should be seized.'

'But I spent all the first lot,' said Mrs Lewis. 'I bought some stuff for the flat.'

'You kept receipts?' asked Harman.

Mrs Lewis's face reddened and Romilly felt a surge of sympathy for her. She believed that Mrs Lewis was telling the truth: she'd gone to the lock-up and found the stash, had no clue where it had come from or what Clive had done to get it, and had simply done what many other people in the same situation would; she'd started filling her pockets.

She was probably a law-abiding woman, but she'd been married to a penny-pinching and essentially crooked man. Romilly decided that they wouldn't push too hard on the receipts. Let the poor cow have a little something, why not? She'd earned it, married to that.

'I suppose I might have receipts somewhere,' said Mrs Lewis, gulping down a mouthful of the hideous cop shop tea. 'Although I don't usually keep receipts. I'm very tidy-minded, Clive was always saying that. The minute something comes through the door, I chuck out the receipts, the packing, everything.'

'We'll need a statement from you,' said Romilly. 'After that, you'll be free to go.'

Mrs Lewis stared at the DI in surprise. 'Really?'

'Yes, Mrs Lewis.' Romilly stood up, glanced at her watch. 'Take Mrs Lewis's statement, will you?' she asked Harman, and left the room.

65

Ruby walked into the Savoy Grill and there he was, as arranged, waiting for her. Thomas Knox. Old school crime lord. Much respected. Much feared. And she must be off her head, to think that she could trust him or believe a word he said.

'Ruby.' He got to his feet, kissed her cheek in greeting.

'Thomas,' she said, and sat down.

'Drink?' he asked.

'Champagne, please,' said Ruby.

Thomas beckoned the waiter, asked for a bottle of Bollinger.

'See, I remembered your favourite. But celebrating? Seems unlikely, right now,' he said, watching her with those cool blue eyes.

'I need cheering up,' she said on a sigh.

'Lots of trouble going down,' he said.

'You can say that again.'

'I was sorry about Rob Hinton.'

'I know. It's devastating for Daisy. So terrible.' Ruby passed a tired hand over her face. 'We only heard yesterday that the police are releasing his body for burial. As his widow, Daisy should make the arrangements, but she's not up to it. So it'll be down to me. And then we have to get through the funeral. I can't imagine how awful that's going to be.'

The waiter came with the ice bucket, uncorked the champagne skilfully, poured them each a glass, and left the bottle chilling.

'Well, drink up,' said Thomas, lifting his glass. 'To better times, yeah?'

'To better times,' said Ruby.

'You know what Winston Churchill said?'

'No, what?'

'When you're going through hell – keep going. So, what can I do?' he asked.

Ruby looked at her old lover with narrowed eyes. 'Maybe I'm wrong to trust you,' she said.

'Maybe you are.'

'Kit doesn't.'

'Kit don't even trust himself. We had a sit-down, you know, Kit and me. Or *do* you know?'

'No. I didn't know that.' Ruby was alarmed. Kit didn't have much of a grip on things right now.

'How did it go?'

'I spoke, he listened. Maybe he believed what I told him. Maybe not.'

'We found the blond git from the heist,' she said.

'Yeah. Kit said. He *also* said that before he could get the guy to talk, he died. Unfortunate.'

She nodded, thinking of Kit framed in her sitting room doorway covered in blood. 'We're all on the lookout for the other one. Kit got an address from the blond, but the black guy had already run from there. Could you keep an eye out too? Pass the word? We want him found, it's urgent.'

'Of course. Anything else?' asked Thomas.

'Pass any information back to me when you get it,' said Ruby. 'Not to Kit.'

Thomas looked at her steadily.

Ruby returned his stare.

'Have you heard of a thing called sodium thiopental?' he asked.

'No,' said Ruby.

'It's a truth drug. I told you I'd prove to you I wasn't involved, didn't I?'

'We got nothing out of the first one. When we get this next one, I want him to talk.' Ruby picked up her champagne glass and drank. 'I want him to sing like a fucking canary. I want to get to the root of all this, and then I want to blast that root out of the ground. What I don't want is trouble blowing up between Kit and you. That ain't going to help.'

'I can get the stuff, but understand this – it's dangerous. It's a barbiturate. It's easy to go too far with it.'

'So long as this bastard tells us what we want to know, who gives a fuck if he dies?'

Thomas's eyes glittered as they held her gaze. He picked up his glass and clinked it against the side of hers. 'You're sexy like this,' he said. 'So, we got a deal? You trust me?'

'We have.' Ruby gazed back at him steadily. 'And I guess I do. I think I have to.'

Silence fell between them. The air seemed to crackle with static as their eyes met.

'I'm not happy,' Thomas said at last. 'In my marriage.'

'Having talked to that airhead you're married to, I'm not surprised.'

'I think you know how this goes by now.'

I can say no, she thought. *But do I want to?*

'I do. Yes.'

'Good.'

Ruby hadn't realized how miserable, how like a coiled spring she'd been, ever since the wedding. Up in Thomas's suite, after two thundering orgasms, she felt the tension of it all slip away from her. Soothed by another bottle of champagne and warmed by Thomas's naked body next to hers, she felt her eyes sting with tears and then she found herself crying hard, for the first time.

'Jesus, it's all so sad,' she sobbed in his arms.

'I know.' He held her tight, smoothed his hands over her shuddering back. 'That's it, sweetheart. Let it go now. Just let it go.'

Ruby pulled away from him after a little while, reached for tissues, dried her eyes, blew her nose. She lay back down, cuddled up close to him. 'They ought to prescribe you on the NHS,' she said with a shaky laugh. 'Take all your tensions away with Thomas Knox.'

He turned to her, fixed her with those ice-blue eyes. 'I've missed you,' he said. 'I've missed *this*.'

Ruby half-smiled. 'What, when you've got such a glamorous young wife?'

'You know the thing about glam young girls? They talk a different language. It's fucking boring. An actual *woman* like you? We understand one another, don't we?'

'Yeah.' Ruby sighed and stared up at the heavy damask canopy over the bed. Toile de Jouy lovers romped up there. If all there was to a relationship was bed, she and Thomas would get along fine. But there was more, wasn't there. She was still playing the part of the mistress, and hadn't she had all this with Cornelius Bray? Hadn't it damned near killed her? Yet here she was, in the same situation. Thomas – like Cornelius – had a *wife*.

Ruby sat up, clasped her hands around her knees.

'I ought to be home, with my daughter. My grandkids are staying elsewhere, because Daisy's been going off the rails. She's blaming everything on Kit, she won't even *look* at him. The whole situation's fucked.'

'And now you've got the funeral to arrange.'

'I have, yes.'

'I think coming here has done you good, though. Given you a break. Relaxed you.'

'Yes. It has.' Ruby tossed the covers back. 'But I can't stay the night. I have to go home. Right now.'

'I'll get the stuff,' said Thomas. 'I promise.'

66

It was Friday morning, nearly two whole weeks since the shootings. Kit sat Ruby and Daisy down in the sitting room and filled them in on what had happened at the lock-up.

'I don't understand,' said Daisy, hollow-eyed and pale as she stared at her twin's face. She still looked at him like she hated his guts. 'Rob had a key to that same lock-up?'

'Yeah.' Kit sat down.

If this was a shock to Daisy, then damned sure it had been a shock to him, too. Rob had always personally done the milk run around there, collecting the money on the arcade that included Clive Lewis's studio. No real reason for it; that was simply the way it had always been. Rob had dished out the jobs but he'd always kept that one for himself. No one had any reason to question it. And now, for the first time, Kit was wondering why. And wondering why was making him feel uneasy.

He'd known Rob, right to the bone.

He *had.*

Or had he just thought so?

Kit thought of the three shots fired at the church. Now he reckoned that for sure one of them had Clive Lewis's name on it. And Rob had a key to the lock-up, so it was quite possible that Rob had been targeted too. Drugs and guns went together like love and marriage. Two shots had found their marks, one hadn't. The third bullet buried in the church door *had* to have been meant for Kit himself, surely? Yet here he was, still standing. For now.

'What are you saying, Kit?' asked Ruby.

'I can't believe it. I don't *want* to believe it. But it could be that Rob was doing a little something on the side,' said Kit. 'Did I say "a little" something? I meant a bloody big something. Shipping coke around the country. There was a stack of money in that lock-up, and Mrs Lewis was stuffing laundry bags with it and taking it home. Probably thought that, with Clive Lewis and Rob out of the way, she could fill her boots.'

'What, *Rob*? Involved in drugs? I don't believe that,' said Ruby, shaken. She was thinking of how sorry she'd felt for Mrs Lewis, that she'd been determined the firm would see the woman right – when all the time the woman had been sitting on a goldmine.

Kit hadn't believed it either; but there was proof. His best mate had been running a drugs operation in secret. Kit hadn't had a clue. *What else did he keep from me?* Kit wondered.

'This could mean . . .' Ruby started, then she stopped.

'Yeah?' asked Kit.

'If Rob was involved in drugs, that's a rough business. And Clive Lewis, too. It could mean that the shootings . . . well, we thought all the bullets were for you, didn't we? But that could be wrong. We thought the gunman had missed his target, but maybe he didn't. Maybe Clive Lewis and Rob *were* the real targets. And he got them.'

'You didn't know anything about this, Daise?' asked Kit.

It was churning over and over in his mind. *Three* bullets. A marksman of sniper standards. Three shots. He remembered Rob saying *We got to have a talk. A* serious *talk.* But

Rob hadn't lived long enough to tell Kit anything; he'd taken it to the grave with him.

Daisy looked startled. 'No! Of course not.'

'He was your fiancé,' Kit pointed out.

'I didn't know. All right?'

'Fine.'

There was silence. Then Ruby said: 'The funeral arrangements. We . . . I have to sort them today.'

Daisy's gaze dropped to the sapphire engagement ring and the plain gold band of the wedding ring on her finger. 'He was my husband.'

'Yeah, he was.' Ruby's expression was dubious. 'But, do you think you're up to this, Daisy? I'll come with you, of course, help you sort everything out, but if you think it's too much . . .'

'You can come with me,' said Daisy. 'But this is my responsibility. I'm going to do it.'

67

It was a dismal way to spend a rainy Friday afternoon. Selecting a coffin. Oak, teak, whatever. What type of handles? Then a lining. Cotton or silk, and what colour. Telling the undertaker with his air of polite businesslike sympathy about the clothes Rob would be buried in. Would there be flowers, or not? Yes, there would. Anyone who wanted to send flowers – the funeral date was set for next Tuesday – could do that. Then on to the florist, with an unspeaking and watchful Daniel at the wheel of the BMW, to get wreaths made up.

Throughout all this, Ruby could see her daughter getting weaker and weaker as the reality of it pulverized her all over again. Rob was dead and gone. Daisy was beginning to accept it now. And after the revelations about the lock-up, Ruby could also see that she was feeling just a little less inclined to blame Kit for the whole sorry mess this had turned out to be.

They called in on what had once been Darkes' flagship department store in Oxford Street. It was strange, coming back here; it reminded her of another life, the life she had led before Kit and Daisy had come back, miraculously, to her. All she had focused on in those days was her precious business, because what else did she have? Fuck all. Now the store had been renamed Silver City, and was under new ownership. They headed straight for womenswear. It was the last bit they had to get through. Picking out a black suit for Daisy with big shoulder pads and a tight kick-pleated skirt, plus a matching hat with a small veil. Mourning clothes that she would wear to her husband's funeral and then throw away. Or burn. Certainly, she could never bear to wear them again.

While Daisy sat silent on the way home, Ruby thought about the lock-up. Her feeling was that Rob had never squared how he felt about the difference in his and Daisy's backgrounds. Deep down, she was sure that he'd felt he wasn't good enough for Daisy. Case in point – he'd dumped her five years back, broken the whole thing off. Eventually they'd got back together, but had Rob ever lost that niggling sense of his own inferiority? Ruby didn't think so.

What she now thought was that the drugs money could have been Rob making up for what he saw as his own shortcomings. Daisy had been raised on stacks of old money by the landed gentry; and Rob? A council estate, his dad Harry a postman. His mother Eunice a cleaner. It was a big difference, and one that Ruby always thought Rob struggled with. Maybe that was it: the cash from the drugs could have made him feel better. Could have made him feel, Ruby thought, like he had something more concrete to offer Daisy in terms of lifestyle.

Christ, maybe trying to impress Daisy actually killed him?

Ruby knew she could never share these thoughts with Daisy. They would finish her.

No, she was going to have to keep them to herself.

68

Ruby got the call from Thomas late Saturday evening, just as she walked through her front door. She was worn out after a long night at the club, thinking that Jenny Rose was never going to be a good enough replacement for her sister Crystal. She'd slipped in the champagne glass tonight, and it had been touch and go whether she was going to fall out of the damned thing altogether. Aggie was shorter. Maybe she would make a better fit. Ruby decided she'd think about it Monday. For now, all she wanted to do was sleep. But it didn't look as if she was going to be able to, not tonight.

'Hold on,' she said, and replaced the phone on the hall table.

Leon had driven her through the few loitering press people at the gates, then to the club and back, while Daniel had remained at the house guarding Daisy. Leon went straight on over to his flat over the garage block, and Ruby was putting the phone down as Daniel came out from the kitchen.

'All OK?' she asked him.

'She's been up in her room all evening,' he said.

'Thanks, Daniel. Goodnight, now.'

He went back into the kitchen and let himself out the back door. Ruby closed and locked it after him. Then she went back to the phone. 'Thomas?'

'We've got him,' he said. 'Your black friend with the dreads and the gold teeth. You sure you don't want Kit in on this?'

'I'm sure. You've got the stuff?'

'Yeah. Remember – it's risky.'

'I've told you, I don't care.'

'I'll pick you up in ten,' he said, and put the phone down.

The warehouse was down near the Albert Docks, empty and disused and echoing. In one far corner of the dilapidated old building stood a cluster of men beside an old workbench. As Thomas and Ruby walked in, they straightened. One of them held lengths of rope. A black man was sitting on a chair. His lip was bleeding. His shoulders were slumped.

Thomas and Ruby walked over and stood in front of the man.

'You got no proof I did a damned thing,' he said.

'You and some others turned over that supermarket warehouse,' said Ruby.

'Nah. Not me.'

'Your friend? The little blond with the bad teeth? It didn't go good for him. My son got hold of him.'

'Don't know what you're talking about.'

'Yeah, but you do. And so we've got a few questions for you, and you are going to answer them.'

Ruby nodded to Thomas. Thomas made a gesture and the boys closed in. They lifted the man off the chair and took him, struggling, over to the workbench. He started yelling as they held him down so that the one with the rope could tie him. They trussed him up, and within minutes he was secure. Then they all looked at her.

First, you had to find the vein. Aware of the circle of men standing around watching her in the damp chill of the disused warehouse, Ruby Darke took the syringe that Thomas handed to her and found the spot. Some of the men were smiling, expecting her to bottle this. Thomas Knox, standing across the bench from her, was looking at her expectantly.

Ruby took a breath and pressed the needle home, hard.

'Christ alive!' said the man tied to the workbench, his back arching, bucking against the ropes that held him. 'Easy there!'

This old place with its crumbling concrete pillars and floors, soaked from years of rain leaking through the roof, soiled from generations of roosting pigeons, was out of the way and nearly derelict.

Which was pretty damned convenient.

Ruby looked down at the tied man without compassion, and emptied the syringe into his vein.

'Easy?' she said flatly. 'You don't get *easy* when you've stepped on our toes. Robbed us blind. Taken the *piss*.'

She drew back from the bound man and looked across at Thomas. 'How long does it take to work?' she asked him.

'Not long,' said Thomas.

They'd talked about it all before. Thomas had said *he* would administer the drug, but Ruby had rejected that idea. Thomas was in the frame, and so part of the object of this exercise was to ascertain whether he was being upfront about his non-involvement in all that had gone down, or not.

'What the fuck *is* that stuff?' asked the man on the bench. He was sweating, although it was cold inside the warehouse.

'It's called sodium thiopental,' said Ruby. 'It's a truth drug. And that's what we want out of you. The truth. Whatever you know, you're going to tell us.'

'Fuck off!'

'You know, this isn't going to end well for you, my friend,' said Ruby. 'It's risky, injecting people, they can even die if there's an air bubble in the syringe. And who knows? I've never done this before.'

'Shit . . .' The man was straining at the ropes without success. His eyes were going out of focus, like he was drunk. His words were starting to slur.

'It's dangerous stuff,' Ruby told him. 'It's a barbiturate. Marilyn Monroe died from a barbiturate overdose – and you know what? I think we'll give you some more, speed matters up a bit.' Thomas refilled the syringe, handed it back to Ruby.

'Who the fuck *are* you?' the man on the table shouted, his eyes wide open and crazed with terror as they stared up at her.

'I'm someone you should never have crossed,' said Ruby.

She plunged the needle in again, injected the stuff into the man's vein.

He yelled, calling them all bastards and motherfuckers, jerking and struggling against his bonds.

Soon, he would start to talk. And then she would begin to know what the *fuck* had been going on. She looked across at Thomas again. Her lover. Her *married* lover, now. Could she trust him? What if this 'truth drug' was something deadlier, something that would wipe the man on the bench out and stop him talking altogether?

Well, if that happened, she would *know* that Thomas was involved.

And what if the truth drug actually worked, and the man said that Thomas was behind all this?

She looked across at her lover: handsome, robust, with his straight blond hair and his icy blue eyes.

Thomas Knox. Local face. Big-noise gangster.

Well, if *that* happened, the game was up.

Thomas would kill her – before she could tell Kit all about it.

69

When Monday dawned bright and clear, Daisy opened her eyes and stared blearily at the ceiling. Then it hit her all over again. Rob was dead. And tomorrow . . . oh fuck, tomorrow they were going to bury him. How the hell was she going to face that? Seeing him lowered into the ground?

I can't do it, she thought.

She thought of her babies, her twins, down in Hampshire with Vanessa. She'd phoned them yesterday, spoken to them, but she felt . . . distant. Detached. It was frightening. Vanessa had told her that it would all be OK. The children were young, resilient. They would forget Uncle Rob.

'And you'll find someone,' Vanessa had said. 'Someone new. Heartbreak doesn't last forever. Life goes on.'

Daisy crawled from the bed, staggered into the shower, washed herself. Combed out her hair, pulled on an old sky-blue, flower-sprigged tea dress. Without so much as a glance in the mirror – who cared what she looked like – she went down to the empty kitchen, made coffee, poured herself a cup and went out the back door, stepping out onto the terrace into a bright, beautiful morning.

It seemed so wrong that the sun was shining when Rob was dead. She sat down in one of Ruby's old Lloyd Loom chairs, feeling warmth on her face, sipping coffee, barely even tasting it. She switched on the old battery radio on the table, heard the opening bars of Sad Café's 'Every Day Hurts'. And it did. Every single awful day. She switched the radio off. She was dreading the future, trying to hold on but failing.

Tomorrow we bury Rob.

It destroyed her to think of it.

So why go on? Why bother?

Daisy put her cup down and stood up, stepping off the terrace onto the well-manicured grass. She had on flat sandals, and the dew brushed coldly at her toes as she walked on down the garden toward the swimming pool. The cover was off, which was silly, it should have been put back on last night to keep the heat in. But this was a chaotic house now. Things could be forgotten. And anyway, what did it matter?

It didn't.

Nothing mattered, not any more.

70

Daniel pulled thc curtains back in his bedroom over the garage, thinking that Leon had been the lucky one – as always – and got the best of this hastily thought-out arrangement. Leon's apartment was at the front of the building, overlooking the front lawns and the drive, but this one was at the back, beside the main gardens. First this had been Rob's place. And then, Rob and Daisy's. So now Daniel was sleeping in the bed the two of them had shared. Christ, some of her clothes were still hanging in the wardrobe. Rob's too. At some point, someone was going to have to clear them out, but for sure *he* wasn't going to raise the subject. It was too bloody painful. He hated being here, living here, but all he could do right now was suck it up.

Gazing out, he saw that there was somebody moving about down in the garden. Was it one of those fucking reporters sniffing around after a scoop? He rubbed the sleep from his eyes, yawning. *Bastards.* Fucking leeches, trying to drag stories out of people when all they wanted was to be left alone.

Suddenly his attention sharpened.

It wasn't a reporter; it was Daisy.

She was wearing a light-blue dress and she was walking slowly, almost dreamily, down toward the pool, which was uncovered and steaming in the cool morning air. The soft morning sun was catching her hair, which flowed down her back in a gold curtain. Daniel held his breath. At the pool's edge, she stopped walking, grasped the hem of the dress, lifted it . . . *What the fuck?*

. . . and pulled it up, over her head.

She's so beautiful.

He knew he shouldn't look, but he couldn't take his eyes off her. He stared at the round, pearly buttocks, the long legs, the slender waist. She turned to toss the dress aside and he got a front-row view of her taut belly and her golden bush.

'Oh Christ,' he murmured, mesmerized. His eyes went to her breasts. They were fuller and heavier than he'd ever imagined, and he *had* been imagining them. They swayed as she moved. The nipples were cinnamon-coloured and they were puckered from the cold morning air. He'd imagined everything: touching those fabulous tits of hers, and kissing her, and pushing her down onto a bed, and – yes – fucking her. With her husband – his brother – not yet even in the ground.

What was *wrong* with him?

Now she had turned away, and was slipping off her sandals. She was stepping down into the pool, very slowly. The water was up to her thighs, covering her hips, her waist, her tits. Her hair floated out, billowing, as the water came up to her neck and she . . .

He felt a jolt of alarm.

She wasn't swimming.

She just kept moving, deeper and deeper into the pool.

'Daisy?' he said aloud, although she couldn't hear him.

Her head was going under.

Now it was submerged.

A shiver of pure fear shot straight through him like lightning, accelerating his heartbeat in a hot rush of blood.

Christ! She wasn't going for a swim.

She was going to kill herself.

71

Kit got a call very early Monday morning. Three-quarters of an hour later, he was down the cop shop sitting across the desk from DI Romilly Kane. No Harman today.

'I wanted to talk to you,' she started in, shuffling papers.

'About what?' Kit watched her hands moving. Long-fingered hands like a piano player's. Then she looked up and her dark-brown eyes skewered him. They radiated intelligence, those eyes. You could see her brain processing data like a computer whenever they looked your way with that unblinking stare. Yes, she was a good-looking woman; but she was also bloody dangerous.

Romilly shoved the papers aside and sat back. 'About your mother.'

'You what?' Of all the things he had expected, it certainly wasn't that.

'Uniform found a black individual, dreadlocks and gold teeth, wandering the streets in Hackney,' she said. 'They thought he was drunk at first, put him in the lock-up to sober up. He was rambling on about a mixed-race woman leaning over him, injecting him with something. Sounds crazy, yes?'

'Go on.'

'In the morning he was found passed out cold, so it was thought best to move him on to hospital. Where they took some bloods which showed something in his system called sodium thiopental. Which is a truth drug, apparently.'

Kit stared at her. 'What makes you think this has anything to do with my mother? There are a hell of a lot of half-caste women in London.'

'Yeah, but not ones who are involved in a murder enquiry. Not ones who are trying to track people down, and who might choose those means to do it.' Kit looked at her steadily. She returned his gaze.

'Prove it,' he said.

Romilly shrugged but her eyes didn't drop. 'I can't. Not unless I could get him to identify your mother in a line-up.'

'Did you try for that?'

'Yep. He got hysterical when I even suggested it. Said he didn't want to press any charges, and now he's checked himself out of hospital and vanished.'

'So what would you like me to do about it?' asked Kit.

'She's quite a girl, your mother. Important part of the firm, yes?'

'We run a legitimate business, detective,' said Kit.

'The bits that can be seen, anyway.'

'No idea what you're talking about,' said Kit.

'Yeah,' said Romilly, eyeing him steadily. 'This is a warning. A shot across the bows, OK? I don't want to hear about anything like this happening on my patch again.'

'Not that it's anything to do with me,' said Kit.

'That's right.'

'Or my mother.'

'Yeah.'

'Noted,' said Kit.

He left the building. Once he was gone, Romilly got on to ballistics. They told her that the calibre of the bullets used in the wedding-day shooting exactly matched the one she'd dug out of the tree near Crystal Rose's shallow grave in the woods. And they were fired from the same gun.

'As we said, it's the type of bullet used by gun clubs all around the country,' said Colin Walker in ballistics.

'Right,' said Romilly. 'Thank you.' She and her team had already been working their way through the gun clubs. So far, nothing. They had to step it up a gear.

She put the phone down and called Harman in. Looked at him. Decided maybe it was better to have him inside the tent pissing out, than outside pissing in. And she could doctor any information he passed on to Kit Miller. It could, actually, turn out to be quite useful that Harman was bent. 'Have we missed any gun clubs off the list?'

'I don't think so.'

'Check it. Let's make sure.'

72

Ruby was having breakfast in the sitting room at the front of the house when Kit rolled up in a fury.

'Problem?' she asked, eating toast. 'You want some? There's coffee here . . .'

'I've just been called in to the nick,' said Kit, pacing around. 'DI Kane's got a stick up her arse about some bloke wandering around Hackney talking about you.'

Ruby's eyes opened wide. '*Me?*'

'He was on the streets talking about a woman injecting him with something. Turned out it was a truth drug.'

Ruby finished her toast and sipped her coffee. She looked icy calm. 'He didn't say anything to the police about me though, did he? I was very clear about that when I last spoke to him. I told him there would be consequences. Dire ones.'

'He was scared shitless, if that's what you mean. Checked himself out of hospital and disappeared. Said he didn't want to press charges, wouldn't look at a line-up, fuck you very much and goodbye.' Kit stopped pacing and stared down at her. 'What is this? You think I can't handle this situation?'

Ruby shook her head. 'Look,' she said. 'Rob was your closest friend and it's hit you hard. And that business with the robbery. It's all piled in on you, I know it has. But, Kit – we want facts, we want answers.'

'You think I mishandled the other bloke.'

Ruby said nothing.

'I told you: it was that stupid fucker Leon who finished it too soon. Not me.' He looked at her curiously. 'So, did you get anything?'

Ruby set down her cup. 'Not that much, as it goes. All he kept saying was "No Knox". Which is good news. It proves beyond all doubt that Thomas hasn't stepped on our toes. But he was frightened of someone else more than Thomas and me. He kept saying that "they" would kill him. That they had a mad bastard who could shoot you dead from a quarter of a mile away.'

Her eyes met Kit's. They were both thinking of the shooter at the wedding.

Kit paced around a bit. 'So the shooter ties into the warehouse job *and* the wedding, and your murdered burlesque girl.' He stopped in front of Ruby. 'And Knox is sound. We agreed on that?'

'He's sound.'

'What about that upwardly mobile slag wife of his?'

'What, Big Tits? She's nothing. Don't worry about her.'

Kit stared at his mother. 'Oh, wait up. You and him . . . that hasn't started up again, has it?'

Before Ruby could answer, there was the sound of running feet and Leon burst into the room.

'Boss? You'd better come,' he gasped out. 'It's Daisy . . .'

73

The second Daisy's head went under the water, Daniel started to move. He snatched up and yanked on his jeans and flew out of his flat door and down the side stairs, hardly noticing what he was doing, he was so panicked.

She's killing herself.

He couldn't let that happen. Wasn't it tragic enough that they'd lost Rob, without having to cope with more grief?

He ran flat out, barefoot, over the dewy grass, slipping twice and righting himself, thinking how long could she survive under the water . . . He didn't know. All he could do was be quick.

As soon as he came to the side of the pool and saw her right in the middle of it, he dived in and swam faster than he'd ever swum before.

Oh Christ, Daisy, please don't do it . . .

She was submerged, right out there in the middle.

He took in a gasping breath of the cold air and dived, plunging through the water, desperation making him fast. Three hard downward strokes and his hand brushed against her hair. He grabbed a handful and she twisted sideways. He lost his grip.

No, no!

He scrabbled around, the chlorine stinging his eyes, and found her again. Grabbed a hank of hair and this time he held on tight. Then he pushed hard upward, dragging her with him.

Daniel broke the surface and gulped down more air and *yanked* Daisy by her hair to the surface too.

She came up. She was spluttering, cursing, *alive*.

Oh, thank Christ.

'What are you *doing*?' she yelled at him. 'Why the hell don't you just *fuck off*, Daniel, and leave me alone?'

She lashed out, furious, sobbing, distressed.

He caught a hefty blow on his cheek, his shoulder. He didn't care, barely felt a damned thing. She was *alive*.

'What the fuck are you playing at?' he demanded, treading water, not letting go of her hair, not caring if he pulled it out by the roots. She wasn't going to do it, he wasn't going to let her.

'I want to *die*,' she shouted into his face.

'Well you fucking well *can't*,' shouted Daniel right back at her. 'You selfish cow. You got kids. You got a mother and a brother. You can't lay all this shit on them, it ain't *fair*.'

'Let go of my fucking hair, you bastard,' she yelled.

'No. Come *on*.' And he dragged her to the edge of the pool, up the steps, and threw her dress at her. She stood there naked, shivering, crying her eyes out.

Daniel looked away, and spotted Leon, coming down the steps from the flats over the garage. Leon, clocking them down by the pool. And then Leon was running for the main house. Raising the alarm.

'Christ's sake, Daise, put your damned dress on,' he told her urgently. 'Leon's seen us and all hell's about to break loose. Get *dressed*.'

Shaking like an old woman, Daisy fumbled her way into the tea dress, which stuck against her wet skin.

'Help me,' she moaned, and Daniel had to turn back to her then, yank the damned thing down over her body, try not to *look* at her body, try not to think about what could have happened if he hadn't drawn back his curtains and seen her coming down here.

Fact was, if he hadn't seen her, Daisy would be dead, floating in the pool, a horror for her mother to find and grieve over. A fresh nightmare. He was shivering himself now, his soaked jeans stuck clammily to his body, the cold morning air puckering the skin on his chest and arms to goosebumps. The shock of it all setting in.

Daisy was covered now. Still crying. But clothed and alive. Not bothering about her sandals, he put his arm around her and started walking, dragging her with him, back up the garden toward the house. Ahead, he could see Leon falling out of the back door, bringing Ruby with him, and Kit. They all started running down toward the sodden pair, and he was glad to see them, relieved.

Halfway up the garden, Daisy collapsed shivering onto the grass and couldn't go any further, and Daniel sat down too, out of gas, out of air, out of everything; swamped by the disaster he'd just lived through, so nearly a reality but avoided because of an accidental peek out of the curtains.

Daisy was alive.

74

Ruby couldn't take it in. She was wrung out with sympathy for Daisy's plight, of course she was, but also – oh for fuck's sake, how could Daisy have even contemplated doing that?

They had sent Daniel back to his flat over the garage to get changed into some dry clothes, then Ruby had put Daisy to bed while Kit summoned the doctor. He came within the hour, and they told him she was in a bad way after her fiancé's death. Not that she had tried to top herself. But that she was very low.

'I've given her something to calm her down,' he said as he was leaving. He handed a bottle of stronger pills and a prescription to Ruby. 'It can take a couple of weeks for full effect, but she will soon start to feel a little better.'

After that, Leon sat out in the hall on door duty and Ruby and Kit went into the sitting room. Ruby collapsed into an armchair. Silent, brooding, Kit sat down opposite and looked at her.

'The funeral's tomorrow,' said Ruby.

'She can't go,' said Kit.

'No. She ain't up to it.'

Kit let out a sigh. 'Christ, if Daniel hadn't seen her . . .'

'Yeah, but he did. And she's going to be OK.'

'You believe that? Seriously?'

'At the moment? After *that*? No, I don't. But somehow we have to stay positive, don't we. Get tomorrow out of the way and maybe the fog'll start to clear. The Lewises are going through this too. Clive Lewis's funeral is coming up soon. You heard anything else about the drugs?' asked Ruby. 'And the stash of money?'

'Nothing yet.'

'I can't believe Rob was doing that.'

'Lots of people live a secret life,' said Kit. 'I just didn't ever think that Rob was one of them.'

'Maybe you didn't know him as well as you thought you did.'

'You could be right.'

There was a long silence.

'It's going to be hard to get through,' said Ruby. 'Tomorrow.'

'Fats will stay here with Daisy,' said Kit. All he wanted now was to get the thing *done*. Yes, it was going to be hard. But everything in his life had been hard, up to this point. What was a little more shit, after all he'd been through already?

75

Tuesday was a day Kit had hoped never to have to endure. The day of his best friend's funeral. Obscenely, the sun came out and it was hot, almost summery. Bright and cheery. Rob should be on his honeymoon, not lying in an oak casket, ready to be shovelled into the cold earth.

The funeral cortège left from Rob's mum's house and Kit and Ruby were waiting at the church, along with all Rob's extended family and many friends and workmates. He'd been a popular guy, a person anyone could turn to, and the crowds massed outside the church reflected that. There were big, elaborate wreaths from all the other gangs, respect was being paid, but all Kit could think when he saw the other major faces there was, *Did you do it? Was it* you *who killed the best friend I ever had? Was it for that thing Rob wanted to talk to me about? Was it the drugs? Or something else, something worse?*

Thomas Knox was there. Kit stared at him and he stared straight back.

Was it you, Knox? Ruby says you're OK, but is it you, playing games?

It was the same church. Rob had died here. Much as he tried not to, Kit couldn't help but glance back at that Georgian building over the road, its thick Virginia creeper bursting with vivid green leaf. He looked at that window, the one where the shooter had been. Such an easy hit. He thought of Daisy, at home in bed, and what had happened yesterday. That *bastard* had wrecked his sister's life.

Also at the church, Kit was angered to see, was DI Kane. No Harman. Just her, dressed in a black trouser suit and white top, watching everyone like a hawk. While Ruby was speaking to another of the mourners, he went over to the policewoman.

'Looking for suspects?' he asked.

'It's what I do,' she said, staring him straight in the eye.

'Yeah? Well, it wouldn't hurt to show a little respect. Maybe be more discreet about it.'

'Mr Miller,' said Romilly carefully, 'I am here on duty. It isn't my intention to offend anyone. Not even you.'

'You making any progress with this?' he asked, a muscle working hard in his jaw.

God, he hated this. Standing here, waiting for Rob's dead body to roll up in a hearse. He *hated* it. The whole thing tormented him. The horror of Rob's death, and this peculiar shit they were uncovering about him.

'Yes. Our enquiries are ongoing.'

'What does that mean? That you're here doing fuck-all when you ought to be chasing down whoever did this?'

'You want someone to vent your anger on,' said Romilly. 'I understand that. So go do it on someone else, Mr Miller. As I said – I'm working. That means I'm too busy to listen to *your* bullshit.'

With that, DI Romilly Kane turned sharply on her heel and walked away.

Bitch!

He almost grabbed her arm, yanked her back. But he stopped himself. No, not today. This was Rob's funeral and it was going to be done *right*. No fights. No disputes.

And at that moment, Rob arrived.

76

It was as bad as he'd thought it would be. Eunice was in bits. Daniel and her partner Patrick were like bookends on either side of her, propping her up. Leon was there too, along with Rob's married sisters and their husbands. The church was packed. And although the vicar droned on about 'a celebration of Robert's life', it was all horseshit as far as Kit was concerned.

He'd wanted the best for Rob. A happy life with Daisy and a peaceful death in bed, at an old age. Not this, *never* this. The ceremony dragged on, eulogy after eulogy being read out, mouthy Leon getting up on his hind legs and saying something nice – his voice half-breaking with sorrow, tears streaming unchecked down his face. Afterwards Kit couldn't remember a word of it. Not a word. There were hymns being sung. Prayers read. And then . . .

The big oak double doors at the back of the church creaked open while the vicar was reading a prayer for the dead. People turned and looked. Ruby was crying, but Kit was dry-eyed, thinking only of vengeance. He turned and . . .

Holy shit!

It was Daisy. Fats was at the door behind her. He saw Kit's look and shrugged.

Couldn't stop her, the gesture said. *Sorry, boss.*

Alone, Daisy walked up the aisle toward Rob's flower-laden coffin in front of the high altar. Now everyone, Ruby included, was turning, looking. The vicar's voice stammered to a halt. The sudden stillness in the building was stunning.

All anyone could hear now was Daisy's echoing high-heeled footsteps. Head erect, she walked on, wearing the tightly cut back skirt suit she had chosen for this occasion, with a red rose corsage on her jacket lapel. She wore the small black hat, her face half-shrouded by its black veil, and her hands were clothed in black leather gloves. Her golden hair was swept up in a chignon. Her lips were painted scarlet, her cheeks were pale.

She walked past all the silent mourners, past her own family and Rob's too. The vicar stood, not speaking, waiting to see what she would do. The echo of her footsteps died away as she reached Rob's coffin. In the heavy, waiting silence of the church she removed her black leather gloves, finger by finger. Slowly, trembling slightly, she reached out one bare hand and laid it upon the gleaming oak of the casket, just in front of a framed picture of Rob that Eunice had placed there.

Daisy stood there for a moment, unmoving as a statue. Then she reached up to her lapel and unpinned the single red rose of her corsage, and laid it on the coffin. She touched the wood again, resting her hand there as if she might feel Rob's still-beating heart beneath it. Then she stepped back, tears pouring down her face, and sat down beside Kit and Ruby.

The ceremony went on.

And finally, out in the sun, when all should have been bright and cheerful and good, Rob Hinton was laid to rest.

77

It would all have gone like clockwork, but when Kit was getting into the car with Ruby – Fats was with Daisy – DI Kane came up to him again and said: 'A word, please.'

Kit looked at her in exasperation. 'Seriously? Today of all fucking days?'

'Any day at all, Mr Miller,' she said flatly. 'Or we can talk down the station, it's up to you.'

Kit stared at her. She meant it. 'Give me a moment,' he said to Ruby. Everyone was getting into their cars, heading off to the wake at Rob's mum's house. He hated these bloody shindigs, sitting around eating cucumber sandwiches and saying what a great bloke the deceased was. What did any of it matter? Rob was gone. It was as simple as that.

'Right,' he said to Romilly, and they walked away from the milling crowds by the gate, back up toward the empty church porch.

As they walked, Kit glanced over to the still-open grave, feeling his innards crease with grief all over again. 'So what d'you want?' he asked, turning his attention back to the detective.

'To clarify a couple of things, that's all,' she said as they stood alone in the porch. 'One: you don't get to talk to me like I'm one of your fucking lackeys. And two . . .' She shook her head. 'No, scrub that. There is no two. *You don't talk to me that way.* You being upset over your friend's death, that's fine. But don't ever think you can take it out on *me*.'

'You what?' snapped Kit.

'Watch your step, Mr Miller. I am *this close* to hauling your arse down the station on any trumped-up charge I can dream up. Don't push me. Because I won't bloody stand for it.'

'Oh. You won't?' Kit stared into her eyes. Fucking *cheek* of this girl. He moved in close to her and Romilly stepped back.

'And don't give me the attitude,' she said. 'I'm not impressed.'

'Right.' Kit eased in, closer still. Cheeky mare. But, Christ, he sort of liked her. And he liked the fact that she spat back at him. It was a long, long time since any woman had dared do that. He saw her pupils dilate, a tell-tale sign. 'Well, detective, let me impress you.' He shoved her back again the church wall.

'What the fuck d'you think you're doing?' she demanded.

'Kissing you,' he said, and did.

She struggled, but he was too strong. When he felt her start to respond, Kit drew back, staring into Romilly's shocked eyes from inches away.

'See? Not so bad, was it?' he asked, his voice husky.

'Get your hands off me,' said Romilly.

Kit let her go. 'Oh, don't play the Victorian virgin. We both knew this was going to happen. And anytime you want to continue with it, just let me know,' he said, and left her standing there.

78

Rob's mum lived on a council estate, in a neat little semi-detached. Cars lined the street. Kit found a space, parked up, and went inside. Daniel and Leon were near the door, dishing out glasses of sherry from a table loaded with food and drink. Kit took a glass of the brown liquid from Leon, threw it back in one. Ew. Sickly sweet. Whisky would have been better. Then he said: 'I want a word with you two.'

They went out into the back garden.

'You know anything about Rob and a large stash of drugs money?' he asked them, flat out.

Daniel and Leon both stared at him. Then glanced at each other.

'You fucking *what*?' said Daniel.

'What the fuck you talking about? Christ, here comes Daisy,' said Leon.

Kit turned. With an upsurge of annoyance, he saw Daisy coming through the crowds of mourners toward him. She'd taken off the hat with the veil, and her face had gone from pale to a greenish white. She'd heard him.

'I've had enough of all this,' she said, her voice shaking. 'I thought Rob was straight, the straightest man I'd ever met. And now this drugs business? I don't believe it.'

Kit heaved a sigh. 'I knew it would hurt you. It's bloody hurt *me*, I know that.'

'Do you think it could be true? *Was* he really involved in that?'

Kit nodded. Daniel and Leon were both looking at the ground.

'It's true all right,' said Kit. 'And Lewis the photographer was shipping the product round the country. Daise . . .' he started, reaching for her. She was right to be angry, disbelieving. Right to be shocked. This wasn't the Rob they all knew. This was a stranger.

But Daisy twitched away from him. She walked off, back into the house.

Eunice Hinton seemed to have shrunk in stature since the day of her eldest son's death. From an ebullient fiftyish blonde, flighty and flirty, she had degenerated into an old woman, her face haggard, her clothes black, her eyes dull.

She was sitting in the crowded living room, her daughters Trudy and Sarah on either side of her. Patrick Dowling was standing nearby, talking in low tones to one of the sons-in-law. He'd been a fixture since Rob's father suffered a fatal coronary four years back; Eunice had wasted no time in scooping up an old boyfriend to fill the vacancy.

Seeing Daisy approaching, Eunice came to her feet, holding out her arms to her daughter-in-law. Her eyes filled with tears; her arms shook.

Daisy didn't respond. Didn't walk into that motherly embrace. She stood there, glaring, hard-eyed.

'Did you know?' she asked. 'Eunice, did you know about Rob and the drugs money in the lock-up?'

'What?' Eunice's face was blank. She looked at Leon, who'd followed Daisy in along with Kit and Daniel. Her mouth formed into a trembling smile and she reached out, rubbed his arm. 'You all right, son?' she said.

Leon twitched away from his mother's touch and her smile died. She turned her attention to Daisy.

'What did you say?' she asked her.

'Did you know?'

'I don't . . .' Eunice started. She dropped her arms, startled by Daisy's tone.

'Did you know?' shouted Daisy.

The hubbub of voices died away into sudden silence. Everyone turned and stared. Eunice looked as shocked as if Daisy had slapped her. Patrick turned and stepped closer.

'Daisy . . .' he said quietly.

'Did *you* know?' Daisy asked him.

'What is all this rubbish?' said Trudy, standing up and giving Daisy a hostile look.

'Rob was running a drugs operation. The photographer was one of his mules, apparently. That's why they were both shot at the church. That's . . . he caused it. It was *his fault* it happened,' said Daisy.

Kit appeared at Daisy's shoulder, trailing Daniel behind him. He grabbed her arm.

'Daise, not today. Come on. That's enough,' he said.

'No, it isn't,' she said, shrugging him off. 'I need to know. Are we the only ones who've been kept in ignorance? Or has he been laughing at all of you too? He's not the man we thought he was. He's deceived us. Taken us for fools.'

'What are you talking about?' asked Eunice, her face ashen now, her whole body trembling.

Trudy and Sarah stepped in, clasping their mother in a protective embrace.

'You'd better go,' said Trudy.

'Yeah,' said Sarah, eyes flashing a threat. 'Right now, or I won't be responsible for my actions.'

'What is all this shit, Miller?' asked Patrick.

The room was silent. Suddenly everyone was watching the two men. Kit smiled, very slightly. Twice, Patrick Dowling had spoken to him like this. There wouldn't be a third time.

'This is Rob's day,' he said quietly. 'So I'm not going to kick your teeth straight down your throat, Patrick. You're upset. We all are. But listen to me. You *ever* talk to me like that again and it will be a different story.' He turned to Daisy and took her arm. 'Come on, Daise. Time to go home.'

79

'What the fuck you playing at?' asked Leon, taking Patrick to one side when Kit and Daisy had departed.

Eunice was watching them uneasily as her daughters busied themselves doling out sandwiches and tea. Trudy and Sarah were bickering over which plates to use, and who had cut the corners off the bloody sandwiches most neatly, but that was them, they were always at it, tearing at each other. Had been almost since the cradle. Eunice was annoyed and embarrassed by that. They had *guests* here. The last thing she wanted, today of all days, was anyone having a kick-off. She'd lost Rob, and she was only glad that Harry hadn't been here to see it. Poor old Harry. Of course, she hadn't *loved* Harry, not for a lot of years, and she hadn't been faithful to him either – there had been a few affairs, which he had never known about – but she had been comfortable with him and she had got used to having him around.

Her eyes strayed to her guests, then back to Leon and Patrick. Rob had been the strong one, the dominant force. He'd never liked Patrick and made no secret of the fact. Leon was the mouthy son, but he seemed to get on pretty much OK with Patrick, which surprised her. She had thought they'd clash, but no; they were usually fine. She knew that Daniel – like Rob – had never taken to Patrick.

But then, Eunice thought, Patrick was *her* choice, not theirs. They'd been childhood sweethearts, but after they'd drifted apart, she'd met sweet, malleable Harry and made a life with him. Five kids – and a cunt like a bill poster's bucket to show for it, according to Patrick, who wasn't one to mince his words.

Eunice thought that Patrick sometimes wasn't very nice.

'What you on about?' Patrick was asking Leon.

'Talking to him like that,' said Leon. 'Don't be bloody stupid.'

Patrick puffed himself up. He could do that, thought Eunice. Like a toad. 'Me, talk to *him*? What about the way the cocksucker talked to *me*? I see him in this house again, I'll kick his arse out the door, that's a promise.'

'Don't push it,' advised Leon. 'Not yet, anyway. Not until things cool down.'

'I speak as I find,' said Patrick. He stabbed a finger at Leon's chest. 'And I speak as I *want*, sonny. That clear?'

Eunice watched them, her son and her partner. Christ, men!

When Harry died, she found that she didn't like being alone in the house at night, not at all. Trudy and Sarah had encouraged her to go out and meet new people, and she had, a few, enjoying the one-night stands, enjoying her freedom. But always coming home to evenings alone.

Then Trudy got a job in Patrick's car dealership, and it turned out he'd known her mother when they were at school, and he was freshly divorced. The stars aligned, Cupid fired his arrow, and Eunice was in a relationship again, and a lot *steadier* with a man about the house. Despite the crack about her cunt. He was a rough diamond, Patrick, you had to make allowances for that. And she did. Lots of them. She was getting a bit tired of doing it, truth be told.

And what was he talking about, not allowing Kit back in this house? *Her* name was on the rent book. *She* lived here, not him. Her, Mrs Eunice Hinton. Harry hadn't been good with money – not at earning it, or managing it. She had controlled the household bills, made sure the rent was paid, worked her arse off with cleaning jobs while the two girls had picked up the slack on the housework at home. Now, Patrick had his feet well and truly under the table and seemed to want to take charge of everything – and she wasn't sure she liked it. She was beginning to think that Harry had been a sweetheart, compared to Patrick Dowling.

'You want to tone it down a bit,' said Leon to Patrick, shaking his head.

'You might arse-lick your way around that big-headed turd, I'm not about to do it,' said Patrick.

'Christ,' said Leon, and left.

80

'How's it going?' the man asked the killer, over the phone.

'It's going,' said the killer.

'What the fuck does *that* mean? Now come on, play straight with me. Have you set it up yet?'

'Set up what?'

'Don't arse me about, you cheeky little cunt. Miller. You got Hinton, you got that pipsqueak Lewis. *Now* get the main man, like we agreed.'

'I'm working on it.'

'In what way?'

'Looking for the perfect site. I don't intend to miss. Not this time. Picking the right place and time is not something to be rushed.'

'Just make sure you finish the bloody job this time. No more arse-ups. All right?'

'Right,' said the killer, and hung up.

Romilly was down the station the day after the Hinton funeral when Harman dropped a sheet of paper on her desk.

'Few more gun clubs,' he said.

Romilly nodded, glancing at the list. It was long. She sighed. They'd already trawled through a load of them, and got nothing.

'I've been thinking about Crystal Rose and the wedding

shooting. Same perp.' She pressed her fingers to her temples. 'He could have been in the club before. Maybe not his first visit. Some men are like that, aren't they?' She threw him a questioning look. 'Like tomcats, always sniffing around the same back door. Wouldn't you say?'

'Wouldn't know,' said Harman, who was married to a woman you wouldn't *dare* cheat on.

Romilly had met Harman's wife Julia at the Christmas party. Julia was a hard-eyed bitch, packed with fat across the shoulders and stomach, her hips weirdly narrow and her legs short but well shaped.

She'd overheard Julia talking to Harman there, and been shocked: Julia's contemptuous tone of voice was one Romilly wouldn't even use on a dog. No, you wouldn't catch *him* going to nightclubs to chat up exotic dancers. He'd be too afraid of the backlash. Pussy-whipped as he was, Romilly suspected that Harman hated having a female boss both in the home *and* in the office. The poor sap had probably been dominated by females most of his life. Maybe that's why the shifty bastard was on the take – he was trying to grab back some control.

'We've questioned all the club staff but no one remembers seeing him before,' said Harman.

'Even so.' Romilly frowned. 'Get Ruby Darke to hand over the CCTVs going back another five months. Get DC Paddick to have a look through them.'

'OK,' he said, and left the room.

Romilly turned and stared at the board. Photos of a rapidly disintegrating Crystal Rose stared back at her. Then she took up the list of the remaining gun clubs, thinking of the wedding, the shooter picking off the photographer and the groom. Nasty business. Vicious on a wedding day. Maybe . . . vengeful? Maybe like, *I have suffered, now it's your turn*? Maybe if Kit Miller was not the target, maybe it was a message to him?

But saying what?

She didn't know.

Her thoughts turned again to Miller. Running toward an armed man with no thought for his own safety on the day of his sister's wedding. So, brave. Obviously. Reckless? Probably. And sexy?

She thought about that kiss outside the church yesterday. To her intense irritation, she had been thinking about it, off and on, for most of last night. And again on waking this morning. When had she last had anything like that in her life? That passion he seemed to give off like sparks from a live wire, that raw, brooding power?

She looked back at the sad remnants of Crystal Rose. Once so pretty, so full of life. Nothing but dust and ashes now. For Crystal, there would be no more passion. No more of anything. She was gone, and all that was left was finding whoever did that to her, and bringing him to justice.

Romilly rubbed her temples. She was getting a headache. Needed some fresh air, needed a break from all this. She thought of hot beaches, warm breezes – and, annoyingly, *again*, Kit Miller.

He was out of bounds. A bad 'un through and through. Not the type of guy she ought to be associating with. And she wouldn't.

She tucked the list of gun clubs along with a batch of photos of the mysterious 'John' into her bag, and left the building.

81

Ruby was in the club mid-afternoon, having a look-see at the accounts and feeling pretty pleased with them. It wasn't the easiest thing in the world, running a club, but this one seemed to be thriving, despite the death of its biggest star. She closed up the club ledgers, put them back in the safe.

Earlier today, she'd phoned through an order to Beirut for some large batches of foreign currency. Later, one of Kit's people would meet the courier at the airport and swap the foreign notes for sterling made from the protection rackets. The couriers would deposit the money at a London bank branch as if it had come directly from Beirut, so that the money seemed to be coming from a legitimate source.

So things were going pretty good on the business front at least, if nowhere else. When she turned back round from the safe, Chloe Knox was standing there, staring at her.

Ruby straightened up fast, clutching at her chest. 'Jesus, Chloe! You startled me.'

Where was Fats? Last she had seen of him, he had been right outside the office door. He wouldn't have let Chloe in here without telling her first.

'You wondering where your ugly-bug minder is? I came in through the front and stood out there in the foyer watching until he went to the bogs. Then I came in.' Chloe closed the door behind her and leaned against it, eyeing Ruby through a forest of false lashes. She was wearing a fox-fur coat. 'You and me, we need a chat.'

'Don't think we do,' said Ruby.

'I told you to stop it with Thomas, and now I am *really* telling you: don't fuck around with him. I mean it.'

'Right. Well, thanks for that. Close the door on your way out.'

'You don't get it, do you?' Chloe was half-smiling. 'He's *mine*. I don't share him. I got the ring on my finger and that means nobody else gets the privilege but me.'

'OK. Now fuck off.'

The smile dropped from Chloe's face. 'You don't want to talk to me like that.'

'Chloe . . .'

'Don't talk down to me, you bitch!' snapped Chloe, and pulled a knife out of her coat pocket and held it out towards Ruby. 'I could cut you,' she said, waving the knife around in the air.

Ruby smoothly reached into her bag on the desk and drew out the .22. 'Sorry, Chloe. I think *this*,' she waved the gun, 'trumps *that*.'

Chloe seemed to shrink a couple of inches. Her arm fell to her side. She glared at Ruby.

'You don't love him like I do,' she said

Not for the first time, Ruby wondered what she was doing, starting it all up with Thomas again. Looking at the woman standing there, desperation in her eyes, Ruby almost felt sorry for the poor cow. It was pretty certain that Chloe *did* love Thomas far more than she did.

Fats was knocking at the door. Chloe slipped her knife back into her coat pocket as he opened the door and looked in.

'Where'd she spring from?' he asked, looking in alarm at the gun in Ruby's hand. 'Everything OK in here?'

'She's got a knife. Left-hand pocket,' Ruby told him. Fats took the knife off Chloe.

'I'm warning you,' yelled Chloe, as Fats shoved her out the door.

82

That evening, Ruby was back at the club, Fats playing bodyguard, and Kit was out and about somewhere. So was Leon. Daniel – and he was pretty pissed off about it – had been left to babysit Daisy again. It wasn't a job he felt equal to, not any more. Not after the drugs and the near-drowning. They were putting a lot on his shoulders and he wasn't sure he could cope. Because he liked her. He'd *always* liked her – a *lot*. And he felt sorry for her over losing Rob. And he couldn't keep his eyes off her. His mind kept replaying that image of her naked by the pool, and it was pervy and disgusting. She was his dead brother's wife.

He was sitting in the hall chair reading the day's paper and here she was again, coming down the stairs in her raincoat and boots and now he was thinking, *Déjà vu, isn't that what they call this?*

Daniel stood up as she approached. She looked pale but seemed to be holding it together.

'Where you going?' he asked, putting the paper on the seat. His guts were clenched with dread. She would want to score again. He knew it. *Now* what the fuck was he going to do?

'Brayfield,' she said, sweeping past him and out the door.

Then she turned and tossed him her car keys. 'You can drive.'

Daniel caught the keys. She was going – at last – to see her kids. Maybe she was finally pulling out of the nosedive she'd been in since Rob's death.

'OK,' he said. 'But I'm phoning Kit first. Tell him what's going on. And I'm leaving a note for Ruby.'

83

You couldn't really appreciate the sheer size or beauty of Brayfield House at night. Set off an unlit lane in the depths of Hampshire, anyone approaching it got a tantalizing glimpse of the gates, and the gatehouse, and then there was the big sweep of the driveway which took you up to a turning circle around an impressive round fountain. Behind the fountain was the bulk of the main house, lights shining out of a few of the rooms like beacons in the country darkness.

Daniel parked Daisy's Mini beside the steps up to the house, which were well lit by a glimmering ancient porch light. They got out, walked up. Daisy knocked at the door.

There was a long pause.

'Are they expecting you?' he asked.

'Yes, I phoned Vanessa earlier. It's a big house.' Daisy started scrabbling in her bag for her key. 'It takes a while to reach the door.'

Before Daisy could get the key in the lock, the door opened. Standing there was a thin, middle-aged woman, scruffily dressed in ripped jeans and a baggy powder-blue jumper. She had pale, watery blue eyes and long, aristocratic, greyhound features. She smiled when she saw Daisy.

'Darling, how lovely.' She opened her arms and Daisy moved in and hugged her, hard. 'The twins will be so delighted, but of course they're asleep now. You'll see them at breakfast.' Her eyes landed on Daniel. 'And this is . . . I think I know the face . . .?'

'Daniel, this is Lady Bray.'

'Vanessa, please,' said Lady Bray, staring at him.

'Daniel is Rob's younger brother. He was . . .' Daisy hesitated. Couldn't say it. Her face crumpled.

'He was at the wedding,' said Vanessa briskly, patting her arm. 'An usher. I know. There were two of you. A taller one, thinner, blonder . . .'

'That's my youngest brother, Leon.' Yeah, Leon was the eye-catching one; he always had been.

'Daniel. Hello. You're more *solid*, I think,' said Vanessa, her eyes holding his. 'You poor boy. Such a shock. Come in, both of you. I've had your rooms made up.'

It was bedlam at breakfast next morning. The kids were screaming with excitement at the arrival of their mother, and Daisy was hugging them so hard that Daniel thought she'd break them. After that, Nanny Jody took them off to the nursery, and Daisy and Vanessa went out for a walk in the grounds. It was damp and chilly but bright, the overnight moisture from the nearby river twinkling like fairy lights on cobwebs strung among the shrubs.

'You don't have to come too,' said Daisy when Daniel followed them out.

'Yeah, I do,' said Daniel, and kept twenty paces back from the two women, giving them space enough for privacy but secure in the knowledge that he could move in if need be.

They passed the circular fountain in front of the house. It wasn't working.

'That's Neptune,' Daisy called back to him as they veered off the path.

'We only switch it on now for public visits,' Vanessa told him.

Daniel paused and looked at the thing. The statue at the centre of the fountain was *huge*, of a bronze man-fish wearing a crown, trident in hand, surrounded by leaping dolphins.

Seeing the house in daylight for the first time ever, Daniel began to understand the depth of Rob's misgivings over his relationship with Daisy. *This* was where she had grown up, in this multi-gabled, rose-red mansion house with cream-coloured corners and a nearby bell tower, which was disused these days, Daisy had told him, and needing refurbishment. The grounds of the place were massive and there was even a pale stone, single-storey mausoleum crouched beside a man-made lake thickly fringed with willows and gunnera and shaded by vast cedars of Lebanon, where all the Brays were buried.

It was toward the lake and the grim little building on its edge that the two women walked, Daniel silently following. Daisy stopped walking a few yards from the building and was looking at the inscription over the door.

Hodie mihi, cras tibi

It always made her shiver. It was Latin for *Today me, tomorrow you.* Meaning that one day, they would all die. They would *all* come to the same end.

'How are you, darling?' Vanessa asked Daisy.

'Oh God, I don't know. Shattered, I suppose. I still can't believe it happened.'

'Ruby is very concerned about you.'

Daisy glanced at Vanessa. Once, long ago, Vanessa had hated Ruby – and she did have cause. Daisy's father Cornelius had conducted a secret affair with Ruby. Vanessa, as his wife, was barren. So when his mistress Ruby became pregnant with twins – Kit and Daisy – it was agreed between Cornelius, Ruby and Vanessa that Cornelius and Vanessa would have Daisy, and they'd paid Ruby off. Only in later years had Ruby been reunited with both her children. And it was only very recently that the icy nature of Ruby and Vanessa's relationship had begun to thaw.

'I know she's concerned,' said Daisy.

'We all are. Of course.'

Daisy's eyes were still fixed on the mausoleum. Her father was buried there.

And her grandparents. And all the Brays who had lived here throughout the generations.

'That's how it ends up, isn't it,' said Daisy bleakly. 'In death and disaster.'

Vanessa reached out and took Daisy's hand. 'That's why it's so important to enjoy your life,' she said. 'And to appreciate what you have. Those beautiful boys.'

'Do you enjoy yours?' asked Daisy. 'I mean, with Pa, wasn't it hard . . .?'

'It was.' Vanessa gave a slight smile. 'But now? I'm content. Horribly upset at all this happening to you, though.' She glanced back. Daniel was twenty paces away, looking around. 'It's always fascinated me how children in the same family can be so varied in their personalities. Rob was quite dominant, quite forceful, wasn't he? This one – Daniel – he's different. Calmer. Quieter.'

'And Leon's full of himself,' said Daisy. 'The one with the loud mouth, Ruby says. What's that?'

Daisy was looking through a screen of ferns and ivy toward the door of the mausoleum. There was something white there on the step. She walked closer, and Vanessa walked with her.

'Oh – that.' Vanessa shrugged. 'Someone leaves them

every year on your father's birthday. The twenty-fourth of February. It's the twenty-eighth now, they're starting to look a bit tired.'

Daisy moved closer. The object on the step of the mausoleum was a bouquet of white roses with ferns and foliage, still in a plastic wrapper and tied with a big ivory silk bow.

She bent down and touched the stalks, looked at the flowers. The white was starting to fade to brown. Soon, they'd be dead. 'You don't know who leaves them?'

Vanessa shook her head. 'No idea. Some woman he had a fling with, I expect. God knows there were plenty.' She looked at Daisy. 'That woman, at the wedding . . .'

'Which woman?'

Vanessa shrugged as if it barely mattered, but her face was troubled. 'The blonde one. Rather common-looking. Big-busted. Heavily made-up. I assumed she was part of Rob's family?'

'You mean Eunice? I saw you staring at her on the day. What about her?' Daisy had to raise a thin, weary smile at that. Vanessa didn't approve of Rob's family. She was painfully class-conscious. She hadn't even approved of *Rob*, at first. But she had come to accept him.

'Is that her name? Eunice?'

'Yes, that's Rob's mother.'

Vanessa looked startled. 'His *mother*?'

'Yes.' Daisy looked at Vanessa more closely. 'What about her?'

Vanessa turned away. 'I thought she looked familiar, that's all, but no, I was mistaken.'

Daisy nodded to where the flowers lay on the cold, green-tinged stone in front of the mausoleum. 'Don't you find that creepy? Someone walking around in the grounds, someone you don't even know?'

'It's a long way from the house,' Vanessa pointed out.

'True, but . . .'

'And I'm not here on my own. Look, there's Ivan over there.'

Daisy looked over to where Vanessa pointed. Ivan the gardener, lean and bearded, was digging away in the long border leading down from the main house. He paused, saw them there. Lifted a hand. Vanessa waved back.

There was a commotion on the nearby path. They turned and there was Jody, the twins racing ahead of her. Matthew came up and flung himself on Daisy, who knelt down and kissed him. Luke followed on more slowly, stopping near to where Daniel stood on guard.

'Sorry, Daisy, they're a bit paranoid about you leaving,' said Jody, breathless.

Which was completely understandable. They'd seen Rob snatched away, so of course they were anxious about Daisy.

'Listen.' Daisy caught Matthew's shoulder and gazed into his eyes. 'Wherever I am, I am *always* with you.'

Matthew eyed his mother gravely. 'Is it true that Uncle Rob is in heaven with Jesus?' he asked.

'Yes, darling. He is.' Daisy's eyes filled with tears. She blinked and swallowed. 'I have to stay with Nanny Ruby for a while, and you have to stay here with Nanny Vanessa. I'll still phone you every day. And you'll be good, yes?' Matthew nodded.

Luke crept closer and slipped his hand into Daniel's. It was unexpected, and Daniel looked down at the boy in surprise. He'd never had much to do with the kids. They'd been Rob's concern, not his. He knew nothing about children and wasn't keen to start finding out. But the poor little fucker! No kid should ever have had to live through what he had. He squeezed Luke's hand.

'I'm going back to Nanny Ruby's tomorrow,' Daisy was telling Matthew, glancing back at her other son, standing there close to Daniel. 'But today, we can do anything we want. OK? You choose.'

84

Sometimes a girl had to do what a girl had to do. So on Thursday Romilly braced herself and paid her folks a visit. Her mother answered the door.

'Romilly!' she said, and spread her arms wide. 'Come in, lovey.'

'Hi, Mum,' said Romilly. 'How are you?'

'Oh, I'm fine, you know. Fine as always.' Mum kissed her cheek, ushered her inside and into the lounge. Through the French doors, Romilly could see her dad mowing the back lawn. 'Yes, look at him,' said Mum, coming up beside Romilly and staring out at her husband. 'That flaming lawn gets more attention than I do. He's forever aerating it, raking it, feeding it, the bloody thing. Cup of tea?'

'Thanks. I'll just . . .' said Romilly, and went out into the garden while Mum went into the kitchen. 'Hi, Dad,' she said over the roar of the Flymo.

Her dad looked up and the Flymo fell silent. 'Hello, sweetheart,' he said, and came forward for a quick peck on the cheek. Stanley Kane was a big man, bulky, and with the calm look of the ex-copper about him.

'You've done something new,' said Romilly, looking at the lawn. The Flymo was on the edge, but in the centre there were lines of open soil radiating out from a central point. 'What's this?'

'Drainage channels,' said Dad. 'You know how the water used to lie here in the winter, cos of the clay. Well, I've dug down, cleared it out, put in gravel for it to drain better, and now I'm cutting around the edges, but that bit I'll reseed later today and it'll be fine. Have to watch I haven't done too good a job, though.'

'Meaning what?' asked Romilly, curious.

'Meaning it might dry out too much now. You know what I'm like, always take a sledgehammer to crack a nut. If that happens, you'll see the pattern of the channels, like herringbones.' He looked at her over his glasses. 'You all right, lovey?'

'Yeah, great.' She wasn't, but she wasn't about to burden him with all her woes. Too much work on her plate, and a feeling that she was on the edge of tumbling into something with a villain, something no sane copper would ever contemplate.

He paused, staring at her. 'This thing with Hugh, is it going to blow over, you reckon?'

Romilly screwed up her face and shook her head.

'Your mother said he cheated on you. That true?'

Romilly nodded.

'Ah, never mind.' Her dad pulled her in for a brief hug. 'Plenty more fish.'

'What, herrings?'

He laughed and dropped his voice. 'Don't take any notice of your mother. If you're happy to be out of it, that's good enough. She's only got her arse in a crease because she can't face her mates down the WI knowing her daughter's a divorcee.'

'Right,' said Romilly, feeling choked all of a sudden. Her dad was always her staunch supporter. Whatever Mum had to say about it, Dad was always on his daughter's side, and ridiculously proud at what she'd achieved in her career.

'Hugh's a bloody lefty milksop, anyway. Fuck him,' said Dad. 'You could do better, any day of the week. Get a real man. Tough as bullets.'

'Job keeps me pretty busy,' said Romilly, thinking – irritatingly – of Kit Miller.

'So long as you're happy, that's fine by me. And remember,' said Dad as Mum emerged from the house with a trayful of drinks and biscuits. 'DLTBGYD, lovey.'

Don't Let The Bastards Grind You Down.

'I won't,' she said.

85

Romilly had so far visited far too many of the London gun clubs on Harman's list, and now she was at a big plush club in Barnes, which boasted a six-lane, twenty-five-metre range. She had been learning all about shooting as she passed through each club, listening patiently as various coaches explained short-barrelled carbines, .22 rimfire rifles, air rifles, air pistols, and the use of telescopic sights.

At the Barnes club, people were coming in and taking up their shooting positions in the lanes. Romilly talked to their coach at the far side of the lanes and showed him two bullets: the one that had embedded itself in the church door, and the one from the woods near Crystal's grave site, just as she had at all the other clubs.

'These are 7.62 millimetre,' he said, turning them over in his hands. 'Used in high-precision target rifles.'

'Used to kill someone, in this instance,' said Romilly.

He handed both bullets back to her. He was thirtyish, calm-eyed, clean-shaven. 'Nasty,' he said. 'Successful?'

'Three shots fired at one scene. Two fatal. One miss.' *And one spent shell missing from the crime scene.*

'Distance?'

'About two hundred yards.'

'Outside?'

'Yes.'

'Is this the shooting at the church? The wedding shooting? That one?'

'You heard about it.'

'Everyone has. Utterly tragic. On the news, you know. Really bad.'

'What do you think?' asked Romilly. 'Can you draw any conclusions?'

The coach sucked his lip. 'Skilled shooter, I would say. There's wind direction to consider, which makes a clean shot tricky at times.'

Romilly thought back to the day of the wedding. The air had been mostly still; very calm. Made the bastard's job easier for him.

'In our inter-club matches,' the coach went on, 'we have wind coaches who sit beside the shooter judging the changing conditions and telling them when to make their shot.'

'This is my shooter's photo.' Romilly took the bullet back and handed him the grainy image of 'John' from the club CCTV.

All six lanes were occupied now, three men and three women setting up their rests, putting on ear defenders, chatting to each other briefly, then setting up their guns, lining up on the targets.

The coach frowned at the photo. 'It's not very clear.'

'It's the best we could get. Do you know him? The only name we have for him – and it might not be his real name – is John. Have you ever seen him in here, or on any of your outdoor ranges, shooting?'

He handed the photo back. 'No. I'm sorry.'

Romilly waved it away. 'Keep it. Show it around, it might ring a bell with somebody.'

'I'm sorry I can't help more.'

Romilly handed him her card. 'If you think of anything

else, contact me. However trivial you think it is, please do that.'

'Of course.'

She shook his hand and stepped away. Then the shots from the lanes began in a fearful volley. Despite herself, Romilly flinched. A nice sport, but a dangerous skill to have. And in the wrong hands – deadly.

Romilly left the club and drove on to the next one on her list. It was the one beneath London Bridge, the Stock Exchange Rifle Club. Kit Miller was standing there at the entrance.

'Something I can help you with?' she asked him.

'Oh, come on. All right, I'm looking around gun clubs. We're *both* doing that.'

'No, *you* come on. I've told you to keep your nose out of police business.'

'Jesus! You're touchy.'

Romilly gave him a glare and turned and walked away.

After a moment's pause, Kit followed and caught her up. Truth to tell, he was half annoyed and half pleased to run into her, and he was also irritated that Fats had apparently missed one or two clubs off his list. Good job he'd checked around himself. He'd be having words with Fats about that. He hadn't been inside this one yet, and with the DI in this mood, it didn't seem like a wise move to do that. Not right now. Later.

'What you up to, Mr Miller?' she asked him. 'Showing the rifle club people the spent shell you nicked from the crime scene?'

'Let me buy you dinner. There's a good Italian in Leadenhall Street. We can walk it.'

'Fuck off.'

'We can talk it all over. Compare notes.'

Romilly halted. 'I thought you didn't know anything. I thought you were pure as the driven snow?'

'My friend just died,' said Kit. 'So I have an interest in this. A big one.'

'I know that. I'm trying to track down whoever killed him.'

'You hungry?' Kit asked.

'Oh, don't give me that.'

'What?'

'The I'm-so-fucking-irresistible crap you're so good at.'

His face lit up in a grin.

Christ, he was annoying! But she was tired, and yes, she was hungry. All that was waiting for her at home was a cold empty house and a TV dinner she'd have to heat through herself. That, and a lot of dead memories.

'OK,' she said.

86

Daniel was glad to fall into bed in the room Vanessa had provided for him that night. All day he'd been keeping a watchful eye on Daisy and the twins as they romped around the grounds of Brayfield. He couldn't help thinking that when she wasn't half out of her mind with grief, Daisy was a great mum to those two boys. A playmate, a friend. A great hugger.

Tomorrow morning, they were going back to Marlow, leaving the twins here with Jody and Vanessa. It had been an eye-opening experience for him, coming here. Given him a better insight into Daisy, and her relationship with Rob.

It was a different world, this place. He'd had lunch in the kitchen, home-made parsnip soup and sandwiches supplied by the housekeeper, and had eaten with silent, surly Ivan there at the kitchen table. Daisy had told him a bit about Ivan – that he was ex-SAS, tough and wiry as a terrier. That Ivan and Rob had clashed once or twice.

Rob and Ivan.

Christ, he would have bought tickets to see that.

Daniel lay in the cosy, chintzy half-light of the bedroom. The moon was full tonight, and he hadn't closed the curtains. Out here in the country, the sky was navy velvet, studded with stars, the moon so white it dazzled. You never saw a sky like that in the city.

He thought of Daisy, in the room next to this one. Daisy, naked by the pool. Daisy in tears. Daisy, laughing with the twins. And now she was starting to depend on him, to lean on him. And in a way he *liked* that, it fulfilled a thousand fantasies, but it also creased him up with guilt. Shit, was he *glad* Rob was gone, out of the way?

No. Of course not. He'd loved his big bruv *so much.* He'd worshipped him.

Yeah, but Leon's right, ain't he? Now you're lusting after his lady.

Daniel knew he was going to have to step back, step away from her. Truth was, he'd always been half in love with her and if he got any closer he was going to get hurt, because she was still in love with her dead husband, of course she was.

Step away.

Step back.

Yeah, that was what he had to do. With his mind made up, he closed his eyes, and was soon asleep.

87

The restaurant was pure Italian cliché. There were red-and-white checked tablecloths, bottles coated with candle wax, and piped mandolin music. It almost made Romilly smile. It was busy in here, packed with customers, but when Kit Miller strolled in a table was – miraculously – found, at once. That sort of killed the humour for her. That, and the way the staff hovered around him, made sure he had the best of everything.

Because they pay him protection? Because he scares them?

Probably both. Christ, was she mad, having dinner with him?

Well, it was only dinner. She reassured herself with that. She ordered the penne, you couldn't go eating spaghetti on a . . . no, it wasn't a date. Only dinner. That was all. In fact, what she was doing – *really* doing – was interviewing a witness.

'Squaring it with your conscience?' asked Kit, when she was quiet, thinking.

That jolted her. So he was handsome, brave, scary – *and* intuitive. 'There's nothing to square.'

'You're having dinner with me.'

'The alternative's a microwave meal for one, so this has its attractions.'

They had wine, breadsticks and chunks of warm focaccia

bread to dip in oil with balsamic vinegar while they waited for their mains.

'So prickly,' said Kit, shaking his head and smiling.

'While I have you here, I may as well ask you some questions,' said Romilly, dipping bread and scarfing it down.

'Like?' Kit sipped his wine.

Romilly was chewing – the bread was heaven – but her eyes were fixed on his hands. 'Like, what's with those?'

Kit put down his glass and turned his hands over. Both palms were silvered with scars, the skin pulled so tight it looked almost opaque.

'Played with fire,' he said. 'Got burned.'

'Care to elaborate?'

'Not really.'

'Got any more interesting marks about your person?'

'Yeah, I have. Got one where a bullet hit me in the chest. Missed my heart by *this* much.' He demonstrated with a movement of thumb and forefinger.

'Wow. So' – she grabbed more bread – 'tell me about yourself.'

'Christ,' he marvelled, watching her eat. 'Do they starve you down the nick?'

'Try this bread, it's great.'

Kit looked at the sad-looking crumbs on the plate between them. 'There's not a lot left. You want me to tell you about myself? No need, is there. Most of it you already know. You've looked into my history pretty damned thoroughly, I'm sure.'

'That's true.' Romilly selected a breadstick and crunched the end between her teeth while she stared at his face. 'Let's see. Kit Miller. Abandoned and raised in a succession of children's homes. Reunited in adulthood with your mother, Ruby Darke, but you'd already been christened Kit Miller and you've stuck with that. Your sister Daisy was raised by

Lord and Lady Bray, but she changed her name back to Darke when she was reunited with her birth mother. That's interesting, that Daisy did and you didn't. Indicates she's closer to her mother. That maybe you resented Ruby for abandoning you as a child. Whereas Daisy – who had a much easier ride, I believe – didn't.'

'Go on,' said Kit, beckoning the waiter for more bread. 'This is fascinating.'

'Borderline criminal . . .'

'Borderline?' Kit echoed. He sounded offended.

'Oh, come on. You used to work as a breaker for Michael Ward, who was a big noise in criminal circles. A real face. Just like Rob Hinton worked as a breaker for you.'

'I run a legitimate business. Security and loans,' he reminded her.

'Isn't that a cover for a lot else?' said Romilly.

'Can you prove this wild accusation, detective?' asked Kit.

'It's detective *inspector*. And that isn't an accusation, it's a question.' Romilly chomped the last of the breadstick down and took a glug of wine. A waiter hurried over with more focaccia, and she pounced on it. 'I expect I *could* prove it, if I could spare the manpower to start digging deeper.'

'Why don't you?'

'Look, here's the thing.' She waved a wedge of bread at him to illustrate her point. 'You ever repeat this and I'll say you're a damned liar. But when they banged up a load of big Mafia dons in New York a while ago, you know what happened? Young punks were running loose on the streets, free to do whatever they wanted without the dons' say-so. It led to complete chaos. A massive hike in unregulated crime. People living in fear. All because someone was super-keen to see those five dons sent down. A year, two years later? New York's finest were wishing they had the dons back, because what they had without them was pure pandemonium.'

'So what else do you know about me?' He was smiling.

'Oh, lots. You had a run-in with Tito Danieri over a girl called Gilda May, who went missing. Her folks never heard from her again.' She nodded to his hands. 'About the time you got the burns, right? I'm guessing Gilda wound up dead.'

Kit stopped smiling. His lips tightened to a thin line and his teasing expression suddenly shut down to hard blankness. 'That's private stuff,' he said.

'Touched a nerve?'

Kit glanced around at the other patrons. 'You wish.'

'And Bianca, Tito's sister. You were linked with her five years ago but she vanished too.'

His eyes drifted back to hers. 'Was I?'

'You were. And Tito wound up dead. That was unfortunate.'

'Certainly was, for him. Look, I hate to disappoint you, but there was nothing mysterious about Bianca "vanishing". She took off to find her family.'

'Tito was her family, surely.'

'I mean her *real* family. Norway. You know about this, I expect.'

Romilly nodded. They were fencing back and forth with words. Parry and thrust. She was almost enjoying it. Then their mains arrived. There was the ceremonial peppering of the penne, some shavings of parmesan, before the waiter departed with a *buon appetito*. God, she'd been starving hungry. Limp and weak with it, literally. As often happened, she'd grabbed a quick bite of toast at breakfast on the way out of the house, and eaten nothing for the rest of the day.

'This is so good,' she said, necking penne.

'You got a good appetite,' said Kit.

'I forget to eat sometimes. Like today. Too busy.'

Kit started eating, while watching her. All that wild, curly dark hair, it was pretty. *She* was pretty, with her solemn, super-intelligent brown eyes, big arched brows, long nose and decisive mouth. He could see she had a good body, despite the unflattering navy trouser suit she wore. She was tall, legs all the way to heaven. Put her in a mini dress, she'd blow your socks off.

Shit, here he was again though. If Rob was still here, he would say, *What the fuck you doin', boss? Girl's a DI. Dedicated to the point of obsession, you can see that. She's bright as a button and quick on the uptake. You won't run rings round* this *one. You think* I've *been living on the edge? Well, so are you. Right now. And you're in danger of going over it.*

Only Rob wasn't here. Kit wished to fuck he was, if only so he could kick his arse and ask him what the sodding hell he thought he'd been playing at, running drugs out of the manor, and not even having the decency to give his boss a heads-up, never even offering him a taste of the action.

Of course, Kit would have turned that down. Drugs was the one thing he wouldn't touch, and Rob knew that. He *knew* how Kit would feel about it. It hurt and angered him all over again when he allowed himself to think about it, the stark betrayal of trust, the rotten feeling that he'd never really known his own best friend at all.

'What?' she asked, catching him staring at her face. 'I got sauce on my chin?'

'A bit.' He leaned over and wiped it off with his thumb. It was an unexpectedly intimate gesture, and Romilly looked flustered all of a sudden.

'So, no husband?' he asked.

'That's private stuff.' She returned her attention to scooping up the penne.

'You don't mind discussing *my* private stuff.'

Romilly looked up at him. 'All right. No husband. He left. I caught him in bed with another woman and he acted like it was all my fault. He said I was married to the job and he was fed up with it.'

'Recently?'

'Yup.'

'I'm sorry.'

Romilly shook her head. 'So was I. For a split second maybe. But it was getting tired, anyway. And too restrictive. I need to keep my mind on this job. Let it flow, you know what I mean? Give the pieces a chance to fall into place. I can't be thinking about dinners and laundry and who last did the hoovering. I guess he didn't like that.'

'No kids?' he asked.

'None. You?'

Kit shook his head.

'Then we're both footloose and fancy-free,' she said, and scooped up the last of the penne and wiped her plate with the last bit of bread. She gave him a bright smile. 'Ain't life grand?'

'Oh sure. My best pal just died. It's great. And then all this stuff with him, things I didn't know about. The money in the lock-up, for example.' Kit put his fork down and looked at her. 'You know, I always thought Rob told me everything. And he always had my back. *Always.* Now, this. It's as if I didn't know him at all.'

Romilly paused. 'Rob Hinton was your minder, wasn't he? Maybe someone's thinking, take out the wall and everything behind it's wide open.'

'They could have got me on the same day they got Rob.'

'That was probably the intention. But you got away.' She looked at him. 'Aren't you scared?'

Kit sighed. 'What's the point of living your life in fear?'

'There were three shots fired at the church. The one with your name on it ended up in the church door. Our firearms experts say maybe the shooter got distracted. Or a sudden gust of wind. Something like that.' Romilly returned his level stare. 'Three murders. All connected. Loosely. Your mate and the photographer. I would have treated those two as a separate deal if not for the fact that the man who killed them *also* appears to have killed Crystal Rose, and was last seen in your mum's club.'

'You're sure about that?'

'He was target-shooting near Crystal's grave site.' She paused, considering. 'It seemed cruel. Don't you think?'

'What?'

Romilly shrugged. 'Your friend could have been shot anywhere, at any time. But no, they went for the wedding day. Inflicting the most hurt. On you, and your mother and your sister Daisy, and on Rob's family. There's two married sisters, isn't that right?'

Kit nodded, ploughed on with the pasta. What she'd said was spot on. It *had* been cruel. And like ripples in a pond, the hurt from it was still filtering outward. Daisy scoring drugs and trying to drown herself. Rob's mother, his brothers and sisters, gutted, bereft. And him. Losing his best mate on a day that should have been so happy.

Yeah, *cruel* summed it up.

'And there are two younger brothers, who both work for you, correct?'

'Daniel and Leon. That's right.' He put his knife and fork down. 'Look, lay off Daisy, will you?' said Kit. 'She's in bits. Devastated. Leave her alone. You want anything else to eat? Coffee?'

'Not for me. I've got to go. And we'll see as to whether or not I have to question Daisy again.' Romilly gathered her bag and stood up. 'And Mr Miller – I haven't forgotten what happened at the funeral.'

'What *did* happen at the funeral?' he asked, all innocence.

The kiss.

It hung between them, unspoken.

'And I haven't forgiven it, either. Be warned. Thanks for dinner.'

Kit shrugged. *OK*. He watched her cross the busy restaurant at a brisk pace and leave. He was half smiling.

Stupid.

But he liked her.

88

Now this was interesting. The killer had been following Miller and now Miller was with that detective inspector woman. They'd gone into an Italian restaurant. Sitting outside at one of the tables, he sipped a coffee and watched them. They were seated way back in the place in one of the banquettes, best seats in the house. Well, of course. For Kit Miller, what else?

He always liked to get to know his targets thoroughly. He'd followed Rob Hinton quite a few times, and Clive Lewis too. Kit Miller interested him most of all. Because the man had presence. And unless the killer was very much mistaken, that female DI was looking at him in a way that was not disinterested. A DI and a villain like Miller? Well, these things could happen. But he hoped the DI wasn't too committed yet, because if she *was*, she was going to get her brittle little copper's heart broken into a thousand tiny pieces, because Kit Miller was already as good as dead.

The killer had sussed out the place to do the job. He'd tested it. Declared himself satisfied with it. Now all he had to do was wait until the moment was right. And it wouldn't be long before he could finish the job once and for all, get his pay, and move on.

The woman was standing up now, hefting her bag onto her shoulder and coming across the restaurant to the entrance. She came out of the door and passed right by the killer's table, then walked off along the road. He looked in at Miller, one last time. Miller was smiling after her.

Ah, must be love …

It was so sweet. But sort of tragic, too.

The killer finished his coffee, and left. He followed Romilly Kane, just for kicks.

89

It was early Friday morning. Three weeks since the shooting at the church in which she had lost her eldest son, and Eunice Hinton was still shell-shocked at the turn of events. When she opened the door to find the Bill standing on the front step, she couldn't suppress an exasperated sigh. Christ! Couldn't they leave her in peace for one bloody minute? Were they *completely* insensitive?

'Mrs Hinton?' Romilly flashed her warrant card. 'DI Kane, and this is DS Harman. Can we come in?'

'I'm just off out to work,' said Eunice. It was the truth: she was standing there in her overall, ready to get the bus and get started. No use moping about the place. She'd picked up her handbag, put on her coat – and now here were the police again, bringing it all back when all she wanted to do was try to forget.

'Only a few minutes,' said Romilly, unmoving.

DS Harman stared beadily at Eunice from over Romilly's shoulder. Eunice felt guilty, like *she* had done something wrong. And she hadn't. But talking to coppers always gave her the jitters. She opened the door wider, took off her coat again and slung it back on the hook. Good job Patrick wasn't here today. He'd give them the rough edge of his tongue – and that would have embarrassed her. Eunice was always polite. Maybe she was what they called a 'people pleaser', but so what? Manners mattered. She thought so, anyway.

'You'd better come in,' she said, and led the way up the hall and into the lounge.

They sat down and Eunice eyed them expectantly.

'So what job do you do?' asked Romilly.

'I clean. I always have, since right back when the kids were small.' Eunice felt defensive all of a sudden. 'There's nothing wrong with being a cleaner. My girls always mock, but I enjoy the work. I like getting places spick and span.'

Romilly nodded and glanced around. The house showed clear signs of Eunice's devotion to her calling. It was immaculate. 'Why do they mock? Do they think you could do better?'

Eunice shrugged. 'I suppose so.'

'And where is it you work?'

'Offices mostly, now. For a big contract company. Used to do it off my own bat, private houses, but not any more.'

Romilly made a note. 'The company's contact details please?'

Eunice rattled the company name and their phone number off. Romilly jotted both down. 'Who disliked Rob enough to kill him, Mrs Hinton?'

Eunice's eyes opened wide in startlement. 'I don't know. How would I know that?'

'You weren't that close?'

Eunice let out a sigh. 'We were close. Very. But Rob was always out and about, doing his own thing.'

'What about the other two?' asked Harman, consulting his notebook. 'Daniel's the middle son, that's right, isn't it? Tell us about him.'

'Daniel's like a rock,' she said. 'He's dependable. Not one to set the world on fire, but a good boy.'

'And the youngest? Leon?' asked Romilly.

Eunice wrung her hands and looked down at the floor.

'Eunice?' prompted Romilly.

Eunice glanced up at her. 'They always say you shouldn't have favourites, don't they. But most women do, I think. *I* did, anyway. As the eldest boy, Rob was very special to me after having had the two girls. I suppose Daniel being in the middle, he sort of got overlooked. Then there was the baby of the family, Leon. Leon was always my *real* favourite. My baby boy, you know?' Eunice gave a shaky smile. 'I spoiled him, I suppose. Couldn't help it. I feel bad about it now. Very bad. Maybe I should have given Rob more affection, but he was so capable, so independent. Maybe I failed him. And Daniel. Losing Rob has made me think much more about Daniel. That he never got the love he should have done. But I've always tried to do my best for my family.'

'What about your husband?'

'My *late* husband.'

'I'm sorry.'

'Harry was a nice man. *Sweet*, you know? Harmless. He was a postman. He passed four years ago now. Only good thing about that is, he didn't live to see Rob cut down in the prime of his life like that. It would have broken him.'

'I'm sure,' said Romilly.

Eunice looked at her watch. 'I'm sorry, I'm going to be late . . .' she fretted. 'The office workers come in at eight thirty, we have to be out by—'

'Can you give me the addresses of your two daughters?' She flipped her notebook open. 'That's Mrs Trudy Fields and Mrs Sarah Pascoe, correct?'

Eunice gave her the addresses.

'No new men in your life? Since losing your husband?' asked Harman. He was thinking that Eunice didn't look the type to retire to graceful widowhood, to embrace cardigans and slippers. Even today, ready for work, it was plain that she'd taken care with her appearance. She had a blonde up-do, and she'd slathered on mascara and lipstick. Her look was busty, brassy, still attractive.

'Oh! Well, my daughters encouraged me to try dating again. I didn't want to, really. But through Trudy I met up with one of my old boyfriends and – yes – I suppose we're what you'd call an item.'

'His name?' asked Harman.

'Patrick. Patrick Dowling, he owns a car dealership out Clacton way. Trudy works there.'

'The address? And his home address?'

Eunice gave her both. Finally Romilly stood up. 'We won't keep you any longer, Mrs Hinton. Thanks for your patience. And if you think of anything that could help us with our enquiries, please don't hesitate to get in touch.'

90

'So how are they?' Ruby asked Daisy when she and Daniel got back to Marlow late Friday morning.

'The twins? Fabulous. Bewildered of course by Rob being gone. Too young, thank God, to understand the full implications.'

'How's Vanessa?'

'Thrilled to have the twins there. Happy as a dog with two tails.'

'Daniel looked after you OK?'

'Yes. Of course he did.'

'I like him.'

'So do I.' Daisy was frowning, wondering why Daniel hadn't spoken a word to her on the way back home – and then he'd just left her to it, gone off to the garage block without another word to her.

'Daisy?' asked Ruby, when Daisy fell silent, staring at the carpet. 'Something wrong?'

'No,' said Daisy with a bright, artificial smile. 'Nothing at all.'

Ruby gazed at her daughter in sympathy. 'This has all been so hard on you,' she said sadly. 'What is it, Daisy? Do you want to talk about it?'

'Sometimes I think I'm going completely crazy,' she said mournfully. 'I want Rob back so much that it hurts. But then I stop and think – I didn't even know him, did I? Not really. He wasn't the Rob I thought he was. He was a dealer, going behind Kit's back, cheating him. What else did he do that I don't yet know about?'

'Nothing, we hope.' Ruby shook her head. 'Maybe that's the end of it. And they'll find his killer soon. They *have* to.'

'I don't think I'll ever rest easy until they do,' said Daisy. *And even then? How was she going to go on, rebuild her life, when it had turned into a train wreck?*

Ruby was staring at her daughter. 'Are you all right?'

'I'm fine,' said Daisy.

'Really? You're sure?'

'Really. Truly. How's it going at the club? Did you ever find a replacement for that poor girl Crystal Rose?'

'Sort of. I think so. One of her sisters is shaping up pretty well as a stand-in. When I watched the act on Saturday night, I was pleased with Jenny. Not a slip in the champagne glass. Not a hair out of place. Even that miserable cow Aggie looked hot in her spangly costume, assisting her sister with lots of cheesy broad smiles and wide-spread *look-at-this!* arm gestures. The punters loved it.'

'Good. I'm glad *something's* working out, anyway.' Daisy paused before adding: 'Did you know that someone lays white roses every year beside my father's grave? And that Vanessa has no idea who does it?'

Ruby squinted at her. 'Well it certainly isn't *me*,' she said. 'It's been a very long time since Cornelius was my favourite person in the whole world.'

'I know that.' Daisy gave a thin ghost of a smile. 'Strange though, isn't it? Wouldn't you say so?'

'Yes. I certainly would.'

'So how was it down at posh towers with crazy Lady Daisy?' asked Leon.

Daniel was on his way up to his place over the garage block when he met Leon coming down the flight of stairs that led to both flats. Leon paused at the bottom, blocking Daniel's way.

'It was fine,' said Daniel. He wasn't going to rise to the bait. Leon *always* tried to wind people up. He seemed to enjoy it, the tosser. He always had.

'Spent the night, yeah?' Leon leered.

'Yeah, we did.'

'Managed to get into her pants yet? Should be easy, the grieving widow.'

Daniel sent him a look of blistering hostility. 'Why don't you shut your stupid mouth?'

'Truth hurts, yeah? You always fancied her, I know that.'

Daniel shoved hard, pushing Leon back against the brickwork, out of his way.

'Ow!' laughed Leon. 'Watch the suit, bruv.'

'I *said*, shut up.'

'Yeah, I reckon you're *glad* Rob's out of the way because—'

Leon didn't manage to finish the sentence. Daniel punched him, hard, sending him crashing back against the wall. Leon stopped laughing, the smile wiped right off his face. When he straightened up, he raised an unsteady hand to his mouth, where blood was dripping from his split lip.

'Fucking fool,' said Daniel, and went on up the stairs.

91

Trudy Fields was sitting at her desk in the far corner of Patrick Dowling's car showroom catching up with the monthly invoices and humming along to 'I Don't Like Mondays' on the showroom sound system when she looked up. Two punters, a man and a woman, were moving down the line of shiny, brightly lit cars toward her.

She put down her pen and stood up, straightening her fuchsia-pink skirt suit, beaming her false professional smile. 'Good morning. Can I help?' she said, crossing the floor to where they stood beside a used Ford.

Not used, pre-owned. Patrick had dinned that into her time and again. *Pre-owned and pre-loved.* Everything in the showroom had been bought for a song, then made to look a treat with a large price tag stuck on the front of it. No matter if the cars were clocked (most were), eaten away with rust (a bucket of Polyfilla sorted *that* little problem out, provided you didn't get one of those smart-alec customers coming in with a magnet in their pocket), or cut-and-shuts, an amalgam of two wrecks sandwiched together, that could be – although Patrick insisted they weren't – a danger to drive. Valeting was one of the big costs here. All of Patrick's cars were presented beautifully, buffed to a high shine, and looked a million dollars.

'Are you interested in any particular make or model?'

she asked. 'Or just browsing? No pressure. Have a good look around.'

Romilly held out her warrant card. 'You probably don't remember me too well. When we last spoke you were rather shaken up. Police. Mrs Fields?'

'Oh! Yes. That's me,' said Trudy, her smile slipping. Oh God. She remembered the woman now. Those sharp brown eyes. And the man. They were going to talk about Rob's death again. She couldn't bear it.

'I'm DI Kane, this is DS Harman,' said Romilly. Her eyes moved past Trudy to the big, red-faced, middle-aged man who sat in a half-glassed office not far behind Trudy's desk. He was on the phone and had half-risen from his seat to stare out at Trudy and the new arrivals. 'Is that Patrick Dowling in there?'

'My boss. Yes,' said Trudy.

'And your mother's boyfriend, that right?' asked Romilly.

'Yes. That's correct.'

'We wanted to talk to both of you. You first, if you don't mind?'

'No. Not at all.' Trudy's smile had faded completely and she looked pale. 'This way.'

She led the way over to her desk and moved behind it and sat down, indicating two free seats in front. Romilly and Harman sat.

'I know this is painful for you,' said Romilly, watching Patrick Dowling put the phone down and come around his desk. 'But I would like to go through what happened on the day of your brother's shooting once again, if you don't mind.'

Trudy nodded dumbly. She *did* mind. It was agony touching on the subject of Rob's death.

'Who's this?' asked Patrick, bustling out of his office door and coming round to stand beside Trudy's chair.

Romilly stood up. 'Police, Mr Dowling.' She showed him her card. 'We have a few more questions for Mrs Fields and for you too in a moment.'

Patrick puffed himself up. 'Well it's bloody inconvenient,' he said hotly. 'This is a place of work. We have customers coming in. Police on the premises when you're selling motors? It doesn't look good.'

'We're not uniform, Mr Dowling,' said Harman, a hard edge to his voice. There were no customers in the showroom in any case. 'However, if you would feel more comfortable closing the premises and accompanying us to the station so that we could talk there, that's fine.'

Patrick's fierce brows drew down over his eyes and his face turned a darker red. He stared at Romilly. Romilly gazed steadily back.

'All right, all right!' he said at last. 'But make it quick, can you? We've got work to do.' He stood there, arms folded.

'We need to talk to you separately. Maybe we could use your office to talk to Mrs Fields in private,' suggested Romilly.

'Right! Go ahead,' he said, and stormed off across the showroom and out onto the forecourt.

The three of them moved into Patrick's office.

'Now,' said Romilly. 'Talk me through that day, Mrs Fields. Take your time.'

92

Daisy came downstairs on Sunday morning to find Ashok, one of Kit's most trusted men, sitting in the hall chair. He folded his paper and stood up.

'Hi, Ashok,' she said. 'Where's Mum?'

'Out. At the club, I think, with Fats.'

'And Daniel?'

'Busy with Kit. Anything I can do for you?'

'Oh. No. Nothing.' Daisy left him there and went into the kitchen. Daniel had been the one minding her ever since Rob's funeral, what was Kit playing at? Or had Daniel *asked* to be taken off that duty?

Bev Appleton turned up at Romilly's door that same night, clutching a bottle of red. She held it aloft when Romilly opened the door in her pyjamas.

'Sunday *night*?' asked Romilly in surprise.

She had been lying on the couch. The great TV dinner had been consumed – beef and Yorkshire pudding, sluiced down with juice and painkillers for a rotten stress headache – and the long evening stretched ahead. Tomorrow she would question Clive Lewis's widow, again, and Rob Hinton's other sister. She was already mapping out the line of questioning. 'What about Brian? Where are the kids?'

'Brian's slumped in front of the telly. The kids are up in

their rooms. I am surplus to requirements, having ironed, packed clean sports gear into satchels, made up lunches ready for tomorrow, cleaned out the loo and vacuumed upstairs. I do that, you know. One week it's the upstairs, the next the downstairs. I have a set routine. It's dull as fuck, but it gets the thing done. When that's out of the way, I have a drink as a reward, before the Monday onslaught.'

'Christ!' Romilly laughed and ushered her mate inside. 'And to think I sometimes get maudlin over the loss of my marriage! I hope you got a taxi, Bev.'

Bev took off her coat and laid it over the newel post at the foot of the stairs. She followed Romilly through to the kitchen. Romilly got out glasses and a corkscrew, laid out some nibbles.

Bev sat down at the breakfast bar and looked at her pal. 'Of course I got a ruddy taxi. Don't worry.' She glanced at Romilly's left hand. Still no rings. '*Is* it lost then, the marriage?'

'Oh, it is.' Romilly applied the corkscrew and got the bottle open. She filled the two glasses and took a seat. 'Lost beyond hope of ever finding it again.'

'Hugh seemed like a good sort,' said Bev, taking a handful of crisps.

'The woman I found him in bed with obviously thought so.'

Bev's eyes widened. Romilly nodded. 'Yep. Told him I'd be late home, then sneaked in at six. And there they were.'

'Was he . . . I mean, did he apologize? Grovel?'

'No, he blamed me. Let's face it, Bev. The man's a complete cunt.'

'Yeah.' Bev half-smiled. 'But cunts are useful.'

'That one isn't. Hugh's about as much use as a spare prick at a wedding. And who knows? Maybe he's right. Maybe this *is* all down to me. You know what the job's like.'

'Yeah, but he's a social worker. Aren't they meant to be understanding types?'

'Well, you should know. And they are, in their work. But day to day, when they're feeling neglected? He's a man, for God's sake. They want to be *numero uno*, don't they. And my job was that. So he went.'

Bev eyed her friend keenly. 'So how are you coping?'

'Oh, fine. Relieved, I suppose. But it's still hard. I get headaches.'

Bev sipped the red. 'God, that's nice. I love late Sundays. A bit of a break before the madness starts all over again.'

'I'm not lonely,' said Romilly, taking a sip. It *was* nice. Took the edge off.

'Did I say you were? Anyway, there are always solutions to that.'

'Oh, *please*. Dive into the whole stupid thing, all over again? You're joking.' Romilly grimaced. 'You know what? It's a relief he's gone. The pressure he put on me . . . it was getting hard to take. I have enough, with the job. I don't need more.'

'Maybe some *uncomplicated* action would do you good.'

'I don't think so. Once bitten and all that.'

'I've been reading this *great* book . . .' said Bev.

'Oh shit. Not another one.' Bev was well known for her passion for self-help books. *Your Life, Your Rules! How to Mend Your Life!* There was literally no end to them.

'No wait. This is just a line from a Taoist teacher. That's all. A single line, but it resonates, I tell you. It goes right to the nub of everyone's problems.'

Romilly sipped the wine again. 'Go on then. Shock me.'

'Well, if you're going to mock . . .' Bev huffed.

'No, no. Go on. I can't wait.'

Bev put her glass down and laid her hands flat on the

93

Romilly was having another shitty day. She'd interviewed Sarah Pascoe, Rob Hinton's other sister, and her husband, then the Lewis woman. She'd listened and watched and realized that she was hitting yet another dead end. So she'd gone back to her office, where PC Paddick told her that there was no sign of their man in any of the six months' worth of CCTV from the burlesque club. She sat there staring at thin air after that, running it all through her mind. Rob Hinton. Crystal Rose. Clive Lewis. All dead. All connected. A single gunman, on the run. A ghost, unfindable.

It was now clear that the killer hadn't been to the club before. On the night he *had* been there, prior to murdering Crystal Rose, he'd paid cash to Joanie the hostess, left them no paper trail to follow.

Frustrating.

She briefed the team, told them how far they'd got. Which wasn't very far at all. Then DCI Barrow called her in for an update. *Something* had to give on this. It was driving her mad. She told him all about Rob Hinton's secret past, the impounded loot in the lock-up, his immediate family and the line of questioning she'd taken with them, and about the gun clubs she'd visited one by one, finding no leads at all.

'It'll come,' he said. 'Super wants a result soon though.'

No pressure then.

Her brain seemed to be stalling, stumbling over one thing: the money in the lock-up. She couldn't think why, but her mind kept going back to that, to Mrs Lewis, to the laundry bag, the impounded loot.

Romilly left the nick with a shrieking tension headache at lunchtime and headed home to take some pills and lie down for an hour. Maybe even eat something. As she parked the car, she saw Sally the barmaid click-clacking past in her ridiculous high heels. Sally upped her pace, her cheeks turning red, her eyes averted. Romilly wondered if Hugh was still fucking her. And then she decided that she didn't give a stuff, either way. She went indoors and straight upstairs – she felt too screwed up to eat. While she was lying on the bed, the phone rang and she heard the answering machine kick in. It was Mum.

'Lovey, how are you? You didn't call at the weekend so I've been worried. I thought I might catch you at home as it's lunchtime.'

Romilly rarely came home for lunch. She worked through, usually, but today she couldn't. Romilly's devotion to her job was just another thing beyond her mother's understanding.

'But it's only a *job*, darling,' she would say.

Only, to Romilly it wasn't a job; it was her whole life.

'And have you spoken to Hugh? *Please* try to sort things out with him, darling, because . . .' *Should never have told her about the split*, thought Romilly.

She tuned out and let her mother witter on.

How to explain the unexplainable? That the thing had run its course, that she felt *nothing* for Hugh any more, and she was glad that the lazy, feckless bastard had gone and given her some much-needed space, because she had to *think*.

None of which her mother would want to hear, or even begin to understand. To Mum, a job was nothing; a family was far more important. And no patter of tiny feet? Romilly had heard that too, over and over again. *You're leaving it very late, you know.* Her mum was desperate to be a grand-parent, but Romilly didn't feel any driving urge to become a mother. She never had. And that was *also* something way beyond her mother's comprehension. Something best not touched upon.

Dad was great. Easy-going, accepting. A delight. But Mum . . .

The answerphone fell silent. Romilly closed her eyes and breathed in, out. Enjoying the peace.

Another half an hour, and she'd go back, start all over. She'd missed something at the lock-up. All that money under the tarp. What had she missed?

The phone started ringing again.

'Oh, Mum, *please* fuck off,' she groaned. This was the way her mother operated. Ring once, twice, three times. Up the stress. *Make* her daughter respond, *make* her pick up.

'Right, I'm doing it OK?' shouted Romilly at the phone, hurling herself across the bed to snatch the damned thing up. 'I'm doing it!'

She wrenched the phone off its cradle. 'Yes?' she snapped, steeling herself for the questions, the emotional blackmail, the whole nine yards.

When are you coming to see us? Are you sure *it's over, you and Hugh? You're not the easiest person to live with, you know, and that's what marriage is all about, give and take.*

Then all at once she had it. The lock-up. Mrs Lewis saying Mr Hinton had a key.

Harman's voice said: 'Great telephone manner. You coming back in? We might have something.'

94

What Harman had was a call from a Mr Janssen at the shooting range in Barnes. Romilly and Harman went over there and met up with Janssen in the plush twenty-five-metre, six-lane, air-conditioned range.

It was currently quiet, echoing, and empty of shooters.

'Thank you for calling in,' said Romilly. 'We appreciate it.'

'No problem,' said Janssen, looking troubled. 'I don't even know if it's relevant. I certainly don't want to lay blame on anyone who's innocent, but . . .' His voice trailed away.

'If you can just tell us what's bothering you, Mr Janssen,' prompted Harman. Janssen wouldn't discuss it over the phone. All he would say was that he had some information, and could they come over. 'It was the picture you showed me. The man in the nightclub.'

'What about it?'

'Well, I've been thinking about it, and he *did* look familiar.' Janssen was shaking his head, looking dubious now. 'I'd hate to cause trouble for anyone,' he repeated.

'Go on,' said Romilly.

'About a year ago,' said Janssen. 'I think he was a member.'

'And?' said Harman.

Janssen still seemed uneasy. 'He was a great shot. A real cracksman. Quite dedicated. Almost Olympic standard, I would say.'

'Yes?' said Romilly when he paused.

Again the head shake. 'I don't want to dump anybody in it.'

'You won't do that, Mr Janssen. Please, tell us.'

'Well . . . it wasn't his shooting that was the issue, it was *him*. There was something *off* about him, you know? Something . . . creepy, a couple of the female members told me. In the end, it was unfortunate, but the committee had to ask him to go.'

'Creepy? In what way?' asked Romilly.

'One of the girls said that he'd spoken to her about dead bodies.'

'You what?' asked Harman.

'Seriously.' Janssen nodded. 'Apparently, John was chatting to her and he started on about how they can identify corpses from dental records, so it'd be a good idea to yank a victim's teeth out before you buried them.'

Romilly and Harman stared at him.

'It really spooked her,' said Janssen.

It bloody well would, thought Romilly, her spine tingling. She thought of Crystal Rose and her missing teeth. Christ! At *last*.

'And that wasn't the only instance. There were others. Suggestions that he'd rather shoot at a *human* target than a paper one.'

Jesus, thought Romilly.

'So in the end, he had to be asked to leave.' Janssen looked indignant now. 'What people don't appreciate is, this isn't cowboys and Indians. It isn't James Bond or some such silly thing. This is a respectable skill, a recognized sport.'

'You've got his address?' asked Harman.

'Yeah, I dug it out. Good job we keep records up to six years back. For the tax man, you know. Come on into the office.'

Janssen led the way into a tiny office that Romilly remembered had been in darkness when she called before. He flicked on a garish fluorescent light to reveal a half-glassed cubicle containing a battered desk with a telephone, and two plain chairs. There was a cabinet stacked with silver trophies on the right-hand side of the office, and on the left-hand side, on a stark magnolia background, were pictures of groups of men and women holding rifles and smiling proudly at the camera.

Romilly stared at the framed photographs. 'Mr Janssen – I don't suppose the man you're talking about would be in any of these shots, would he?'

'Well, I . . .' Janssen looked around. 'It hadn't occurred to me, but I suppose . . .' He went over to the wall behind the desk. 'These are older ones. That's December last year, this one's January . . .'

He was scanning the faces, moving from print to print. 'Ah look. Yes. Here.'

Romilly joined him and looked at the man he indicated. 'John' was standing at the far end of the group, a little apart from the others. A very tall, thin, narrow-jawed, unsmiling, dark-haired man. His expression was closed-off, very intense. He was staring at the camera, holding his rifle cracked like all the other people in the group, but somehow looking . . . *apart*, she thought. Not one of them.

'Did he use a club rifle, or did he have his own?'

'God. I can't be one hundred per cent sure after all this time. But I think . . . yes, I think he had his own.'

'You've had no instances of club rifles going missing?'

'No. None.' He took a sheet of paper off the desk and handed it to Romilly. 'I wrote the address down for you.'

She felt a surge of hope that almost deadened the pain of her banging headache, and tucked the paper in her pocket.

'And his phone number?' she asked.

'No. Sorry. And the address is his uncle's, not his own. He works away a lot, apparently.' Harman was squinting at the print with 'John' in it. 'Um,' he said.

'What?' Romilly's attention sharpened at his tone.

'That big bloke at the other end of the group.'

Romilly looked at the man Harman was indicating. She peered closer. Her stomach tightened in shock.

'Oh yeah.' Janssen peered at the man. 'Everyone felt doubly bad at letting John go, because *he* recommended him for membership in the first place.'

Romilly and Harman were looking at the man in the picture. He was big, florid-faced, with fierce eagle eyes, thick grey hair and bushy eyebrows.

'That's Patrick Dowling,' said Romilly. She fumbled the piece of paper out of her pocket and stared at it. 'This is Patrick Dowling's home address. D'you mean this "John" lives with him?'

'No. He doesn't. John moves around in his work a lot, apparently, so it was most convenient to have us contact him if we needed to at Patrick's address,' said Janssen. 'Patrick's been a member for about three years now.'

'And he proposed this "John" person?' asked Harman.

'Yes, that's right,' said Janssen. 'John's his nephew.'

95

Romilly and Harman went back to Patrick Dowling's car dealership. Trudy was there at her seat, and Patrick was showing a flashy red BMW to a middle-aged couple. When he saw the police arrive, he smilingly told the couple to get in, have a feel of the car, and then he came over to Romilly and Harman with a face like thunder.

'What the fuck d'you lot want now?' he demanded.

Romilly said: 'Mr Patrick Dowling, you are under arrest and may be charged as an accessory to a serious crime. You do not have to say anything, but . . .' She went on, reading him his rights.

Patrick's mouth had dropped open. 'You fucking *what*?' he roared, not listening.

'Please accompany us to the station, Mr Dowling, where you will be questioned,' she concluded.

Trudy was watching, open-mouthed. So were the couple in the BMW.

'Or do we have to cuff you?' asked Harman.

'Right. All *right*. I'm coming. This is all a mistake. A *big* mistake. I warn you, I'm a friend of the chief constable. Trudy!'

Trudy jumped.

'Look after the dogs, all right?' She nodded.

'Soon as you can,' prompted Romilly. She heard the

clicking of canine claws on the lino in the office. Curious, she went to the door and looked in. Three Pekinese dogs were in there, their leads tied to a chair. They yapped and snarled at her as she came into view.

Just as charming as their owner, she thought.

Later that same day, Romilly was updating DCI Barrow in his office.

'Patrick Dowling is in tight with Eunice, and her boys work for Kit Miller, so this could be a takeover bid aimed at bringing Miller down. Dowling's a car dealer, he's in the trade. He could easily have sourced the van used in the supermarket warehouse robbery,' said Romilly.

This was the bit of the job she loved the most. It was as satisfying as when she'd played pairs as a kid. This card matches *that* card. Slowly, the whole thing would fall into place. It was the best feeling in the world. The shooter was Patrick Dowling's nephew, his brother's kid. Not right in the head. And Patrick had exploited the younger man's strangeness.

'Probably the van's been scrapped by now, but we'll run through all Dowling's connections,' said the DCI, his eyes gleaming. He loved this too.

'I've pulled him in,' said Romilly. 'We're questioning him right now.'

'Get that showroom of his locked down. And his home address, get a team in there, search it. Careful, though. Our shooter could be hanging around. Let's make Patrick Dowling really start sweating.'

'It's done.' Romilly nodded. She already had people climbing all over Patrick Dowling's workplace and his home address. Patrick had huffed and puffed about it – it seemed to be what he was best at, projecting a big, bluff, bullying demeanour to the world in general – but fuck him. It didn't cut any ice with her.

'Good work. Still not found the nephew?'

'Not yet.'

She left his office and went back to her own, thinking of the Kit Miller connection, that the robbed supermarket warehouse was on his 'manor'. The warehouse job could signal the start of a serious turf war. She'd thought first that it was one of the old established mobs, but here was Patrick Dowling, coming out of left field at her. And for as long as John Dowling was on the loose, Miller was under threat. Throwing out Thomas Knox's name during the robbery she now believed had been a blind to lead them all in the wrong direction. No, Patrick was in the frame now. *Right* in it. All they had to do was make him crack.

Meanwhile, the Clive Lewis funeral was tomorrow, at the crem, and she was going to be there.

96

Another fucking funeral, thought Ruby when they all assembled at the crematorium next day. Daisy hadn't come, but Kit was there and quite a few others too – including that police detective, giving everyone the evil eye as they gathered to pay their respects to the departed. The service was short, and throughout it Ruby kept her eyes on Mrs Lewis at the front, near to where Clive Lewis's coffin sat on the dais.

The vicar droned on, and when the curtains opened and the coffin slid out of sight, Ruby was glad to get outside again, into the fresh air. It was done.

'Can I have a word?' It was the detective inspector, Romilly Kane.

'You can have one,' snapped Ruby. 'In fact, you can have two. Why don't you piss off and do your job, instead of hanging around us like a bad smell?'

'I'm doing my job, Miss Darke,' said Romilly, unfazed. 'I've got someone connected to the case in custody and I'm hoping to round up your son-in-law's killer very soon now.'

Ruby looked at her sharply. 'Oh? This person you've got in custody and the shooter, are they one and the same?'

'No. They're not.'

'It's all taking a bloody long time,' said Ruby.

'These things do, sometimes,' said Romilly.

Truthfully, Romilly was worried. They'd already detained Patrick Dowling for nearly twenty-four hours and he was proving a tough nut to crack, responding to their questions with a string of 'no comments'. She'd left Harman chipping away at the bolshie old sod, but she didn't hold out a lot of hope. Any longer, and they'd have to apply to a judge to keep him and that could easily go either way.

She didn't want him slipping out of her grasp. He could vanish, go to ground. *She* would, in his place.

'Excuse me,' said Ruby, and walked away, in the direction of the tear-soaked widow.

'Hi,' said Kit.

Romilly turned and there he was. Black suit, white shirt, bright blue eyes. Handsome as the devil.

She felt her stomach do a neat little back-flip.

'Hi, yourself,' she said.

'Making progress, detective?'

'Some. We've traced the shooter back to a particular gun club.'

'Which one?'

'The one his uncle Patrick Dowling belonged to. It's in Barnes.'

That jolted Kit. He thought of Patrick, and his connection to Rob's family and therefore to him. And Fats hadn't told him about any gun club in Barnes. Christ, could that have been deliberate?

Could *Fats* be involved in this mess?

'Let's walk,' he said.

They strolled along the car-lined driveway of the crem, heading for the gate. Fats tailed them, at a distance. Romilly glanced back. Other people were moving back there, chatting. Kit's mother was among them, talking to Mrs Lewis.

'So you're still keeping bodyguards around you,' she said, looking at Fats.

'I'm still a target, right?'

'It doesn't seem to worry you much.'

Kit gave a thin smile. 'I'm with a detective inspector. I think I'm safe.'

A car was turning into the gates up ahead of them. Behind them, car engines were starting up. Everyone was off for tea and cakes at Mrs Lewis's place, going to toast Clive Lewis the drugs mule and say what a great man he'd been, contrary to all the evidence.

'I heard you tell my mother that you had someone in custody,' said Kit. 'You pulled Dowling in?'

'Yes. I have.'

Kit stopped walking. Turned and stared at her. 'Let me just check something. This is the same Patrick Dowling who's an item with Rob's mother? The car dealer? *That* bastard?'

Romilly nodded. The car was still coming toward them, heading in from the gate. A BMW.

'Was that son-of-a-bitch *cunt* involved in Rob getting offed?'

'We've yet to prove it.' Romilly was watching the car approach. Tinted windows. She couldn't see the driver. And . . . she felt the hairs on the back of her neck rise. Something felt wrong.

'Well, when are you *going* to?' he asked, facing her.

'There's more. I checked with Mrs Lewis because something was niggling at me about the lock-up and the money. You remember she said Mr Hinton had a key?'

'Yeah. Of course I do.'

Romilly paused. 'She didn't say *Rob* Hinton.'

'She . . .' Kit froze, staring at her face. 'So which Hinton did she mean?'

Romilly was still watching the car. Suddenly the engine roared, it *screamed*, and the car was coming fast, like lightning. She shoved Kit Miller away from her, hard, and dived the other way. She felt a *clunk* and a burning pain lanced down her shoulder as she rolled dizzily, end over end, landing up on the grass in a heap.

Bedlam broke out. Romilly looked up blearily, everything tilted at the wrong angle, and saw Kit scrambling back to his feet. The man who'd been trailing him at a distance was now chasing after the car, but it was speeding away around the big turning circle, people leaping out of its path, and then it was back at the gates and it was gone.

'Shit! You OK?' asked Kit, running over to her. 'Fucker hit you.'

Her arm really, really hurt. Her head spun. Suddenly, she felt sick and disorientated.

'I'm OK . . .' she started, and then she was gone, out cold.

97

This time Daisy didn't have Ashok or even Fats to fall back on. When she came downstairs, it was Leon who was sitting in the hall, on duty. Her heart sank at the sight. No Daniel. She hadn't seen him for days, ever since they'd come back from Brayfield. It was pretty clear now that he was avoiding her. She'd thought they'd grown close over the past weeks, that they were friends, united in their grief over Rob; but obviously he didn't feel the same, and that really hurt her.

'Going somewhere?' asked Leon.

'Yes. Out,' she said, pausing to place the note she'd written to Ruby on the hall table, then carrying on to the front door.

Leon stood up, blocking her way. 'Not on your own. Kit's orders.'

'Where is Kit?'

'The Lewis funeral.'

'Right.'

'So where to? I'll drive.'

'Just out.'

Daisy was thinking of being stuck in a car with Leon. But she couldn't drive on tranquillizers: she didn't feel steady enough for that. The pills were kicking in, calming her down, and she was grateful for it. Now, she could hardly get her head around the fact that she'd tried to drown herself. She had kids. What the *hell* could she have been thinking?

'OK. No problem, I'll drive you,' said Leon. He was looking irritable; nervy.

'I'd prefer Daniel to do that,' said Daisy.

'Daniel's busy.' Leon was smiling now, but it wasn't reaching his eyes; they were cruel, and cold. 'Got a soft spot for my big bruv, have you? Remind you of Rob?'

Daisy tensed. 'That's a fucking horrible thing to say.'

'Just saying, that's all.'

'Well don't. *This* is why I'd rather have Daniel than you, Leon. He doesn't give me lip like you do.'

Leon's lips tightened. 'Oh, what? Have I *offended* Her Majesty?'

'Why don't you just shut your mouth and give your brain a chance to catch up, you moron?' snapped Daisy. 'I'm going out and I *don't* want you with me.'

She walked out to the car, aware of Leon following. Christ, she loathed him. He was a *total* pain in the arse.

'Tough,' he said, grabbing the keys off her. 'It's me or nobody.'

They got in the car. Leon switched on the radio, turning the dial until it hit a different station to the one Daisy usually listened to. It was Squeeze and 'Up the Junction'. Leon cranked the volume up until Daisy winced.

'So where are we going?' he shouted at her over the noise.

'Brayfield,' said Daisy. Fuck's *sake!* She'd just have to put up with the mouthy sod.

98

Romilly came out of A & E after several hours of waiting, checks, X-rays and consultations. She felt shaky and drained and her left arm was in a sling. Kit Miller had driven her there and was still waiting for her.

'All OK?' he asked.

'Just twisted my arm and got a bit of a shaking up, that's all,' she said, feeling stupid. 'It's sore, but a few days and it'll be right as rain.'

'You still look white.'

'I'll be fine. If you can drop me home . . .?' Harman had taken the car back to the cop shop and he had let her know that he was currently applying for an extension of Patrick Dowling's twenty-four hours in custody. She hoped he'd get it. For now, all she wanted was her own bed and some sleep.

'Sure. No problem.'

Having Kit see her home made Romilly painfully aware that her little terraced house – that was supposed to have been her pride and joy – was in fact a project she'd never yet tackled and now barely had the strength for. When she'd moved in, before she'd met and married Hugh, she'd had such plans for this place. Knock through into the kitchen, open out the rooms. Decorate. Tidy the garden up, maybe even get it professionally landscaped.

Somehow, none of that had happened. Instead, Hugh had kept his shabby old pad but moved in with her when they married. As well as being deeply commitment-phobic, Hugh had proved himself a useless do-it-yourselfer. Any job he grudgingly tackled on the house was bodged, and usually cost a fortune to put right. Then there were arguments over employing tradesmen to do the work. They charged too much, Hugh always insisted, and a full-blown fight invariably followed. In the end, it had all proved too fucking stressful, so Romilly had thought: *sod it*. And the place had fallen into disrepair.

The pressure of the job, the early starts and late nights, the broken weekends, the full-throttle concentration that was required of her, had all impacted not only on her marriage but on her house, too. None of the improvements she'd intended had been done, and she was starting to doubt they ever would be. This was a bad-memories place now, and she wouldn't be sorry to leave it. The porch light still shorted out, the path to the front door was thick with weeds and a fast-growing rogue buddleia. The hallway was dark and depressing. The kitchen was a tiny box with a faultily wired dishwasher that often sent the whole property plunging into blackness, and the previous owner's ghastly scarlet Venetian blinds still hung dustily at the bathroom window. It irritated her every time she went in there.

The whole *place* irritated her now.

'What you need,' Bev was forever telling her with a jokey smile, 'is a wife.'

And she knew Bev was right, no doubt about it. A cleaner would be good, too, if she ever got around to organizing one. Lower-class guilt held her back on that; Mum would throw a fit if she heard that her daughter employed a cleaner. Mum kept her house *spotless*. Of course she did. She had fuck-all else to do.

Romilly considered that it might be nice to have a housekeeper too, to organize bill payments and stuff like that, because she kept forgetting to open the post. She never forgot work stuff, of course. *Never.* And a cook would be nice, to keep her from starving. Yeah, Bev was right. A wife. That's what she really needed.

'Nice place,' said Kit, following her in through the front door.

Romilly made a humphing sound and sent him an amused glance.

'What?' he asked.

'You don't have to be polite. It's a shithole. Tea?' she asked, heading for the kitchen.

'Yeah, sure. Let me.' He moved into the kitchen and grabbed the kettle and filled it. 'Sit down. Take a rest, for God's sake.'

Romilly sat on a bar stool and watched him moving around her poxy little kitchen. She was reflecting on the splendid irony of life. He'd driven her here in a shiny new Bentley and she knew damned well that him and his family lived in considerable splendour. Their lives were nothing like as chaotic, pressured or downright shabby as hers. But wasn't she supposed to be the good guy? Wasn't Kit Miller supposed to be a crook? So why wasn't *she* living it large? And why wasn't *he* shut away at Her Majesty's pleasure, sewing mailbags, instead of being obviously minted and having flunkies fix his meals and wipe his gorgeous arse?

Kit busied himself while Romilly sat there, watching him.

'You're domesticated,' she said at one point, when he put two cups of tea on the work surface.

'Is that such a surprise?'

'Dunno. I guess I thought you'd have staff. Doing the cooking, ironing your drawers, mopping your brow, etcetera.' She sipped the tea. Hot and sweet.

'Toast?' he asked, and when she nodded he got a loaf out of the freezer and started organizing that. Then he brought the plates over with knives, butter and jam, and sat down beside her. 'Arm really sore?'

'A bit, but it's eased off now. I'll take some more pain-killers.'

'Where are they?'

'That cupboard. There.'

Kit got them. Sat down again. Looked at her struggling to butter her toast. He took the knife out of her hand and did it for her. Romilly watched him. He was so damned good-looking, so *gorgeous*.

'What?' asked Kit, catching her staring.

'Nothing,' she said.

'Right.' Kit paused in the buttering. Then he leaned in and very gently kissed her.

'I told you to stop doing that,' said Romilly.

Kit gave the ghost of a grin. 'Shoot me,' he said, and kissed her again.

When Romilly started to kiss him back, he pulled her in closer.

'Ow, ow, *ow*,' said Romilly, wincing.

'Sorry,' he murmured against her mouth, relaxing his grip.

Then the bell rang.

'Shit,' said Kit. 'Just when things were getting interesting. Expecting someone?'

'No.' Romilly was glad of the interruption. She felt hot, right to her core. God, the man certainly knew how to kiss. He only had to *touch* her, and it was like electricity zapping through her veins. And that was bad. Very bad indeed. 'Can you . . .?'

Kit went out into the hall and opened the front door.

'Oh!' said Hugh, standing there on the doorstep.

'Who is it?' Romilly called through.

Kit gave Hugh an expectant look.

'Hugh,' shouted Hugh back, stepping into the hall. Kit stopped him with a hand on his chest. 'Hold up, pal.'

'I'm Romilly's husband,' said Hugh, his face reddening with anger.

'You want him in here?' Kit called back to her.

'Let him in,' she said.

Kit stood aside and let Hugh walk ahead of him into the kitchen. Then he followed.

'What's up with your arm?' Hugh asked her.

'Had a bit of an accident, but it's fine. Mr Miller brought me home.'

Hugh was still looking at Kit like one animal catching another trespassing on its territory. Kit was looking amused.

'What did you want?' asked Romilly.

'Oh sorry, am I interrupting something?' Hugh asked sourly.

'No,' said Romilly. 'You're not, and even if you *were*, it's no business of yours.'

'There's no need to be like that.'

'There's every need. We're over. And I told you, I don't want you back here. What the hell do you want?'

'I came for my cassettes. Up in the spare room,' he said.

'Go and get them then,' said Romilly.

Hugh went off up the stairs and Kit looked at Romilly. 'You want me to go up with him? Make sure he don't nick the family silver or something?'

'You're finding this very funny, aren't you?'

'Sorry.'

'Thanks,' said Romilly. 'For all your help today.'

'Least I can do. I think you saved my frigging life. Thought you said I was supposed to end up shot. Not run over.'

'Different MO,' said Romilly. 'Doesn't add up. Our shooter's a neat person, a creature of habit. Hitting people with cars is messy.'

Kit looked at her face. 'So . . . what? He's changing tactics?'

'Unlikely.'

'You mean we've got two people trying to top me now, instead of one? Terrific.'

'I didn't intend to save your life,' said Romilly.

He looked at her. 'What's *that* mean?'

'What it says. I . . . acted on instinct, I suppose. You weren't looking. I shoved you out of the way. Nothing heroic. I just did it.'

'Well – thanks anyway. Eat your damned toast.'

Romilly ate it, took some tablets, drank some tea, and began to feel a bit steadier. Hugh came thudding back down the stairs and stood in the kitchen doorway. He shot a wrathful glance at Kit, then looked at Romilly.

'I thought we could talk. Like civilized human beings,' he said.

'I think I gave up on the idea of talking to you, Hugh, when I caught you riding the local bike.'

'Listen, Romilly . . .' said Hugh.

'Did you hear what she said?' asked Kit.

'Who the fuck asked you?' said Hugh.

Kit straightened up. 'You want me to throw this tosser out onto the pavement?' he asked her.

'I'd like to see you try,' said Hugh.

'Trust me – you wouldn't,' said Kit.

'Stop it, the pair of you,' said Romilly. This situation was embarrassing, and it was about to turn into something farcical. 'Hugh – bugger off.'

With a last furious glance at Kit, Hugh left, slamming the front door closed behind him.

Romilly looked at Kit. 'I don't want to even talk about it,' she said. 'OK?'

'Fine. So tell me. You were saying something before the car hit you. About the money in the lock-up. If it wasn't Rob the Lewis woman was talking about, who was it? She said Mr Hinton. And Rob always managed business on that side of town.'

'I checked with her. It wasn't Rob she was talking about. And it wasn't Daniel. It wasn't even Patrick Dowling, calling himself Mr Hinton. It was Leon.'

Kit stared at her face. 'What the *fuck*?'

'That's what she said.'

Kit was silent, taking that in. Leon! What was the little bastard playing at?

'You know, I can't remember the last time I blacked out like that.' Romilly ran shaking hands through her hair. 'Primary school in assembly, I think.'

Kit's attention came back to her. 'Thought you were a goner.'

'Made of tough stuff, us Kanes. We bounce well.' Romilly finished the tea. 'Thanks.'

'Had enough?'

She nodded. He'd caught her in a weak moment. If Hugh hadn't interrupted them, *anything* could have happened. And the worst thing? She'd wanted it to. Suddenly she wanted to say, *Look, take care*. All at once she felt that putting Kit Miller in the ground would be like destroying a vital, beautiful animal. It had to be the meds they'd given her at the hospital, or the shock of the impact.

'No problem.' Kit gathered the crocks together and took them over to the sink, washed and dried them, put them away. Placed the butter and jam back in the fridge. Put the pills back in the medicine cabinet. 'Right, I'm off now. You get your head down, OK? Couple of hours, you'll feel better.'

They went out into the hall.

'Thanks,' she said again, as he opened the front door.

Kit turned and looked at her. The bloody girl was a hero. And he was getting *much* too pleased to see her, every time he did. *Bad* move. 'Get some sleep,' he told her. Suddenly his eyes were teasing. 'Oh – and *stop* trying to get to first base with me, OK? It's getting embarrassing.'

Then he turned away from her and all the humour left his eyes to be replaced by something more deadly. First thing, he wanted a sit-down with Fats – and then, a fucking good word with that cunt Leon.

99

Later that same day the sitting room door opened at Ruby's place and Ashok said that Lady Bray was here to see her. It had been a day of surprises, none of them welcome. That car, speeding through the crowds of the crem, heading straight for Kit. And that woman had saved him, the detective inspector called Romilly Kane. It had shocked everyone, seeing Kane lying there unconscious. All right, Ruby disliked her instinctively, because she was filth: but she was still someone's daughter. Then the ambulance had come, and Romilly had regained consciousness, and it didn't look as if it was too serious. But someone had tried to get Kit, and missed. No doubt about that.

'I should have phoned ahead,' said Vanessa.

Ruby shook her head. 'It's fine, not a problem. It's been a bit of a day, that's all.' She was trying to be polite, but she was mystified to find Vanessa here. They had never been bosom buddies, ever. There was too much history between them for that.

'Can I get you something to drink?' asked Ruby. 'Tea, coffee?'

'No, thank you.'

Ruby sat down on the sofa and indicated that Vanessa should sit, too.

'OK, what is this?' asked Ruby. 'I don't think you've ever been here before, so why now?'

'It's a nice house,' said Vanessa, looking around.

'It is. I worked hard to get it.' Ruby was thinking that this whole Victorian villa could fit into the hallway of Brayfield House, Vanessa's palatial home.

'There was something I wanted to talk to Daisy about, if she's in?'

'She's not. She went down to Brayfield to see the twins. She left a note. You must have passed each other.'

'Oh.' Vanessa's face crumpled. 'I really should have phoned ahead, shouldn't I? But it's been troubling me and I just got in the car with Ivan and he drove me. He's outside, waiting. Silly of me.'

'What's been troubling you?' Ruby was watching her old enemy curiously. Vanessa was always so cold, so composed. But today she looked . . . rattled.

'When she came down to the country, Daisy and I were talking about all that's been happening in your family. Rob's death was terrible. Awful. I'm so sorry.'

'It's been hard to get through,' said Ruby, wondering where all this was going.

'That day. The day of the wedding . . .' said Vanessa.

'Yes?' said Ruby when she hesitated.

'Rob's mother – Eunice, isn't it?'

'Eunice Hinton. What about her?' Ruby had noticed Vanessa eyeballing Eunice on the wedding day, and had thought it odd; but then, with all the horror that had followed, she had forgotten about it.

Vanessa paused as if in thought, then went on: 'I got such a shock when I saw her there. Realized who she was. The mother of Rob and those other two boys. Daniel and . . . Leon, isn't it?'

'That's right. And the two girls. Sarah and Trudy.' Ruby frowned. 'How do you know Eunice, Vanessa?' It seemed impossible that Vanessa would ever have mixed socially with Eunice. They were from different classes entirely. There was a huge yawning gulf between them.

'Oh Lord.' Vanessa gave a shaky laugh. 'Where to start?' She looked at Ruby with an accusatory glance. 'I believe you are familiar with our London house . . .?'

Christ, after all this time, to drag that up again! Yes, Ruby knew the London house. She'd gone to bed with Cornelius Bray there, back in the day when she'd been a Windmill girl. She'd been hopelessly in love with Cornelius, and unaware at first that he was married to Vanessa. But he was. And so Ruby had become his mistress. Maybe that was her calling in life, to always be the 'other woman'. She'd never yet been a wife. And suddenly, that was beginning to hack her off.

'I know the London house, yes,' she said. 'What about it?'

Vanessa took a breath. 'Well, she worked there. Back in the sixties.'

'Eunice did?' Ruby thought about that. Well, why not? She knew Eunice cleaned offices now, but that didn't rule out that she had cleaned private houses, too.

'Yes. She . . .' Vanessa hesitated.

'She what?' prompted Ruby.

'Not for long. Six months at most. But . . .' Vanessa was pulling at the sleeve of her coat, her eyes not meeting Ruby's.

'Oh, come on, Vanessa. What's the big mystery?' asked Ruby, impatient.

Vanessa's eyes raised and rested on Ruby's face. 'It's embarrassing,' she said. 'But you knew him, didn't you? Just as well as I did. You weren't the first and you certainly weren't the last, either.'

Ruby was frowning. 'I don't know what you're saying.'

'I'm saying that Cornelius had an affair with her. Well, hardly an affair. More a fling. The housekeeper reported it to me. And sacked her, of course.'

'Eunice?' Ruby could hardly take this in. Eunice and that randy goat Cornelius? Ruby had her own deep regrets where Cornelius was concerned. Oh yes, she'd been in love with him back in the day when she was still young and stupid. But she had soon come to know him for what he was. A chancer. A user. And a bully. *That* was Cornelius Bray. He'd made her pregnant, given her Daisy and Kit. Then he'd paid her off, snatched pure-white Daisy off her for him and Vanessa to raise, and disposed of Kit like so much unwanted baggage.

'When I saw her at the wedding, I recognized her straight away,' said Vanessa.

'But I didn't think you'd have much to do with the staff at the London house. I know you prefer the country.'

'I told you: the housekeeper was a reliable, respectable woman and she was loyal to me. She saw what was going on and told me. Too late, as it happens.'

'Too late for what?'

'This Eunice person was pregnant with Cornelius's child when she left my employ.'

Ruby's mouth dropped open in shock. She stared at Vanessa. 'No,' she said, shaking her head.

'I'm telling you the truth,' insisted Vanessa, wringing her hands. 'This is why I wanted to see Daisy, talk to her. She asked me about something when she was down at Brayfield. I'm afraid I lied to her about it. Someone lays white flowers outside the mausoleum where Cornelius is buried, every year on his birthday. Daisy asked did I know who left them there, had I seen them, and I said no. But that wasn't true. I *had* seen them putting the flowers there, and I *did* know who it was. It was her. It was Eunice Hinton.'

Ruby was thinking of Rob, Daniel, Leon, Trudy and Sarah. Five children that everyone believed to be the product of Eunice's marriage to Harry Hinton.

'Initially, I had no idea it was her doing it, and naturally that bothered me. So Ivan set up a camera, and it filmed her coming there, laying the flowers. I was puzzled, so I hired someone. A private detective. I wanted to find out who she was. It was him who made the connection with our London house, that she had once worked there. And he found out more about her, too. Much more.'

'So what happened to this child? Did she get rid of it, have it adopted or something?'

Vanessa shook her head once: no.

'Did she lose the child? Miscarry?'

Again the shake of the head.

'So . . . she kept it? What about her husband, what the hell did he have to say to it all?'

'The husband never knew, apparently. Poor man, he thought the child was his own. Or ignored his own suspicions on that score, if he had any, I suppose.'

Ruby was trying to take all this in. So who . . .? Rob? She felt a sickening lurch of the stomach as she realized that Daisy could have been about to marry her half-brother.

'Please tell me it wasn't Rob,' she said, aghast.

'No. It wasn't him.'

'One of the girls?'

Vanessa shook her head.

'Christ! That only leaves Daniel and . . .' Ruby stopped dead as she thought of Leon. Pale blond hair and startling blue eyes and a permanent chip on his shoulder over something or other. His mother Eunice's spoiled, hateful favourite. Her baby boy.

'It's Leon,' gasped out Ruby, a hand flying to her mouth. 'Oh Christ! It is, isn't it? He even *looks* a bit like Cornelius.'

Vanessa gazed at Ruby and slowly nodded. 'Yes. It's Leon,' she said.

100

Ruby went straight over to Eunice's place after Vanessa left. She hammered on the front door, but got no answer.

Quickly she went down the side of the building, in the alleyway running between the two houses, stepping past the bins, unbolting the gate that led into the back garden. Ruby went to the half-glassed kitchen door and tried the handle. It was locked. She went to the window. The blinds weren't down, she could see in. She cupped a hand over her eyes and . . .

She could see Eunice sitting there at the kitchen table, head in hands. Ruby knocked at the window. Eunice's head lifted, her hands dropping. To her shock, Ruby saw blood on Eunice's face. She got to her feet – *lurched* to her feet – and came to the back door, unlocked and opened it. She stood there and stared at Ruby. She looked dazed. There was an inch-long cut on her left eyebrow, oozing blood.

'What the hell's happened to you?' asked Ruby.

Eunice shook her head. Her eyes were glassy, unfocused, and her face was very pale. Ruby realized that Eunice was on the point of passing out. She stepped inside, easing Eunice back with her, taking her to the chair she'd just vacated.

'What happened?' she asked again, kneeling down in

front of Eunice's chair, taking the bloodied tissues from her shaking hands and pressing them firmly to the wound. Eunice winced but sat there and allowed Ruby to staunch the flow of blood. Her dress was spattered with it. It was on the floor, and the table. But Ruby was relieved to see that it seemed to be slowing. 'Eunice? Can you tell me? Did you fall or something?'

Eunice's shoulders started to shake. Tears filled her eyes and a sound came out of her mouth, a guttural roar of pain. 'Oh *God*,' she moaned.

Ruby watched her in alarm.

'I'm so sorry.' Eunice sobbed. 'Oh God, poor Daisy. It's all such a fucking *mess*.'

'Look, keep this pressed right there, OK? I'm going to make us some tea and then you can tell me about it. All right?'

Eunice nodded and took the tissue while Ruby put on the kettle, found tea bags, milk, and sugar – plenty of it – for Eunice. She made two mugs of tea and set them on the table, took the blood-soaked tissues from Eunice and put them in the bin. The cut over Eunice's eye was barely seeping now, but Ruby fetched a square of clean kitchen towel and handed it to Eunice, who nodded a feeble thanks and applied it to the wound.

'How did that happen?' asked Ruby, indicating the cut.

Eunice took in a gasping breath. Tears were pouring down her face and dripping onto her bloodstained dress.

'Eunice?' asked Ruby.

'It was Leon,' said Eunice.

'What . . .?' Ruby stared at her. 'Leon *hit* you?'

Eunice was nodding, biting her lip, the tears still flowing.

'But why?'

Eunice gulped painfully. 'Because I was going to tell

Daisy. I was going to tell her everything. I told him so this morning. I said it was wicked, it was awful, and I couldn't go on with it a second longer. And then he hit me, told me to keep my mouth shut, or else.'

'You were going to tell Daisy about Leon's parentage?' said Ruby.

Eunice's eyes flicked up in shock. 'How do you know about that?'

'Vanessa Bray just paid me a visit. She told me she'd always known about it. You and Leon. The visits every year to put the flowers at the door of the mausoleum. So it's true. Leon really is Cornelius's child. Jesus! That makes him half-brother to Daisy and Kit.'

Eunice's shoulders slumped. Then her head lifted and her eyes met Ruby's. 'All right. Yes. It's true.'

Ruby was still for a beat, taking it in. 'Your husband . . .?' she asked.

'Harry? He never had a clue. Poor bastard.'

'All right. Tell me the rest of it. Spit it out.'

'I heard about you, all those years ago,' said Eunice, her eyes suddenly bright with malice. 'The staff at Lady Muck's house, they talked about you and him.'

Ruby wished the floor would open up and swallow her. Christ, the madness of youth! She had been so in love with that bastard Cornelius, had gone to the London house with him, had made love with him upstairs there. *Not* her finest or smartest move. But she had conceived Daisy and Kit there. Out of all the chaos, at least she'd got them. She had that to be thankful for.

'We're not here to talk about me, Eunice,' she said, her voice hard.

Eunice gave a shrug, her mouth drooping. 'Well, you're not bloody perfect, are you? Far from it.'

Ruby eyed her coldly. 'I loved him once, Eunice. *Really* loved him. I wasn't just bored with my marriage. I didn't even *have* that. So *get on with it*, will you?'

'All right,' said Eunice. 'But you won't like it, any of it.'

101

Eunice took the kitchen towel away from her face. It looked as if the bleeding had stopped. She put the red-stained towel down on the table, beside the two mugs of tea. Then she let out a sad, weary sigh.

'Ah, Jesus! What's to say? I had four kids to feed and I was married to a bloke who earned next to fuck-all. And then Lord Bray took a shine to me. He paid well, too.' Her cheeks reddened. 'I know what you're thinking. That sounds like I was a brass or cheap or something, but I wasn't. Not at all. I . . . I *obliged* him and he paid me for it. I was a real looker in them days, you know. Still am, some say. I was working there in the house and he was there too, sometimes, in his study. And so . . . it happened. More than once. Christ, my life was so fucking dull that I was glad of it. Harry was never all that in the sack.'

'And you had Leon,' said Ruby, thinking of poor bloody Harry being taken for a mug, raising another man's child.

'Yes, I did. I felt bad about it, but it was easy, deceiving Harry. I made sure to get the dates close, and Harry was kept well in the dark. He never questioned it, not once. No need to. He was convinced that Leon was his, same as the other kids.'

Ruby was standing over Eunice, arms folded, glaring

down at the woman. 'So all these years, you've kept it a secret from everyone?'

'No, not everyone. I wish I had. I told Leon when he turned sixteen,' said Eunice. She gulped down a breath and shook her head. 'I thought he deserved to know where he really came from. He's got blue blood running in his veins, how could I not tell him that? I always made a big fuss of him. I . . . I was dead keen on Cornelius Bray. Oh, I know he was above me. But he *liked* me, you know?'

'He liked fucking you, Eunice. Cornelius would have fucked a pig if it stood still long enough.'

'Well, you *would* say that, wouldn't you? Cornelius was good to me – but then his bitch of a wife found out we'd been together, and sacked me.' Eunice's eyes lit up with spite. 'That cow. I recognized her at Rob and Daisy's wedding. She's aged badly, hasn't she? For all her fucking aristocratic bloodline, she's turned into a right old crone.'

'Get on with it, Eunice,' said Ruby.

'Leon was so special to me. *Very* special. He still is. Not that he has much to do with me any more, not since I told him. But . . .' Her voice trailed away.

'What?' asked Ruby.

Eunice heaved a sharp sigh. 'I wish to God I hadn't said anything. I wish now that I could snatch it back, the decision to do that, because . . . it changed him. Before that, he was my little boy, golden and beautiful, a little angel, full of mischief. Soon as I told him, a change came over him. He took it bad. He was bitter. Angry.' Eunice's eyes met Ruby's and they sparkled with more tears. 'He called me a common whore. Right to my face. And you know what? My boy, my sweet baby, he *slapped* me. I couldn't believe it.'

And now he's punching you in the face, thought Ruby. Things were getting worse. 'It must have been a hell of a shock for him,' said Ruby. 'If he believed up to that point that Harry was his father.'

'Anyway, it made him nasty. He threatened to tell Harry. I mean, what good would that have done? Harry was innocent. An old-fashioned man. I don't think Leon ever did tell him. I hope not, for Harry's sake.'

Ruby was silent, taking all this in.

Eunice went on: 'He got resentful, my boy. Started going on about the life he should have led. He was Lord Bray's son, after all. He was working alongside *another* of Lord Bray's sons – Kit – and Kit had so much: he ran the manor, he had *everything*, and what did Leon have? Just the odd jobs Kit or Rob thought to put his way. He was a dogsbody. He didn't feel appreciated in the least. And don't even get me started on how he ranted on about Daisy.'

Ruby's attention sharpened at that. 'What about her?'

'He said she was a spoiled cunt and she'd been raised in the lap of luxury in a mansion out in the country, and what did *he* have by comparison? Nothing. A postman for a dad, scraping a living, a council estate to grow up on. Burned-out cars and gang warfare and dog shit on the streets. He was envious. Full of bile. Life had short-changed him, while others had been lucky. He reckoned Rob had been the luckiest of all. That he'd hit the jackpot, marrying Daisy, because she's going to inherit Brayfield House, isn't she, which is worth a damned fortune.'

Ruby stared at Eunice uneasily. She was remembering Daisy saying, *Get Kit to sack Leon. I don't like the way he talks to me.*

She thought of Leon, one minute charming, the next in a foul mood, sneering around the house. She'd believed it was just youthful attitude, too much testosterone and not much sense to temper it. That he'd grow out of it, become a more mature and rounded individual like his older brothers Rob and Daniel.

But would he?

Then she thought of him doing that odd little dance to a Michael Jackson track in her kitchen – with his brother barely cold in his grave – and she felt a chill hand touch her spine, sending a shiver of dread right through her.

'Leon always seems so edgy,' she said. 'Uptight.'

'Yeah,' said Eunice, and her face was sad; over the course of their conversation, she looked like she'd aged ten years. 'It's my fault. If I hadn't told him, he'd have been none the wiser, nothing would have changed. But I did, and God – how I regret it. I'll regret it until the day I die. And there's more. That's not all of it.' Eunice started to cry again. 'There's more, and it's worse. Far worse.'

102

'Go on,' said Ruby. Neither of them had touched the tea. Her mouth was dry and she felt consumed by dread. Whatever Eunice was about to say, she felt sure she did *not* want to hear it.

'I've been stupid. I've been *such* a bloody fool,' said Eunice helplessly, her shoulders shaking, the words almost lost as she sobbed her heart out. 'Patrick. You know Patrick?'

Ruby nodded. She'd last seen Patrick Dowling at Rob's funeral. She'd always disliked him; he was a pompous, puffing windbag of a man, bloated with self-importance.

'We went out together, years ago when we were young. After Harry died, I was so lonely. It seemed like a miracle when I found Patrick again. My daughter Trudy works for him at his car showroom, and so we met. I thought it was luck.' Eunice dabbed at her reddened eyes. 'Just coincidence. But it wasn't, I can see that now. Not really. Anyway, we started going out again. He was so *attentive*, you know? I almost believed he loved me. But of course it wasn't me he was interested in, was it? It was my family. It was Rob, Daniel and Leon. It was the way they were all connected to your boy, to Kit, working for him. That was where his real interests lay.' Eunice raised her eyes to Ruby's and her mouth lifted in a pitiful smile. 'No fool like an old fool, eh?

Once he was in, he started getting nasty. Insulting me. Showing his true colours.'

'And . . .?' said Ruby when Eunice paused.

'It was Leon that Patrick fastened on to most of all. In no time, they were in tight together, those two. Leon envied Kit. And I reckon Patrick saw a chance to force his way into Kit's manor, shove him aside. He'd use my boy. Leon knew all about how Kit's business worked, didn't he? Course, Rob and Daniel did too, but they were loyal. Rob especially was so close to Kit, they were real mates, those two, weren't they?'

'Yeah. They were,' Ruby agreed, staring down at Eunice, feeling fury starting to take hold.

'You know what I think?'

'Go on,' said Ruby.

'I think Rob found out that Leon and Patrick were planning something. And Rob was going to tell Kit, tell everyone. So they decided he had to go.'

Ruby felt a chill sweep over her. 'You think Leon was involved in his own brother's death?'

'Christ, that sounds cold, don't it? But Leon resented Rob ever since his sixteenth birthday. Rob was dating Daisy at that time. They split up and it all died down. But they got back together, and when Leon heard Rob was going to marry Daisy, he was green with envy. *Sick* with it. Because when Daisy inherits that pile of loot, as her husband, Rob would be in on it too. I don't think Leon could stand the thought of it, not when he knew *he* was Cornelius's son.'

Jesus. Ruby thought of Leon standing up there at the front of the church, reading the eulogy at Rob's funeral. Tears had been streaming down his face. *Fake* tears. The tears of an accomplished actor, a devious liar. Even from his grave, Cornelius Bray was still managing to ruin lives.

He had wrecked hers, and her children's. Now his bastard child had caused Rob's life to be snatched from him.

Eunice reached up and caught Ruby's arm in a surprisingly hard grip. 'Patrick was behind that warehouse robbery. I can't prove it, but I *know* it. He hates Kit and he wants to take over his manor. He probably agreed a share-out of his part of the job with Leon in return for inside info about Kit's dealings. And that job was only the start.'

'Do you think Patrick was behind the shootings at the church?' asked Ruby.

Eunice bit her lip and nodded, her eyes brimming with more tears.

'My poor boy, my poor Rob,' she sobbed. 'He didn't deserve that. Dying that way. When he should have been so happy.' Eunice gulped down a breath and continued: 'I think it was Patrick's nephew that did it. He's *mental*, that boy. Obsessed with guns. I only met him once, and he's all handsome and smiley, but there's something wrong behind his eyes, you can see it. He makes your skin crawl.'

'Why did the people who did the heist say that Thomas Knox was involved?' Ruby wondered out loud.

'Blaming the Knox gang was meant to rattle Kit even more, make him doubt those around him, people he'd trusted. I tell you, Ruby, and I'm not joking – Patrick and Leon together? They're dangerous.'

'But why Thomas? Why him? Why not name someone – anyone – else?'

'Knox once turned Patrick down on a deal he wanted in on. It was years ago, but he never forgot it, he was always droning on about it. And I suppose he saw his chance to make trouble for him. He always held a grudge. Oh God, Ruby! I've caused all this. Caused Rob to die, and that poor little photographer. It's all my fault.'

Ruby looked down at Eunice coldly. 'Yeah,' she said. 'It is.'

Then she leaned over and Eunice recoiled at the sudden icy rage she could see flaring in Ruby's eyes. Ruby raised a quivering finger and pointed it straight in Eunice's face.

'Do you know what you've done, you stupid cow?' she ground out, teeth clenched, fury barely contained. 'You've killed one son to save another. And by doing that, you've destroyed my daughter, ruined her happiness. You stupid *bitch*!'

Ruby raised her hand, her whole body shaking with the force of her anger.

Eunice gave a cry and recoiled into her seat, cowering, waiting for the blows to start.

But then Ruby froze and reason came back into her eyes. Her hand dropped to her side.

'Nah,' she said quietly. 'A smack upside the head's too good for you. And Leon's already done that, hasn't he? No mother should ever have to take that from one of her own. Your punishment will be to go on living with what you've done for the rest of your miserable life.'

'Ruby—' croaked out Eunice.

'No!' Ruby held up a silencing hand. 'I don't want to hear another *word* out of your mouth, and you ever come near me or mine again, you'll regret it, you hear me? I've had enough. I'm going.'

103

Patrick Dowling had lost a lot of his bluster during the long hours he'd spent down the nick. At first he'd claimed special relationships with everyone from county judges to chief supers. The team were surprised he hadn't pleaded a special relationship with God Almighty, because he seemed to be working up that way. He said they'd pay for this, he'd have their jobs, he'd sue, they were in *big* trouble.

'And I don't need a fucking lawyer,' he said. 'I'm a well-respected local businessman.'

'So you have been advised of your right to counsel, and you have refused,' said Harman, who was conducting the interview with a female DC sitting at his side.

'You're happy to answer questions, without a brief present?' Patrick nodded.

'Get the fuck on with it, can't you?'

So they'd got the fuck on with it. And as matters proceeded, Patrick Dowling shrank before their very eyes. He stopped trying to play the hard man, issuing threats, and reverted to saying 'no comment'. The twenty-four-hour detention period was extended. They told him about the incriminating evidence they'd found in his office, connecting him to a scrap yard where they had found parts from a dark-green van that forensics had tied into the supermarket warehouse robbery back in January.

'So where's the money from that gone? Where's your share, Patrick?' Harman asked.

'No comment,' said Patrick. He was sweating.

'You could be in a lot of trouble here, Patrick,' Harman warned him. 'Worse than robbery. We have evidence that you are linked to a man who has committed three murders. *Three*. Witness statements confirm that this man is your nephew. Where is he, Patrick?'

'No comment,' said Patrick.

Romilly came into the interview room, her arm still in a sling. As she did so, young DC Phillips rose from her seat. Romilly slipped into it. The DC left the room.

Patrick looked at Harman. Then at Romilly. A trickle of sweat wormed its way down the side of his brick-red face, although it wasn't hot in the room. Finally he said: 'Chap you *ought* to be persecuting in all this is that fucker Miller.'

'Why's that?' she asked, when Harman said nothing.

'Well, he runs the rackets, don't he? That warehouse pays him protection, I heard. It was probably an inside job, I reckon. *He* took it,' said Dowling. 'Him and that mother of his, they're bent, the pair of them.'

Romilly stared at him. She stood up, went to the door, called the DC over and had a word. Then she closed the door and came back and sat down.

'Patrick,' she informed him, 'the evidence is in *your* office files. The scrap yard where we found what's left of the vans does regular business with you. And apparently you are a shareholder in that business, too. What do you have to say about that?'

'I've changed my mind. I want a lawyer.'

104

Kit caught up with Fats at Ruby's place.

'Fats! What the fuck. You missed a club off that list and it was the one we needed.'

Fats stared, frowning. 'You what?'

'You heard. The one at Barnes. Patrick Dowling and his nephew shot there. You miss it? Or was it missed for a reason?'

Fats grew very still. 'What you saying, boss?'

Kit looked at him cold-eyed. 'You *know* what I'm saying.'

Fats was silent for a long moment, shaking his head.

'Well, come on. What the hell's happening here?' said Kit, wondering where the fuck his life was going these days. Rob deceiving him, and now Fats? Was *Fats* involved?

'I didn't make out that bloody list,' said Fats stiffly. 'Leon made it out and passed it back to me.'

Leon again.

'I need to speak to that little shit. Where is he?'

'Right now? No idea.'

Ruby walked into her study, snatched up the phone.

'Thomas?' she said when he picked up.

'Yeah. Ruby?'

'Do you know Patrick Dowling?'

'Dowling? Yeah. Sure I do. What's this about?'

'Did he want in on a deal with you? Did you turn him down?'

'He did. And I did. Bloke's full of shit. What is this?'

'His boys mentioned your name at the warehouse job to cause trouble for you. Watch yourself – I mean it. Dowling's been nicked but his nephew did the shootings at the wedding.'

'Christ.'

'And he's still on the loose.'

She put the phone down. Hearing voices in the hall, she went out; Fats, Ashok, Kit and Daniel all turned and looked at her.

'Kit? Daniel? Come in here, will you? I want a word.'

As soon as the three of them were seated in the sitting room, Ruby launched straight into it.

'Where's Leon?' she asked.

'Thought he was here,' said Kit grimly. 'I'm looking for him too. I want a fucking word with that little cunt.'

'Vanessa called on me earlier. Then I went over to see Eunice,' she said.

'Oh?' said Kit.

'Her partner Patrick, and Leon – they've been working against you, together.'

Kit and Daniel were both staring at her.

Ruby pressed on. 'I went to see Eunice because of something Vanessa told me. It was very important. Shocking, really.'

'Go on,' said Kit.

He was thinking of the Barnes gun club missing off the list that Leon had written up – the one that could have led them straight to Patrick, and his weirdo nephew. And now he was *also* thinking about Leon blowing the blond bloke's head off with that grenade out on the marshes – when it looked like he'd been about to tell them who was the ring-leader behind the warehouse heist. And the lock-up. Leon had the key to that. *Not* Rob.

Ruby was staring at Daniel. 'I'm sorry, Daniel. This isn't easy to tell you. But it seems your mother at some point in her life had an affair with Cornelius Bray – Daisy and Kit's father. Vanessa's late husband.'

'You *what*?'

Kit was staring at his mother's face. 'Vanessa told you this?'

'She did. And . . .' again Ruby's eyes went to Daniel. 'Eunice confirmed it.'

'She—?' Daniel started, then stopped.

'It's the truth, Daniel.'

Now he was staring at her, open-mouthed. 'Good Christ, you're serious,' he said.

'I am.'

'She admitted it?'

'She did.'

'Fuck!' Daniel got to his feet and paced around, running his hands through his hair in agitation. He stopped in front of Ruby. 'When did this happen?'

'The exact dates I don't know. Years ago. How old are you?'

'Twenty-six.'

'And Leon is . . .?'

'Twenty-three. Rob's a fair bit older than us. It's a family joke, Mum had her kids in two batches. First Trude, Sarah and Rob, then five years later came me, then Leon.'

'So the affair happened about twenty-four years ago.'

'Wait. Wait! You're saying she actually had a kid with Bray? What about my dad, did he know any of this?'

'Your mother don't think so.'

'You're telling me it's Leon? Leon is Bray's kid?'

She nodded. 'I'm sorry.'

'Daisy and me, we're related to Leon?' asked Kit.

'Yes, but . . . look. There's more. Eunice was concerned because she told Leon on his sixteenth birthday and he reacted badly. According to her, from that moment on, Leon hated Kit and Daisy – and even Rob, because he was marrying her and she was going to be worth a lot of money.' Ruby paused, her eyes filled with sympathy for Daniel. 'Leon thought he was entitled to a lot more than life had given him. And he resented Kit, Rob and Daisy for doing well, when he hadn't.'

'Holy shit,' said Daniel. He knew Leon was a pain in the arse, but *this* . . .

Had Leon *always* been the way he was now? He tried to remember. No. Looking back, Daniel didn't think so. Leon *had* been different after he hit sixteen. After that, he'd become moody. Cruel.

And now he saw why; their mother had finally told him the truth.

'Jesus, I can't believe it,' he said.

'It's all true. Eunice says when she threatened Leon that she was going to tell what she knew about him and Patrick, he hit her. He left her there in the kitchen, bleeding – that was how I found her.'

'Is she all right?' asked Daniel.

'She's OK. Shaken, but OK.'

'Christ, I'd better get over there . . .'

Kit stood up. 'Wait. Just a minute,' he said to Daniel. Then he turned to Ruby. 'What exactly did she know about Leon and Patrick?'

Ruby told him, and suddenly Kit felt a huge weight lift from his shoulders. Rob hadn't betrayed his trust. He hadn't been about to tell him that *he* was involved in the drugs trade on the morning of his wedding day; he'd been planning to tell him what he'd discovered about Leon and Patrick. But he'd left it too late. They'd already decided to strike. They'd been building their own empire behind the scenes, and somehow Rob had found out about it, so they silenced him. They'd rid themselves of Clive Lewis, too. Most likely he'd been wobbling, threatening to bail and reveal their secrets. And Kit should have died too, on that same day. All neat and tidy. But he'd survived.

'Shit! Where's Daisy?' he asked.

'Brayfield. She left a note,' said Ruby.

They all went back out into the hall. Ashok was still there, sitting by the door.

'Did you see Daisy go out in her car?' Kit asked him.

'Yeah, I did. She passed me as I came in. But don't worry, she wasn't alone. If she had been I'd have stopped her. Leon was driving her.'

There was a moment of total, dead silence.

'Oh God,' said Ruby faintly.

Then the doorbell rang. Fats went and opened it. Two uniformed policemen were standing there.

'Can we speak to Mr Kit Miller?' one asked.

Kit stepped forward, his mind still fixed on Daisy and Leon. 'What?' he asked.

'If you can accompany us to the station, Mr Miller, and assist us with our enquiries . . .?'

'You *what?* What enquiries?'

'It's pertaining to a robbery. And Miss Darke, is she here . . .?'

'I'm here,' said Ruby, stepping forward.

'Both of you, please. Quick as you can.'

Kit and Ruby looked at each other. 'Daisy . . .' started Ruby, snatching her coat from the hall stand.

Kit looked at Fats and Daniel. This was Daniel's brother

they'd been talking about. But Kit reckoned he knew where Daniel's loyalties lay. He lowered his voice so that only Fats and Daniel could hear him.

'Get to Daisy. Hear me? Get to her *quick* and make sure she's safe.'

105

It had been a frightening drive down to the Hampshire countryside. Leon was a crazy driver, darting at breakneck speed between cars, shooting through gaps that Daisy herself would never have attempted. All the while, he'd been talking. And none of what he'd said made her feel good.

'I bet it was nice, wasn't it?' he asked her.

'What?' she snapped back, grimly tensed for impact as he swerved the Mini around a ten-ton truck.

'Growing up in the lap of luxury.'

'I don't know what you're talking about,' said Daisy.

'Yeah, you do.' He glanced at her.

Look at the road, you fool, thought Daisy. *Keep your damned eyes on the road!*

'I *mean*, being raised in the ancestral pile. Nice place, yeah?'

Daisy didn't reply. Everything Leon said was sneering and sour. They'd passed Ashok coming into the drive as they were coming out, and Daisy had cursed her luck. If she'd come downstairs ten minutes later, she'd have avoided this and been sitting here with Ashok instead. She watched the road, and wished a police car would come on the scene, wished someone could tell this *idiot* to slow down.

'Must have been good, getting the full five-star treatment,' he said.

Daisy'd had enough. She swivelled in her seat and stared at him. 'What the hell are you talking about?' she asked hotly. 'Why do you have to mock things all the time? What's *wrong* with you?'

'Me?' Leon grinned, and she could see he was pleased he'd got a rise out of her at last. 'Nothing wrong with me, Daisy. Just wondering what it must be like to have all that. As opposed to *nothing*.'

Daisy straightened in her seat. The road flashed by, cars honked. *Christ*, she'd be so glad when they got to the house.

'Your family are OK,' she said, thinking of his dad, Harry. She'd *loved* Harry. He'd been so welcoming to her, right from day one.

'What? My mum's a whore and my "dad" was a wash-out. A nobody, all his life.'

Daisy was startled by that. 'Harry was a nice man.'

'Where the fuck does "nice" get you in this world?'

'It gets you further than being a complete pain in the neck,' said Daisy.

'Is that a dig?'

'Take it how you want.'

They'd turned off the main roads now and Leon was speeding along curving country lanes. Daisy was tense as a bowstring, anticipating tractors, horses, bikers. Any one of which could spell disaster. They careered over the bridge where the gin-clear river fed the watercress beds, and she nearly cried with relief when he turned the Mini into Brayfield's drive. They shot past the gatehouse and Leon roared on up the driveway, bringing the Mini to a skidding halt inches from the Neptune fountain at the front of the house.

'Whewee!' he said, killing the engine, looking up at the vast building in front of them. 'What a place, eh?'

Daisy pulled her hands through her hair, feeling shattered. 'You're a moron, Leon,' she said tiredly, reaching for the door.

Leon shot out a hand and stopped her. Daisy looked at him.

Leon leaned in close. His face wasn't friendly. 'You had all this,' he said through gritted teeth. 'And I had fuck-all.'

'Leon—' Daisy started, not knowing what to say.

'Poor little sis, so bewildered by it all,' Leon pouted.

He saw the question in her eyes and shook his head.

'I'm not calling you that because you were married to Rob – briefly. God, that was sad, wasn't it? Poor old Rob. But not to worry, I think Daniel's ready and willing to step into the breach.'

'That's a filthy thing to say,' spat Daisy.

'But true, yeah? Just like it's true that you're my sister, Daisy. You and me, we got the same blood, but you did better out of it than me, didn't you?'

Daisy stared at him. 'You're mad,' she said, hoping that Ivan or Vanessa would have heard the car on the drive and would come to investigate. She'd always found Leon annoying, but today he was behaving so strangely. And he was talking crazy too. She actually felt threatened by him.

'Not mad, no. Given the shitty end of the stick? Oh yes. Certainly.'

'What do you mean?'

Leon released her hand. His grip had been crushing. Daisy flexed her fingers.

'Oooh, sorry, did I hurt woo?' Leon asked in a baby voice, pooching his lips. Mocking her.

He was *always* taking the piss. She was sick of it.

'You didn't hurt me, Leon. You just do my head in, that's all. Now explain to me what you're saying. It doesn't make any sense.'

'Well, how can I say this delicately?' Leon made a face as if thinking. He tapped his chin. 'Got it. Right.' He turned to her with a bright smile. 'Once upon a time, about twenty-four years ago, your father fucked my mother. They had an itsy-witsy baby boy: me. So my lovely "dad" as you put it, is not my dad at all.'

106

Daisy was shaking her head. 'You're telling me that my father had an affair with *Eunice*? How is that possible? How could he have even known her?'

'What, how could he have known a common little nobody like her? Well, she skivvied up at the family pile in London. And bad old Cornelius no doubt saw my mother's very appealing arse wobbling around the place behind a Hoover and thought, *Hey, that looks good, why not shag it?*' Leon's eyes were suddenly sharp on Daisy's face. 'He paid my mother to have sex with him, you know. Your dear old dad. Of course, my *proper* dad was a pauper. And I'm guessing a bit underpowered, sexually. So my lovely mother got a double whammy from Cornelius Bray. A nice bit of hard aristocratic cock to liven up her dull little life, and a juicy payout.'

'This can't be true,' said Daisy, shocked.

'She told me. My dear mama. On my sixteenth birthday I got a bike, I remember. I expect your dad paid for that. Never forgot that bike. Dark blue. I was standing right by it, out in the front garden, when she broke the news. Told me who I *really* was. It was a bright sunny day. I dropped the bike and hit her. Called her a filthy whore. Which she was, and is. And I never rode that bike. Couldn't face it. Left it there 'til it was nicked. Which didn't take long, where I grew up.'

'That's awful,' said Daisy. Maybe it even went some way to explaining why Leon was always such a pain in the rear. 'Did Eunice tell Harry?'

'No.' Leon leaned his head back and exhaled slowly. 'But I did. On his deathbed. As the last breath was leaving his body. I was the only one in the room at that moment and I. Just. Couldn't. Resist.' Leon smiled as he emphasized each word. Daisy felt sick at the thought of Harry lying there, dying, having to listen to Leon's bile. 'He looked *puzzled*, that was all. He looked like the loser he was. And then he died. I would have liked more of a reaction, really.'

'That was bloody cruel,' said Daisy. 'You didn't have to do that.'

'I sort of enjoyed it,' said Leon, turning his head toward her, smiling. Then he looked at the house. 'What a fucking place,' he said, his voice low with wonder. 'I've seen it before, you know. Followed my mother here, when she was putting flowers on dear old Dad's grave.' His head turned and once again their eyes met. 'You know what's occurred to me, Daisy?'

Daisy shook her head: no.

'This sounds a bit *wicked*, but bear with me. You know what?' His voice was light, thoughtful. 'It crossed my mind quite a long while ago that if anything happened to you, anything sort of *fatal*, who would get all this when Lady Bray kicked off and died?'

Daisy took a breath. Her head had gone light and her heart had speeded up to a wild pace while Leon spoke, and now she was *praying* for Vanessa or Ivan to show up, stop this. He must be completely insane, given the terrible things that were spewing out of his mouth.

'And what about Kit?' Leon mused, pursing his lips, thinking it over. 'You were the only *acknowledged* child of

Cornelius Bray, but then – you see – how about this? Lady Vanessa is such an honourable sort. And I've got a feeling she might even push things Kit's way, if anything happened to you. Don't you think so?'

Daisy shrugged. Christ, he really was mad.

'They can prove parentage now, can't they?' Leon was saying, almost to himself. 'Well, Cornelius Bray is lying in that mausoleum down by the lake – right over there – and my mother leaves flowers at his grave every year. I saw her do it. Again and again. *Every* year. Dozy cow. Probably imagined herself in love with that bastard. His remains are laid out there. So I could prove the link, couldn't I? I could prove I'm his son, and Mummy dear would back me up, she'd agree to it in a heartbeat, she'd do anything to win back her little boy, you know.'

'You're mad,' said Daisy shakily.

'No, it all makes perfect sense. So if you had some sort of accident – such a shame, but these things do happen, don't they – then Kit would have to go too, in case he made a claim.'

'Patrick and me, we agreed we'd take out Rob and that stupid photographer bloke. What a twat. All I wanted was for him to carry on the drugs stuff, but he was getting jumpy. He said he reckoned Rob was on to us, that he was going to tell Kit, and so he wanted *out*. Oh!' Leon sat up straight. 'Hang on. I'm forgetting the kids. Your little twins.' He made a clicking noise of regret with his tongue. 'It's not very nice, is it? But the fact is, they'd have to go too, wouldn't they? Sad but true. Or they'd get all this – and you know what? I'm not going to let that happen. Not when I've finally got the chance to make things swing my way.'

She couldn't listen to any more of this. He'd been in on killing Rob, his own brother, and that poor sod the photographer. And having told her all this, was he going to let her live? She didn't think so, not for a moment. Daisy wrenched open the car door and scrambled out. She crossed the drive and ran up the steps, but she could hear Leon hot on her heels. He was right behind her, and coming fast.

107

Daisy let herself in with her spare key – no time to rap on the door, no time to wait for Vanessa or Jody to answer it. She flung the door open and almost fell into the hallway, pushing the door closed behind her. Or she tried to. Leon stuck his foot out and shoved forward. Daisy staggered back several paces and he came in, closing the front door quietly behind him. He was smiling.

'What, weren't you going to ask me in? That's downright rude, Daisy, and I thought a girl who'd been raised in Posh Towers would know better.'

Daisy backed up until her shoulder blades hit the carved newel post at the foot of the grand staircase. Then a female voice from overhead called, 'Daisy?'

She turned her head and there was Jody, coming down the stairs, her face curious. And – oh Christ! – there behind her came the twins, Matthew and Luke.

'What's going on? I didn't expect you today,' said Jody. She looked at Leon. 'Oh! Hi, Leon.'

Daisy didn't even recognize her own voice when it came out. It was ragged with panic and desperation. 'Jody!' She tried to calm herself. If she told Jody to call the police, or Kit, Leon could kill her right now. If she could keep him talking, keep him *engaged*, maybe she had a chance of survival. 'Listen, Jody, everything's OK. But there's been a security alert. So go upstairs to the nursery, take the twins in there and lock the door.'

And call Kit, she thought, but daren't say it.

Jody's smile froze on her face and her foot hovered over the next step down. Then Daisy's words sank in and she stepped back. Matthew was shouting 'Mama!' and coming down. Luke was following.

'Do it!' shouted Daisy when Jody hesitated. 'Don't let them down here!'

Jody grabbed Matthew's hand. And Luke's.

'Where's Vanessa?' Daisy called up. *And Ivan*, she thought. She desperately needed Ivan, right now.

'They went out – up to town, I think,' said Jody, tugging the boys behind her up the stairs and along the landing. A moment later she was lost to sight. Daisy heard the nursery door shut, heard the key turn in the lock. She looked at Leon.

'Not very sociable,' he said, shaking his head. 'My nephews, yeah?'

'They're nothing to do with you,' said Daisy coldly. 'Just as I am nothing to do with you.'

Leon stepped away from the door. 'So,' he said, flinging his arms out. 'What now, Daisy?'

'You've never been inside here before, have you?' said Daisy, thinking fast.

'No. Strangely enough, I've never been invited.'

'Well,' Daisy gulped, 'let me show you around this place you covet so much and see if you still feel the same afterwards.'

Leon stared at her, and for a moment she thought he was going to say, No, don't bother.

'Why wouldn't I feel the same?' he asked instead.

'Because it costs a fortune to run, you know. It's crippling, keeping the place going. Vanessa's opened part of it to the public to try and help with the running costs. But it's a struggle.'

'My heart bleeds.'

'The roof needs replacing, but all we can do is patch it because of the expense involved. A total refit would run into millions.'

'You're making me cry,' said Leon.

'Come on,' said Daisy, starting off along the hall. 'I'll show you.'

108

The phone was ringing at Ruby's. Ashok picked up.

'Can I speak to Kit?' said a woman's voice.

'Who's this?' asked Ashok.

'Jody. The twins' nanny. It's urgent.'

'He's not here. Nor is Ruby. Can I help?'

Jody told him about Daisy turning up with Leon, that she'd said there was a security alert, and that Daisy seemed nervous.

'You know what? This might sound stupid, but I think she was scared of him,' said Jody. 'Of Leon.'

Ashok looked at the phone. He didn't know *what* the fuck was going on. 'Listen, Daniel and Fats are on their way down there. They left about an hour ago, so they should be with you soon.'

'All right,' said Jody, and put the phone down.

Would Leon follow? wondered Daisy. Or would he drag her to a halt and break her neck right now?

She knew he could do it. Easily.

Fear was making her tremble, but she knew she had to stay outwardly calm in order to buy as much time as she could. She walked into the blue-and-gold drawing room that led out onto the garden with the long borders. It was

Vanessa's favourite room, strictly private, never opened to public view.

Leon let out a low whistle. Daisy turned and looked at him, seeing the stark avarice in his eyes.

'Jesus, *look* at this,' he murmured.

Daisy was staring at the fireplace, wondering if she could get across the room fast enough to snatch up one of the implements hanging there. She didn't think so. 'It looks fabulous, I grant you, but see – the ceiling mouldings are cracked from the damp and the tapestries badly need a clean, they're full of dust. It all costs, Leon. And it's not cheap, not on this scale. Come on.' Daisy walked past him, back out into the hall, and went into another room, even grander than the first, decorated in rose-gold and with muted pink brocades on the furnishings. 'This one doesn't get used much. The public are allowed in here.'

'Is that . . .?' asked Leon, indicating a large painting hanging over the fireplace of a big, handsome, blond man wearing ermine and long flowing robes.

'That's my father. Cornelius Bray.' Daisy indicated the other paintings hanging all around the walls of the big room. 'And all these are his forebears. Grandfather. Great-grandfather. And so on, right back to the eighteenth century. That's Vanessa, when she was twenty-one, right there.'

'She was a looker,' said Leon.

'Yes. Come on,' said Daisy, and led the way back out into the hall on unsteady legs.

What else to show him?

'This is the library,' she said, opening a door into a massive wood-panelled room lined with books.

'Christ, how many books in here?' he asked, gazing around in wonder.

'About five thousand.'

Daisy stepped back out into the hallway. She wanted to get away from him now. He made her feel sick. He *was* intending to kill her, she knew that.

Leon stepped out of the library, pulling the door closed after him. Their eyes met. Hunter and hunted.

'What's up, Daisy?' he asked her. 'You going to run now?'

'Yes,' she said, fear and panic suddenly overwhelming her.

She ran.

109

'How far now?' asked Fats.

Daniel, at the wheel with his foot pressed hard on the accelerator, glanced at him. 'Couple of miles, that's all.'

'You think he's done anything?' asked Fats.

'I don't know. Leon? Anything's possible,' said Daniel grimly, thinking of Daisy, alone and unprotected, down in the country with his fuckwit brother for company. It wasn't a cheering thought. Bearing in mind all that he now knew, he was afraid Leon would do something desperate and that Daisy might not come out of it alive.

He floored the accelerator and hoped to Christ the police didn't stop him. The speedo was on eighty-five miles an hour. It didn't seem fast enough. He pushed it to ninety.

Daisy knew every inch of this house, she'd spent her whole life here when she was not up in town with her Aunt Ju. Catching Leon by surprise with her sudden action and turn of speed, she sprinted off along the passage toward the east wing, tore through the padded green baize door that led down into the kitchens below stairs, slamming it behind her. Then she hared through the kitchen with its old range and walls hung with rows of copper pans and unlocked the back door. She heard Leon coming down the stairs as she tugged at the key, needing to lock it from the outside.

It wouldn't come out.

And she couldn't take the time to keep trying.

She went outside, slamming it behind her as she heard Leon coming across the kitchen flagstones. She ran along the pathway at the back of the house, glancing back in dread as she heard the kitchen door open and close. He was coming.

He's going to kill me.

Total fear fogged her brain. She was about to die. Jody might have phoned for help. Or she might not. Who knew?

Daisy ran over the lawn to the family chapel, thinking it would be unlocked. She turned the big circular handle, but it wouldn't open. It was locked up tight and she could hear Leon's footsteps getting closer and closer.

She ran on, snatching up a three-foot stick from among the thick shrub on either side of the path. She reached the clearing in front of the bell tower and thought with sudden despair that *that* must be locked, too. She was on a curve in the path, and for a moment she couldn't see Leon.

She ran over and tried the handle. It turned, and the door swung inward with a groan like a coffin lid lifting after long dry years. There was no key. She pushed the door closed very gently, trying to be quiet. It was dark and damp in here. The scent of ancient mould and moss tickled her nose. Maybe he hadn't seen her coming in. Maybe she'd got lucky. Maybe he'd pass on by.

Daisy, paused, gasping for breath, and looked up at the rafters in the tower. The bell-pull hung there, still and silent; no one ever rang it now. She could see the massive circular bell with its clapper high above her head. To the side of where she stood, crumbling stone stairs wound up around the interior edge of the tall building. Glancing fearfully back at the door, she started up them. She had gone up thirty of the hundred steps when she heard the door creaking open.

Oh Christ!

He was here.

110

'Oh, Daisy!' Leon called.

She didn't answer. Stepping as quietly as she could, she carried on upward.

'I know you're in here!'

Daisy said nothing.

'What's the use of running? You're only putting it off. Might as well get this over with.'

Now she could hear him starting up the stairs behind her. Trembling, sweating, she walked on. Her grip on the stick was loosening. She wiped one damp palm on her dress and tightened her hold. Fuck it! Whatever he had in mind, she wasn't going down without a fight. She had the twins. She had her family. This bastard had been responsible for her losing Rob. One way or another, he *had* to pay for that. She had to live long enough to do him some harm. She *had* to.

'Daisy, Daisy . . .' he was singing, like this was some cheerful little jaunt, like he wasn't following her up the tower with every intention of killing her stone dead.

Fuck you, Leon, she thought, but her brain was stalling. He was stronger than her, fitter, faster. When she reached the top, what then? She wasn't familiar with the inside of the clock tower, it had been closed for years. One day, it was intended that restoration should take place. Some of the rafters were disintegrating. She didn't know the details. All she knew was that it had been off-limits for as long as she could remember.

Now, she was inside it. And climbing, climbing. Seventy, eighty, ninety steps. Ninety-five. One hundred.

She was at the top of the stairs. She stepped off and onto a wood floor. She was in a room, at the centre of which hung the huge bronze bell. It was lighter up here, the air fresher. There were two windows, glassless, through which a howling breeze was coming, ruffling her hair, drying the nervous sweat on her brow. She walked toward one, hoping to see someone – anyone – outside down there, someone she could shout to for help.

All she saw was greenery. The gardens. The landscaped lake. The mausoleum.

She went to the other window and a fearsome fluttering erupted in her face. A manic draught and ferocious flapping made her close her eyes with a shriek and step back. A pigeon! The thing flew out of the window, even more startled by the unexpected encounter than she was. Then she felt the wood beneath her feet give and groan. Quickly, she stepped off it, gasping in shock. Christ! She looked down. The wooden planking was full of wormholes. She reached down a hand, touched it. It felt friable and light. Rotten.

And now Leon was coming.

'Oh, Daisy . . .' he cooed, laughing at her, knowing he had the upper hand.

Now she could see him, his blond head appearing as he slowly climbed the last of the stairs, as if he had all the time in the world. He was smiling. Daisy clasped the stick more firmly in her hand and prepared to fight for her life.

111

Daniel swung the car off the lane and into the driveway of Brayfield. They flashed past the gatehouse on the left and the car streaked up toward the house. He slammed on the brakes in front of the fountain of Neptune, right beside Daisy's empty Mini. He and Fats got out at a run and tore up to the door. It was unlocked. They went in.

'Daisy!' shouted Daniel.

Nothing.

'Daisy! You here?' he bellowed.

Christ, what if they were too late . . .?

'Who's that?' came a shaky female voice from somewhere over their heads.

He looked up and saw Jody the nanny leaning over the banister on the landing. She looked pale, frightened.

'Where's Daisy? Is she all right?' he called up while Fats went off along the hall, looking left and right, throwing open doors.

'Daniel? She said there was some sort of crisis going on. She was with Leon. I called Ruby's place to let Kit know.'

'Where are they?' he asked. Fats came back to the hall, shaking his head.

'I heard them go down to the kitchens,' said Jody. 'I think they went out the back door from there. Daniel?'

Jody looked down, her face taut with strain. 'I think Daisy was running away from him. I think she was *scared*.'

'You stay here,' Daniel said to Fats. 'Look after Jody and the twins.'

Then he was gone at a flat run, heading for the green baize door that led down to the kitchens and from there to the back of the building.

112

As Leon came into view, Daisy ran forward and swung the stick as hard as she could. It struck his head with a fearful *whack* and Leon fell sideways, almost – but not quite, dammit – losing his footing. If he'd done that, he could have tumbled end over end right down to the bottom and broken his rotten neck, and she would have been glad.

Leon fell against the side wall of the tower, bracing himself with his hands. As Daisy watched, blood started to seep out of a wound, colouring the blond hair with crimson. First it seeped, then it dripped. Good. She'd hurt him. His face was screwed up in pain.

Daisy took another swipe at him, thinking of the twins, her babies, and that if she let him come up further she was never going to see them grow up. Worse still, their own lives would be in danger so long as this bastard was alive. She swung as hard and as fast as she could, her mind focused on stopping him at any cost.

On the downswing, Leon caught the stick in one bloodied hand. His eyes turned on Daisy and she saw pure venom in them.

'Fucking *bitch*,' he spat out as blood leaked steadily from the gash on his head and dripped down over his face, turning it into a fright mask. He yanked the stick toward him, taking Daisy with it. She stumbled forward with a yell, falling to her knees, the skin scraping back from her palm as he pulled the stick from her grasp.

He was coming further up the stairs and now *he* held the stick, not her.

Oh Christ!

Daisy lurched to her feet and then she heard it: Daniel's voice, way below them, out in the grounds.

'Daisy!'

She ran to the far window, away from Leon.

'Daniel!' she screamed, looking out there, desperate to see him. She couldn't. And he probably couldn't see her, either. 'I'm in the . . .' she started, and then agony erupted in her arm as Leon swung the stick at her.

She fell, unbalanced by the weight of the blow, her upper arm a sea of pain. Clutching at it, she rolled, narrowly missing another hefty whack with the thing, and kicked out, catching the side of Leon's knee. He staggered, letting out a roar of rage, and fell on her, throwing the stick aside, clutching her throat in his hands.

Daisy couldn't breathe. He was choking her. His weight was crushing her. She felt consciousness flicker in and out as he increased the pressure. Above her he bled, red droplets falling onto her, his face twisted, bloodied, demented. She felt everything go hazy, and thought *Oh God, the twins, he'll kill them . . .*

She had to fight back, but she couldn't.

She was floating away, losing her grip on reality.

It was all going, fading away into nothing.

113

Then suddenly her throat was free and Leon's crushing weight was gone. Daisy looked up, gulping in great lungfuls of air, hardly able to believe that she was still alive, and saw Daniel lifting Leon up bodily, shoving his younger brother away from her.

Now the two brothers were fighting, grappling with each other, landing punch after punch, the cut on Leon's head staining their fists and clothes. Daisy crawled shakily to her feet and backed up, away from them. She leaned weakly against one of the windowsills, felt the stone crumbling under her fingers. Then she looked at the boards she had trodden on earlier. She wanted to call out a warning to Daniel, but she daren't distract him.

Don't tread there, Daniel. Please don't!

Leon was heavier than her, but Daniel was heavier still. If he stepped where she had stepped, he'd go through. She knew he would. Leon punched Daniel hard and he fell back, so close to that weak mouldering patch of floorboards that she almost yelled out in terror.

'You rotten little shit!' Daniel shouted, clouting Leon right back. 'Picking on women? That's about your mark, isn't it, you *tosser*.'

Leon was actually grinning through his mask of blood. 'Got the hots for her, aintcha?' he taunted.

Daniel hit him again. Leon went reeling back, then straightened, spitting out a tooth, and the grin dropped from his face. He waded back in, throwing vicious lefts and rights, forcing Daniel to retreat.

Daniel was on that weak patch now.

She could hear the floor creaking and groaning under Daniel's weight.

'Daniel, don't!' she shrieked, and caught his fist on the backward swing and with all her remaining strength *pulled* him back toward her, off that weakened section of board.

Daniel staggered back, and Leon saw his chance. He leapt forward, *thundered* forward, toward his older brother, to finish the job.

The wood didn't groan this time; it splintered with an ear-splitting *crack*. Leon looked down in bewilderment. Then, just as he tried to move, to save himself, the floor opened up beneath him, shreds of rotted wood falling away, and he fell.

114

When Leon's body hit the floor fifty feet below, there was only a dull, final *thud.* Up in the bell tower, Daniel and Daisy stood frozen, staring at each other. Then, slowly, Daniel leaned over and looked down through the gaping hole in the floorboards. Catching at his arm for support, Daisy looked too.

Leon was stretched out on the slabs down below, spread-eagled like a starfish. A slowly expanding pool of blood was seeping out around his head, staining the stones dark red.

Daisy drew back, thinking she was about to throw up. Her arm hurt. Her knees too. She was shivering with the aftermath of fear. She sat down gingerly beneath the window. Carefully stepping away from the hole in the rotted section of floor, Daniel slumped down beside her. He was breathing hard. They both sat there for long moments, exhausted, wrung out.

'I thought you were dead,' said Daniel finally, when he could speak.

'He was going to kill me,' Daisy managed to say. 'He wanted this. Brayfield. Eunice told him that my father was his, too . . .'

'I know. She told Ruby, and Ruby filled us in,' said Daniel tiredly.

He leaned his head back against the stones. His knuckles were red-raw from the fight, his suit spattered with blood. When he looked at Daisy his eyes were full of despair. 'This is going to do Mum in,' he said. 'Leon was always her favourite. We all knew it.'

'Maybe she actually *loved* my father. Maybe that's why she thought Leon was so special.'

'Who knows?' said Daniel. 'I only hope my dad was none the wiser.'

Daisy turned her head and looked at him. Her eyes filled with tears. 'Leon said he told Harry all about it, right before he died.'

'Christ.' Daniel put a battered hand to his eyes, his face contorted with pain.

'I'm sorry,' said Daisy.

'It's not your fault.' He wiped angrily at his eyes, dropped his hands. 'Thanks for telling me the truth.'

Daniel clambered to his feet. He held out a hand and Daisy stood up, too.

'We've got to get out of here,' he said, indicating with a nod of the head the hole through which his brother had quit this life. 'And we've got to tidy the mess away down there. Listen, Daise – when we get down to the bottom, go straight over to the house and tell Fats to come here. And then stay there, upstairs with Jody and the kids. OK? Don't come back out. I'll tell you when it's all clear.' Daisy nodded. She knew how this must be hurting him. Leon was his brother.

'Daniel,' said Daisy.

'What?'

'Thanks,' she said, and leaned forward and brushed a kiss against his cheek.

'Come on,' he said, drawing back. Then he took her hand and carefully led the way back to the stairs, and down.

115

When Daisy, Daniel and Fats got back from Brayfield, Ruby fell on her daughter with a cry of relief.

'I was so frightened when they said you were with Leon! Are you all right?' Ruby crushed Daisy to her in a tight hug.

'I'm fine,' said Daisy, but Ruby's hug hurt her bruised, aching body and she had to suppress a flinch of pain. Her arm where Leon had struck her throbbed hotly; tomorrow it would be black with bruising, she knew it.

Kit was looking thunderous. 'Where is he?' he asked Daniel, taking in his bloodstained knuckles and bruised face. 'What the hell happened to you?'

'We had a fight,' said Daniel. He glanced at Fats. 'Leon ran off after that. He knows the shit's hit the fan, boss. He won't come back.'

Daisy looked at Daniel, the awful secret thrumming in the air between them. Daniel looked away.

Leon's dead.

And Daniel killed him.

'Things been OK here?' asked Daisy, trying not to meet Daniel's eyes, trying to act as if everything was normal when in fact she felt shaken to her core. But Daniel had told her before they left Brayfield, *say nothing.* Even Fats had been sworn to secrecy, and to her surprise he had agreed to that. She didn't know what he and Daniel had done with Leon's dead body. She didn't even *want* to. It could just as easily have been her, or Daniel, laid out dead at the bottom of that tower. The very idea was enough to make her shiver.

'Mum and me got hauled into the nick for questioning,' said Kit.

Daisy stared at him. 'No,' she said faintly. 'Oh *no*.'

But Kit was smiling. 'Yes, Daise,' he told her, amused as always by Daisy's attitude. Kit and Ruby might be into all sorts, but Daisy? She never got involved in the business. 'We were questioned about the warehouse robbery. And we know nothing about it, do we? So we were released without charge.'

Kit was thinking that they'd got off lightly. Surprisingly so. Their insider, DS Harman, had conducted the interview with some green DC beside him. There had been no sign of DI Kane, and Kit wondered about that. Had Romilly put Harman in there deliberately? Maybe she *knew* about Harman being Kit's man, and knew that because of that he'd pull his punches. In which case, Kit was being shielded. It was an interesting thought.

'Leon's up to his neck in all this,' said Kit. 'He's in tight with Patrick Dowling. So I want him found. And so do Old Bill.'

116

Patrick Dowling was finally spilling the beans. Well, some. Not about the money. That had been divvied up, shared out, and he said he didn't know where his partners in the warehouse crime had gone with it. Upcountry or abroad, most likely. He had devised the raid, hired a crew. Planted the seed of misdirected suspicion by having one of the gang name Thomas Knox during the raid. He could give more names, to lessen his own sentence, if they wanted him to. They did. He gave the names.

'You had your nephew shoot Clive Lewis and Robert Hinton,' said Romilly, as she sat in the interview room across the table from Patrick.

Her shoulders ached with tension and she could feel the gnawing onset of another stress headache, but she was ignoring it, surging ahead because this had been her goal for weeks, and now she was nailing Patrick Dowling's fat arse once and for all.

'All right. I admit it. I wanted Hinton out of the way because he'd found out about the drugs operation. At the same time, Lewis was getting too chicken to go on with what he was doing, the situation was heating up, and me and Leon thought he might tell your lot. We were certain Rob Hinton was going to tell his boss Miller about it, so yes, I had my nephew do the job on both of them.'

'Three shots fired,' said DC Paddick, a gangly hawk-nosed young man, who was sitting in. 'Who'd the shooter miss, Patrick?'

'You don't have to answer that,' said his brief, a bald, angular man wearing heavy black-rimmed glasses.

'What fucking difference is it going to make now?' Patrick huffed. He turned his attention back to Romilly. 'John was meant to get Miller too. Clear him right out and make way for me to take over that side of town. He said there was a puff of wind and he missed. He'd have taken another shot at it, but Miller was on the move, coming toward him, so there wasn't time.'

'Where is your nephew now, Patrick?' asked Paddick.

'Fuck knows.' Patrick took out a handkerchief and dabbed at his brow. His face was brick-red with tension. His eyes looked defeated.

'The Barnes gun club gave your address as his, too,' said Romilly.

'That peculiar fucker don't live anywhere. He drifts around the country. I don't have an address for him. If I want to get in touch with him, I contact my brother Bill and if John rings him – which don't happen often – then Bill can pass on that I want to get in touch, and John contacts me.'

'Him and your brother, they're not close?' asked Paddick.

'You're fucking joking! Broken home, that. John's mother scarpered when he was nine. Bill's a drinker. Think he was knocking that poor cow Abigail about, but I can't prove it. Maybe the kid too, who knows? Maybe that's what sent the lad over the edge.'

Fuck, thought Romilly. They were in for a nationwide search for the shooter.

'He's still going to do it,' said Patrick.

Romilly and Paddick stared at his face.

'I hired him to do the three. The weird little bastard has this compulsive nature, d'you see? I gave him twenty grand at the start, but refused to pay him the other twenty because he'd only half done the job. He got two of the three, but he missed Miller. So he'll be looking to finish Miller off. He don't give up until he's *done*, you see. Never.'

Romilly and the DC exchanged looks.

'You're sure there's no one he'd get in contact with? No girlfriends? Male friends? Anything?' asked Paddick.

Patrick was silent, bushy brows drawn down over his bloodshot eyes. He shook his big high-coloured head.

'This is important,' said Romilly. 'Think. If Miller gets hit, that'll increase your sentence – you'll go down as the instigator of three murders.'

Patrick chewed his lip and then said: 'He turns up for our mum's birthday. Or he used to. His gran raised him after Abigail left, he didn't want to stop with his dad.'

'When's her birthday, Patrick?' asked Romilly.

'March fifteenth.'

Next Saturday.

'Give me her address,' said Romilly, and he did.

Then she formally charged him.

117

The killer was sitting in his hired VW Beetle as he watched Romilly Kane come out of the police station, get in her car, and drive away. It was almost sad, that he was going to have to wipe out Miller when she seemed to be so keen on him. But there you go, that was life. Get involved with people and it's certain you're going to get hurt.

He had his place all sorted out. Time to finish the job. Complete his contract.

Romilly tracked Kit down next day to his office behind Sheila's restaurant.

'Can I have a word?' she asked.

Kit nodded to Fats, who went outside and closed the door behind him. Kit, sitting behind his desk, looked up at her expectantly.

'Quite the little empire you got here,' she said.

'Pays the bills,' said Kit. 'Take a seat. What can I do for you, detective?'

Romilly sat down, took out a notebook and pen from her bag. 'You can tell me where you go, what you do.'

'What?'

'Do you have a set routine? Would someone be able to watch you, and know that at a certain time you were going to be at a certain place?'

Kit sat back and stared at her.

'I'm not looking to trap you, Mr Miller,' she said when the silence dragged on. 'I'm trying to keep you alive.'

'Why?' he asked, standing up and coming round the desk.

'Why?' *Stay on the other side of the desk, for God's sake.* 'Because you're a citizen and I'm a copper. It's my duty to protect you.'

'What about Patrick Dowling?' asked Kit.

'We've charged him and he won't get bail. As for the rest of the gang who were involved in the warehouse robbery, there's an alert out on the lot of them. We've rounded up a couple already.'

'And the missing money?'

'Some of it. Not much.' This annoyed Romilly no end. She liked things tidy. She wanted all of the gang and all of the money. She suspected she wasn't going to get either. 'The problem we have at the moment is tracing the shooter Patrick hired to take out Clive Lewis, Robert Hinton and you. It's Patrick's nephew: John Dowling. It seems he won't give up until you're dead. And here I am, trying to prevent that and catch his arse at the same time. So tell me, where do you go on a regular basis? Where would anyone *know* where to find you at any given time? Here, for instance. Do you keep regular times here?'

Kit shook his head. 'I suppose so.'

'Mr Miller, what I believe is this: John Dowling is going to stake you out somewhere you go regularly. So come on. Help me out.'

Kit stared at her. 'Your hair's different.'

'You what?'

'You're wearing it down. Not tied back.'

'So?'

'It looks nice.'

'Mr Miller . . .'

'How's the arm? I see the sling's off.'

'It's fine. Mending.'

'Mum's place,' said Kit.

'What?' Romilly was thrown.

'Mum's club in Soho. I go there every week on a Tuesday. Twelve o'clock.'

'For what purpose?'

'To see my mother and take her out to lunch,' said Kit. *And to wash a little money*, he thought.

'All right.' Romilly made a note. 'Anywhere else?'

'No. Clubs, restaurants, snooker halls – it's all hours.'

'I'm guessing John Dowling already knows that. There are shops opposite the burlesque club, that right?' Romilly trawled her memory for details. 'With flats above them?'

Kit shook his head. 'Some of them are never used. Thought of buying a couple and coining the rent, once. Some are used as stock rooms. Don't think anybody lives up there.'

'That's a gift for him. He'll probably be up in one of those and pretty soon he'll take his shot at you.'

'There's a word I don't like in there: "probably". What if he doesn't? What if he thinks he'll pick me off somewhere else?'

'He might. This bloke's a perfectionist. He settles in, rehearses the shot, then takes it. And he doesn't do head shots. He goes for the chest, every time. That's the pattern. His MO. Our people say he'll stick to that, he won't vary.'

'And the only reason you're here, telling me all this, is because you're a copper and I'm a citizen. Right?'

'We have a safe house,' said Romilly, ignoring the question. 'Would you go there?'

'What – hide away?'

'Yes. Hide away.'

'No. I wouldn't do that.'

'Look . . .'

Romilly's voice trailed away as without warning he jerked her out of her seat and into his arms. 'Mr Miller,' she started lamely, feeling his hard muscularity weakening her resolve, melting it like ice on a boiling hot day.

'Call me Kit.' He was lifting her hair now, kissing her throat.

'Kit.' She had to suppress a moan as his teeth nipped at her ear, his hot breath scorching her skin.

'Yes, honey?' He raised his head and grinned into her eyes.

'This is serious,' she said. 'And I think we should both concentrate.'

'I *am* concentrating. On seducing you.'

'Mr Miller.' Her voice was sharper now.

'I told you: Kit.'

'Stop it. That's *enough.*' Romilly broke free of his embrace and stepped back. She was trying to breathe steadily and failing. Dismally, she was aware that her face was flushed and her nipples were rigid. If she sat back down, she might just burn a hole in the seat. 'Let's return to the subject in hand, shall we?'

'OK. Right.' Kit sighed. 'But can we do this and walk at the same time? I got places I got to be.'

'Yeah, sure.' It would be a relief, not to be in an enclosed space with him.

Kit led the way out of the office and into the main body of the restaurant, where waiting staff were starting to set up the tables ready for lunch. Fats fell into step behind Romilly as Kit went over to the big glassed front door. On either side of the door, there were massive plate-glass windows so that prospective diners could look in and see what a buzzing place it was.

As Kit opened the door, the plate-glass window on his left exploded.

118

It was pandemonium for minutes after the window blew in. Glass sprayed out over the whole of the restaurant, waitresses screamed, tables were knocked over, glassware was dropped, crockery smashed, cutlery was hitting the floor. Then a series of small pops, and suddenly Kit knew what this was.

It was *him*. That twisted bastard John Dowling hadn't set himself up opposite Ruby's club; he was somewhere over the road right here.

Kit dived for the floor, dragging Romilly with him. His skin was crawling as he waited for one of the shots to find him. He could feel Romilly's body crushed beneath his chest, but he didn't dare move, take his weight off her.

He got a flashback of Rob, lying half-dead and blood-spattered outside the church.

Ah Christ, no. Nobody else. Please.

The pops stopped suddenly. There was a shocked silence, then one of the waitresses started to cry.

'Everyone all right?' Kit called out. 'Stay down. Don't move.'

'You OK boss?' said Fats.

'Yeah. I'm fine.' Kit moved his position a fraction, glass crunching underneath him, a shard of it stinging his palm as he shifted his weight to let Romilly draw breath. 'Romilly?'

She wasn't talking. Her eyes were closed.

'Romilly?' he said urgently. There were shards of glass in her hair. 'Jesus! *Romilly.*'

She was very still. Kit felt panic starting to rise in his airways, compressing his chest.

Then her eyes flicked open. 'Has it stopped?' she asked.

'I think so. You hurt?'

'No, I think I'm OK.'

Thank Christ.

'Everyone all right?' Kit called.

One by one, the girls answered. They were OK.

Romilly was trying to sit up.

'Not yet,' said Kit. 'Everyone – crawl to the back wall and then into the office. Don't stand up.'

They all started to move over the broken glass, toward the back, out of sight of the shooter. Once they were all in the office, Romilly phoned in to the nick to raise the alarm.

119

It was shocking for Daniel, seeing the damage that Leon had done to Eunice's face. There was a ragged-looking purple cut over her left eyebrow, and the area all around it was blackened by bruising. She looked subdued, as well she might, as she poured him a cup of tea in the kitchen. She didn't have her usual make-up on, and it made her look her age. Finally she sat down with him at the table and Daniel braced himself, because for the first time in his life, he knew he was going to have to lie to his mother.

'Have you seen Leon?' she said, straight away.

'Recently? No. And I'm not likely to. He's run off. If he hadn't, he'd have gone down with Patrick.'

'Yeah, but he must come back sometime, mustn't he?' she asked, and it hurt Daniel to see the pitiful hope in her eyes.

No, he won't, because I killed him.

'Mum.' Daniel shook his head. 'He can't come back. He won't. He wouldn't dare. If the cops don't get him, Kit will. He wants Leon's arse roasted over a slow fire.'

'But he—'

Anger started to take hold of Daniel. He hated this. Telling her lies. Concealing the truth. But he had to. He had no choice.

'Listen, will you?' he said sharply. 'Leon was working with Patrick. They were running the drugs, building up their money, getting everything in place for a takeover. They were going to kill Kit to get him out of the way. And the photographer, because he was a weak link. And Rob, because he'd got wise to what they were doing and he was going to blow the whistle on them. Together they were planning to grab Kit's manor. So no. Leon won't be back. Not now. Not *ever*.'

Eunice started to cry.

Daniel handed her a handkerchief and she dabbed at her eyes, wincing as she touched the left one.

'I'm sorry,' he said more gently.

'It isn't your fault,' she sniffed.

Yeah, it is.

Eunice was blinking, her eyes red-rimmed and sorrowful as she gazed at Daniel. She heaved a heartfelt sigh.

'You're a good boy,' she said shakily.

'I'm not,' he said.

'Yes, you are. I think that really, you were always the best of the three. The steady one. The *good* one.'

Daniel shrugged and took a mouthful of tea, feeling uncomfortable. Oh yeah, he was good all right. Lusting after one brother's wife, and killing the other one. Yeah, he was a prince among men.

'You're all I've got now,' said Eunice, managing a watery smile. 'Oh, I've still got the girls, but you're my only boy. And I don't think you ever got the attention you deserved.'

There was the noise of a motor outside, then someone started hammering at the front door.

'Now who's that?' said Eunice tiredly.

Daniel got up from the table and went through the hall and opened the door.

Ashok was standing there.

'What the fuck?' asked Daniel.

'We got to get over to Sheila's. Someone's taken a shot at Kit.'

120

Next day, Daniel was sitting in the hall chair reading a paper when Daisy came down the stairs. She hesitated at the foot of them and looked at him. He kept his eyes on the paper, but Daisy *knew* he was aware of her standing there.

'Daniel?' she said.

He kept reading. 'What?' he asked.

Daisy walked over to where he sat. She took hold of the paper and pushed it down. Daniel looked up at her. His face was cut and bruised and Daisy felt such a wave of compassion for him that it nearly swamped her. He'd fought for her. Rescued her. But now he wouldn't even *talk* to her, and that hurt her beyond belief.

'Something the matter?' he asked.

'Yes, there's something the matter,' said Daisy. 'It's *this*. It's the way you are with me. I don't like it. How long are you going to keep this up? I'd really like to know.'

'I'm doing my job,' said Daniel. 'You're my boss's sister and I'm looking out for you. Nothing's changed.'

He stood up, tossed the paper onto the chair, brushing past her.

'Wait! Where are you going?'

He was walking away from her, heading for the kitchen. Ignoring her, like he always did now.

'Daniel, *please*!' Daisy ran after him and caught his arm. She stepped around him, looked up at his face.

'What?' he asked. But he was like a block of wood. She couldn't touch him. Couldn't reach him.

She gulped and tried again, her eyes pleading as humiliating tears started to flow.

'Daniel . . .' she said faintly.

'What? Daisy, I've got things to do.'

'Look,' she said. 'I know I'm a pain. I know I'm one of those stupid bloody addictive personalities, that I need a crutch sometimes just to get through the days. Something bad happens – something *terrible*, like Rob being snatched away the way he was, like this *maniac* trying to get to Kit – and I crumble. I *know* that.'

'He didn't succeed,' Daniel pointed out, but yesterday had been a nasty shock for them all. When they'd got to Shelia's and seen the extent of the damage, and learned that John Dowling had targeted Kit again and got away, everyone had felt just that little bit less safe.

'But he *could* have succeeded. Daniel – I know everyone thinks of me as crazy Daisy – if it's not drugs it's the drink . . .' Hot colour flooded into her cheeks. 'But please, please – don't turn your back on me like this,' she whispered in desperation.

She'd got through to him at last. She could see it, straight away.

Daniel blinked, swallowed. Looked away, then back at her face.

'I won't do that. I never would.'

Daisy nodded and bit her lip. 'You promise?'

'I promise.'

'Good. I'm so glad,' she said, and he went off into the kitchen, where Ruby was making coffee.

121

'Has something happened with you and Daniel?' Ruby asked Daisy five minutes later. 'He just shot through here and out the back door without a word to me.'

They were sitting in the kitchen, drinking their coffee. Daisy started nervously and looked at her mother in surprise.

'What?' she said.

'There's been an atmosphere between the two of you that you could cut with a knife. What's going on?'

'Nothing. You're imagining things,' said Daisy, standing up and pacing restlessly.

She'd hated being at odds with Daniel. She had come to depend on him. She felt *safe* with him around. Daniel the overlooked one, the forgotten middle son. How had she not seen him before, solid and dependable as an oak? How had she not known how valuable, how *precious* a person he truly was?

'I want the twins back soon,' she said.

'Not yet,' said Ruby.

'When then?'

'Look, Daisy – Patrick Dowling may be safely banged up, but his nephew's still on the loose. He tried to get Kit again yesterday. And have you forgotten? Leon's still out there somewhere.'

Daisy had a horrible vision of Leon, eyes wild with fear, falling through the rotting boards in the bell tower.

'Kit's no fool. If the police don't work this out, he will.'

'But he's stepping into dangerous territory. If only Rob was here . . .' she stopped speaking. 'Sorry,' she said.

Daisy's innards were creased with pain as she thought of Rob. Her love, lost to her forever. And . . . it hurt, that she hadn't really known him. Understood him. Seen the pressures he was under.

'The shooter's still out there,' said Ruby. 'He's still after Kit. He still hasn't fulfilled his contract.'

'It'll be all right,' said Daisy, taking her mother's hand.

'Do you believe that?' Ruby shook her head. 'Because you know what? I don't.'

122

That evening, Ruby was meeting Thomas at the Savoy, their usual placc. Monday night. She wasn't really in the mood. There would be dinner, followed by sex in a suite of rooms he would have booked in advance. This was the way it always went, for them. Here she was, fulfilling her usual role of mistress. She'd never – unlike Big Tits – been accorded the status of *wife*.

No one had ever asked her to marry them. She was clearly mistress material, and the men in her life had always seen her that way. Now . . . frankly, it grated. What was wrong with her, that no one had so much as *asked* her to be their missus? Other women had to beat marriage proposals off with a stick. Why not *her*?

'You're not up for this tonight, are you?' asked Thomas over dinner.

Ruby had been quiet, saying little. She put down her knife and fork – the steak was fine, but tonight it almost choked her. 'Worried about Kit,' she shrugged. *And thinking that this is going nowhere.*

'He's a big boy,' said Thomas.

'Rob Hinton was a big boy too. He's dead.'

'Anything I can do?'

'Nothing.' Ruby started eating again. Soon, she put her

knife and fork together, drank some champagne. Let out a sigh.

Thomas put his knife and fork down too. His dinner was only half-eaten.

'Not you too?' said Ruby.

'Fact is . . .' said Thomas.

'Fact is, what?'

'I have some news. And I thought I ought to tell you. I wouldn't have told you tonight had I thought we were going anywhere this evening, but clearly we're not.'

'What news?'

'Chloe's pregnant. I went out yesterday and bought her the Mercedes she'd always wanted, to celebrate.'

Ruby put down her glass. 'Oh. Right.' Pregnant! And he'd bought her a car. *Lovely*, she thought sourly. Then she had a vision of the car speeding through the crem grounds, heading for Kit and the detective inspector. But . . . *she* had been walking right behind them. And Big Tits was a demented cow.

'What was her old car?' she asked.

'Vauxhall Cavalier. She hated the thing.' The car at the crem was a BMW.

Ruby sat back, her dinner forgotten, staring at his face. Once, she had almost believed herself in love with him. But that was the past, and now . . . things were different. Much as she disliked the bumptious tart, how could she go on with this if Chloe was expecting a child? *She'd* been treated badly as a pregnant mother, and there was no way she could inflict that on someone else. Not even Big Tits.

'So . . . I don't want her upset,' he said.

'Of course.'

'I think we should maybe cool things off a bit.'

'What, until after the baby's born? Then it's game on again?' asked Ruby.

'Rubes . . .' he said, shaking his head, catching the sarcasm in her voice.

Ruby placed both hands, palms down, on the tabletop. 'Of course that's not a problem you have with me, is it? I'm right in the menopause, no chance of a pregnancy with *this* lady.'

'Come on, Ruby . . .'

'No, I appreciate what you're telling me. She's your wife. That's something special. Although, at your age? A kid's going to run you ragged.'

'We can still be friends.'

'I'm not interested in being your friend, Thomas. In fact, I'm not even interested in being your mistress any more.' Ruby gathered up her bag, pushed back her chair, stood up. 'It's been fun, revisiting this thing of ours. But truthfully? It's been over for a while. And now? It's *really* over.'

123

Romilly had a trip to make. En route, she detoured to her local pub, took a little nosey around the car park at the back, then resumed her journey. She drove through nose-to-tail traffic until she was out past Barking and Rainham on the A13. At last the countryside opened up in front of her, green and lush. She kept her foot to the floor until she reached Southend-on-Sea, then she turned in when she reached a row of Victorian semis. She got out of the car, opened a squeaky little gate, hearing the screaming of seagulls and smelling the ozone-fresh tang of the ocean. She walked over tan and black tiles up to a blue-painted front door, and rang the bell.

A young man with a black beard opened the door. Romilly flashed her warrant card at him, and he ushered her inside. She followed him along a short passageway and then left into a lounge decked out in black leather sofas with red cushions to match the curtains at the big sash window that looked out onto a fence at the side of the property.

A tall, dark and broad-shouldered man in white shirt and faded jeans was standing in front of the window, sunlight streaming in on him, making his black hair gleam. He half-turned when she entered the room. The younger man withdrew, pulling the door closed behind him.

'Well,' said Romilly. 'You look pretty bloody lively. Considering you were supposed to be a corpse by now.'

'Thanks,' said Kit. He glanced around the room. 'Have to say, your safe house ain't all that.'

She shrugged. 'It's a safe house. We're not entering it for the Home of the Year. Sorry if it's not up to your usual high standards. How are you?'

'Bored,' said Kit, coming over to where she stood. 'He got away again. He was *right there*.'

Within a quarter of an hour of her phoning in to the incident room, police had been swarming all over the restaurant and the streets outside and the buildings across the road. They'd found where John Dowling had almost certainly been firing from, but he'd left no casings this time. The bullet that hit the plate-glass window had buried itself in the carpet about five inches from where Kit had been standing when he opened the door. If he hadn't turned back to look at Romilly at that instant, he'd have been toast.

'Good news is, John Dowling isn't certain whether he hit his mark or not. Hopefully, he thinks you're dead. We're certainly not going to disabuse him of that notion. The heat should be off, but the safe house is prudent,' said Romilly.

'I'm doing this under protest,' said Kit.

'Noted. But by being here you're not only protecting yourself, you're protecting all those people around you.'

'So what happens next?'

'We wait.'

Kit sighed. 'Oh, great.' He wanted to get his hands on that fucker so badly he could almost *taste* it now.

'Not for long,' said Romilly. 'Just over a week, that's all.'

'Right.'

'Let's take a stroll,' she said.

124

They walked along the beach, with the funfair in the distance, Ashok following twenty feet behind them. There were other people down this end, but not many. The wind was beyond bracing, it was bloody cold. The sea tossed and churned, gulls shrieking as they hovered above the crashing waves, riding the foam-flecked wind.

'You're quiet,' said Kit, picking up a stone and throwing it into the sea.

'Hm? Yeah.' Romilly was watching him. Alive and well, and bent as a hairpin. His minder strolling along at a distance behind them, stopping when they stopped, walking when they walked. 'Shook me up, that business at the restaurant. Never been actually *fired* on before. And I thought he'd got you. I really did.'

'Were you sorry about it? Devastated? Cut to the quick?'

Romilly had to smile at that.

'You're pretty when you smile.'

'Where'd you find that chat-up line? In a Christmas cracker?'

'Detective.' Kit caught her arm and pulled her in closer, shielding her from the ferocious wind with his body. They were face to face suddenly, his eyes locked with hers. 'God's sake, Romilly . . .'

'Don't you fucking dare kiss me again,' she said.

Kit grinned. 'Why? What you going to do about it?'

'I told you the first time. I don't forget, and I don't forgive. Remember?' Behind them, she could see Ashok standing still, looking around. Watching Kit's back.

'Yeah? Well maybe I'll risk it,' he said, and did.

When he drew away from her, Romilly's eyes were closed.

'Not so bad, eh?' he whispered against her mouth.

'Shut up,' she said, and he kissed her again.

Finally, Kit drew back. He carried on walking. So did Ashok. After a moment's hesitation, Romilly followed in Kit's footsteps, thinking of her dad's words. *A real man. Tough as bullets.*

Shit, this was bad.

It was also the most excitement she'd had in about a zillion years.

'You ever see that old film, *Get Carter*? They shot him on a beach, right at the end,' said Kit.

'That was a head shot.'

'That's right.'

'No one besides my DCI and me – and laughing boy back there – knows you're here. And no one followed me here.'

'We could go back to the house,' said Kit. 'The bed's pretty comfy.'

'I came down to touch base with you, that's all, not to jump your bones.'

'Shame.'

'And to say it's on for Saturday at Grandma Dowling's place.'

'He *always* shows up there on her birthday? You're sure?'

'Always, according to Patrick Dowling.'

'Good luck with that then. Oh – and I've got something for you,' said Kit.

He dug in his jacket pocket, pulled out a 7.62 spent shell casing and dropped it into her hand.

'You did take it. I knew it,' she said.

'Guilty,' said Kit with a grin. 'Now, about the bed . . .'

125

'I shouldn't be doing this,' said Romilly.

'No, you shouldn't,' Kit agreed. He bit her ear, quite hard. 'You are a very, *very* bad girl.'

'Ow,' Romilly complained, smiling and rolling over to snuggle in to his chest.

Kit had sent Ashok out so they'd have the place to themselves. Then they'd gone upstairs and Romilly had suddenly felt as shy, as uncertain, as a teenager.

'What am I doing?' she asked him.

'You want to change your mind? The door's right there. No pressure.'

She didn't want to change her mind. This had been building between them for weeks, and it was at boiling point now. Desire had wrestled with sense for too long. Romilly shook her head. Kit kissed her, and before long they were tearing at each other's clothes, and then they were both naked, devouring each other with a passion that took them both by surprise. Sex with Kit Miller was nothing like it had been with lazy, laid-back, soft-bodied Hugh; sex with Kit was like being put into a washing machine on fast spin. The man was an *animal* in bed, cheerfully lustful and yet at the same time oddly tender.

Now they lay together, exhausted.

Romilly propped herself up on one elbow and stared down at him, when she finally got her breath back.

'You're too damned good-looking for your own good,' she pointed out.

'You're a hard cow.'

'Also, you're a bastard.'

'Yeah, I think we're quits,' said Kit, smiling and pulling her in for another kiss.

'I can't believe I'm doing this,' she breathed.

She'd fantasized about this, but really? She'd never believed that it would actually happen, never believed that she would ever *let* it. Yes, she'd fancied him like crazy almost since their first meeting. They'd been flirting, both enjoying the thrill of the chase, the forbidden nature of what was threatening to happen, but had either one of them ever truly believed that this was a viable relationship?

Romilly winced as she thought of his file down the nick. The list of his possible failings as a model citizen was lengthy. Racketeering, money laundering, intimidation, sale of stolen goods, income tax evasion, failure to report off-shore accounts and holdings. Oh, and the possible murder of Tito Danieri – which, granted, had never been proved. Kit was a very bad man, and hadn't she always been a straight-down-the-line copper? Hadn't she always been unshakable in her honesty and her devotion to her job, delighting in bringing criminals to justice?

Yes, she had. Yet here she was now, naked in bed with a gangster.

'I ought to go,' she said, drawing back from him.

'Mm,' said Kit, kissing her again. He slapped her bare arse, hard, and sat up. 'Come on, detective, let's grab a shower if all this is still tormenting you so much. Shame. I was hoping for round two.'

He'd picked up on her thought processes again. Romilly

sat up too, ran a hand down his hard-muscled arm, kissed his shoulder. He smelled *so* good. And he was so dangerously appealing.

'Kit . . .' she started.

'What? You going to tell me this can't go anywhere? I already got the message.'

'I'm a copper.'

'I got that too.'

'In any other circumstances . . .'

'I know.' He turned his head, kissed her very gently. 'Don't stress over it. Come on. Shower.'

126

On Thursday, Romilly phoned the shooter's grandmother to ask if she could drop in. On Friday, Romilly and DC Phillips called on her. Romilly flashed her warrant card and asked to come in. Phillips followed suit. Looking bewildered, the old lady led them through to a richly ornamented front room, stuffed with seaside memorabilia, old tea sets in display cabinets, and piles of old newspapers. On the mantelpiece there was a pile of brightly coloured envelopes. Birthday cards, Romilly thought. For tomorrow.

The old lady cleared a space on an Ercol sofa for them to sit, and took her blanket-covered chair by the gas fire. The very first thing out of her mouth stopped both Romilly and DC Phillips in their tracks.

'This isn't about that girl on the news, is it? The dancer?' she asked, frowning at them with anxious eyes.

Romilly and Phillips exchanged a glance.

'Why do you say that?' asked Romilly.

'You said you wanted to talk about my grandson John. His dad's a nutter, you know. I won't even let him over the threshold. Haven't for years. *Is* it about the girl?'

Romilly chose her words carefully. 'Would you please explain why you would say that?' The woman puffed out her cheeks in a sigh. 'Oh God,' she said.

'I'm sorry about this,' said Romilly, and she truly was.

Poor old girl, not much in her life except the occasional family visit, and after tomorrow there wouldn't even be that to look forward to. But appearances could be deceptive. The woman could be covering for her grandson. John Dowling could be upstairs right now, listening to them down here talking. Who knew? Romilly wanted to look around the place. Suss it out. 'Do you have a bathroom I could use?' she asked.

'Yes. Upstairs, first on the landing,' said the old lady.

Romilly shot DC Phillips a glance. *Keep her talking.*

She went up the stairs and pushed open the loo door, closing it loudly. Quietly, she moved along the landing, opened another door, then another. Down below, she could hear Phillips making conversation with the old lady, keeping her busy. She walked into what looked like the master bedroom, taking it all in. A single bed, a dressing table. Everything old, dusty, out of fashion by thirty years. She crossed to the window and looked out. Someone was keeping the back lawn cut, anyway. A neighbour perhaps. It looked neat enough but for a depression or two in the grass, and the flower borders were weed-free.

Romilly went out of the master bedroom, and into the loo. She flushed the chain, rinsed her hands before returning downstairs. She smiled at the old lady and sat down again beside DC Phillips.

'Your garden looks nice,' she said. 'Who does it for you?'

'My son Bill used to. But since I won't have him in the place now, the council send blokes round. Ex-offenders or something. Never the same lot twice.'

'Mrs Dowling, if you can tell us what you mean about your son Bill, that would help. You're saying he – John's father – is a nutter? What do you mean by that?' she said.

'He's not right in the head.' The woman stood up shakily, took a couple of steps to the mantelpiece and took down a framed photograph. She handed it to Romilly. It was a picture of a smiling red-haired woman holding a tiny sand-coloured dog in her arms. There was a big man, surly faced, standing beside her, and in front of them was a young boy.

John, thought Romilly. There was something in his eyes, something feral, something *wrong*.

'John's dad used to get drunk, raging drunk, and beat up his wife. My son! He's a bastard, and it was a nasty business.' The old woman's mouth trembled. 'I liked Abigail. She was all right. Used to have a cute little dog – a lapdog they call them, don't they? A chihuahua. There she is. Kiki, Abi named her. Sweet little thing. She doted on that dog. Then one day he said she'd left, run away. John was only young at the time. About nine, I suppose. Left, my arse. *I* knew the truth. I still do.'

'What is the truth, Mrs Dowling?'

'We were friendly, me and Abi, very close. She wouldn't have just run off and not told me where she was going. I think . . . I think he killed her.'

Christ, thought Romilly. 'So he was violent in the relationship?' she asked.

'Yes, he was. Poor little cow'd be black and blue, time and again. Don't know how she stuck it. Maybe because she had the kid. But I'm telling you, *he* ain't right either. He's like his dad, dead behind the eyes. After Abi went, John used to stay over here with me, a lot. I practically raised him. But I knew John wasn't the full shilling. When I saw that about the missing girl on the news, and they showed a picture of that man walking through the club with her, I knew it was him. I just *knew*. I couldn't tell on him though, could I? He's *family*.'

There was a long silence, broken only by the ticking of the clock on the mantelpiece. Romilly stood up and replaced the framed print up there. Then she turned to the old lady.

'We have to talk to him, Mrs Dowling. And he'll be here tomorrow, won't he?'

The old lady nodded. 'He never misses.'

'In that case I'll be here too. And Mrs Dowling?'

'Yes?'

'I'm sure you can see now that this is urgent. We have to stop him. We can't let what happened to Crystal Rose ever happen to anybody else. So this has to be between us. A secret. All right?'

The old woman sighed, and nodded. 'Yeah. All right.'

127

On Saturday morning, the street outside Mrs Dowling's house was staked out. To all appearances, it was just another Saturday, cars parked up, people walking their dogs, mowing their lawns, nothing to see. But in some of those cars there were police officers, and an innocent-looking van along the road was packed with the armed officers.

'He comes around eleven and stays for lunch,' Mrs Dowling had told Romilly the day before. Now it was eleven o'clock, and no John.

Everyone was getting fidgety. Perhaps the old lady had tipped off the bastard? DC Phillips suggested as she sat in one of the yard's rusty undercover cars with Romilly, both of them anxiously watching the house.

'She wouldn't,' said Romilly, although she wasn't entirely sure. 'She thinks the bloke's a creep like his dad and that's he's done Crystal Rose just like his dad did his mum. She was literally *shuddering* with disgust when we spoke to her, wasn't she. No. She wouldn't do it.'

She wanted – *so* badly – to feel this bastard John Dowling's collar, to haul him down to the nick and squeeze everything out of him, if it was the very last thing she ever did.

Christ, maybe it does run in the family, she thought. Bill the father was bad, according to the old lady. And the son too.

And as John Dowling had already killed more than once, well, didn't they say it got easier? Thinking of that blank-eyed boy in the photograph, she knew that they had to shut him down, once and for all. She glanced at her watch. Fuck! Ten past eleven. Where the hell was he?

'Ma'am,' said Phillips.

He was there.

John Dowling had pulled up in a yellow VW Beetle and was now walking toward his gran's property. Phillips was talking into the radio, telling everyone the target was here. Then Romilly and Phillips slumped down in their seats. John Dowling, triple murderer and sharpshooter. Fuck, this time they *had* to get him.

Romilly watched him, thinking how strange it was, that a man so elegantly dressed, pin-neat, actually fairly attractive with his dark hair and eyes, could in fact be such a loathsome monster underneath it all.

'We'd better . . .' she started, and then something happened.

There was the faintest of noises, and . . . 'What the fuck . . .?' asked Romilly.

John Dowling flinched – and collapsed.

128

DC Phillips was yelling into the radio, police were pouring out of vans. Romilly was hardly aware of jumping out of the car and running full pelt with Phillips over to where John Dowling lay.

Dowling was flat on his back and there was blood.

But . . . it wasn't on his chest. And there was only a little of it. Surprisingly little.

She knelt on the pavement beside him. His eyes were wide open, staring in surprise at the sky. And there, neatly placed at the centre of his forehead, was a bullet hole.

'Oh Christ . . .' gasped Romilly as other officers crowded around the corpse.

Somebody grabbed her arm and hauled her back to her feet.

'We have to clear the area,' someone said, and in a daze Romilly hurried back to the car.

She couldn't believe it.

They'd almost *had* the bastard.

And now someone had beaten them to it.

129

Two days after John Dowling breathed his last, Daniel drove Daisy down to Brayfield to collect the twins.

'I've missed them so much,' she told him as they turned into the gates, passing the disused gatehouse on their left. Daisy stared at it as they did so. 'Ma and Pa gave me that gatehouse. I used it once, had a wild party there and ended up in hospital.'

Daniel shot her a look.

'I know. I was young and I was extremely stupid and I was in a bit of a mess.'

'Like . . .?'

'I'd found out that Ruby was my mother, not Vanessa. That my father'd had an affair with Ruby. And that I was one of twins and Kit was my brother. It was a lot to take in. Too much, I think. I reacted badly.'

Daniel shot her another look. 'What, you? Don't believe it.'

Daisy started to smile. 'Are you mocking me?'

'Maybe a bit.'

'Well, don't,' said Daisy, but she was still smiling, when since Rob's death she had never believed she would smile again. It was so good, having Daniel back at her side.

The car shot on up the driveway. Daniel parked it beside

the circular fountain of Neptune, and switched off the engine. Daisy got out, and so did he.

'Can we walk for a bit? Would you mind?' she asked.

'I don't mind,' said Daniel, and they set off down the meandering path that led to the mausoleum and the lake.

On the way, they passed the bell tower. Daisy paused there, looking up, remembering that desperate struggle, remembering she had almost died that day. And instead, Leon had perished.

'Can I ask . . .?' she started, then hesitated.

'Don't.'

'I have to. What did you and Fats do with Leon?'

'You really want to know? You sure?'

'I'm sure,' she said.

Daniel walked on and Daisy fell into step with him. They went further, down to where it was mossy underfoot, where the cedars of Lebanon hung low over the pathway, forming a dark green tunnel that led to the family mausoleum. Daniel stopped there in front of it, gazing at the inscription over the pale marble doorway.

Hodie mihi, cras tibi

'What does it mean?' he asked her. 'Latin, is it?'

Daisy nodded, thinking that Rob would not have asked, even if the ancient text was puzzling him. Too afraid of showing his ignorance. Whereas Daniel didn't see anything wrong in admitting he didn't know a word of Latin. He really *was* more solid than Rob, more stable, less easily intimidated by class barriers.

'It means "Today me, tomorrow you",' she said, her face sad. 'In other words, we're all going to die. Those inside the crypt are dead now, but one day we will be, too.'

'That's fucking grim,' he said.

'It is. But it's a reason to live life to the full, isn't it. Grab it by the throat.' Daisy paused. 'Where is he, Daniel? Where is Leon?'

Daniel thrust his hands into his pockets and looked at the ground. 'You're sure . . .?' he asked.

'I want to know.'

Daniel nodded. Then he looked her in the eye. They were so like Rob's eyes. The same khaki green. But they were also completely different. Calmer. More accepting. Daisy looked into those eyes and realized she could tell Daniel anything and it wouldn't shake him. And that her wealthy background meant nothing to him. It neither worried nor enticed him, and that was so different to Rob's reaction.

'He always wanted to be part of Cornelius Bray's family,' said Daniel, his voice low. 'So we granted him his wish. He's sharing a coffin with his dad right now. In there.'

'Oh God,' said Daisy.

'You OK?'

'Yes. Fine.'

Daniel's eyes left her face, looked beyond her. 'Vanessa's spotted us. She's in the garden and she's got the kids with her. Jody too. You sure you're all right?'

Vanessa was calling her name. Daisy turned. Out there in the sunshine, beyond the shade of the darker borders, was Vanessa, a twin tugging at each hand, Jody running behind. Daisy waved. They all waved back.

'I'm OK,' she told Daniel, and realized, for the first time since losing Rob, that she really was.

'Good,' said Daniel, and followed steadily behind her as she led the way out onto the lawn.

130

Kit was down The Grapes in one of the private dining rooms round the back. Fats was at the door, Ashok out in the bar. Within ten minutes, the man arrived. He was grizzle-haired, hook-nosed; an elderly gent with a stooped back and with a hearing aid big as a plum protruding from one ear.

'Hiya,' said Fats, and ushered him into the room, moving back outside and closing the door behind him.

Kit stood up and walked over when the man came in. He shook his hand.

'All right, Peach?'

'Fine, fine,' said Peachy. Aside from loving Sinatra and collecting small arms and having once been an ace safe-cracker, Peachy was also ex-army, where he had been employed as a sniper. He might be deaf as a post now – as his wife Lil told anyone who would listen – but his hands were steady as rock, and his eyes were still sharp as an eagle's.

'Take a seat, Peach,' said Kit, and they sat down. 'Get you a drink?'

'Nah, too late in the evening for me, Mr Miller. Don't want to be up pissin' half the night.'

'OK, Peach. I just want to say, you done good. And thank you.'

'Scum like that, walkin' about,' said Peach in disgust. 'Old Bill gets them and then you have to keep the rotten twisted bastards in comfort for the rest of their natural? I don't see it, do you?'

'No,' said Kit. 'I don't.'

He pulled a brown envelope out of his jacket pocket.

'Five grand, as agreed. Plus a bonus.' He pushed the envelope over the table to Peachy.

'No need for that.' Peachy frowned as he picked up his payment.

'There's every need,' said Kit. 'Rob was my brother. My comrade. You understand that, I know you do. No one gets to wipe him out like that, and live.'

Peachy nodded. 'I'm grateful to you, Mr Miller.'

'Get Lil something nice, yeah?' Kit smiled.

'I'll get her a new bog, I reckon. She wants one of them "en suite" efforts put in. This'll cover it and some spare left over. Thanks.'

'No problems then?' asked Kit.

'It was a piece of piss,' said Peachy.

131

It wasn't exactly a perfect ending to proceedings, but it was neat so you couldn't complain.

'So that's that,' said Harman, sitting in Romilly's office, twirling back and forth on the swivel chair.

'Nearly,' said Romilly.

She was still royally pissed off about this. No prizes for guessing who'd beaten her to the draw on John Dowling. She'd almost handed it to Kit Miller on a plate; that was the most galling thing about it. She'd told him when the perp was going to be at his gran's place, and he had picked him off like something in a turkey shoot.

'We got Patrick Dowling,' said Harman, ticking items off on his stubby fingers. 'Several of the warehouse gang too. The money? Some of it, and there's more to come, more arrests to be made. That's ongoing, but it should be doable. We got our triple killer red-handed, with the gun tucked away in the back of that hired VW. All right, *someone* got him, but what the fuck, he's done for and that's a fucking relief to all concerned.'

Romilly nodded, doodling on a notepad, turning it all over in her head. Something about the whole thing was still bugging her, she didn't know what. She didn't like loose ends. She kept thinking of Patrick Dowling and his brother Bill, who the killer John had sometimes got in touch with.

Bill the drunken wife-beater. Then her thoughts turned to her own father, out in the garden, planting seeds in the greenhouse.

What is it? What's missing?

She couldn't get it, not yet. Irritating.

The phone rang, and she snatched it up. She listened, said, 'OK, sir,' and replaced the handset.

'DCI wants a word with us both,' she told Harman.

'Right,' said Harman, and they left her office and went off along the corridor, past the bigger open office where Phillips and Barry Jones and the others worked, and into the DCI's.

'Take a seat,' said James Barrow, ushering them in and going behind his desk. Romilly and Harman sat down. So did Barrow. Then he said: 'We're starting to wrap this up now. We want to find the shooter who wiped out *our* shooter, of course. Evidential checks are done on the Patrick Dowling case, and Crown Prosecution's happy to go ahead. And now – Harman – it's time we had a chat.'

132

Harman started in surprise at that last bit. 'What about?' he said.

'There's nothing worse than a bent copper,' said James Barrow, his eyes hard as they rested on Harman's face. 'And that's what you are. Isn't it?'

'*What?* I don't know—' said Harman.

'Spare me that,' snapped James, his voice rising to a shout. 'You hand in your warrant card today and clear your desk and then you fuck off out of it. You're off the force, pending enquiries. Now go home, out of my sight.'

'What the fuck . . .?' Harman's face was a picture of surprised dismay.

'You've been working as an informant for a criminal gang,' said James. 'And I'm not having it. Get out.'

Harman got to his feet; he looked almost dazed. Then he went out the door, slamming it closed behind him. In the silence that followed, James and Romilly exchanged a long look.

'Kit Miller will plant someone else in here if Harman's gone,' said Romilly.

'I know that.' He stared at her. 'I'm wondering who it will be.'

What the DCI *didn't* know was that she was indirectly responsible for John Dowling's death because she had told

Kit he'd be there on his gran's birthday. And she wasn't going to tell him.

Christ, she'd been getting too close to Kit Miller. *Far* too close. She knew it.

'If there's nothing else, sir . . .?' she said uncomfortably. Had he heard something about her and Kit?

Barrow eyed her beadily. Then he said: 'Not right now, no. Off you go.'

133

Later that day, Romilly got home and found the post on the mat. A decree nisi was there – Hugh was suing *her* for divorce. The cheeky sod. Unreasonable behaviour. Well, good. She'd already decided that tomorrow she would wrap this up, phone the estate agent. Time to put the house on the market and move on. She'd never much liked it, anyway.

In the evening, she went down to her local and into the snug and rang the little bell on the bar top.

Kevin the landlord came through.

'Is Sally about?' asked Romilly. 'I'd like a word.'

'I'll get her,' said Kevin.

Sally came through, saw Romilly, and stopped dead. Her face hardened.

'What do you want?' she asked.

'Well, I'd like you to stop trying to run me over, for a start,' said Romilly.

'What?' Sally's face went bright red.

'Christ, never go into crime in a big way, will you? You haven't got the face for it. You look guilty as sin. And you are, aren't you?' Romilly shook her head and stared at Sally in disgust. 'I thought Kit Miller was the target that day at the crem, but he wasn't, was he? The target was *me*, and you got me.'

Sally was chewing her lip and looking desperate.

'Don't bother denying anything,' said Romilly. 'I clocked the car and the reg number before I passed out cold. Force of habit. And I came round the car park last week to check out the motor. BMW. Tinted windows. It belongs to Kevin, and he lets you use it sometimes. He let you use it on the day of Clive Lewis's funeral at the crem. You're not fucking Kevin as well as Hugh, are you? No, scrub that question. I'm not even interested.'

'I wouldn't do that to Hugh,' said Sally, her mouth trembling. 'I'm not *cold* like you are.'

'Cold? Honey, you don't know me so don't even pretend you do.' Romilly leaned on the bar. Sally moved sharply back, away from her. 'I got the decree nisi in the post today, so pretty soon Hugh is going to be free as a bird. But do yourself a big favour and don't hold your breath waiting for commitment from him, because he hasn't got the *balls* for that.'

'Are you . . . are you going to . . .?' Sally couldn't even get the words out.

'What? Am I going to feel your collar? Drag you off down the nick?' Romilly cocked her head to one side and eyed Sally speculatively. 'You're not worth the paperwork. But do anything like that, ever again, and your shapely little arse is going to get *fried*. You hear me?' Sally nodded.

'Good,' said Romilly, and left.

134

Rather than go home to her empty house and yet another crappy TV dinner, Romilly drove on over to her folks' place. Dad answered the door.

'Hello, lovey,' he said. 'What a nice surprise.'

'Hi, Dad,' said Romilly, giving him a peck on the cheek and a hug, inhaling the familiar comforting scents of tobacco and Old Spice aftershave. 'Thought you'd be out in the garden.'

The days were getting lighter. Her dad always got into a panic at this time of year, planting seedlings, potting plants on. The garden became a hive of activity.

'I was. Just came in to wash my hands and grab a drink, and I heard the bell. Mum's down the bingo.'

'How's it all going out there?' asked Romilly as he led the way through to the kitchen.

'Fine. You want a drink?'

'Water's OK.'

He filled two glasses and took them out onto the patio, putting them on the white plastic table. He sat down in one of the chairs there, and Romilly sat too.

'It's starting to look a picture,' she said, gazing around the garden in admiration.

'All this dry weather's made it difficult. Now I'm having to get the hose out all the time. Heard you made big strides with that warehouse robbery. Got the man responsible. And the triple killer too. They ought to give you a commendation for that, girl.'

Romilly didn't think she deserved a commendation. But she said nothing. She thought that she'd been a fool. She'd let her feelings get in the way of logic, started to fall for Kit Miller in a big way – and that annoyed the fuck out of her.

'Dad? I think I've met someone,' she said.

He looked at her in surprise. 'Well, that was quick. After Hugh, I mean.'

'It was unexpected. It's knocked me sideways, really.'

'Is he a copper?'

'Nope.' Romilly screwed her face up. 'He's . . . pretty amazing. But not entirely kosher.'

Her dad gazed at her. Then he looked off down the garden. 'You'll do whatever's right, lovey. I've always known that.'

But what *was* right, now? She felt bewildered by all the possibilities opening up before her. And bloody scared, too.

'So what's the problem, with the dry weather?' she asked, to get her mind off Kit.

'I put in drainage channels, I told you last time you were here, remember? Cleared out the clay, put in gravel. I said at the time, if we get too dry a spell that herringbone pattern is going to show right through. Look, the grass I seeded on there has taken OK, but you can see the depression in the lawn, see the pattern where I dug it out.'

Romilly looked. She could see it. 'So what do you have to do about that?'

'I'll have to fill it in with some more soil. Raise the level. Which isn't too bad, but I could have done without it. I've got the tomatoes to pot on, and the sweetcorn's got to go in, and the sticks for the beans got to go up . . .'

Romilly tuned out. A thrill of intuition was making the hairs on her arms stand up.

'Dad?'

'What, lovey?'

'I've got to go.'

135

First she had to get the nod from DCI Barrow to go ahead.

'Romilly. You're a fucking good detective, but you know what? There's a thin line between genius and utter bloody madness, and I've yet to decide which one applies to you.'

'Yes, but I think—'

'I know what you think. We've done all that.' DCI Barrow slapped his hand down on the desk, making his framed family photos jump. 'Yes! All right! Go ahead. Now *get out*!'

Then there was the old lady to appease, which proved easier, although she wasn't overjoyed at the prospect of it, and who could blame her.

Both those hurdles cleared, it was a matter of getting a small earth mover into the back garden of John Dowling's grandmother's property, getting the forensics people in with the tent, then having Derek Potts ready on site to do the necessary.

'I don't know what you think you're going to find,' said Mrs Dowling to Romilly when the whole damned circus showed up at her door.

'The last time you saw your daughter-in-law Abigail, Mrs Dowling. What happened that day?'

'What? Well . . . she came to see me. She had the little dog with her, Kiki.'

'What was Abigail wearing, can you remember?'

'A lilac dress. She wore a lot of lilac. She had red hair and it suited her colouring.'

'What happened next? After she showed up here?'

'She said she was leaving him. Then Bill showed up, and there was an argument. I left them to it, went off down the shops. When I came back, she was gone but Bill was still here. He said she'd gone home.'

'Didn't you say he used to look after the garden for you?'

'He did. That's right. He couldn't do it now, of course. The drink's on him too much for that and I won't put up with him coming here.'

'Round about that time, did he dig over that patch of lawn beside the far rose border? The part that looks sunken?'

'I can't recall. It's possible, I suppose. He used to be quite keen on gardening. But after Abi left, he seemed to lose interest.'

'Can I go upstairs?' asked Romilly.

The light was starting to fade, and as she looked out of the back bedroom window the slanting angle of the sun made one of the depressions in the lawn out there even more apparent. It was roughly six feet by three. She watched as the tiny digger started up, started in, working carefully to scoop off the top layer of soil. It began to go deeper, moving slowly, slowly. Then it pulled back and men started in with spades.

What if there's fuck-all in there?

Christ! She couldn't even think about that. James Barrow was pissed enough with her as it was. *This* would tip him right over the edge. Romilly went downstairs and out into the garden to watch more closely. Derek was standing at the edge of the lawn, overalled, bag in hand, ready to work.

What if there's nothing for him to work on? What if I've wasted everyone's time and all these resources? Barrow's going to go apeshit.

Suddenly a cry went up from one of the men and they stopped digging. Lights were switched on and the tent was pulled into position. Romilly and Derek moved inside. One of the workers was scraping away at something yellow-white in the lamplight.

Romilly felt her heart spasm in shock.

It was a rib, and it looked human. A scrap of tattered lilac fabric was clinging to it.

136

They stood watching in silence as the work went on. Darkness fell. Finally, the whole skeleton was revealed.

'Female,' said Derek, moving in for a closer look. 'The skull's crushed on the right side. A fatal blow, I would think. And – this is odd, given what we discovered at Crystal Rose's burial site. All the teeth have been pulled.' Derek looked at her. 'You said *two* sites back here, I believe.'

Romilly nodded. Poor bloody Abigail. She stepped outside the tent with Derek, and indicated the other dip in the lawn. It was a lot smaller. The arc lamps flicked on, flooding the garden with cold blue light. The men started digging again, while Romilly and Derek sat on the back step, out of the way of the workers.

It didn't take long, this one. Soon they'd unearthed another skeleton, a fraction of the size of the first one. The photographer moved in, the flash lighting up a mouldering leather collar around its neck, with a brass nametag attached. Romilly and Derek went over. When it was cleaned, they could see the name *Kiki* engraved upon it.

Romilly stared down at the tiny, pitiful grave. She hadn't wanted to be right. But here was proof; she was.

'Poor woman,' said Derek. 'And her little dog, too. Tragic.'

'Yeah,' said Romilly, and called DC Phillips over. 'Bill Dowling,' she said. 'Let's bring him in, shall we?'

Bill Dowling was sitting in front of the TV scratching his balls and emptying a can of Special Brew down his neck when the doorbell rang. Patrick Dowling's brother looked a lot like Patrick – big and fleshy – but Bill also had the mottled corned-beef colouring and unfocused eyes of the devoted alcoholic.

'What the fucking hell . . .?'

If it was some daft sod selling something he was going to give them a mouthful. He lurched out of the chair and went through to the hall and from there to the front door. He flung it open, ready to give whatever *moron* was standing there a piece of his mind. He stopped short when he saw two uniformed coppers standing on the step.

'Mr William Dowling?' asked one.

'Yeah. Who wants him?'

'Mr Dowling, I am arresting you on suspicion . . .' started the other one.

'What the *fuck*?'

The officer went on reading Dowling his rights.

'New evidence has recently come to light,' he concluded.

'What? What the fuck you talkin' about?'

'We have unearthed remains at your mother's property that appear to belong to your wife, sir,' said the copper.

Bill sagged against the wall. 'I'll get my coat,' he said.

137

The day after the excavation, Romilly was writing out the report on Abigail Dowling's murder. Odd that, about the teeth. The father using the same MO as the son. Bill had somehow *taught* young John that little trick. It made her feel nauseous to think of it.

Having done her paperwork, she went along the corridor to where Phillips, Paddick and Barry and the others worked. Through the open door she could see that Harman's desk was cleared; he was gone, and good riddance.

As she stepped through into the big office, a ragged cheer went up and everyone clapped. Barry was grinning, opening a box on his desk. DC Phillips was smiling at her.

Paddick too. And the others. Bev Appleton came in and stood there, grinning like a Cheshire cat.

'What's this?' asked Romilly.

'It's a bloody hat-trick, Romilly,' said Bev. 'Patrick Dowling for the warehouse job, the shooter dead, and now that poor woman's killer brought to book after all these years.'

'There's missing money still. And people,' Romilly reminded her.

'And fucking Harman's out on his ear,' said Barry Jones, thrusting the open box under Romilly's nose. Chocolate éclairs, apple turnovers, vanilla slices. 'That's something to be thankful for, losing that cocky git at last. Have a cake, and don't be such a tight-arse. It's time to celebrate.'

Romilly took an éclair. Bev winked at her and selected an apple turnover.

'Any calories in these, Barry?' Bev asked.

'Guaranteed calorie-free,' he said.

'You're a very poor liar,' said Bev. She sighed. 'I'm going to flatten that poor bloody horse when I start my lessons next week.'

'You're going to do it then?' asked Romilly, delighted for her old mate.

'Yep. And what about your little ambition, hm? The one we discussed.'

'What ambition's that?' asked DC Phillips, her brunette plaits bobbing as she dived at a vanilla slice.

'Never you mind,' said Romilly.

138

Romilly phoned Kit at Sheila's restaurant.

'Detective,' he said in greeting.

'Mr Miller.'

'Something I can do for you?'

'Possibly. Can you call round to mine? Say . . . nine o'clock tonight?'

'What's this about?'

'Can you just come? I don't want to discuss this on the phone.'

'All right. I will.'

Kit was there on the dot. As he walked down her pathway, he noticed that there was a For Sale sign up in the front garden. He rang the bell. Romilly opened the door, ushered him inside.

'Moving on, detective?' he asked.

'Yeah. Can't wait.'

'I heard there was all sorts of fallout from the Dowling case. A buried body? Some woman who went missing years ago?'

'You heard right.' Romilly stared at his face. 'Tell me, did you *also* hear that our three-times-killer got shot? Fatally? Through the head? As he was on his way to see his grandmother?'

'I did. Shocking,' said Kit.

'Ain't it just. Oh – and Harman's gone. I'm sure you'll miss him.'

'I *won't* miss him. Man's an arsehole.'

They walked through to the kitchen. Romilly opened a bottle of red, held it up. 'Want some?'

'OK.'

'Excuse me,' she said, having taken a gulp from her glass. 'Just a minute, there's something I've got to do.'

She left him there and went upstairs. Kit took a sip of the red. It was cheap and raw, but passable.

Then he heard her call out.

'Hey, Kit! Can you give me a hand with something up here?'

He put his wine glass down on the worktop, went through to the hall and up the stairs. At the top of the landing he looked into the first bedroom. Romilly was there, fiddling with something on the brass headboard of a double bed.

'You OK?' he asked, coming into the room.

She turned toward him. 'I am absolutely fine,' she said, and to his surprise she came up to him, placed her hands on either side of his head and kissed him, long and slow.

His arms snaked around her, pulling her in closer. Then Romilly eased back, turning, taking Kit with her, pushing him down onto the bed.

'This is nice,' he said, and then Romilly closed the cuff in her hand around his wrist, and snapped the other one shut on the brass headboard.

Kit looked at her. Then at the cuffs, chaining him to the bed.

'You know, I don't have to be *tied down* to cooperate, detective. You don't have to just help yourself to the goods. I'll behave, I promise.'

'Oh, you certainly will,' said Romilly, unbuttoning his shirt.

She slid her hands inside, feeling his heat, his muscularity.

'I would return the favour and undo *your* shirt,' said Kit, giving the cuffs a tug. 'But you got me at a slight disadvantage here.'

'Well, we can't have that, can we?' said Romilly, and unlocked them.

Kit pulled her between his legs and started stripping off her clothes.

'I'm still hopping mad about that whole thing,' she said, feeling breathless, feeling her blood literally fizzing with desire. This was what she'd wanted, almost from the first minute they'd met, whether he was a bad 'un or not.

'Yeah? But you're like me, aren't you,' said Kit, pushing her bra aside so he could touch her naked breasts. 'You like living on the edge, pushing the boundaries. It excites you. *This* excites you, being with me. Admit it.'

'I admit nothing,' gasped Romilly, lust flooding through her.

'Then, Romilly Kane, I'm afraid that I am going to have to *force* a confession out of you,' he said, and pulled her down onto the bed and into his waiting arms.

139

Six months later . . .

The day had come when the stonemason was going to erect Rob Hinton's headstone. He finished work on it in the morning, then all the family gathered in the graveyard late in the afternoon. Eunice was there, with her daughters and their husbands. Daniel was also there, standing near to Daisy, and Kit and Ruby were there too.

A dear son and a beloved friend
Much missed, much loved

It was a beautiful headstone, grey granite with the inscriptions picked out in gold. Eunice and her daughters placed wreaths against it, then Daisy laid a bouquet of red roses.

'I still can't believe he's gone,' said Daisy, giving a crying Eunice a comforting hug. Her eyes met Daniel's, over his mother's head.

Back in February she'd married Rob Hinton. Then had come death and multiple shocks. Secrets unveiled, shaking them all to the core, making them doubt him. But it had all been lies. That rattlesnake Leon had been the deceiver, the schemer, the drug baron – not Rob.

'You OK, Daise?' asked Kit, putting an arm around her shoulders.

'I'm OK.' Daisy hugged him. 'Kit? Look . . . I owe you an apology, and I never gave it. I'm so sorry for the way I acted when Rob died. I feel so bad about it. I blamed you. And I shouldn't have. I see that now.'

'Don't be daft. It's all forgotten,' said Kit.

Ruby was quiet, staring at the headstone. 'It's hard,' Eunice told her, wiping away a tear. 'Losing Rob. And Patrick being sent down for so long. And now I don't even know where my Leon is.'

Daisy and Daniel exchanged a glance, but neither said a word.

Kit and Ruby lingered near the grave after the others went back to their cars. They could relax now. All threats were past. Kit's gun had gone back into the glove box of the Bentley; Ruby's was back in her study drawer. They could take a breath, knowing that Peachy had done the business on that sick bastard John Dowling. Ruby was watching Daisy and Daniel, standing a little apart from everyone else, heads together, talking.

'Is there something, d'you think? Those two?' she asked her son.

'What? No. Anyway, she's a bit older than him,' said Kit. 'And she's not over Rob. I don't know if she ever will be.'

'Daniel don't seem to care very much about the age difference.' Ruby looked at Kit. 'And what about you? Anybody in your life these days?'

'Nah, nobody,' said Kit.

'Then what the hell's *she* doing here?' asked Ruby, looking over toward the cemetery gates.

Kit followed her gaze. Romilly Kane was standing there, watching them all.

'You're not getting into anything with her, are you?'

'What, that copper? Don't be mental. You still seeing Tom Knox?'

'Nope,' said Ruby, watching her son sceptically. 'He's got a young wife and a baby now. And I'm out of there.'

'Those Rosettes worked out? After Crystal Rose?'

'They're fine.' Ruby thought of poor Crystal Rose, meeting John Dowling and her fate, all in one night.

Wrong place, wrong time, she thought.

She gazed at Rob's grave. You had to be cautious in this life, never stray too close to the precipice, always take care. But right on the edge was where they always seemed to be, her and her kids and the people who worked for them. She prayed for calmer waters in the future. For peace. But then – peace had never been their business. So she didn't hold out a lot of hope.

'I'll just . . .' said Kit.

'Yeah,' said Ruby, and watched her son as he walked over to where Romilly Kane stood waiting.

140

'Hi,' said Romilly when Kit joined her by the gate.

'Hi, yourself. How's it going?' he asked.

'Barrow's signed me off for a couple of weeks. Says I'm shattered after my divorce and everything. And maybe's he's right. It's been a bit of a year, all in all. I've sold the house, kicked out my husband, and . . . well, there's you, isn't there. And although he didn't *say* he knew about us, I think he does.' She grimaced. 'I think he's figuring out what he intends to do about that.'

Kit glanced around, then pulled her back behind the brick pillar beside the gate and kissed her, long and hard. 'So the house is sold, but you've got nowhere else, not yet?'

'Not yet, no.'

'You could move in with me.' He nuzzled into her neck, making her shiver. 'I got a nice place. Near Belgravia. You'd like it.'

'Kit,' she said, almost laughing. 'You're a very bad boy. And I'm on the side of the angels. It couldn't work.'

Kit shrugged. 'Hasn't worked too badly, up to now.'

And that was true. They'd had months of passion, great debates, lots of fun. Weirdly, they suited each other. They had similar intellects, they were both driven. But . . . she couldn't ignore the fact that they were on opposite sides of the fence.

'Listen,' said Romilly, freeing herself from his arms. 'I have to go.'

'Meet me tonight. The Italian place. Eight o'clock.'

The little Italian restaurant near London Bridge had become 'their' place over the last few months.

'OK,' she said, and kissed him again, lightly.

Kit thought that if Rob could see him, right now, falling like a ton of bricks for DI Romilly Kane, then he'd kick his arse. *Hard.* But right now, he didn't even care.

'I think this break will do me good,' said Romilly. 'Give me time to think it all over, work out what I want.'

'And what *do* you want? Exactly?' asked Kit.

Romilly grabbed his tie, pulled his head toward hers, and kissed him hard on the lips.

'You know what?' she murmured against his mouth. Her eyes danced with teasing light as they gazed into his. 'I think I'm looking at it.'